Nobody asks the question “what t!
“*What if* a woman ruled in the W d
everything for the only man she ever loved . . . and the only career she ever wanted?” The answer is *The Justice,* a page-turning, heart-stopping political thriller by one of the best storytellers in America. Packed with Oval Office intrigue, insider details, and an unpredictable plot that never stops, *The Justice* is a faith-seeking thrill ride through the District. Fasten your seat belts!

—LIZ CURTIS HIGGS, AUTHOR OF *MAD MARY: A BAD GIRL FROM MAGDALA*

A tale of political intrigue and spiritual renewal at the highest levels of government, and a welcome reminder that God cares about both people and nations. Angela Elwell Hunt once again demonstrates her tremendous range in weaving a story of ambition, passion, and the values that matter most.

—JAMES SCOTT BELL, AUTHOR OF *THE NEPHILIM SEED*

The Justice is enthralling! In her crisp, compelling style, Angela Hunt presents an intriguing and sometimes sobering look at the dangers inherent in the trappings of power. Throughout this page-turning tale, the hope of redemption shines.

—DEBORAH RANEY, AUTHOR OF *BENEATH A SOUTHERN SKY*

The Justice's tightly written political intrigue reads like tomorrow's headlines. If it were any more realistic, they'd be arguing about it on CNN.

—DEANNA JULIE DODSON, AUTHOR OF *IN HONOR BOUND*

In *The Justice*, Angela Hunt doesn't just transport me into a fascinating world of power politics, she yanks me there by the scruff of my neck and doesn't let go until the final word. I never know what to expect, but I always know the next trip with Angie will be better than the last.

—HANNAH ALEXANDER, AUTHOR OF *SACRED TRUST*

In a brilliant, one-of-a-kind story, Angela Hunt plunges the reader into a world of political intrigue and moral corruption. *The Justice* is woven with fine threads of truth that will resonate long after the last sentence is read.

—DENISE HUNTER, AUTHOR OF *REUNIONS*

Just when I thought Angela Hunt couldn't possibly write a more engrossing, thought-provoking book than *The Note*, she comes up with another winner. Don't make the mistake of starting this book at night—you won't be able to put it down!

—COLLEEN COBLE, AUTHOR OF *HEART FULL OF LOVE*

THE JUSTICE

ANGELA HUNT

W PUBLISHING GROUP™
www.wpublishinggroup.com
A Division of Thomas Nelson, Inc.
www.ThomasNelson.com

Published by the W Publishing Group, Nashville, Tennessee, in association with the literary agency of Alive Communications, Inc., 7680 Goddard Street, Suite 200, Colorado Springs, Colorado, 80920.

Library of Congress Cataloging-in-Publication Data

Hunt, Angela Elwell, 1957–
The justice / Angela Hunt.
p. cm.
ISBN 0-8499-1631-3
1. Women presidents—Fiction. I. Title.

PS3558.U46747 J87 2002
813'.54—dc21 2001046872

Printed in the United States of America
1 2 3 4 PHX 9 8 7 6 5 4 3 2 1

Other Books by Angela Hunt

The Note

The Immortal

The Truth Teller

The Silver Sword

The Golden Cross

The Velvet Shadow

The Emerald Isle

Dreamers

Brothers

Journey

With Lori Copeland:

The Island of Heavenly Daze

Grace in Autumn

A Warmth in Winter

With Bill Myers:

Then Comes Marriage

With Grant Jeffrey:

Flee the Darkness

By Dawn's Early Light

The Spear of Tyranny

Web page: www.angelahuntbooks.com

One often passes from love to ambition,
But rarely returns from ambition to love.

—La Rochefoucauld, *Reflections*, 1665

A man's character is his fate.

—Heraclitus

ONE

As an act of whimsy, or perhaps pique, on June 6, 2003, Fate gave Daryn Jane Austin the most impressive birthday gift of her forty-eight years: the presidency of the United States.

Awakened by the screeching of the Nokia on her nightstand, she sat up in darkness and glanced at the glowing clock as she reached for the phone—3:30 A.M. Such an hour rarely brought good news, and only a handful of people had her private cell phone number. So either something had happened to her parents, or . . .

Bracing herself, she cleared her throat. "Yes?"

"Madam Vice President, this is Anson Quinn."

The name registered immediately, as did the noticeable absence of an apology. Quinn served as head of the Presidential Protection Detail, the Secret Service branch specifically dedicated to guarding the president. If this were anything other than the direst emergency, protocol would have demanded that he apologize for disturbing her sleep.

As a flock of worries took wing, she struggled to keep her voice low and level. "What's the trouble, Agent Quinn?"

"A crucial situation has developed. A car will pick you up in ten minutes."

She pressed her hand to her brow, willing her fingers not to tremble. "Am I needed at the White House?"

"You'll be taken to George Washington University Hospital." Quinn paused a moment, then spoke in a tone heavy with portent. "They've sent for the chief justice as well."

Daryn's hand fell to her lips. She could think of only one reason Quinn would roust that venerable old man out of bed: President Craig Parker was dead or dying. In an effort to maintain the illusion of order, the chief justice of the Supreme Court would administer the oath of office to Parker's successor before daybreak, before the morning newscasts . . .

The chief justice would administer the oath for *her*.

Her fingertips clung to her lips, which had gone cold and still, then adrenaline surged and she found her voice. "I'm on my way."

Snapping the phone off, she crossed to the closet in three strides. After flicking on the light, she squinted in the brightness, then reached for a black suit that reeked of authority and solemnity.

She grabbed the ivory silk blouse that never wrinkled, then crossed the darkened bedroom and tossed the hangers on the bed. Dressing in the stream of light from the closet, she struggled to anticipate the aftereffects of something that had happened in another darkened bedroom a few miles away.

President Parker, who'd appeared hale and hearty at a state dinner a few hours ago, must have had a heart attack. If it proved fatal, she would become the tenth vice president suddenly to assume the office.

And the first woman.

She stepped into the skirt, yanked the zipper upward, then slipped her arms into the jacket sleeves. Moving to the mirrored wall behind the bed, she fluffed her short hair, then wet a fingertip and wiped a leftover mascara smudge from below one eye. She'd forgo makeup; no one would expect a national leader to appear pink and blooming in a moment of crisis.

Satisfied with her face, she took a half step back to check her head-to-

toe reflection, then drew a deep breath. This wasn't the look she had imagined she'd adopt when she became the first female leader of the free world . . . still the juxtaposition of dark suit and pale complexion *would* make a striking photograph.

An image to resonate through the ages—and to make her father proud.

●

As a quartet of uniformed motorcycle officers led the way, a black limousine whisked Daryn over largely deserted streets. A light rain had begun to fall during the night; now it steamed on the still-warm asphalt while traffic signals splintered in their liquid reflections.

Six escort sedans accompanied her car, each occupied by Secret Service agents. Three agents rode with Daryn. Troy Stock, chief of her own protective detail, kept her company in the back and scowled at every intersection. She usually sat alone in the rear seat; she usually traveled with only two escort vehicles. The president, on the other hand, traveled with a minimum of twenty-four.

Was she, in fact, already president? Impossible to know for certain, and impolitic to ask an agent who was not supposed to know more than the vice president . . .

She wiped her damp palms on her skirt and returned her gaze to the road. After Quinn's call she had envisioned the worst-case scenario, but anything might have happened tonight. Craig Parker may have been only incapacitated. According to the Twenty-fifth Amendment, in case of a temporary disability, the vice president was empowered to act as president until the president recovered. Perhaps the chief justice had only been summoned as a precaution. Perhaps—

Stock's rough voice scraped against her nerves. "Right on time," he said, punctuating his last word with the clunk of the door handle.

The parking lot of George Washington University Hospital gleamed beyond the limo's darkened windows. Anson Quinn sprinted forward with an umbrella as the car rolled to a stop at the curb.

The ozonic smell of rain struck Daryn as Quinn opened her door. Powerful and confident, the agent stood with one arm propped on the car, the bristles of his gray hair glowing in the arc-sodium lights. "The president and first lady arrived five minutes ago," he announced without preamble. "The doctors are still working on POTUS, but there's no pulse. We want to get you in place before they pronounce him."

There's no pulse . . .

The words rang in Daryn's brain like the somber tolling of a funeral bell. In this day of respirators and defibrillators, how could the president of the United States not have a pulse?

As she stood a rising wind came whooshing past, lifting her hair from her ears and whipping her skirt tight around her legs. Crouching slightly, she hunched beneath the shelter of the proffered umbrella, then matched her pace to Quinn's as they hurried past a flashing ambulance toward the safety of the building. "What happened?" She lifted her voice to be heard above the pounding of their footsteps.

"Firelight called us at 0300," Quinn explained, using the agents' code name for the first lady. "Apparently he got up in the night, then collapsed on his way back to bed."

Daryn considered the news in silence. At sixty-three, Craig Parker was as fit as any president in recent memory, and he'd passed each of his yearly physicals with flying colors. During the 2000 election, they'd made a point of jogging together at every campaign stop, and Parker had easily kept pace with Daryn's long-legged stride.

She caught Quinn's eye. "Mrs. Parker is here?"

"Affirmative. Firelight is inside, waiting for you. The chief's ETA is four minutes. The doctor plans to pronounce POTUS as soon as the chief arrives, then the justice will administer the oath of office." Quinn hesitated, and for an instant Daryn thought she caught a glimpse of personal concern in his dark eyes. "Firelight knows it's important for her to stand by your side. She's been prepared; she's ready to follow procedure."

A pair of plain-clothes agents in trench coats pulled the glass doors open as Daryn and Quinn approached. "I can't recall there being an established procedure for this," she whispered as they passed through the doorway. "This is happening so fast."

"Everything happens fast these days," Quinn answered. "Crenshaw's calling the shots and he didn't want to give the vultures time to circle. As soon as POTUS is pronounced, you'll be sworn in. No quibbling allowed."

Pressing her lips together, Daryn stepped back as Quinn closed the umbrella and handed it to another agent. Few Americans outside Washington knew that Curtis Crenshaw, Parker's chief of staff, had been the de facto second-in-command ever since Parker took office. As Parker's campaign manager in the past election, Crenshaw had been the one to toss Daryn's name into the pool of prospective running mates when Craig Parker decided to run as an independent. She'd reluctantly agreed to the political ménage à trois, understanding that in exchange for the historical honor of becoming the first female vice president, she would placate the women's movement, charm the Southern vote, and remain pretty much out of sight when and if the White House was won.

The former vice president, Al Gore, had maintained four offices in the capital: one in the West Wing of the White House, one in the Old Executive Office Building, one in the Dirksen Senate Office Building, and one off the floor of the Senate. Since the inauguration, she'd been allowed to oversee her duties in two: the ceremonial office near the Senate chamber and the vice-presidential office in the OEOB. Crenshaw had taken Gore's old office in the West Wing.

Standing in the hallway, she brought up her hand and swiped a damp hank of hair from her forehead. She had never intended to stay in the background. Like so many women who lived and worked in a man's world, she had planned to play the game well, do excellent work, and then run for the presidency on her own merits—against Parker, if necessary. But now fate had taken a hand, turning the tables on Parker and Crenshaw and the entire crew who ran the West Wing.

"Daryn."

She turned at the soft voice and saw Helen Parker approaching in a floral housecoat of cotton, the sort of thing older Southern women wore to do housework. The top snap hung open, and through the V-shaped gap Daryn could see the worn lace of a pink nightgown.

"Mrs. Parker, I'm so sorry." Daryn bent to embrace the woman, who felt wooden in her grasp.

"They say it was an aortic aneurysm." Helen Parker did not look at her, but seemed to be staring at something Daryn couldn't see. With two fingers she picked at the lace of her neckline. "He was standing there, holding his back, then he fell onto the bed . . ."

Not knowing what else to do, Daryn placed a hand on the pale woman's shoulder. The human touch seemed to awaken something in the older woman, and her gaze shifted to Daryn's face. Her mouth twisted; the blue eyes softened with pain. "Time to do our thing for the country, then." Her hands fluttered over the robe as if she would smooth out a host of imaginary wrinkles. "Jackie stood by Lady Bird and LBJ when he took the oath, so I'll need to stand by you. I want everyone to see. To know we . . . intended to finish the course."

"Mrs. Parker?" One of the aides approached, a steaming foam cup in his hand. "We have coffee for you. If you'd like to sit a moment while we set up . . ."

Shuffling forward, her legs white and spindly above a pair of brown leather loafers, Mrs. Parker let herself be led away. Daryn felt pressure on her elbow and turned to see Quinn gesturing to an open door guarded by two other agents in dark glasses. She followed, then nodded to the slender man who sat on a vinyl sofa in the small room. "Hello, Peter." She extended her hand. "It's good to see you, even if I do regret the circumstances."

Peter Chang, official White House photographer for the Parker administration, stood and shook her hand. His usually animated face seemed locked in neutral, as though he hadn't decided what sort of expression fit the situation. "I'm not sure why I'm here, Madam Vice President," he said, his hand falling back to the camera hanging from his neck. "But I'm ready."

"Thank you, Peter. I'm sure everything will be made clear in a moment."

From the corner of her eye, Daryn saw Quinn turn slightly and press his hand to his earpiece. The agents in the hall lifted their heads, and without being told, Daryn knew what Quinn's next words would be.

"The chief justice has arrived." His focused gaze shifted to Daryn. "We'll bring him to you."

He left the room, leaving Daryn with Peter Chang, who swayed nervously on his feet. "Please, Peter—" she gestured to the worn sofa against the wall—"make yourself comfortable."

With a grateful smile, Chang sank to the couch and began to rummage in his camera bag. Daryn turned to the wall and crossed her arms, then glanced at her watch—3:53 A.M., and her life's significance was about to take a quantum leap upward. Something within her crowed at the thought, but she tamped her rising emotions. In the days and weeks ahead of this momentous hour, she needed witnesses to testify to her calm, her courage, and her compassion for the widow. No matter how intense her feelings, she could not dissolve into tears or trembling. Either extreme would be extraordinary for a man, unforgivable for a woman.

She straightened as the sound of approaching footsteps reached her ear and turned toward the door in time to see the chief justice enter, followed closely by Anson Quinn and Helen Parker.

Chief Justice Marshall Haynes, a gaunt man with a shiny head and weary eyes, gazed at Daryn with a resigned smile on his lined face. "Good morning, Madam President," he said, his Texas drawl evident despite twenty-five years of life within the Beltway. "Shall we proceed?"

Shock flew through her. *Madam President.* Somehow she smiled and nodded at the old gentleman. "I'm ready."

She stepped forward, then suppressed a sigh as an aide scrambled to find a Bible. During the wait, Daryn turned to the first lady, who stood with her arms stiffly wrapped around her waist, her eyes focused on some inward horizon. "I'm so sorry," Daryn whispered, hoping for some sign of unbending. "We'll do all we can to preserve the dignity of his legacy, of course."

The first lady's eyes seemed to focus, then her slack face contorted in a grimace. "It was nothing—" her hands tightened upon her arms—"a little backache, that's all. He took aspirin and went to bed early. And then he got up and went into the bathroom, then he came back and fell. I called for help right away, and they worked on him, but he was gone from that first minute. He was there and then he just . . . left me."

Daryn slipped an arm around the woman's shoulders. Moving silently in the background, Peter Chang set to work, but Daryn shot him a *not-now* glance, and he lowered the camera.

A moment later Quinn returned with a Bible and handed it to Haynes. Catching Daryn's eye, he added, "From the nurse's station."

As Helen Parker held the Bible on her open palms and Chang's camera began to click in earnest, Daryn placed her right hand on the worn, leather cover and repeated the oath of office after the chief justice: "I, Daryn Jane Austin, do solemnly swear that I will faithfully execute the office of the president of the United States . . . and will to the best of my ability preserve, protect, and defend the Constitution of the United States."

Chang's camera flashed.

●

After driving to the White House under a warm mantle of darkness, Daryn walked into the large secretarial alcove outside the Oval Office and breathed in the scents of paper, leather, and power. Three desks occupied this space, mute testimony to the work that disseminated from the room beyond. On each of the desks, a small electronic device displayed a blue screen, on which Daryn could read POTUS: Oval Office. The fields for FLOTUS—first lady of the United States—and VPOTUS—vice president—were blank.

She glanced at the matching palm device in Quinn's hand. He had just tapped in her present position, as scores of other agents would as she moved throughout the fifty-five-acre White House grounds. Any one of her aides would only have to look at one of the desktop devices—which were located throughout the mansion and OEOB—to know where she could be reached.

Daryn had seen the gadgets before but had never thought to inquire how they worked. Now she turned to Quinn, who stood behind her. "My whereabouts are revealed on this thing all the time?"

"Yes," Quinn answered, "but not in detail. When you're in the family quarters, all the screen says is *residence.* And when you're in the Oval, that's as detailed as the device gets. We don't have agents outside your private study or—"

"The bathroom." She laughed. "What does it say when I'm away from the White House?"

Quinn grinned. "Probably ARON—away for the remainder of the night—but I'm not sure. We check our devices at the desk whenever the president leaves the premises, and where the president goes, we go."

"One more question, Agent Quinn." She reached out to caress the silver shell of the appliance that would reveal her every move to hundreds of people. "There's a slot here for the vice president, yet I don't believe I was ever tracked before today." She tilted her head and looked at him. "How did Parker explain that?"

Quinn swallowed hard and thrust his hands behind his back. "I don't know, Madam President. Perhaps . . . because you didn't maintain an office on the grounds."

Clever of him to use the word *maintain* instead of *have.* Implying that she'd chosen to work at a distance from the pinnacle of power.

Helpless to halt Quinn's discomfiture, she averted her gaze. "Perhaps you're right. But when I appoint a vice president, we will restore the West Wing office. It'll be nice to see your screen fill up again, won't it?"

She ran her fingertips over the polished desk, moving away from the shiny gadget. The presidency would result in huge adjustments to her personal lifestyle, for as vice president she'd been able to retain a measure of privacy. But she could not regret anything attached to the Oval Office. She'd worked for this position all her life, and she would learn to work within the system. After all, if forty-three men could manage it . . .

A dim lamp burned on the desk belonging to the president's personal secretary, Soon Yi Park, and a matching ray of light blazed from beneath the curved door leading into the Oval. Daryn glanced toward it, doubting that Miss Park had been notified of her employer's sudden demise. So who . . . ?

She moved forward, put her hand to the knob, and found it locked. The person undoubtedly plowing through the Oval Office had to be Curtis Crenshaw, Parker's chief of staff.

She pressed her forehead to the cool wood, finding joy in an unexpected lagniappe. Now, with the reins of power firmly in her hands, she could finally admit the truth—she had never liked the man.

At her hesitation, Quinn cleared his throat. "Is there something I can do for you, Madam President?"

"Yes. I seem to be locked out of the Oval Office."

Turning, she flashed him a smile with steel beneath it, then stepped aside as he hurried forward. From a pocket he produced a key card, then the door swung open, startling the disheveled man who sat in the executive chair behind the desk.

"Good morning, Mr. Crenshaw." Entering behind the agent, Daryn offered the greeting with a polite nod. "So kind of you to get things in order for me."

At least Crenshaw had the decency to flush. Standing, he gestured toward a stack of leather folders. "Daryn, it's good to see you. I thought I'd try to sort things out before you came in, remove anything that might be personal. I didn't think you'd appreciate finding one of Helen's grocery lists among the presidential papers." He lifted his hand to wipe his forehead, revealing fresh sweat stains on his blue dress shirt. Crenshaw hadn't gone to the hospital. He had been hard at work here for the last two hours—doing what?

"Curtis—" she softened her voice as she walked toward him—"three things. First, I am very sorry for your loss. I know you and the president were friends as well as coworkers." Reaching the desk, she lowered her voice and placed her hands on the edge, leaning toward him. "Second, I believe you should call me *Madam President* from this moment forward. I was elected to fill this job and I have every intention of doing my dead-level best to meet that responsibility. And third—" she gave him the brightest smile she could muster—"I want you to step away from the desk and leave everything exactly as you found it."

Crenshaw's eyes, she noticed now, were red-rimmed and watery. Either his devotion to Parker or his adoration for the Tinkertoys of power had been genuine.

"I appreciate the concern," she said, resuming her normal tone, "but the discovery of a grocery list wouldn't bother me. Nor would I be tempted to call the tabloids if I found a love letter from a starry-eyed college intern." She placed her hand atop the presidential seal on the uppermost folder. "Thank you, Curtis, for your help, but I'm sure you'd like to be alone to collect your thoughts."

Crenshaw said nothing, but tapped the desktop with his fingertips, then pointed to a single sheet in the corner of the blotter. "Tomorrow's schedule. Miss Park always places it on the desk the night before. The master calendar, of course, is kept by the Office of Presidential Scheduling and downloaded to the president's computer." He jerked his thumb toward the hallway that led to the private study where for generations presidents had accomplished the real work of the office. "I expect we'll cancel everything until further notice."

"I'll have the scheduling office see to it." Daryn fixed her face in lines of somber humility. "I'm sure Jacob Thrasher, my chief of staff, will be calling upon you in the next few days. We'll offer every assistance to Mrs. Parker as she plans the funeral, and I expect you'll extend the same courtesy to Jacob as he oversees the transition."

A change came over Crenshaw's features—a sudden shock of sick realization. *Yes,* she wanted to add, *you backed the wrong horse and now you're outta luck.*

Ignoring his stricken silence, she walked around the desk and stood next to him, holding her ground until he retreated. "Now," she said, resting her hand atop the president's desk, "would you be so kind as to call Jacob Thrasher? Tell him to meet me at the Naval Observatory ASAP. We'll make the first announcement from the vice president's mansion."

She paused. "I'm assuming you've already alerted the White House press secretary?"

Only the tightening of the muscles in Crenshaw's throat betrayed his emotion. "Morgan's in her office."

"We'll want to have a statement prepared for the 6:00 A.M. network news. Statement first, I suppose, followed by a press conference at 7:00. Run the idea by Ms. Morgan and let's hear what she thinks."

Daryn knew she was treating Crenshaw like a secretary, but on several occasions in the past three years he'd treated her with far less respect. She had been elected to the office of vice president, her constituents had helped put Parker, an independent from nowhere, in the White House, and then she had been relegated to meetings with women's groups and Georgia peanut growers. She'd been willing to pay her dues and wait, to wear pizza-sized corsages and attend an endless succession of mind-numbing social events, but Fate, bless her heart, had decided to end the testosterone-based partnership from which Daryn had always felt excluded.

Payback felt rich.

A look of irritated despair passed over Crenshaw's features. "I'll send Morgan in." He turned and moved toward the door, his gait wooden. As he passed Quinn, Daryn thought she saw the flicker of a smile cross the agent's face.

Sinking into the tufted leather chair, she gave the agent a nod. "Thank you, Mr. Quinn. I appreciate your help in what could have been an awkward situation."

He lifted one shoulder in a slight shrug, murmured, "No problem, Madam President," and followed Crenshaw out the door.

Finally alone, Daryn placed her hands on the desk and took a deep breath. The Oval Office . . . belonged to her. She had dreamed of the day she would sit behind this desk, but she'd planned on being older and far more experienced. As the daughter of Edward Austin, who'd served as both a Georgia governor and state senator, she'd grown up as a political princess, but it wasn't until she entered the game herself that she began to learn the hidden rules and truths kept from the public.

During her terms in the Georgia House and Senate, she'd learned how to bargain; during her term as governor of the Peach State, she'd learned how to win through diplomacy. But during the last campaign—and in her two and one-half years as vice president—she had learned that national politics was an entirely different game, with higher risks, greater rewards, and the most amazing opportunities.

Now she sat in the seat of power.

On impulse, she reached for the center desk drawer and pulled it open. Ronald Reagan had found a welcoming note from Jimmy Carter inside this drawer, but Daryn knew she'd find nothing to welcome her to the job. Craig Parker had not planned on vacating the office for at least another eighteen months.

She smiled as she inventoried the items in the presidential drawer: one roll of cinnamon breath mints, two pens decorated with a tacky representation of the presidential seal, a tablet of yellow sticky notes, a half-dozen paper clips, a comb, complete with dangling gray hairs, and a section of newspaper folded to reveal a half-completed crossword puzzle. No spy decoder rings, no invitations to dine with the queen of England, no encrypted punch card revealing the identity of Watergate's Deep Throat.

She closed the drawer and pushed the chair back to inspect the carved desk more closely. This had been George H. Bush's desk, pulled from storage because Parker had always admired the former president. Clinton had used JFK's desk, seeing himself, no doubt, as heir to the assassinated president's charm and celebrated compassion.

Daryn wrinkled her brow. This desk was attractive and functional, and she would use it for a few more weeks. But she'd order a new desk at the first opportunity, something sleek and less clunky, perhaps something from a Georgia manufacturer. In generations to come other presidents, eager to touch something used by the first female commander in chief of the United States, would summon the graceful *Austin* desk from storage.

The thought of future generations brought a worry in its wake, and her hand went automatically to the plastic card in her suit pocket. A stone-faced military attaché had given it to her a moment after she had taken the oath of office. She'd been told to keep the card within reach at all times, for it contained the go-codes necessary to launch a nuclear strike.

A tremor of mingled fear and anticipation shot through her. Somewhere in the shadows outside, a uniformed military officer carried an arm-stretching briefcase referred to as the "football." The football—such an innocuous name for such a deadly device—contained top-secret plans for launching what could easily become World War III.

Leaning forward, Daryn pressed her hands to her temples. She wanted to be president, but she hadn't asked for the responsibility on a dark June morning while most of the nation slept in blissful ignorance. Reagan had declawed the Russian bear, Clinton had benefited from the bear's confusion, but now the bear was restless—and the Chinese dragon an ever-growing threat . . .

Without thinking, she picked up the cordless phone and punched in a familiar number. A sleepy female voice answered, and Daryn asked immediately for Governor Austin. "I know he's asleep, but wake him, please. I'm his daughter."

The live-in nurse knew better than to argue.

Exhaling slowly as she settled back to wait, she swiveled the leather chair, absorbing details of the historic room: two lovely sofas before the fireplace, delicate wing chairs and antique tables, priceless art from the National Gallery, a guarded doorway to the main hall, an unguarded doorway to the president's private study, bathroom, and dining room. Turning further, she saw a niche in the wall, topped by a graceful shell-shaped fan vault. The shelves in the niche were laden with framed photos of President and Mrs. Parker with their nieces and nephews, the largest of which featured the presidential family at his January 2001 inauguration. She made a mental note to bring the silver-framed portraits of her parents from the vice-presidential mansion. She might add Chang's picture of her oath taking this morning, depending upon how somber the final shot appeared. She didn't want anything dark and depressing in this room, not when tourists and wide-eyed eagle scouts regularly traipsed in for meetings with the president.

Following the gentle curve of the room, Daryn's gaze slid to the wide French doors that opened to the South Lawn and the outdoor walkway constantly monitored by the Secret Service. Soft yellow lights gleamed over the flagstones, sending shafts of light through the heavy bulletproof glass. She turned again, her gaze finally shifting to the door through which she had come.

She ran her hand through her hair, wondering about features of the office she could not see. She knew the Secret Service's presidential protective command post lay beneath the Oval, and from somewhere in this room a secret tunnel led to the family quarters. For months back in '98, Americans had buzzed about private spaces in the Oval Office, wondering how Clinton and Monica Lewinsky had managed to be alone . . .

"Hello?"

The quavering voice snapped her back to the present. "Daddy?"

"Daryn? You all right?"

"Yes, Dad. I'm . . . president."

Silence hummed over the line, and Daryn closed her eyes as her throat tightened. She owed her presence in the Oval to the man at the end of the phone line, she had worked her way upward for him, but she couldn't voice those thoughts without weeping and she had no time for tears . . .

"Oh, my." Her aged father exhaled the words in a hoarse whisper, as though they were too momentous to utter in a normal voice. "Did somebody shoot Parker?"

"An aneurysm, Dad, very sudden. Turn on the TV; you'll hear all about it. And tell Mom, okay?"

"I suppose . . ." She could almost see his brow wrinkling. "I suppose they'll have a quick ceremony, then. Probably not enough time for us to come up there."

"Gee, Dad, that'd be nice, but I took the oath of office about an hour ago. It's done. I'm in the Oval Office now."

Silence again, broken only by the heavy ticktock of an antique schoolhouse clock on the wall.

"My daughter, the president." His voice filled with the old vibrancy that had once shivered the halls of the Georgia governor's mansion. "Make Georgia proud, Daryn. You make *us* proud, you hear?"

Pressing her hand to her forehead, she nodded, too overcome to speak. "I will, Daddy," she finally said, suddenly feeling all too much like the sixteen-year-old girl who'd been caught smoking pot at the most exclusive private school in Atlanta. "I'll do my best."

Amazed at her dad's ability to make her feel like a dependent child, she disconnected the call and dropped the phone into her lap. Her eighty-eight-year-old father would cross the bedroom, shake his wife's shoulder, and tell her that their daughter had just become president. And Constance Austin, who had probably planned nothing more for the day than a trip to the pharmacy, would rise and assume the identity she'd set aside when Edward Austin retired from Georgia politics. Except now, instead of playing Former Governor's Wife, Constance would star as Presidential Mother.

Maybe, if things went well, Constance would finally forgive the daughter whose teenage rebellions had cost her the governor's mansion. If things went *very* well, Daryn might one day be able to stand before Congress and introduce her father, the man from whom she had inherited her height, blonde hair, and an overabundance of lofty dreams.

Daryn sighed as her gaze fell upon one of the pictures of Mrs. Parker, a woman who had never let Washington go to her head. Daryn's mother, on the other hand, had been intoxicated by mingling with Georgia movers and shakers, so this latest development would undoubtedly send her on a bender of ecstasy . . .

A tentative knock broke into her thoughts. As Daryn lifted her head she saw Natalie Morgan, the White House press secretary, standing in the north doorway.

Daryn welcomed the woman with a tired smile, then gestured to the folder in her hand. "Do you have our official statement?"

"I've come up with something that should be suitable," Natalie said, crossing the deep blue carpet in the center of the Oval. "Any of your personal comments can, of course, be worked into the text. CNN has the full story; they've been running it since 4 A.M. Chang released the photos, and there's a pack of press around the hospital waiting for Mrs. Parker. The usual White House correspondents have been arriving since five."

Daryn studied the typed statement. The typical government prose was heavy on compliments for a fallen public servant and sprinkled with enough biographical information to serve as a eulogy in case no one tuned in to watch the funeral . . . which, given Parker's bland administration and the competition offered by one hundred cable channels, seemed an all-too-likely scenario. Craig Parker had been a fine man, but not an especially colorful chief executive. Then again, perhaps his pedestrian personality was a blessing. Daryn privately believed the American public had overdosed on color in the Clinton years.

"I'll make my statement from the vice president's mansion," she said, crossing through a redundant paragraph. "Until we get things sorted out, direct any inquiries to my chief of staff, Jacob Thrasher. And, for the record, I will not be moving into the Oval Office or the White House until after the funeral. The public will want to know that we allowed Mrs. Parker time to grieve."

Natalie Morgan nodded. "And the statement?"

"You've made a good start." Daryn gave the woman a smile. "I'll add a few things, and you can release a transcript after I deliver the statement at the Naval Observatory. Now—" she bent to glance out the French doors behind the desk—"the sun is rising, and I need to slip away without being seen by that pack of reporters. How would you suggest I do that?"

Natalie Morgan managed a small, tentative smile. "Follow me, Madam President. I'll lead the way."

TWO

PAUL SANTANA HAD ATTEMPTED TO TRAIN HIS body to wake with the rising sun by sleeping with the blinds open. In the gray dimness of June sixth he reached out and snapped off the alarm at two minutes until six, sparing himself and his wife from its bone-rattling blare.

He blinked in the stillness, then forced himself to sit up. In the twin bed next to his, Maria still slept, her breaths punctuating the heavy quiet with an even rhythm. His glance did not linger on her side of the room. He used to enjoy studying her rounded profile in the slack innocence of repose, but ever since she'd put on a few pounds she tended to grow flustered and uncomfortable if she woke to find him watching her. He tried to respect her wishes, and he could not bring himself to steal pleasures in sleep she would not willingly give in wakefulness.

Shuffling into his slippers, he pulled his robe from the foot of the bed and left the bedroom. A moment later he stepped from the chill of the air conditioning and moved through the muggy warmth of a south Florida morning. A faint breeze rustled the palmettos clustered around the sabal palms. The shrubs at the edges of his tiled front porch hummed with the sounds of crickets, promising another scorching afternoon.

Bending, he picked up the paper, pulled it from its plastic sleeve, and scanned the headlines. The Miami mayor was in trouble again, and the

Cuban community planning yet another prayer vigil for Elian Gonzalez, the ten-year-old boy who probably didn't retain a single accurate memory of his short sojourn in the United States.

Paul slapped at a droning mosquito as he skimmed the story. Some of the Elian supporters mentioned were his clients, and he respected their strong anticommunist views. But the more attention they drew to Elian's long-lost cause, the more opportunities they gave Castro supporters to tout the victory of Cuban socialism over Western capitalism. Just last week Paul had read a newspaper story in which Cuba's vice president claimed that the victorious battle for the return of Elian Gonzalez had demonstrated the goodness and effectiveness of socialism and solidarity . . .

He slammed the front door more forcefully than he had intended. After a guilty glance up the stairs where his wife and daughter slept, Paul moved into the kitchen, where the automatic coffee maker had just finished brewing the perfect pot. "Try finding one of these gadgets in Cuba," he muttered, reaching for a mug.

After pouring his coffee, he punched the power button on the under-the-counter television, then pulled a package of bagels from the fridge. The tiny screen bloomed with living color, then a somber voice filled the kitchen. "This is a CBS News Special Report: the Death of a President."

Sinking to a stool at the kitchen bar, Paul stared at the television, his mind whirling. The camera focused on a trench-coated correspondent standing before the iron gates at the White House.

"This is Steve Dasher," the reporter began, "continuing our coverage of President Craig Parker's sudden death. The first lady is still at the hospital, but we expect her to be leaving for the White House at any moment. Vice President Austin was sworn in as president this morning at 4 A.M. by Chief Justice Marshall Haynes. Our nation's first female chief executive is expected to make a statement momentarily."

Paul caught his breath as the shock of discovery hit him full force. Daryn Austin, president? He looked at the bagel in his grip and saw that his hand trembled.

Why? Years ago his rational brain had accepted the fact that his old friend had won the office a heartbeat away from the presidency. He had even considered sending a note of congratulations. Though his mind had eventually skated away from that inclination, he'd been honestly happy for her, quietly thrilled that she'd come so far.

And today . . . she was *president.*

"We take you now to the U.S. Naval Observatory, site of the vice-presidential mansion," Dasher was saying. "The president is about to make a statement."

As his fingers tingled in an adrenaline rush, Paul dropped the bagel to the counter and tented his hands. Odd, how after all these years, he could still feel nervous for her. The camera took him to an indoor scene, where it focused on an American flag standing before a blue curtain. As the lens swung to the left, he saw a lectern bearing the presidential seal.

"Ladies and gentlemen," a sober man in a black suit announced, "the president of the United States."

Every man and woman in the crowded room stood as Daryn appeared. A moment of silence followed her short walk to the lectern, then a smattering of the assembled reporters broke into applause. And why not? Despite the somber circumstances, history had just been made—the first female president of the United States had stepped up to deliver her first official statement.

Though he'd seen a hundred pictures of Daryn in the last few years, Paul found himself looking for signs that the event had changed her. She stood as slim as a pleat in a black suit, her expression serious and reserved, her faint smile tinged with sadness. He felt an instant's squeezing hurt at the sight of that sadness, then reminded himself that he no longer had a right to care.

A wealth of golden blonde hair framed her slender face, a face that seemed unmarred by the passing of years. Paul unfolded his hands, cupping his chin in his palm as the camera zoomed closer. The new president acknowledged the applause with a polite smile, then cut it off with an uplifted hand. Daryn had always known the proper and expedient thing to do.

"Thank you for coming, ladies and gentlemen," she said, clearly tempering her natural energy to suit the sad occasion. Paul resisted a guffaw—as if any reporter in his right mind would stay away from *this* historic press conference.

Daryn glanced down at her notes, then lifted her chin for the camera. "Just before 3 A.M. this morning, in the family quarters of the White House, President Craig Parker collapsed. The first lady called immediately for help, which was given within seconds, but though the White House medical staff worked diligently to save his life, their efforts failed. At 3:39 A.M., at George Washington University Hospital, President Parker was pronounced dead. Cause of death was attributed to a ruptured abdominal aortic aneurysm."

She paused, her graceful brows drawing together in an agonized expression. "I will defer any medical questions to President Parker's doctors. Now I join you in grieving the loss of Craig Parker, a great president and an exemplary human being. He was a compassionate public servant, a devoted husband, a leader of integrity and vision. He brought a measure of dignity to the office of the president; he exhibited leadership both in and out of the spotlight. He will be deeply missed by his wife, his colaborers, and the nation."

A tremor passed over her face, and a spasm of grief knit her finely-arched brows. Paul felt his own heart constrict at the sight, an involuntary response that time had not been able to eliminate.

"The doctors have assured me that President Parker did not suffer. For that knowledge we are grateful, yet we regret being denied the wisdom of his parting words. I believe he might have echoed the thoughts of another American president, Zachary Taylor, who died in the same bedroom where President Parker collapsed. Just before taking his last breath Taylor said, 'I am about to die. I expect my summons very soon. I have tried to discharge my duties faithfully. I regret nothing, but I am sorry I am about to leave my friends.'"

At this, Daryn looked directly into the camera. "Mr. President, your summons came too quickly. But you have nothing to regret, and you discharged your duties with excellence and compassion. And we, your friends, are sorry you have left us so soon." She turned, sweeping the assembled reporters with a tremulous smile. "We will offer every consideration to the first lady, and we will continue to rely upon the goodwill, cooperation, and faith of the American people. I do not accept the responsibility of this office lightly, but will discharge my commission to the best of my ability." Pausing, she gripped the lectern with both hands. "A day after succeeding to the presidency after FDR's death in April 1945, Harry Truman stood before an assembled group of reporters and said, 'Last night the moon, the stars, and all the planets fell on me. If you fellows pray, pray for me.'"

She hesitated a moment, and as the camera moved closer, Paul saw a shimmer in her eyes. "I'd like to echo Truman's sentiment, but must make one small amendment. Considering how the gender makeup of the press pool has changed over the last fifty years, I'd have to say 'if you *people* pray, pray for me.' Thank you."

Voices rose as she left the platform, reporters shouting questions, but Daryn disappeared through the blue curtain flanked by a retinue of men and women in dark suits. CBS News returned the screen to Steve Dasher, who still stood outside the White House. The news director must have caught Dasher off guard, for a shell-shocked expression occupied his face until he snapped to attention and lifted his microphone.

Stunned and shaken, Paul raked his hand through his hair. "Well," he murmured, his mind's eye occupied by the image of Daryn at the lectern, poised and in complete control. "You got what you wanted, didn't you?"

"What?"

His wife's soft voice startled him. He turned in time to see Maria enter the kitchen, a vitamin bottle in her hand. She'd been cancer free for nearly three years and seemed convinced that the vitamins were keeping her healthy.

"Just talking to myself." He nodded toward the vitamins. "Want me to pour you some juice?"

"I can get it." She moved slowly toward the refrigerator, her slippers softly slapping the tile. "What's happened? You have that look on your face."

Paul glanced at her—how closely had she looked at him?—then turned back to the television. "The president died last night. An aneurysm. Apparently he had no warning."

She paused with her hand on the refrigerator. "That's terrible."

"Tragedies happen. And now we have a new president—our first female commander in chief."

"Your old friend." Maria said these words in an inflectionless voice, and for a moment Paul could not look at her. He'd never been entirely honest about Daryn, preferring to believe that ancient history deserved to remain buried and undisturbed. But Maria knew him, could interpret his silences and his averted eyes, and still the refrigerator door had not opened, so she was standing there, waiting for some kind of reassurance . . .

He stood and reached for her, pulling her softness into the circle of his arms. Even during her illness, which doctors had treated with lumpectomy and radiation, she had retained her rounded figure and full face. Her body had recovered, but the diagnosis of cancer had devoured something at her core, an incorporeal essence invisible to x-rays and undetectable to all but the man who'd married her. Maria had once wanted many things; now she wanted only to live a private, pampered, and protected life because she'd had *cancer*.

"I knew Daryn Austin ages ago," he said, cradling her dark head against his chest. "She probably doesn't even remember my name."

Maria tipped her head back, a smile finding its way through the mask of uncertainty. "How could anyone forget Paul Santana? There's never been a man so handsome, so intelligent, so utterly *encantando* . . ."

"Never as charming as Maria Santana," he countered. He bent and pressed a kiss to her forehead, then shifted his gaze to the television. The first lady—the *former* first lady, he corrected himself—was leaving the hospital on the arm of a tall man he recognized as Curtis Crenshaw, the late president's chief of staff. Helen Parker, who wore a trench coat belted around her waist, walked with her eyes downcast. As the relentless camera swooped closer, he saw her chin waver. The woman the papers had dubbed the "Determined Dowager" would face a difficult adjustment in the days ahead.

Maria had followed his gaze. "The poor woman," she whispered, her hand rising to her throat.

He squeezed her soft shoulder. Helen Parker had lost her spouse without warning, undoubtedly a difficult situation, but Paul felt as though he had been losing his wife for years. Maria was well, the doctors said, and as soon as she'd passed five cancer-free years they'd consider her cured, but still she lived like a semi-invalid, shrinking from intimacy, his gaze, any semblance of a normal married life . . .

Something in his gut shriveled at the thought of another two years of this eggshell existence. Releasing Maria, he returned to his bagel and tepid coffee. "I'd better hurry to the office," he said, lifting his mug. "Any change in the political landscape makes my clients nervous. This is going to pack a double whammy—a new president, *and* a woman."

"And you?" Maria regarded him with a faintly speculative gaze. "Are you nervous?"

Paul forced a laugh. "Why should I be? As the first female president, Daryn Austin will be far too busy to monkey around with South Florida politics."

●

In his Adams Morgan apartment, Republican Senator Hank Beatty, reigning senate majority leader, switched on the TV in his darkened bedroom and watched the most recent broadcast. His aide had called at daybreak, and Hank had passed a couple of hours waking his party faithful with the news. As an independent in a Congress dominated by Republicans, the late Craig Parker had been pretty much a lame duck ever since his inauguration. He'd won by running on a platform that called for an end to partisan games, then he'd landed in Washington and discovered that political football had only two teams, neither of which was interested in drafting *him.*

Hank wanted to kick a cat whenever he thought of the past election. Craig Parker wouldn't have stood a snowball's chance in hades if he hadn't had a movie star brother willing to stump for him in the New Hampshire primaries. Zane Parker, the handsomely aging star of a trilogy of space adventure films, had pulled on a flannel shirt and joined his brother on the road in a rented Winnebago. That fancy schmantzy party-on-wheels drew the media like a convention draws pickpockets, and by March both the Republican and Democrat front runners knew they were in serious trouble.

Hank, one of a half-dozen Republican contenders, had quietly withdrawn from the campaign. Better to bide his time than run against a fellow naive enough to honestly believe he could change Washington. Hard to beat a man who told his audience, "Vote for the candidate who promises least; he'll be the least disappointing." And the movie star angle was killer. Not even a Kennedy could have prevailed against a stubbled, flannel-shirted Zane Parker.

Any idiot could see that Parker had added Austin to the ticket to broaden his voter appeal among women and Southerners. Never mind that she'd had no national experience, never mind that she was relatively young and single and decidedly closedmouthed about some of her opinions. She'd been thrilled to come along for the ride—who wouldn't be?—and the Parker-Austin ticket had squeaked through the election, winning by forty electoral votes.

But now Parker was history, and that Georgia gal was planning to move into the Oval Office. Hank smiled, amused by the thought. Everyone on the Hill knew that Parker had kept Daryn Austin mostly out of the loop. Most vice presidents were nothing but spare tires; Daryn Austin had been a pretty china doodad in the display case. Now she'd be the first woman president, hip hip hooray, and if those idiots in the West Wing could keep her in line for eighteen months, this odd time-out would stop in 2004 . . . and the two teams would continue the game.

Sinking to the edge of his bed, he pulled a package of cigarettes from the nightstand and focused on the pretty blonde woman on the TV screen. CNN was replaying Austin's speech, and undoubtedly they'd follow with yet another analysis. How many times would they run that clip today? Craig Parker had died at a decidedly inopportune hour—too late for the paper media and on the graveyard shift for the network reporters—but now that America was awake and downing its first cup of coffee, CNN would make certain Daryn Austin was celebrated from sea to shining sea.

He drew deeply on the cigarette, then exhaled through his nose. Parker had died on Friday, too, which meant this Austin news would dominate the weekend unless the new president messed up and did something really egregious, like trying to upstage the widow.

Naw. He took another drag, then set the cigarette on the edge of his nightstand while he unbuttoned his pajamas. Austin might have been out of touch, but she was no fool. She had good handlers, and they said she'd been a capable governor of Georgia. She'd won that office on her daddy's coattails, of course, worming her way in on the strength of somebody else's good name. But she couldn't have come all this way without learning a thing or two.

He had to hand it to her. Daryn Austin had walked into the Oval Office without the benefit of a single supporting vote. Seemed almost unconstitutional.

Snorting, Hank knocked his cigarette ashes into a half-empty glass of water, then took another long drag. President Daryn Austin would make history, have a few months in the sun, and doubtless inspire a thousand headlines about hair and hems and other female hoo-ha. And the lady just might need some guidance to see her through the next few months.

Dropping his cigarette into the glass, he picked up the phone and dialed his chief aide. "Justin," he snapped, forgoing any greeting, "get me an appointment with Austin as soon as you can."

●

After doing a perfunctory inspection of an engine, twenty-two-year-old Clive Wilton wiped his hands on a grease rag from the bin and stepped from the steaming heat of the garage into the air-conditioned lobby of Art's Automotive Repair. With Glenda Rosenberg's perfectly healthy Plymouth up on the rack and not due to come down until $600 had passed (about four hours, according to Art's estimate), Clive was surprised to see her brother Samuel sitting in a plastic garden chair next to Art's stack of faded *Playboys.* Sam's money was green enough, but he was still a Jew.

Art had taken a seat on the other side of the room. With his lunch spread on the footlocker that passed for a coffee table (and held, Clive knew, about a hundred back issues of *The White Race Report*), the wiry boss kept his attention fixed on the small black-and-white television on a stand in front of the window.

"Hey, Rosenberg." Clive shot Art a quick glance. "Your sister's car's not ready. Could be the differential, or maybe the transmission. We haven't exactly decided yet."

"I don't give a flying fig about that car," Rosenberg answered, his attention riveted to the TV. He leaned forward, his elbows pressing into the stiff crease that bisected his dress pants. "Take a load off, Clive, and take a look at this. I can't believe what I'm seeing."

Stepping closer, Clive saw a vaguely familiar woman on the television. "Who's that?"

While Art chewed his banana and peanut butter sandwich, Rosen-Jew supplied the answer: "Our new president, that's who. Parker died last night."

Clive leaned against the wall. "Somebody shoot him?"

Swallowing, Art thumped his chest. "Something popped in his gut.

Anyway, the guy's dead and we have a woman in the White House. Whoop-de-do."

"Oh, man." Clive crossed his arms as a name rose in his brain. "Isn't she somebody-or-other Austin? I don't follow politics much."

"You should." Rosen-Jew folded his prissy-clean banker's hands together. "When the president sneezes, the world reaches for a tissue. Whatever this woman decides about taxes, laws, schools—it's all going to affect you someday."

Clive smiled, scratching at his goatee. "I don't see how. It's not like anybody in Washington is going to care what a woman does. Everybody knows women were meant to serve men, and nobody's gonna listen—"

Rosenberg flapped his hand in Clive's direction. "Hush up now, she's about to talk."

"She's been talking all morning," Art drawled, mumbling around another mouthful of peanut butter. As proprietor, nobody would tell *him* to hush up. "And I've only got one thing to say—they need to put *her* picture on the dollar bill instead of that dusty George Washington. Her assets look like U.S. prime . . ."

Frowning, Clive closed his eyes, unwilling to listen to the woman or the crude talk that sometimes clouded this room like a visible haze. Being employed by a man who would work on the cars of Jews and blacks was hard on a guy's conscience—but working for a man who thought a woman would make a good president might be more than a proud white American could take.

●

At nine o'clock, after a mind-numbing day, Daryn returned to her bedroom in the vice president's mansion, then closed the door and leaned against it, staring at the crisply made bed. Only eighteen hours had passed since she rose from the fourposter, but she felt as though she'd aged a lifetime since her head lifted from the pillow.

After kicking off her black leather pumps, she shrugged out of her jacket and tossed it over the wing chair in the corner. She picked up the remote and turned the television to CNN, then muted the volume as she watched her own face fill the screen.

President Austin. The title felt like a badly fitting bra, apt to pinch if she turned the wrong way. The thought brought a twisted smile to her lips. Not many of her esteemed predecessors would identify with *that* metaphor . . .

This afternoon, like a ball in the children's game of hot potato, she'd been passed from meeting to meeting. She sat through quick emergency briefings from Quinn, director of the Presidential Protection Detail; Alexander O'Leary, White House counsel; Samuel Tomlin, executive director of the CIA; Lincoln Walker, director of the FBI; and a trio of unsmiling military men whose names she hadn't caught. After dinner she had been introduced to William Templeman, the chief usher of the White House, a discreet and distinguished thirty-year veteran who'd be helping her move *in* once the first lady moved *out.* She'd shaken hands with a few dozen other White House staff members, including the president's personal secretary, Soon Yi Park, and directors of the Offices of Presidential Scheduling, Presidential Personnel, Political Affairs, Public Liaison, and Communications. Finally, she'd met over two dozen members of the PPD assigned to protect the president. After a quick adjustment, the director of the Secret Service assigned the presidential team to cover her at the Naval Observatory, while temporarily dispatching the VPPD to cover Mrs. Parker, who would be granted Secret Service protection for as long as she lived.

Watching the PPD scramble, Daryn realized that these men and women didn't care for change. The sooner she lived at the White House, where they had mapped every crook and cranny, the happier they'd be.

The Secret Service agents weren't the only ones on edge today. Everyone from the director of the CIA to Miss Park had looked at her with wary expressions behind their sorrowful smiles, and Daryn knew they were thinking of their careers. She now had the authority to replace anyone holding a so-called *patronage position*—and nearly six hundred people on the White House staff alone had been appointed to serve at the pleasure of the president. If the circle were extended to include all patronage positions in Washington, nearly sixty-five hundred judges, advisers, agency heads, and bureaucrats now looked to her for continued support and job security.

No wonder they were handling her with kid gloves.

They needn't have bothered. After her initial surge of adrenaline wore off shortly after dinner, she'd been functioning on automatic pilot. Now she was so tired her nerves throbbed, and she wanted to wash her face, get out of these clothes, and crawl beneath the covers . . .

She was just about to step into the bathroom when she heard a knock at the door. Wishing she could ignore it, she called, "Mrs. Jones, is that you?"

The door opened. Her housekeeper stood in the hall with her cook, chauffeur, and Troy Stock, the head of her former Secret Service detail. Wearing a wide smile, Mrs. Jones held up a blazing chocolate cake as the small group chanted, "Happy birthday, Madam President!"

Daryn tipped her head back and howled with laughter.

THREE

SADLY, HISTORY OFFERED SEVERAL FINE EXAMPLES of presidential funerals. Daryn was not surprised to hear that the woman who'd been brave enough to face the White House photographer in a cotton housecoat decided to model her husband's funeral service after Abraham Lincoln's.

For two days Parker's body lay in state in the Capitol Rotunda, where crowds of mourners and curious tourists lined up to pay their respects. Cameras, Daryn was relieved to hear, would be forbidden in the rotunda, along with shorts, halter tops, and protest posters.

On Monday evening, the night before the memorial service, Helen Parker appeared on a Barbara Walters's television special, where she spent the better part of an hour lauding her husband and reciting his many accomplishments. On Tuesday, a team of black horses carried the casket to the National Cathedral, where the chaplain of the Senate delivered the eulogy. At the service's conclusion, the elaborate funeral procession moved to Union Station, where the widow boarded a train that would carry her and her late husband to California, Parker's home state and final resting place. Every train depot between Washington and Los Angeles, Barbara Walters announced, would be draped in black bunting.

For her part, Daryn signed a proclamation declaring Tuesday, June tenth, a National Day of Mourning. Every government building was to fly its flag at half-staff, and every American citizen was reminded to pause at noon for a moment of silent meditation.

Her first presidential act brought her no joy, but Jacob Thrasher, warming to his new role as White House chief of staff, seemed thrilled to inform her that her approval rating soared after the proclamation.

During the days of public mourning, Daryn tried to remain beneath the media radar. She attended the funeral within a clutch of other dignitaries; she placed a wreath upon the casket when it rested in the rotunda. She gave no interviews and told the White House press office to hold all press releases.

From the clutter of her vice-presidential office she watched the Barbara Walters interview and couldn't help noticing that Helen Parker referred to her only once, when Walters asked if Daryn Austin would be able to handle the job she had inherited. "If she weren't fit for the job, Craig wouldn't have chosen her as his running mate," the first lady snapped, and Walters let the matter rest.

Daryn wasn't surprised by the first lady's answer. Helen Parker had found herself in a difficult position—she had loved her husband, she had done a good job of managing the often thankless position of first lady, and she had taken extreme pride in her husband's accomplishments. Daryn had always suspected that Helen was less than enthusiastic about her husband's decision to attempt to break the gender barrier in a national campaign, but the election was now old news. Even if Mrs. Parker had been a vivacious Austin supporter, it would have been difficult to rejoice at Daryn's ascendancy without regretting the event that made it possible.

No, she couldn't expect public support from Helen Parker's camp. Support from Congress hadn't been exactly overwhelming, either. The female members, of course, had immediately issued press statements expressing sorrow at Parker's passing and congratulations for the first female president. She'd received cards and calls from several key congressmen and senators, including the House and Senate majority and minority leaders. But none of them came to visit; so they were either unwilling to run the gauntlet of photographers and commit their faces to film, or they didn't think the major media would be active on the weekend.

One congressional representative, however, did pay her a visit, arriving after dark on Saturday night. The Honorable Senator from South Carolina and Senate Majority Leader, Hank Beatty, appeared at the vice president's mansion to offer condolences and quiet congratulations. Though the conversation was inconsequential and his manner friendly, Daryn soon realized that he had called to sound out her intentions about the future.

"I'm assumin', of course," he'd said, shifting his bulk in a guest chair, "that you're plannin' to hold to the course President Parker set for this nation. That's fine. I liked Parker and I like what he's done so far."

All Parker had done, Daryn refrained from pointing out, was save a few additional acres of wetlands and issue a handful of proclamations to honor teachers, healthcare providers, and the United Nations. His efforts to do more had been stymied by both houses of Congress.

At this point Beatty narrowed his eyes and pointed an index finger toward her. "It's no secret, Madam President, that Parker wanted to be the head coach, and we all know he didn't accept much input from his teammates. So I'm sure a bright young woman like yourself is bound to have ideas of her own. How about sharing some of them with me? I just may be able to help you get those ideas through the Senate, do something to help you make a mark on the office while you're here."

Daryn smiled, wondering how a man who worked in an office all day had acquired a tan. A tanning booth? Perhaps. His smile, especially when he grinned like the Cheshire cat, looked positively dazzling against his tanned skin. The better to charm voters down in South Carolina, where wealthy landowners liked to spend time on the golf course . . .

"You are very kind, Senator." She inclined her head in a small gesture of gratitude. "But I believe it'd be foolish to discuss my plans before I've even moved into the Oval Office."

He watched her for a moment, his eyes alive with speculation, then he leaned forward. "If I may be direct," his voice fell to a conspiratorial whisper, "let me cut to the chase. Your boss was having a heck of a time getting anything done in Washington, and you'll have the same problem. But there's another election approaching, and if you really want to make your mark on this town, you have a great opportunity staring you straight in the eyes."

Daryn raised a brow. "Indeed?"

"You bet. My people are exploring the idea of putting my name out for the upcoming primaries, and I'll need a running mate. Your boss made it in on the independent ticket, but I think we both know he wouldn't have won diddly if not for that brother and the Winnebago road party. But if you can see your way clear to toss off that independent party nonsense and join the GOP, I think we could investigate a few scenarios—"

"Senator." She stopped him with an uplifted finger. "While I admired President Parker tremendously, I don't plan to spend the next eighteen months signing useless proclamations. Whether I run for reelection or not, I'm going to do the job I was elected to do—which means doing what I think best for the American people. The late president and I ran on a platform that placed people over politics, and I don't think I can cast that mandate aside now." Tilting her head, she allowed herself to lapse into the Georgia drawl she'd spent years trying to eliminate. "Why, if I did that, I'd be seen as a traitor at worst, and an opportunist at best."

Beatty jerked at his sleeve. "Parker had no mandate. People over politics? What in the world is that supposed to mean?"

"It means—" she gave him a smile with teeth in it—"that I care less about positioning and politics than I do about people—individual people, not corporations and caucuses. And if I do consider running for the 2004 election, I don't think I'll sit on the sidelines for anyone, not after running the country for a couple of years. That just wouldn't be a practical use of my time."

Beatty departed with a great deal of polite posturing, leaving her to wonder if he would have made such a brazen offer if the meeting had occurred in the Oval Office. Perhaps not; the building itself seemed to confer dignity upon the person behind the desk.

But Beatty was from the old school, and probably still tended to think of women as ladies who did nothing but lunch and run Junior League thrift sales. Later, at Parker's memorial service, she could have sworn he was searching for potential running mates as he surveyed the crowd in the cathedral.

He wanted her job, no doubt about it. Pity she had no intention of giving it up.

●

As the funeral train pulled out of Washington's Union Station, a team of White House staffers went to work. As one group moved the Parkers' belongings out of the family quarters, another moved Daryn's boxes in. Another squad of staffers moved her personal office furnishings from the OEOB to the Oval Office, so she could officially and publicly begin the work she'd inherited.

By the time Daryn returned from the train station, the transition had been accomplished with remarkable discretion. The dense formal floral arrangements Helen Parker favored in the White House reception areas had been replaced by the lighter, taller sprays Daryn preferred. In the Oval Office, the photos of the Parkers' nieces and nephews had been replaced by Daryn's photos of her parents and a black-and-white shot of her taking the oath of office. The busts of Eisenhower and Lincoln near the fireplace had been replaced by figurines of Dolley Madison and a newly commissioned bust of Franklin Delano Roosevelt. The dark blues and reds Parker favored had vanished; now the carpets and walls gleamed in Daryn's preferred shades of ivory and gold.

The transformation had occurred in a matter of hours, and once again Daryn was impressed with the diplomacy, tact, and efficiency of the people who would control every aspect of her life for months to come.

She'd just settled into the chair behind her elegant new desk (ordered from a premier Georgia furniture company) when Thrasher rapped on the door, then thrust his head into the room. "Madam President?"

"Come in, Jacob." She stifled the urge to grin at him.

Thrasher let out a long, appreciative whistle as he looked around. "Nice digs. What'd they do, bring in a guy with a magic wand?"

"I wouldn't be surprised." She propped her head on her hand. "What about your office?"

"I'm all moved in, right next to Al Gore's old place."

"Don't you mean Crenshaw's?"

His smile widened. "There's not a scrap of Curtis Crenshaw remaining within three miles of here."

Daryn shot him a warning glance. "Don't write him off so quickly. If there's one thing I've learned, it's that men like Crenshaw are bad pennies; they always turn up again. If you write them off, they'll turn up working for your enemy."

Giving her a look of mock horror, Thrasher sank into the guest chair. "Say it isn't so. We have *enemies?*"

"Dozens, and we're only getting started." She slouched against the armrest, feeling comfortable for the first time in days. "Did you see Senator Beatty at the cathedral? I swear he was counting heads in the crowd, probably trying to scope out vice-presidential candidates."

"For your campaign, or his?"

"Either. Which brings me to our next priority—we need to nominate someone to fill that upstairs office right away. It won't be easy, since both houses have to confirm. But if we act quickly, the honeymoon effect might see us through."

Thrasher crossed his leg at the knee. "You want someone temporary . . . or permanent? Extricating yourself from a partnership that's not working will be difficult if you plan to run in 2004."

"I plan to run." She paused, letting the words resonate. "I also plan to win. I'm here, I have the office, and I plan to use it to full advantage." Swiveling her chair toward the photo-laden shelves in the wall niche, she glanced at the picture of her father. "My father taught me that possession is precious. If you surrender an inch of ground, you might as well lie down and play dead. You're done."

Thrasher looked at her in that cautious silence in which diplomatic words were sought and carefully stitched together. "I always wondered why your father didn't run for a second term as governor."

Daryn shrugged. "He meant to, but I got in his way—school trouble, the typical high-school rebellion stuff, but he knew the papers would kill him with it. He thought he could take some time off and run again later, but the party had new favorites by the time I got my act together. So he had to settle for the state senate."

"It must not have been that bad." Thrasher spread his hands. "I mean, if you'd been in real trouble, it would have come out in your own campaigns."

"The winter of my discontent wouldn't make headlines today, but that was years ago, in the Deep South, and I was the governor's daughter." She gave him a wintry smile. "It's not real life, Jacob; it's politics. And the truth of the matter is that I cost him a run at the White House. He had grand ambitions in those days . . . and the smarts to see it through."

"I've heard he was a regular firecracker."

Daryn laughed. "Sometimes he was. But I remember that he did some real good. We used to get letters—well, Daddy got letters, and his assistant would let me read them while I waited to see him. People would write to him, women and children who'd lost husbands and fathers, men out of work for one reason or another, and Daddy would help them. That's when I saw what public service was all about." She shrugged. "And that's when I knew I wanted to do what he did."

A crystal-clear memory, unexpected and unsettling, crept into her thoughts. At five, she'd been consigned to the care of a nanny while her father campaigned. She remembered watching him on the black-and-white RCA Victor television set, leaning forward in spellbound delight as people praised the lanky man from Atlanta. "That's your daddy," the nanny said, nodding at the television as she clicked her knitting needles. "The *best* man in Georgia."

A few nights later he won the biggest election of his life, and the Austin house bustled with the sounds of victory. Over her mother's protests, her father arranged for Daryn to be interviewed by a select group of reporters, and one smiling young woman knelt in the living room and asked if Daryn's daddy had any special names for her.

Overflowing with confidence, Daryn nodded.

"And what is that name, sweetheart?"

In a childish treble that echoed through the living room, Daryn said, "Daddy calls me 'Later Sugar.' That's what he says every time I try to hug him."

One of daddy's tall campaign assistants had swooped down and picked Daryn up, declaring that she needed a nap, but thanks to one and all for coming.

Her father had never allowed her to be interviewed again.

Closing her eyes, she listened to the absence of sound in the Oval Office. The bulletproof windows muffled most of the noise from outside, and the heavy carpeting and thick walls shut off the interior sounds as effectively as if she'd been dropped into a bomb shelter—which, she mused, she probably had. The door leading to the secretarial area was partially open, though, and through it came the distant chirping of telephones and fax machines . . . the music of her life.

"So, are you sure you want this for another four years?" A trace of unguarded concern lingered in Thrasher's eyes as he looked at her, and her heart warmed at the sight of it.

"Darn right. And I want another term in 2008. Just last night I was praising the powers that be that Parker lived past the halfway point of his term."

Thrasher squinted at her. "Mind explaining that one?"

"The Twenty-second Amendment. If he'd died in the first half of his term, we couldn't run more than once."

"So this way you could have two and a half terms." A note of awe filled his voice, but not a trace of disbelief, and Daryn appreciated his confidence. Thrasher had been with her since her days in the governor's mansion, and in all their years together he had never been anything but capable, confident, and loyal. At thirty-six, he would be one of the youngest men ever entrusted with the daily operation of the Oval Office, but he had divorced his wife soon after coming to work for Daryn and considered himself wedded to her career ever since. "It's not that I didn't appreciate the comforts of married life," he'd confided to her right after his divorce, "but I just don't have time to manage both work and marriage well."

Daryn had silently agreed with his sentiment. She had never married, either, though she'd maintained a few casual dating relationships. But while a married male politician actually benefited from marriage, a married female politician frequently suffered for it. No husband wanted to undertake the "wifely" duties that were considered the sacred tasks of first ladies across the fifty states, and no female leader could afford to walk demurely beside her husband in public.

Few people knew she had been in love once, and when she came to the crossroad of choosing between her man and her job, she weighed her options and chose the latter. Every woman she knew was either quitting work and surrendering to the safety of marriage or going crazy trying to balance family and employment. Daryn had studied enough economics to understand that the reason women earned less than men had nothing to do with law and everything to do with life choices—women who chose to divert their time to marriage and child rearing paid the price by devoting less energy to their careers.

She couldn't afford to pay that price. Her teenage shenanigans had cost her mother four more years as Georgia's first lady and her father another term as governor. She owed her parents, and upon reaching maturity she learned how to pay in currency they valued. She'd begun to downsize her debt in college, giving them bragging rights to her success as president of her sorority, then her leadership role in Yale's legal services organization. Even after falling in love, she kept a guard on her heart, knowing she could never surrender completely to a husband when she owed so much to her parents. Especially her father.

So she had decided against marriage and children and love . . . though the perquisites of power had certainly compensated for her sacrifices. She liked living alone, and, if she exercised discretion, she could invite a man to her apartment any time she chose.

Now she stared across the Austin desk and wondered how her life would change. The White House family quarters upstairs gave her nearly two full floors to occupy; she could invite whomever she wanted to spend the night in the spacious rooms and no outsider would be the wiser. But better, for a time at least, to err on the side of caution. She was entering uncharted waters, a smooth sea fraught with hidden currents and risks.

The thought of sleeping alone in the presidential residence sent a sudden chill down her spine.

"Jacob, I want you to call someone for me. Invite her down for a White House weekend."

Thrasher pulled his pocket PC from his coat. "Who?"

"Professor Octavia Gifford, formerly of Yale Law School. She's retired, but still living in New Haven. If the number's not listed, the school will have it."

The corner of Thrasher's mouth rose in a wry smile. "That's the beautiful thing about working out of this office. Everyone takes my calls."

Daryn swiveled her chair to look out the window. "The professor was a tremendous influence on my life. I think she'd get a real kick out of coming here."

She waited, half-expecting a wry comment about how she was still trying to impress her teachers, but apparently the Oval Office had shaved some of the irreverence from Thrasher's style. "I'll get right to it," he said, standing. "Did you want her to come this weekend?"

"Friday afternoon would be good—make sure the scheduling office knows to reserve a couple of hours."

As Thrasher walked away, Daryn stood and walked to the wide French doors. The expanse of the South Lawn stretched toward the black iron fence in the distance, and beyond the fence, the tall outline of the Washington Monument caught her gaze and lifted it toward a darkening sky.

How many presidents had stood and regarded this view? And for how many years could she call it her own?

FOUR

AS THE POCKET PC ON HER DESK CHIMED, DISCREETLY warning her of another appointment, Daryn stood and extended her hand to the last six members of the cabinet to offer their resignations.

"Please understand, I believe in President Parker's agenda," she said, giving them each a heartfelt smile. "I appreciate your willingness to resign, but I want you to continue the wonderful work you're doing."

John Norton, attorney general, gave her hand an extra squeeze. "You're doing a fine job, Madam President. We'll do our best to keep Parker's legacy alive and well."

She waited until the last cabinet member had left the Oval Office, then unsmiled. She'd made the same speech to two other sets of cabinet members. Truth be told, she wouldn't mind seeing some of them vanish into the woodwork, but she didn't want to cause a commotion as she struggled to find her footing in Congress and the White House. She needed a safe harbor, physically and politically, in which to prepare for the election that would grant her administration the legitimacy she'd need to make a real difference.

The intercom buzzed softly on her desk. "Yes?"

"Madam President, Ms. Gifford has arrived."

"Thank you, Ms. Park. Please send her in."

When the curved door opened, Daryn greeted her old professor with a smile. Octavia Gifford seemed shorter than Daryn remembered, and her face more lined, but her brown eyes still snapped with the intelligence that had impressed Daryn in law school. The professor wore her hair pulled back in the same tight bun Daryn recalled from her law school days, but now the dark hair was liberally streaked with gray.

Professor Gifford offered her hand, but Daryn drew the woman into a heartfelt embrace. "Professor Gifford!" She breathed in the faint scent of lilacs. "You don't know how many times I've wanted to see you over the years!"

When Daryn released her, the professor stepped back and gave Daryn a quick head-to-toe examination. "You've filled out a bit since your days at Yale, President Austin."

Daryn laughed. "Not too much, I hope. They tell me the camera adds ten pounds, and I seem to be facing cameras every time I go outside these days."

"You look fine. But you were quite thin in your younger years. A twig, really."

"I was a lot of things, including foolish." Daryn gestured toward the matching sofas that faced each other in the center of the oval carpet. "Please, let's sit and catch up."

Miss Park, who had lingered in the doorway, stepped forward. "Madam President, would you or your guest like coffee?"

"Yes, please." Daryn sank onto the sofa opposite her teacher, noticing how the older woman perched on the edge for a moment, then gradually relaxed into the luxurious upholstery.

"I thought someone was playing a joke on me at first," Octavia said, her voice quavery with age and what could have been anxiety. "Imagine, the president inviting me to the White House? But then I remembered that you have always been good about keeping in touch."

"You've given me good advice through the years." Daryn leaned forward, planting her elbow on her bent knee. "I only wish I could have visited you more often. But once the dust settled here, I knew I wanted to bring you to the White House. I was hoping it'd be a treat for you."

The professor laughed. "That's the understatement of the year, my dear. Everyone else in town will be positively emerald with envy."

"I'm not entirely altruistic in my motives, Professor. I was also hoping to pick your brain, if you'll pardon the expression."

Octavia's fine, silky brows rose a trifle. "Whatever for? I'm certain you have an entire cabinet of capable brains at your disposal."

Daryn shrugged. "The cabinet members *are* capable, but they're also mired in politics. I wanted a fresh opinion, and I particularly wanted yours." She lowered her voice to a near whisper. "Professor Gifford, as the first female president I've already made history. But I want my administration to be notable for more than its gender."

Inside a net of wrinkles, the professor's eyes gleamed with the clear, deep light that burns in the heart of a flame. "Then make a name for yourself by paving the way for true change. Don't be frightened of this place. Think of Washington as a college, complete with anxious freshmen and cocky seniors and all the petty rivalries that go on between the dorms and classrooms. The people in this town are political adolescents, and you, my dear, are the chancellor."

Laughter floated up from Daryn's throat. "I never thought of it that way, but the analogy is perfect. Congressional recesses even line up with a school year."

"And the two-party system is akin to college football, each led by the ranking senior quarterback—in this case, the majority and minority leaders of the House and Senate."

Gripping the edge of the sofa, Daryn leaned forward. "Which team, would you say, is winning this year?"

"The Republicans, of course," Octavia answered, her hand rising to touch her hair. "The Democrats have lost too many players. And they're constantly earning penalties."

Daryn hooted. "That's rich! Oh, how I wish my father could hear this!"

"Think about it," Octavia went on, folding her hands, "if we took a survey of our congressional representatives—providing we could get honest answers, of course—I'm sure we'd discover that 99 percent of those who work on the Hill were precocious, overachieving teacher's pets who regularly made the honor roll and volunteered to be hall monitors. They grew up thinking they were somehow superior to everyone else, so, upon reaching adulthood, what could they do but enter politics?"

Daryn's smile stiffened. "Um . . . I was one of those overachieving honor roll students."

Reaching forward, Octavia patted Daryn's hand. "So was I, dear. There's nothing wrong with being wired this way, but it's helpful to understand the mind-set you'll be addressing. Just remember—in this school, you're the boss."

Daryn smiled, wishing the professor's analogy were as simple as it sounded. The American president did have considerable power, but a stern board of directors governed the American system of checks and balances. According to the professor's analogy, the directors would be the Supreme Court . . .

"Madam President, I brought you a gift."

Startled from her thoughts, Daryn stared. "That was thoughtful, but I didn't expect—"

"Of course you didn't, that's why I brought it. Here."

The professor reached into her large straw purse and pulled out a brown paper gift bag—a heavy bag, by the look of it—and dangled it in the space between them. "Sorry I didn't wrap it. I've always tended to be lackadaisical about that sort of thing."

Pleased that the professor had thought to make a personal gesture, Daryn grasped the bag by the plastic handle and peeped inside. "Shall I proceed with the unveiling?"

"Please do."

Slipping her hand into the bag, Daryn gripped a cool, ceramic object, then pulled out an alabaster statue of a man with two faces, one looking left, the other, right.

She placed it on her palm. "Let me guess—Janus, right? One of the Greek gods."

"Roman." The professor's voice brimmed with approval. "The god of beginnings; of the past and the future; of gates, doorways, and bridges. And the god of peace."

"How appropriate." Shifting, Daryn placed the creamy statue on the antique table next to the sofa. "I suppose you meant for me to be reminded of good beginnings . . . and peace, perhaps?"

Amusement flickered in the professor's dark eyes. "My dear, I would never telegraph my intent so openly. I thought of you when I saw the two faces."

Daryn managed a petulant smile. "I hope you aren't referring to my character in college. I have matured since then."

"No, dear girl, I was thinking of the two personas every successful politician must develop—the public persona and private person. I've seen far too many wonderful people sacrifice themselves on the altar of government. You must take care to reserve space for yourself, not to allow intrusion, not to carry the burdens of one life into the arena of the other."

"Far easier said than done," Daryn drawled, "when you live in the company office."

All traces of anxiety had fled from the petite woman, replaced by the bold passion Daryn remembered so well. "I know, but I have faith in you. If anyone can survive a term here unscathed, I believe you can."

Daryn leaned forward and propped her hand beneath her chin, absorbing the professor's words. "I know it sounds trite—" she met Octavia's direct gaze head on—"but I really want to make an impression on this office, so I'm going to run next year. But for all their talk about how it's about time we had a female president, Congress is watching me like a hawk, ready to swoop down at the first sign of weakness. The media is poised to report on the least little mishap, whether it's a fashion fiasco or a staffing snafu—"

"So tread carefully for the next eighteen months. E. B. White once said that a candidate could easily commit political suicide by coming up with an unconventional thought during a presidential campaign, and the remainder of this term will be your campaign, Daryn. So work quietly, deeply, and lay a subtle foundation for the work you intend to do in the years ahead."

The professor smiled, touching her hair again. "After you've proven you can govern without rocking the old-boy network too severely, you'll win by a landslide. Administrate successful programs, install successful people, then run again. Don't pull a Clinton and try to change everything in the first six months. Save your most ambitious programs for that final term, then go for broke. If all goes well, you'll have had *ten years* in which to influence government from the ground up."

The professor's gaze shifted, wandering about the room for the first time. "Do you realize how few presidents have had ten years of leadership? FDR had twelve, but then Congress passed the Twenty-second Amendment to prevent anyone from again serving four terms."

Daryn closed her eyes. Ten years would seem like an eternity. She hadn't yet held the office for ten days, but her life had been filled with minute-to-minute responsibilities, large and small. She'd doubtless adjust to the pace and grow accustomed to back-to-back meetings and the bundles of priority memos, correspondence, and reports she found on her nightstand every night. She had begun to understand Truman's comment about how a president either stayed on top of things or he'd soon find that things were on top of him.

In ten years . . . at the end of this adventure she'd be fifty-eight, too wired to retire, and too settled to start a new career. But if she could do something worthwhile while in office, make substantial changes and improvements, perhaps she wouldn't mind retiring to the lecture circuit or a presidential office in downtown Atlanta.

"Being the first woman vice president was a great honor," she said, opening her eyes. "And until last week I was content to occupy that place until Parker had finished his term. But now I find myself in a different situation—" she waved her hand, indicating the glorious office—"and I don't want to squander the opportunity. It would be easy to get caught up in administration and policy papers, but as the first woman here I feel I need to exceed everyone's expectations."

"What's stopping you?" A smile curled upon the older woman's thin lips. "Dare to dream of the things that will change the warp and woof of our society. Find the courage to articulate your dreams, then do whatever it takes to make your dreams happen. You'll never again have the opportunities, the power, and the personnel to make this kind of sweeping change." She leaned forward, clasping her blue-veined hands. "Think, Daryn. What would you like to see happen when you are elected to this office?"

Looking away, Daryn exhaled softly. "Honestly? I'd like to see . . . the homeless fed. The elderly housed and cared for. Children who know more about books than television. Women with complete reproductive control, including free contraceptives and abortion, should it be needed. I'd like to eradicate guns on the streets, legalize marijuana for medicinal purposes, and make certain no mother sends her son to die on foreign soil during my watch." She gave Olivia a brief, distracted glance. "Sounds like pure Cinderella talk, doesn't it?"

The professor shook her head. "All new ideas sound a little crazy at first. Make your list of dreams, and make things happen. The road will be rough, but even if you don't see complete success, you'll have changed the way we think. That's a tremendous step forward."

Raking her bangs from her forehead, Daryn nodded. "Any thoughts about the upcoming election? Eighteen months doesn't give me much time to strategize."

Octavia's nostrils flared slightly. "What I think about political campaigns in general isn't going to help you at all. But there is one piece of advice I could pass on, though it may sound trivial: Get a dog."

"I beg your pardon?"

"When it comes to persuading the electorate, there is nothing more important than having a wife, kids, and pets. Since you don't have the wife or the kids, a pet will be more important than ever." The hint of a smile lit her eyes. "Americans are mad about dogs. And if a dog loves a candidate, people figure the candidate has to be lovable."

"I don't know," Daryn said, laughing. "I've never had a pet."

"Dogs are magic. If you'll check the news archives, you'll find that Bill Clinton, an avowed cat man, got his Labrador retriever in the same month he told Monica Lewinsky she'd better come up with a cover story about her repeated visits to the Oval Office."

Daryn blinked. "What sort of dog would you recommend?"

Smiling, the professor cocked her head slightly. "A toy breed would be the most manageable, but men would see a tiny dog as proof that you're too frou-frou. You need something big."

"A Doberman? A Rottweiler?"

"Those breeds would suggest that you're weak and need protection. No, I'd recommend something large and friendly. A mastiff, perhaps. If you have the patience for two animals, couple it with a golden retriever. Everybody loves goldens."

Daryn smothered a smile as she considered the image of a huge beast lounging on the sofa in the Oval Office. The only mastiff she'd ever met had been a drooling mass of muscle, easily 250 pounds. But the dog had been impressive.

"Maybe I'll keep the dog upstairs," she said, running her hand over the spotless upholstery.

"I'd recommend a kennel and I'm sure there's one around this place. The dog's only important for photo ops and the occasional jaunt to Camp David. But you may actually grow attached to the animal."

Daryn fell silent as the door opened and Soon Yi Park pushed in a tea cart. As the secretary poured coffee into the delicate White House teacups, Professor Gifford smiled. "You certainly seem to be well tended. Is there anything you need?"

"Yes. A wife. Someone to deflect the constant attention directed toward my hair and clothing." She accepted a cup from her secretary. "Did you know that the *Post* did an article last week on my *shoes?* The writer filled the piece with quotes from podiatrists saying I was a bad example because high heels put extreme pressure on the knees. According to the *Post*, an entire generation of American women will be in dire need of arthroscopic surgery just because I chose to wear three-inch heels to President Parker's funeral."

"Don't let the petty people get to you," the professor said, accepting her coffee. "As for the other—I assume you are going to nominate a vice president to finish out this term?"

"It's a top priority."

"Good. Select a man who's married and let the second lady of the land take the heat for fashion and whatnot. You have more important things to oversee."

"By the way, Ms. Park—" Daryn caught her secretary's eye—"see what you can do about finding a mastiff breeder in the D.C. area. I'd like a young puppy, but past the housebreaking stage. Male, I think, and in good health."

The secretary didn't even blink. "Massive? That's a dog?"

"Mas-*tiff.* A big dog. The sooner a puppy can be delivered, the better."

The secretary nodded. "Anything else?"

"No, thank you. You can leave the cart; we'll serve ourselves."

The secretary left without a backward glance, and the professor's gaze followed her. "She seems quite competent."

"She's excellent. Discreet, reliable, and agreeable to overtime. Sometimes I think she lives here. Sometimes I think three-quarters of the staff lives here."

"You need a capable staff. Let them handle the routine duties so you can focus on the bigger picture." She paused. "What is your most pressing concern?"

Daryn bit her lip. She trusted few people totally, but Octavia Gifford had always been on the short list. The woman had no political ambition and she abhorred the mainstream press.

"I'm most concerned with learning the intricacies of the position," she said. "Parker and Crenshaw did a good job of keeping me at arm's length. Heaven knows there are so many White House staffers the place ought to run itself, but there's a prevalent paranoid concern over power—who's close to it, who has the president's ear, who's getting what perks. Working over at the OEOB, I was fairly out of the loop."

Octavia spooned sugar into her coffee. "I once read that the American vice president was like a man in a cataleptic condition—he could not speak, he could not move, he suffered no pain, and yet he was perfectly conscious of everything going on around him."

Daryn chuckled, though the statement was anything but funny. "That's a pretty accurate picture of how I felt, except there were times I wasn't conscious of much. The president and I had lunch once a week, often with the first lady, but Parker kept the conversation perfunctory. He utilized his chief of staff far more than me."

Octavia raised a brow. "And that chief of staff is—"

"Gone." Daryn grinned. "One of my first acts, actually. He had insinuated himself between me and Parker one time too many. My chief, Jacob Thrasher, has been with me for over six years."

"It's important to surround yourself with people you can trust." Octavia picked up her cup. "The cabinet?"

"All good people—and I'm going to let them do their jobs for the remainder of this term."

"Wise move." The professor sipped her coffee, then smiled at Daryn over the rim of the delicate china. "Whatever happened to that young man you dated in law school? The handsome Hispanic fellow?"

A jolt of unbidden emotion ripped through Daryn's soul, but a lifetime of lessons in camouflaging emotion served her well. Looking up, she gave the professor a calm and practiced smile. "Paul Santana? Last I heard, he was practicing law in Miami. He was a key player in the Elian Gonzalez situation."

"Really. On whose side?"

Daryn lowered her gaze to her coffee cup lest her eyes reveal the emotional tumult Paul's name always elicited. "Elian's Miami family. He has solidly aligned himself with the Cuban community."

The professor made a soft *tsk*ing sound. "A shame he had to take on that case. It was a no-win situation. Impossible to declare victory when the choice is between democracy and a parent's right to his child."

"I know. In any case, Paul has kept a low profile since Elian went back to Cuba."

Unable to still the trembling of her hand, Daryn lowered her coffee cup to the saucer, hoping the professor wouldn't hear the rattle of the china. Paul Santana. Since college she'd lived only a handful of days in which she hadn't thought of him, but she'd learned how to manage the memories. Even in times like these when, like hunger pangs, they sliced through her center and demanded attention, she could shove them behind the curtain of her thoughts and promise to address them later. On those nights, on *most* nights, she would lie on her bed, her body half-asleep but her brain busy taking each memory from its hiding place and savoring it, breathing in its fragrance and tasting it from a dozen perspectives. Two years with Paul had given her a veritable storehouse of memories, but she had her favorites: the look of frank admiration he always gave her when she entered the room in a new dress; the time he had laughed with abashed pleasure when, after six months of living together, she could still recite every detail of their first meeting; and the delightfully casual way he said, "Hello, lovely" whenever she picked up the phone . . .

Suddenly remembering who and where she was, Daryn jerked the curtain over her treasured recollections and sipped her coffee, letting the silence stretch. Professor Gifford's common sense and encouragement had been just what she needed, an unbiased voice to assure her she was moving in the right direction. The thing Daryn needed most in Washington was an honest friend with no ulterior motives.

She lowered her cup to the saucer. "Would you, Professor, consider a position in Washington? I could always use another adviser, and you've always seemed like the last person on earth who'd pursue a selfish agenda."

The professor tipped her head back, the room filling with the high peal of her laughter. "Oh, Madam President," she finally said, wiping a tear of mirth from her eye, "you have a delicious sense of humor."

"I wasn't kidding."

Octavia's smile softened. "No, dear, I know you weren't. But Washington is not for me. You think of me as unadulterated, and you're probably right, at least to a point. But ten minutes after the first report that I'd been seen having lunch with the president, my objectivity would be up for sale."

"You've never seemed the type who could be bought."

"Everyone, Daryn, has weaknesses. I might not be the sort to take a financial bribe, but I expect there are other ways I could be tempted." She set her cup on the delicate saucer, then crossed her hands at the wrist and focused on Daryn's gaze. "Education for poor children, reproductive freedom, environmental crusades . . . The right lobbyist, the right cause, and I could become as rabid as the next fellow, coming up here to pull on your ear and demand attention." She shook her head. "No, my dear, I'm deeply honored, but I think I'll keep to my home in New Haven and tend to my summer garden. You may be the most famous of my former students, but there are others who occasionally call."

"Would you mind that? An occasional call? Or the random question that must, for obvious reasons, remain off the record?"

"I'd be honored to hear from you," she said, her voice low and sincere. "I would be grateful for your trust."

In a wave of relief, Daryn smiled. Though she'd taken pains to wear a brave and confident face, until this moment she had felt strangely alone and unready for the task ahead. But Professor Gifford, fount of wisdom, would always be a phone call away.

"What you need in an adviser," the professor added, "is someone who's known you for years, someone with integrity. And someone who hasn't been spoiled by the Washington powerbrokers." One of her brows arched. "Your father, perhaps?"

Daryn shook her head. "Though Dad would love living in Washington, I'm afraid his health won't permit it."

The hint of a smile lit Octavia's eyes. "What about Paul Santana?"

"Bring Paul to Washington?" Though something inside her bubbled at the idea, Daryn took care to temper her smile. After all, Paul the memory might not match Paul the present man. "As a lawyer?"

"Doesn't the president need lawyers?"

She forced a laugh. "Of course, my *lawyers* need lawyers. The president has a chief counsel, a deputy chief counsel, and more than a dozen associates who work for them—I'm not even sure how many."

"Then you could use another good man."

"Perhaps . . . unless he's attached to *his* summer garden."

The professor's dark eyes sparkled wickedly. "Unless he's changed drastically in the past twenty-odd years, I doubt Paul Santana spends much time in the garden. Mr. Green Jeans, he wasn't."

Daryn shot her professor a look of agreement, then stood. "Did you bring an overnight bag? I'm giving you a choice—you can spend the weekend either in the Lincoln Bedroom or in the spare bedroom next to mine. The Lincoln Bedroom is more notorious, but the room next to mine was JFK's."

Professor Gifford had stood; now she stopped in midstep and threw Daryn a startled glance. "I could sleep in John Fitzgerald Kennedy's bedroom?"

Daryn grinned. The professor had been an ardent fan of Kennedy's, often ending her classes with quotes from the "Ask not what your country can do for you" speech.

"The very place," she said. "They tell me Jackie occupied the master suite, and though she and JFK spent an uninterrupted hour together every afternoon, the president actually bunked next door. If, however, you'd prefer the Lincoln—"

"Are you kidding?" Octavia moved forward with a great deal of eagerness. "Lead me to Kennedy's room. I might not come out all weekend."

FIVE

HIGH ON A MOUNTAINSIDE OVERLOOKING TETON Village, Clive joined the True People meeting in a ramshackle wooden building which crouched amid the evergreens at the end of a rutted dirt road. Morning sunlight shone through the open windows and the chinks in the clapboards, spangling the pine floor and walls. Shifting in a rusted metal folding chair, Clive crossed one blue-jeaned leg over the other. A thin ribbon of sweat wandered down his back; not even the pounding of the ladies' rattan fans and the slow circular orb of a ceiling fan overhead could dispel the heavy heat of a June afternoon.

He nodded as the speaker pounded the wooden stand with his fist. "Government structure is not and never has been the problem," Jimmy Griffin said, his voice commanding the room. "Until last week this country had always managed to understand the importance of having a white man at the helm. The Romans recognized whites as the ruling class, so did Hitler's national socialists. It is only when the Jewish pestilence infiltrates society that we see such anomalies as women in the White House, Jews on the cabinet, and blacks in the Congress. Our forefathers, who bled and *died* for the freedom of the White Race, are surely turning over in their graves!"

A chorus of agreement echoed from the men on the right; while a little flutter of admiration ran through the knot of women on the left.

"We must retake that which has been stolen," Jimmy went on. "White society must advance and regain our ground, then we must be certain that the man in leadership is the best *man* available, and that he is committed to White Racial loyalty. That *woman* in the White House is proof that God has turned his back on us. Because we have forfeited our position, because Anglo-Saxon white men have stood idly by while Jews and blacks and women took our God-ordained places of leadership, God has given our nation over to them. The children of white men are now oppressing them, and women are ruling over us. Have you noticed that the white man's women are no longer classified as white? They are minorities, thrust into the same group as the Jewish contamination and the black animal!"

A murmur of voices, a palpable unease, washed through the room as Jimmy picked up his Bible. "Isaiah 3:12 predicted it: 'As for my people, *children* are their oppressors, and *women* rule over them. O my people, *they which lead thee* cause thee to err, and destroy the way of thy paths.'"

He lowered the Bible with a thump. "Due to his own negligence, the Anglo-Saxon white man has now become an object of ridicule. The whore of Babylon, who sits upon many waters, is leading this nation astray. Rise up, oh men of God! Rise up, White Men of America! Before it is too late!"

Another chorus of agreement followed, but Jimmy lifted his hand. "Be silent, brothers and sisters. Don't give me your words; give me your action. Be still and think about what you need to do for the White Race."

The silence that followed was like the hushed moment when a doe caught the hunter's invasive scent and froze, intuiting that life and death wavered upon the next thin minute. Clive followed Jimmy as he moved to the tall wooden chair on the platform, and kept his eyes upon him as another member began to close the meeting with an announcement about a covered dish dinner after the meeting next week.

Clive had never been so stirred, not even on the first Saturday he discovered this mountain outpost of the True People. Jimmy was absolutely right; Clive had seen the proof even in Art's Auto Repair. Art might have gotten a few jollies over cheating the Jews, but still he accepted their cars. Wasn't that a dangerous compromise? And wasn't Clive himself compromising by working for a man who would roll out the welcome mat for anyone with a credit card?

He lowered his head as shame washed up from his collar, flooding his neck with heat. He didn't need that job. The trust fund provided by his dead parents provided more than enough for a simple existence.

On the way out of the building, he paused on the porch to shake Jimmy's hand. "Fine talk you gave there, brother." Clive hesitated on the threshold. "I especially appreciate the call to action. I'm going to do something, too, soon as I figure out what needs doing. I'm thinking about quitting my job, maybe moving up into the mountains to consider a few things. I figure I can live off the land for a while, maybe do some odd jobs while I figure out how to help the White Race—"

"Bless you, son." Jimmy put both his big hands around Clive's. "Right now, you can certainly pray. That witch in the White House only has a few months to serve, and then we'll get a white man back in control. But in the meantime, we'll need you to pray she does no damage."

"I will, sir." Clive spoke with as much quiet firmness as he could muster. "You can count on me to do my part."

"Glad to know there are young folks like you around, son."

Releasing his hand, Jimmy turned to the next member, sending Clive out into a glorious summer Saturday rich with promise.

SIX

THREE DAYS AFTER THE PROFESSOR'S SUGGESTION, a pair of Secret Service agents ushered Mr. Clifford Johnson and a five-month-old male mastiff to the Oval Office.

"Oh, my." Stepping out from behind her desk, Daryn gave the animal a dubious gaze. "He's still a puppy?"

"Twenty weeks, ma'am," Mr. Johnson said, extending a hand. "And out of the finest pair of mastiffs in the country right now. You'll not find a pedigree like his in the entire world."

Daryn bent down, bracing her hands against her knees. The fawn-colored dog had the biggest feet she'd ever seen on a canine, but his eyes were clear gray inside a deep black mask. The expression was pure sweetness.

She looked up at the breeder. "Not the brightest bulb in the pack, was he?"

"Aw, ma'am, don't let that puppy face fool ya. This pup could guard the White House all by himself, if you had a mind to let him. Mastiffs were born and bred to guard English castles back in medieval days, but we've bred 'em gentle in the last few years. Had to, you know, since we started showing 'em. Can't have a show judge sticking his hand in the mouth of an animal that wants to eat him alive."

Daryn offered the dog her hand.

"Don't know that I'd ever stick my fingers in front of a strange dog," Johnson muttered, speaking more to his Secret Service escort than to her. "One snap and those fingers would be flat gone."

Wordlessly Daryn folded her fingers into her fist. The dog, however, seemed more inclined to sniff than bite, and after a moment of perfunctory whiffing, he settled onto his haunches and gave her a jowly grin.

"Does he have a name?" she asked.

"Tyson's Majestic Washington," Johnson said, slipping his free hand into his jeans pocket.

"That's a lot of name."

"Well, ma'am, he'll be a lot of dog. He's 150 pounds and still got a stretch of growing to do. His 260-pound daddy was the number one mastiff in the country for five years running."

Daryn wiped her hand on her skirt. "Let's hope Tyson helps me do as well as his daddy." She took the leash from the breeder, then stooped to rub the big, dark head. The dog closed his eyes while a two-foot tail began to thump the carpet. Daryn couldn't help laughing.

Bill Templeman, chief usher of the White House, stepped into the room. After nodding to Mr. Johnson, he said, "We have a kennel prepared in the residence. We've laid down a nice vinyl floor and put in a doggy bed." He hesitated, then gestured toward the leash. "I can take him upstairs now if you'd like."

Tyson, enjoying the head scratching, lowered himself to the floor, forcing Daryn to follow. "Um—" she explored his oversized ears—"maybe he can stay here for a while. He can nap beside the desk. If he gets rambunctious, I'll call."

The breeder grinned. "Mastiffs don't generally get rambunctious," he said, pulling on his ear. "Sleepin' and eatin' is about all they like to do."

Daryn made a face. "I was hoping for something to present a vigorous picture—"

"Oh, he'll look vigorous, all right." Johnson shoved his other hand into his pocket. "For about ten minutes. Then he'll be ready to come inside for a nap."

"Perfect." Daryn grinned. "We'll keep the photo ops to ten minutes from now on." She looked to Thrasher, who had slipped into the room behind the dog's entourage. "Keep that in mind, will you? Unless it's a state dinner or something, all White House photo ops will now include the dog. And they'll be short and sweet."

Tyson the Magnificent dropped his head to the carpet and let out a china-rattling snore.

"You'll love him once he gets to know you," Johnson promised. "These here are one-man dogs. They like pretty much everybody, but his sun will rise and set with you."

Exactly what she needed—a friend. Daryn extended her hand toward the dog breeder. "Thank you very much, Mr. Johnson. I'm sure Tyson and I will be very happy together." After shaking his hand, she inclined her head toward Thrasher. "My chief of staff will make sure you are properly compensated."

"There's no need for that, ma'am. I'd like to give him to you. It'd be an honor to tell folks one of my pups is growing up in the White House."

"That's very kind of you, Mr. Johnson, but the White House Gift Office needs to keep appropriate records." She spread her hands. "You know how it is—we can't do anything without filling out a form in triplicate. So if you'll go with Mr. Thrasher, he'll make sure you receive the proper forms."

"Thank you, ma'am." Johnson turned, then paused. "Do you think we could have a picture made? You, me, and the dog?"

Not at all surprised by the request, Daryn shrugged. "Why not?"

Before she could pick up the phone, Peter Chang appeared in the doorway, his camera around his neck. He grinned at Daryn, then bit his lip at the sight of the snoring dog. "Um . . . does he move?"

"Not unless he wants to," Johnson answered, moving to stand beside Daryn. The Secret Service agent in the doorway tensed, but Daryn lifted her hand, signaling him to relax. Johnson seemed as gentle as the dog.

The breeder knelt at her feet, then nudged the sleeping puppy. "Tyson, wake up. You want a cookie?"

Snapping to alertness, the dog lifted his head.

Daryn whistled. "What was the magic word? *Wake?*"

"Naw. Just say *cookie,* and he'll do whatever you want him to."

"Would that be a chocolate chip or sugar cookie?" Daryn joked, positioning herself behind the dog's bowling-ball-sized head.

"It's a dog biscuit, ma'am," Johnson answered, clearly missing the joke. He stood in a somber posture, his hands hanging limply at his side, and for a moment Daryn wondered if he'd been planning to slip an arm around her waist. *Yessir, me and the lady president are tight!* Funny, how many people now claimed to know her well . . .

After two quick clicks of the camera, Mr. Johnson stepped away, thanked her for the honor, and allowed her to thank him again for the puppy. While the agents escorted the visitor out, Tyson stretched out on the carpet, rolled onto his side, and resumed his snoring.

Miss Park came to the door and stared at the somnambulant animal. "You want him taken upstairs?"

Daryn shook her head. "Let him sleep. If we're going to become friends, we might as well get used to each other."

"But Mr. O'Leary is on his way to see you."

Daryn stared out the window, considering the situation. She'd asked for this appointment, so O'Leary was bound to be curious, if not actually anxious, about the meeting. A dog might help diffuse the situation.

She bent to rub the sleepy dog's head. "I don't think Mr. O'Leary will mind. Tyson's not going to bother anyone."

As she waited, she mentally reviewed what Thrasher had told her about Alexander O'Leary, the counsel to the president. At forty-seven, O'Leary probably fancied himself at the pinnacle of his career, though the anonymity cloaking most White House staffers would prevent him from garnering real fame or fortune until he left his presidential appointment. His present job paid $123,000 per year, not much when he had a family to support and two daughters in a tony private school. He had undoubtedly planned on leaving the White House at the end of the Parker presidency, then capitalizing on whatever glory the position exuded on his résumé—trouble was, Parker had died before his name had developed any sort of pleasing patina. A large part of O'Leary's future, Daryn realized, now depended upon her.

The relationship, however, was symbiotic. She needed a solid counsel, and she'd heard nothing but good things about O'Leary. The White House counsel functioned as a sort of ethics officer. He and his staff read the papers, watched White House operations, and threw red flags when the president's positions, personnel, or policies came anywhere close to conflicts of interest or embarrassing situations. She didn't plan to get into trouble with the ethics police, but one never knew what could happen.

O'Leary, red-haired and as freckle-faced as the stereotypical Irish boy next door, walked into the Oval Office a few moments later. Daryn saw him every morning during the senior staff meeting in the Roosevelt Room, but this was the first time she'd asked to meet him alone.

"Good morning to you, Madam President." He stretched out his hand, but she thought she detected a trace of nervousness behind his smile.

"Thank you for coming, Mr. O'Leary," she said, stepping over the dog. "I appreciate your taking time from what I know is a very busy schedule."

"My calendar is always at your disposal." Moving toward the sofa she had gestured to, he pointed toward the dog. "Would you be thinking of him as a prospect for a new rug?"

She laughed. "A new companion. The residence can be lonely at night, and someone thought the sound of snoring might be comforting for me."

O'Leary's answering chuckle sounded forced. He stood in front of the sofa, but didn't sit. "Truth to tell, I have to admit I'm curious as to why you'd be wanting to see me." His freezing blue eyes glinted with worry. "Is this about the tax reform package?"

Daryn waved her hand as she approached. "I'm going to let that move forward despite my personal reservations. President Parker spent a great deal of time on that package, and for once I think both houses of Congress are inclined to agree with him."

"It's about the antidrug campaign, then. We've done extensive research to refute the First Amendment challenges to our antismoking advertisements—"

"I didn't call you in to talk about the First Amendment, Counselor."

O'Leary's face flushed to the strawberry color of his hair as he followed her example and sank onto the sofa. "Well, then. Perhaps I should stop spouting off and let you tell me why we're meeting."

She smiled, grateful for his late attempt at humor. In staff meetings O'Leary seemed about as cheerful as an undertaker.

"It's about your staff, Counselor."

His flush deepened. "I run a tight ship. If there's been a leak—"

"No leaks that I'm aware of, Mr. O'Leary. No, I'm not unhappy with anyone. In fact, I think you can appreciate the fact that I've done my best to keep Parker's staff intact. Except for Mr. Crenshaw, no one has been asked to leave."

The grim line of his mouth relaxed slightly. "Sure, and I've noticed."

Daryn nodded. "I just want to be sure we're on the same page. As I consider your staff, however, I can't help thinking that this might be a good time for you to add an associate—perhaps even a deputy counsel."

Confusion and wariness warred in his eyes. "I don't think we're understaffed. There are sixteen lawyers employed by the White House counsel's office—"

"I think we should increase the number to seventeen. At the last Rose Garden press conference I noticed that your legal staff seemed, well, rather WASP-ish."

The lawyer stiffened. "Don't you know that among our legal staff are four women, two African-Americans, one Asian-American, not to mention me, an Irishman?"

"But the Hispanic population has just become the largest minority in this country, or haven't you read the latest census figures?" She spoke gently, not particularly wanting to arouse his infamous ire. "I applaud your diversity, Alexander, but I think it's time we hired a Hispanic lawyer—one with clout in the Latino community."

Pressing his hand to his square jaw, O'Leary stared at the carpet. "I'd have no problem with hiring a qualified Hispanic lawyer, none at all. But I doubt there's money in the budget. If we were to hire someone new, someone else would have to go."

"This is the White House, with over sixty-five hundred positions to fill. Move someone out and make room." She gave him a smile. "Call it a promotion. I'm sure there are at least a dozen agencies in Washington who could use another legal eagle."

O'Leary stroked his chin. "I'm still a wee bit confused. We're not in the public eye. The average American has no idea what the White House counsel's office even does, let alone who works in it. So—if I may speak frankly—how is your hiring of a Hispanic lawyer going to matter?"

"Because we're hiring an American hero, and you'll make him your deputy counsel." She broke into a wide, open smile. "I want the country to see that this administration is committed to racial diversity, and I have the perfect man for the job—Paul Santana, of Lopez, Bentley, Kremkau, and Stock in Miami Beach. I'd appreciate it if you'd submit his name for the background investigation immediately."

O'Leary's brow furrowed. "Santana—and wasn't he the lawyer who lost Elian Gonzalez?"

"He's the lawyer who *won* the undying loyalty of nearly every Latino in Florida," Daryn countered. "And he's a bright attorney who hasn't bought into his firm's partnership. So I have a hunch he'll be warm to a job offer."

The White House lawyer said nothing, but stared at Daryn. She had the feeling his eyes were attempting to probe what his words could not, but she could no longer be intimidated. O'Leary, Thrasher had reminded her, was a sharp and determined strategist, but he was not the president.

The lawyer dropped his hand. "I'll submit Santana's name to the Office of Presidential Personnel, then. The routine often takes a few weeks, but they can start the background checks immediately—"

"Let them take as long as they need, but Paul Santana will have a clean record. I'd stake my life on it."

"You know him, then." The words were flat and faintly accusatory.

"I haven't spoken to him in over twenty years, but I know his character. He's a visionary, a man who'll work to his last breath to serve whatever cause he's adopted. I think it's time we put that kind of tenacity to work for us."

O'Leary nodded, then pressed his hands to his knees. "If there's nothing else—"

"Just my thanks for a job well done, Counselor. My office is always open to you."

As O'Leary closed the door behind him, Daryn took advantage of the solitude to survey her new pet. The dog was awake now, but his gray eyes were half-closed, still heavy with sleep.

"You're just a big doofus, aren't you?" she whispered, kneeling next to him. On a whim, she lowered herself to the carpet and propped herself on one arm, caressing his velvet ears with her free hand. "We could use a doofus around here to lighten the mood. And I could use a friend."

A memory, a safe one, flitted past her face like the wings of a butterfly. She and Paul had once stopped by a pet store, and he'd begged her to let him buy a puppy.

"Come on," he'd said, his eyes as woebegone and adorable as those of the beagle in the pen. "You need a friend to keep you company when I'm in class."

She'd refused, listing a dozen reasons why they couldn't have a dog: the landlord would have a fit if the carpets were soiled, she and her parents had never been dog people, how could he expect her to find time to feed and walk and worm an animal while she was working for her degree? In the end they'd gone home empty-handed, Paul walking with his arm snugly around her, but still with that lost puppy look in his eyes . . .

"If I had it to do over again," she whispered, lowering her head to whisper in Tyson's ear, "I'd buy the dumb dog in a heartbeat."

SEVEN

On the twenty-fifth of June, just as Paul was settling in to watch a Wednesday night baseball game, a special announcement cut into the broadcast. A moment later the station's logo faded to a blue curtain and the presidential seal, then Daryn Austin strode out to meet the assembled group of reporters.

Paul straightened in his chair. He'd heard nothing about a scheduled presidential address, so this was no ordinary press conference.

"Good evening," Daryn said, her lovely countenance serious as she faced the press. "Two days ago, during a routine flyby over Iraq, one of our new F-22 jet fighters went down in Iraq. I have spent the last two days in the Situation Room meeting with the National Security Council. Our deliberations resulted in a recommendation that a Navy SEAL team be dispatched to reconnoiter the area and bring our missing pilot home."

The flicker of a faint smile crossed her face. "I'm happy to report that Captain Henry Wilt is now safely en route to Edwards Air Force Base in California, where he'll be debriefed. He was rescued without mishap, and details of the mission are classified. The SEAL team, which will not be identified, also returned safely." She swept the room with a confident smile. "Are there any questions?"

A flurry of hands filled the lower part of Paul's TV screen, then someone asked about the plane.

Daryn nodded. "Unfortunately, the jet had to be destroyed. As you may know, the F-22 Raptor combines stealth design with the supersonic, highly maneuverable long-range requirements of an air-to-air fighter, and its integrated avionics are cutting-edge technology. We could not allow that information to fall into enemy hands, so Captain Wilt, quite properly, destroyed the plane."

Another hand rose. "What about the cost? Aren't those planes worth millions?"

"The cost," Daryn said, arching a brow, "is inconsequential compared to the worth of a human life. We were primarily concerned with rescuing Captain Wilt. We can always build another plane."

"What made the plane go down?"

"Why was it flying over Iraq?"

"Was Saddam Hussein aware that we violated his boundaries?"

Cool as a professional assassin, Daryn lifted her hand and restored order. "We have been conducting flybys over Iraq for years as part of the U.N.-brokered peace agreement. The crash was apparently the result of weather, and yes, I'm sure Saddam knew we had a man down. That was why we acted with all due haste, secrecy, and efficiency."

Without another word, she smiled, paused to shake the hand of a uniformed military man standing behind her, and walked away, leaving the press pool with all the important facts and none of the tantalizing details.

Impressed, Paul folded his arms and stared at the television. "Bravo, Daryn," he whispered, the corner of his mouth rising in a smile. "Courage and grace under fire. You have just proved yourself a president."

●

The next Monday, Paul's secretary routed an unusual caller into his office.

"Paul Santana?" The voice on the phone was unfamiliar, but it carried enough authority to reflexively tighten the muscles of Paul's forearms.

He looked through the doorway toward his gray-haired secretary, who was eavesdropping with more enthusiasm than usual. Again, just in case he'd missed it, Agnes mouthed *the White House.*

Paul shifted his gaze toward his desk. "This is Paul. How can I help you?"

"Alexander O'Leary, White House counsel."

Paul felt his stomach drop. Though he'd known Agnes wasn't the type to joke around, the confirmation of her announcement sent a frisson of alarm through his bloodstream.

"What can I do for you, Mr. O'Leary?" He turned his chair toward the wall, unwilling to let Agnes read his anxiety on his face. In twenty-two years as an attorney, he could count all his calls from any branch of the federal government on two hands. And all of those had sprung from the Elian Gonzalez case, not exactly a pleasant memory.

In rising disbelief he listened as O'Leary explained that a position had opened in the White House counsel's office. Not just any position, but that of deputy counsel, the man second in command to the president's lawyer.

Daryn's lawyer.

He drew a quick breath as understanding flooded his brain. Daryn had arranged this, and he couldn't begin to imagine why.

"I'll be honest, Mr. Santana," O'Leary was saying, the hint of a smile now in his voice. "The salary isn't spectacular, but the perks are substantial. Most of our associates are recent law school graduates, but they're the brightest and best. The intensity level is quite high, however, and if you're the type who likes to invest your time in issues that matter, well, this may be the perfect place for you."

Paul shifted in his chair, conscious of a small stirring of curiosity, but fought it down. Daryn Austin, president or not, belonged in his past.

He cleared his throat. "Well, Mr. O'Leary, the offer is certainly an honor. But I'm afraid I'm going to have to decline."

The line hummed for a moment, then O'Leary added, "Wouldn't you like some time to consider it? I can overnight a package with a salary proposal to your office. We don't need an answer right away, if you take my meaning."

"Thank you, but no. I've put down roots in Miami, and I'm afraid they're deep. At this stage of our lives, I don't think my wife and daughter would be thrilled by the thought of moving to Washington."

O'Leary deepened his voice. "Perhaps I should add that this offer comes directly from the president. She specifically asked me to contact you."

Paul forced a polite chuckle. "Then thank President Austin for me, but I'm afraid I'll have to decline what is an admittedly tempting opportunity."

The White House lawyer would not be denied. "I appreciate your loyalty to your family, but I really must insist that you take a few days to consider our offer."

Leaning back in his chair, Paul grinned. "Is this a private line?"

"Yes."

"She really put the screws to you, didn't she?"

O'Leary laughed. "Sure, and didn't she say you were a bright one! Well, I think I can safely say no one wants to disappoint her in the honeymoon phase. We keep waiting for her to take a broom and clean house."

"I can't believe Daryn would be unfair. The woman does have principles."

"Yes, but we're not quite certain what they are."

Paul chuckled, feeling a sudden wave of compassion for the man. The passing of twenty years had surely changed Daryn Austin, but she had always been persistent. Some character qualities did not fade with time.

"I'll talk to my family and to the head of my firm," Paul promised. "But my inclination is to decline."

"Understood. But if the president asks me, at least I'll be able to say you're considering the offer."

After thanking O'Leary for the call, Paul hung up, then tented his hands and stared at the floor. Go to Washington? Ten years ago he'd have jumped at the offer. He'd have done almost anything to pry Maria from the bosom of her family, and Cristina had been young enough to adapt to a new place. But since the cancer Maria had become doubly dependent upon her family, and Cristina couldn't decide what to wear without consulting her circle of friends. Though, at eighteen, Cris was about to leave the nest, how would she feel if they moved and she had no nest to return to?

And Daryn . . . Reluctantly, he forced himself to think of her. Over the years he'd draped memories of Daryn in mental barbed wire, and now he winced out of habit. He'd grown accustomed to hearing her name on the news, inured to the sight of her photo in magazines, but O'Leary's call had summoned memories of the young woman Paul had known, the girl who had taken his heart, his future, and wormed her way into his soul . . .

She'd asked for him. She wanted him in Washington.

And he'd be the worst kind of fool to open himself up to that kind of pain again.

"Well?" Agnes leaned in the doorway, her eyes alight and her mouth pursed into a knot. "Was that really the White House?"

"It's a confidential matter, Agnes." Shifting out of his meditative pose, Paul turned back to his desk and riffled a set of papers. He glanced up. "And shouldn't you be going to lunch now?"

Agnes took a half step back, as though the words had stung, and gave him the look a schoolmarm might give a recalcitrant student. "I'm leaving."

Sighing, Paul watched her go. That simple call had already begun to wreak havoc in his life, and he ought to end the speculation right now. He could call O'Leary back, tell him thanks but no thanks, and let the White House lawyer deal with the fallout.

He hadn't been entirely honest with the man. Even apart from his reluctance to be near Daryn again, he hadn't leaped at the opportunity because he wasn't exactly eager for a career in government. The battle over Elian had wounded him, though only Maria and Cristina knew how deeply.

The pain went far beyond personal pride. The little boy's Miami relatives had trusted him to prevent his forced return to Cuba, and Paul's all-too-public failure had resulted in another feather for Castro's propaganda-laced cap. Even now, photos of Elian's father, Juan Miguel Gonzalez, regularly appeared in the Cuban press. In the photos, Juan Gonzalez wore a hero's smile and always stood next to a high Communist official.

By far the worst barb was the oft-repeated opinion that Paul's failure to protect Elian from Communism meant that Elisabeth Broton, who drowned in her attempt to reach the safety of the United States, died for nothing.

Dropping the papers in his grip, Paul confronted the truth: his encounters with the U.S. government had done little to encourage his belief in the American system. He still believed in freedom, and as the son of Cuban refugees he probably cherished it far more than the average American citizen. But the Elian situation had taught him that in the American mind freedom no longer ranked as the most important virtue. Diplomacy ranked higher, as did political correctness. The authorities had held their fingers to the prevailing societal winds and made a value judgment that tore Elian from a loving family and negated a courageous woman's self-sacrifice.

"Señor Paul?" Agnes wrapped softly on the door, and this time her eyes were gentle. "I have to know, are you going to work for the White House?"

Paul shifted his gaze to meet hers. "Afraid not, Agnes."

A smile lifted the corners of her pink-painted mouth. "Oh. I am sorry."

"Don't be," he said, pushing up from his chair. "No sense in crying over spilled milk, is there?"

EIGHT

ANSON QUINN WHISTLED AS HE PASSED THE security checkpoint at the entrance to the Old Executive Office Building, then paused by the desk to punch an old friend. "Hey, Quinn!" The uniformed agent flashed a grin. "You slumming down here today?"

"Not a chance," Quinn answered, moving toward the hall that led to a branch of the mammoth White House Correspondence Office. "Came to see someone a lot better looking than you."

Leaving the uniforms to their job, he moved down the corridor, nodding at several of the people he passed. Most of them wore good-for-one-day V-passes, indicating that they were part of the volunteer staff. Though he occasionally encountered an exception, a majority of the folks in this office were white-haired, retired, and eager to fill their time with something productive.

The woman he'd come to see, however, was neither retired nor white-haired. Spying her through a window in the Presidential Greetings Office, he pulled the door open, crept forward on tiptoe, and pressed a finger to his lips as an elderly woman caught his gaze. Her brow lifted, but she said nothing as he swooped in and planted a smacky kiss upon the brunette's neck.

His wife pulled back, giving him a look of equal parts pleasure and reproach. "Anson! Mrs. Terwilliger will think I'm cheap."

"Don't go putting thoughts in my head," the older woman said, watching Anson with faint amusement. For an instant a note of wistfulness stole into her expression. "Sure wish someone would come up and do that to me."

Anson dropped into the empty chair beside Gayle, then nodded toward the labeled boxes on the table. "Who are you congratulating today? Antiques?"

"Eagle Scouts," she answered, pulling a signed card from a stack. Without breaking her rhythm, she slid the card into the envelope, sealed it with a swipe of a sponge-tipped applicator, then smoothed the edge with her fingertips. She picked up a fountain pen to address the card, then paused. "Mrs. Terwilliger's doing today's congrats for one-hundred-and-one-year-olds, if you want to put your name in."

"Very funny, Wife." He paused, watching her begin to write. Long and curving, her handwriting had always seemed an extension of her lovely grace.

Without looking up, Gayle said, "So—what brings you down here? Are you bored?"

"How could I be bored?" Lacing his hands behind his head, he stretched out in the chair. "I've got the most exciting job in the world."

"Then why aren't you out protecting the president?"

"Because the president's in, and there's already a full team over there."

Mrs. Terwilliger's eyes widened. "You're one of the president's men?"

Anson felt the corner of his mouth twist in a wry smile. "I'm not sure you phrased that correctly, ma'am. I'm one of the agents assigned to her protective detail."

"He doesn't put in extra hours, is what he's trying to say," Gayle added, giving him a smile. "I like him home with me when he's not working."

Mrs. Terwilliger's smile turned to a chuckle. "I can't say I blame you."

The door behind him opened, ushering in a breath of fresh air and a new set of footsteps. Reflexively, Anson turned in time to see another volunteer, a red-faced balding man with a V-pass swinging from his neck.

He dropped a gray mail tray to the table, then stood and pressed his hands to the small of his back. "Tarnation," the guy groaned, making a face. "I'm getting too old for this lifting."

Looking at his wife, Anson jerked his thumb toward the mail tray. "I thought this stuff went to the New Executive Office Building to be sorted."

"It does," Gayle answered, glancing past him. "But then it gets hand-carried to the appropriate office."

As the deliveryman turned toward the water fountain, Anson glanced into the tray. These letters, rubber-banded into manila folders, had already been opened and read. Through the gap in the folders he could see that most had the envelopes clipped or stapled in the upper corner. He glanced at the side of the tray, where a label in block lettering read *Secret Service Protective Research Division.*

The guy had picked up the wrong tray. Anson waited until he had returned from the water fountain, then reached out and swiveled the tray so the red label faced the sweating volunteer. "Sir, do you see this label?"

Bending, the man peered at it. "Yeah."

"Does it say *Correspondence Office?*"

More peering. "Well, look at that. But this is the tray they gave me."

"It's the wrong tray, sir. If you want to go get the correct tray, I'll take this one to the proper office."

The man frowned, looking for the first time at Anson's face. "I don't think I should do that."

Anson pulled his ID badge from his shirt and dangled it before the man's eyes. "I'm with the Secret Service and I'll hand-carry it to the proper office myself."

The old fellow glanced once at Gayle, as if she had some say in the matter, then nodded. "Okay." Wiping his hands on his pants, he looked toward the door. "I gotta go out again in this heat?"

Standing, Anson shrugged. "I don't think there's any rush. Take ten, cool off, then go out."

Grinning, the man came around the table and slid into the empty chair next to Mrs. Terwilliger. She tilted her head and shot Anson an *are you trying to fix me up?* look, and Gayle's mouth twitched, a sure sign she was trying not to smile.

Anson picked up the tray, kissed his wife on the cheek, then slipped out into the hall. In the elevator to the ground floor, he obeyed an instinct born of idle curiosity and peeked at the letter at the top of the banded stack.

Dear White House Witch, some fool had written, *the White Race is against thee, and thou art in danger of hellfire . . .*

Blowing out his cheeks, Anson scanned the letter, grateful that he didn't have to read this kind of thing every day. The guys in the research division, though, were pros at sorting through ranting diatribes and loony letters.

Curious, he pulled the page forward and looked at the envelope, attached by a paper clip. The writer had been clever enough to leave the return address blank (he was always amazed at how many idiots threatened the president and told the Secret Service exactly where to find them), but he'd mailed the envelope from Jackson, Wyoming.

He glanced at the signature. No complete name (again, a sign of relative genius), but instead an obscure one: *Jehu.*

Wondering if the name meant anything significant, Anson slid the letter back into the folder and stepped off the elevator.

●

"You told them *no?*" Maria's dark eyes had gone as round as her dinner plate, and even Cristina had stopped eating. Both women stared at Paul as if he'd suddenly sprouted a horn in the center of his forehead.

He kept twirling spaghetti on his fork. "I said no." He kept his voice light. "I said I was happy in Miami, that we had roots here, and so I wasn't interested."

"Dad!" Cristina's voice filled with the anguish only a teenager could produce. "You turned down the *White House?* Are you crazy?"

Maria's gaze shifted to her daughter. "Don't disrespect your father," she chided, then she turned to Paul. "Are you *loco?* This is the opportunity of a lifetime! How many Florida lawyers get invited to work at the White House?"

Paul shrugged. "None that I know."

"You see?" Maria thumped the table with her small fist. "You should call him back tomorrow. Tell him you've reconsidered."

"Call him quick," Cristina pointed her fork at him. "Before he fills the job with someone else."

Exasperated, Paul dropped his fork. "What's the big deal? It's just another law firm. I hear the salary's not even that great."

"Dad, it's the White House!"

"It's Washington, D.C. The capital of our country." Maria's eyes flashed with the fire inherited from grandparents who had been born on foreign soil. "The home of the free and the brave."

Sighing, Paul turned to his daughter. "I didn't think you'd want to leave your friends."

Cristina gaped at him. "Dad, I'm leaving home in a month. I'll be making all new friends at college."

Paul opened his mouth to protest, but his wife cut him off. "I know what you're thinking," she said, her voice firm. "And I've got news for you, Paul Santana. They have doctors everywhere, good ones. And I can get my checkups in Washington as easily as I can get them here."

Bewildered, he looked at her. "I wasn't thinking about the doctors; I was thinking about your family. You're so close to your father—"

"I can call my papa when I need to. Besides—this isn't forever, is it? Won't we be coming back?"

Glancing away, Paul picked up his fork and prodded his spaghetti. "Sure, we could come back. The election's in less than eighteen months. If President Austin loses, I'm sure most of her staff will leave to make room for the new guy."

"You see?" Maria tapped the table, triumph in her eyes. "We'd be right back."

Paul shot her a warning look. "What if Austin wins?"

Uncertainty crept into Maria's expression. "Well—"

"So what?" Cristina cut in. "I think it'd be great if she wins. It's about time we elected a woman to office." She turned to her mother, gently gripping Maria's arm. "So you'd be in Washington five or six years, Mama. That's not the worst thing in the world."

Maria eyed Cristina with a critical squint. "That is a long time."

"You'd be closer to me. I could come home from college on weekends. Cambridge isn't that far from Washington."

Maria's chin quivered. "You'd really come home?"

"At least once a month. Maybe more." She grinned at Paul. "It might be fun to hang out with a guy who's working in the White House."

Drawing a deep breath, Maria shifted her attention to Paul. "Let's go."

Paul shook his head. "You're not thinking about the stress. I don't want to put you through the move and the adjustment."

"Pablo," she lowered her voice to a more intimate level, "do you think for one moment I could be happy knowing I'd held you back? If the White House needs you, you should go. I'll go with you, and we'll stay for as long as you want to. Then we'll come home."

He closed his eyes, inwardly wincing as he backed toward the thought of Daryn Austin. Would Maria's attitude change if she knew she was pushing him toward the one woman he had never been able to forget?

At a complete loss for words, he caught his wife's hand and squeezed it.

"And another thing," Maria continued, her eyes burning a hole through him, "you shouldn't let yourself be burdened by a sense of obligation to the law firm. Let Papa and the others get along without you for a while. All these years you've worked for them, and they've never made you a partner. After all this time, you'd think they'd appreciate all you've done."

Stricken silent by a guilty conscience, Paul released her hand. Mr. Lopez and the other partners at the firm had invited him to join them, several times in fact, but he'd never felt free to accept their offer. First, he hated the appearance of nepotism, and everyone knew he had married Mr. Lopez's daughter. Second, buying into the partnership would mean paying thousands of dollars he didn't want to spend on himself—not while he had a daughter who dreamed of Harvard and a wife who lived with a cancer phobia. Papa Lopez had slyly hinted that something could be arranged, but Paul had always refused.

"Well," he said, twirling spaghetti again. "It would seem I misjudged the situation. But we're too deeply entrenched in Miami."

"Paul, listen to me." Maria's birdlike hand reached out and grasped his sleeve. "What do you owe this city? Nothing. The people turned on you after Elian; they forgot all you did and how you suffered on that boy's account. You owe Miami nothing; you owe the firm nothing. And we, your wife and daughter, want you to do great things. We want you to go. The White House needs you."

A memory surfaced from a distant tide pool, Daryn in her robe with her hair wet from the shower, smelling of Irish Spring as she wrapped him in her arms and tugged on his earlobe. *"Don't go to class,"* she had whispered, a smile bathing her face in light. *"I need you here."*

Coughing, he thumped his chest, hoping the action would explain the sudden color in his complexion.

Cristina frowned. "You all right, Dad?"

Catching his breath, he looked from Cristina to Maria. "I wouldn't say the White House *needs* me. I'm sure they called because . . . well, because President Austin is an old friend. It's not like they called because they've heard about my exemplary prowess."

"You're connected, Dad, and you don't have to be ashamed of it." A smile overtook Cristina's indignant features, displaying the investment of several thousand dollars in orthodontia. "I plan to milk it all I can. I was thinking I'd be a nobody among the blue bloods at Harvard, but now everything's changed. Can you imagine what my roommates will think when I tell them my dad is a lawyer for the White House?"

Paul froze, then brought his hand up to his chin. "Are you sure?" he asked Cristina. "It'll mean a major move. The weather's different up there, so you'll be saying good-bye to warm Christmases and summers on the beach."

Cristina snorted. "I'll be living in Massachusetts, Dad. Come February, Washington will feel warm in comparison."

He took his wife's hand. "A move would be asking a lot of you. Moving a household is a lot of work."

She turned her hand to grip his. "We'll hire a moving van and someone to help with the unpacking. We'll rent the house out, so we won't have to bother with selling it."

"Well." As defenseless as a buck with its hind foot caught in a steel trap, he swallowed, then looked at the two women who ruled his universe. "I suppose I could speak to Papa Lopez tomorrow."

Maria squeezed his hand. "Call the White House first. Ask them if the job's still open."

He nodded slowly. "I believe it is. O'Leary said he wanted me to take a couple of days to think about it. Apparently he didn't want to give President Austin bad news."

Maria released his hand. "I don't know your old friend the president," she said, reaching for the French bread, "but I think I'm beginning to like her."

As his ladies began to talk of glorious days ahead, Paul lifted his glass of iced tea while one particular anxiety that had been lapping at his subconscious suddenly crested and crashed. Now that his obvious excuses had been shot down, his hidden heart bobbed like a decoy on a lake, vulnerable and exposed. Dealing with refreshed memories of Daryn was difficult enough, but if he went to Washington, he'd have to deal with the woman herself . . . and he was frightened to death by the thought that she might have more than business in mind.

Immediately, common sense castigated him. Only an egotistical fool would assume that passion had instigated her call, and he was far too realistic to be egotistical.

Still . . . why else would she contact him?

For some reason she wanted him in Washington, and the reason probably had nothing to do with his reputation, intellect, or even his racial background. There were thousands of intelligent, savvy lawyers who'd be delighted to work in the White House, and probably scores of Hispanic lawyers who'd leap at the chance. But she hadn't called the brightest and best and most eager.

She'd called *him.*

And if he went to Washington, she'd want to see him.

He pulled off a hunk of bread, forced it over his dry tongue, and nodded mindlessly at something Cristina was saying.

He wasn't certain he could work for Daryn Austin. He respected her, even admired her, and he had followed her career closely enough that he thought he knew what sort of political stands she'd be taking in the coming months. And, to be fair, this position might not involve intimate or even close contact with her; he might spend all his days in a crowded office surrounded by file boxes. But somehow he doubted he could go to Washington without ever having to confront the feelings that had once raged between them.

That thought sent panic rioting within him.

Excusing himself from the dinner table, Paul tousled his daughter's hair, kissed his wife's cheek, and carried his dishes to the sink. As he scraped the suddenly tasteless spaghetti into the garbage disposal, he blocked the sounds of female chatter from his mind and tried to focus his blurred memories.

He and Daryn had parted in May 1979, just after his graduation from law school. A month after her miscarriage. Their emotions had been rubbed raw by the stresses of finals and fear and passion, but she'd let him drive away from her apartment free from promises and commitments. He had planned to stay in New Haven for another year, working for the Jerome N. Frank Legal Services Organization while she completed her coursework, but a friend of his mother's had called him about an opening at the Miami law firm of Lopez, Bentley, Kremkau, and Stock.

He'd moved home and taken the job, worked from dawn through dark to chalk up his share of billable hours, and crammed to pass the Florida bar. During those frantic months he wrote Daryn and received newsy notes in response—she'd been busy, too, burdened with studies and exams and volunteer work at the legal services office. And then, as May 1980 rolled around and Paul prepared to ask her to join him in Miami, she wrote to tell him she had decided to return to Atlanta and eventually run for a spot in the Georgia House of Representatives.

He understood, of course. In those days one of Daryn's most charming qualities was her devotion to her father, the stately man who had ruled Georgia with a velvet hand. She wore her pride in him like a crown, though the strain of maintaining his reputation sometimes brought on a royal headache. Later, after Paul had learned to love Daryn, he realized that the driving force behind her pride and devotion was an unquenchable thirst for her famous father's love.

He'd tried to meet that need himself. He had promised her his heart and life, but by the summer of 1980 he understood that he could not give her what she lacked.

I'm not so foolish as to think I'll win the election right out of the gate, she'd written. *But I'll be doing pro bono work out of an Atlanta legal services office, and sooner or later those people are bound to remember that I pulled them out of a scrape. And those are the folks who will send this woman to the House.*

Apparently they did remember, though the fact that she bore the same surname as one of Georgia's favorite governors worked in her favor as well. Monitoring her career from Miami, in '82 Paul sent a telegram of congratulations when she won her seat in the House, followed by another four years later when she won a seat in the Georgia State Senate. He sent flowers when she won the gubernatorial election and received a preprinted form letter in reply.

He didn't send anything when Parker put her in the vice president's office. That was the year life nearly drowned him—immersing him in struggles with a strong-willed fifteen-year-old, the Elian Gonzalez case, and his wife's cancer treatments.

Paul had married Maria, his boss's daughter, in the same year Daryn charmed her way into the Georgia House. And over the years he had come to appreciate Maria, but the feeling she evoked in his breast paled in comparison to the white-hot passion that had boiled his blood in college.

Was that passion a natural by-product of youth? If he'd met Maria at twenty-two instead of twenty-eight, would he feel different toward her now? Perhaps. Or maybe the difference lay in the two women—Maria was small and dark, lovely like his mother, while Daryn was tall, blonde, and every inch a WASP.

At forty-nine, Paul had learned to be honest with himself, and now he could admit that at least some part of his feeling for Daryn sprang from the pride that suffused him when she walked on his arm. When they were together, the world couldn't help but notice the Cuban scholarship student and second-generation immigrant who had won himself a golden girl.

After stacking his dishes on the counter, he dried his hands on a dish-towel. He didn't know why he had loved Daryn Austin more than any other woman in his life, but now he cherished his wife and adored his daughter.

The thought of Washington was invigorating, but he wasn't eager to put those commitments to the test.

●

As Paul moved down the hall toward his den, Maria rose from the table. "Help me with the dishes, Cristina."

She smiled, pleasantly surprised when, for once, the girl didn't suddenly remember a call that had to be returned. "Do you think he'll really do it, Mama? Work at the White House, I mean?"

Maria shrugged as she carried the empty spaghetti bowl to the sink. "Your papa does what he thinks is right. And if he thinks he can help the president, he'll go."

Amid the clattering of silverware, Cristina piled the remaining dishes in a stack, then carried them to the counter. "I think it'd be so exciting. I have no idea what those people do all day, but it has to be more interesting than helping immigrants process their INS applications."

Maria gave her daughter a reproving look. "Your father's job is important. If someone hadn't helped *his* father, do you think you'd be here? You wouldn't."

"Maybe." Leaning against the counter, Cristina crossed her arms. "Is the president really an old friend of Dad's?"

"He says she is."

"How good a friend? I mean, it's not like we've ever gotten a Christmas card from her."

Maria picked up a saucepan and held it under a stream of running water. "I don't know, Cristina. They went to law school together."

"But Dad went to school with hundreds of people. None of them have called to offer him a job."

Maria put her hand in the water, testing the temperature. "Maybe none of them have jobs to offer."

"Hey, Mom." Cristina leaned forward on the counter, her eyes shining. "Do you think they were, like, boyfriend and girlfriend?"

"This water." Maria twitched her fingers in the tepid stream. "It takes so long to get hot."

"You didn't answer my question."

"I don't like to waste time on foolish words." She jerked her head toward the table. "Wrap up the rest of the bread, will you? Be sure to use the good plastic wrap, the kind that clings. That other brand is useless; I don't know why I bought it."

Grinning, Cristina moved toward the table. "My dad might have *dated* the president," she said, her voice a singsong chant. "My dad might have *kissed* the president!"

"Cristina." Maria laced her voice with rebuke. "Don't repeat such things. It's not dignified."

In response, her daughter grinned, then glided toward the pantry, her feet moving to the rhythm of her ridiculous chant.

Pressing her lips together, Maria turned off the water, then picked up the plastic scrubber and took a halfhearted swipe at the sauce-encrusted pot. Why didn't Loupe clean up after cooking? The woman insisted on leaving at five, and that meant Maria or Cristina had to clean at the end of a long day, at an hour when their energy was low and their tempers short . . .

No. This wasn't a problem of temper or tiredness; this was the old fear, the feeling that rose to assault her like the chill of a sudden fever.

Despite the warmth of the water on her hands, despite the heat radiating from the glass window above the sink, Maria felt the cold clamminess of panic beneath her arms, along her stomach, behind her knees.

"Stop it." Maria whispered the words. "You are being foolish. Your husband is a good man. And if we go to Washington, all will be well."

Please, God, let him be a good man. Keep his heart faithful and true, and bring us home safely, home to friends and family who will keep us safe . . .

"Did you say something, Mom?"

"Nothing, dear." Turning on the water again, Maria summoned her energy and began to scrub to the rhythm of her prayers.

NINE

CURLED UP ON A SOFA IN THE LIVING ROOM OF the White House residence, Daryn ate her dinner off a TV tray and tried to concentrate on the intelligence briefing in her hand. A CNN newscaster droned from a television against the wall, but the top-of-the-hour story was a repeat that didn't concern her.

The cell phone in her pocket buzzed, and she frowned as she recognized the number in the screen—the Secret Service was calling. "Yes?"

"Madam President," a somber voice intoned, "Alexander O'Leary is in the downstairs lobby. Would you like to see him now, or should he schedule an appointment?"

She straightened. "Send him up." She tossed off the afghan that covered her legs and bare feet. "I'll see him immediately."

She slid into her slippers, dropped the silver serving dome over the remains of her dinner, and tucked the briefing behind an embroidered pillow. After running her fingers through her hair, she walked to the mirror and checked her silk blouse and pants—still a presentable outfit, though a bit wrinkled. But O'Leary wouldn't expect perfection at the end of a long day.

Two minutes later, she called "enter" when the Secret Service rapped on the door. O'Leary entered and shook her hand. "Thanks for coming right away, Counselor," she said, pointing to a wing chair near the sofa. "Please, have a seat."

He sat, a little stiffly, then his gaze focused upon the TV tray. "If this is a bad time—"

"Nonsense, I'm just glad I didn't have a state dinner or something to keep me from seeing you." She looked pointedly at the manila envelope in his hand. "Something tells me you haven't come about the tax reform program or our antismoking ads."

"No." Smiling, he pulled a page from the envelope, then passed it to her. Her heart leaped at the sight of a familiar handwriting at the bottom of the fax—Paul Santana's signature.

Holding her breath, she skimmed the letter. Paul Santana was honored by the invitation and thrilled by the opportunity to serve his country as part of the White House counsel's staff. If approved, he and his family were planning to move as soon as the White House office required his presence . . . Again, it was an honor and a privilege to work for President Austin's administration.

She read the letter again, hoping for some sign of her first name, but the missive was formal, polite, and unerringly proper. Pure public Paul.

Still . . . he was coming.

She returned the letter to O'Leary. "Anyone reading that would think he hadn't had a single hesitation," she said, her mouth curling in a wry smile.

O'Leary saw the smile and chuckled. "He gave me a flat refusal when I spoke to him yesterday. Cited his roots in Miami, family commitments, loyalty to his firm—"

"But something changed his mind."

His brow quirked. "And would that have been you?"

She threw up her hands. "I might have called him, had he proved entirely stubborn, but I didn't." She brought her hand to her shoulder, rubbing at the weariness in her neck. "I think you'll like Paul. He's an exceptional lawyer and he'll be a valuable member of our team."

"I have no reason to doubt you, Madam President."

She exhaled in an audible rush. "So—he's willing to come. Where do we stand with the paperwork?"

"We'll send the FBI out to handle the field check," O'Leary said, "and someone will be dispatched to do the personal interview to be sure there are no skeletons rattling in his closet."

"There aren't. This guy is a boy scout."

"Sure, but we'll make certain of that before we bring him in. Once that interview has cleared, we'll send out the forms—the personal data statement, the waiver permitting us to review his past tax returns, the questionnaire for the FBI, the financial disclosure statement—"

"He's going to despise all that," Daryn interrupted, raking hair off her forehead. "He's going to hate my guts before he even gets here."

"The price we pay for serving our country." O'Leary stood and buttoned his suit coat. "And now, if you'll excuse me, I'll be letting you get back to your dinner."

Daryn let him go, then sank onto the sofa and curled her legs beneath the afghan. Paul Santana—lawyer, crusader, and her former lover—would soon be working under her roof. Soon he'd be issued one of the elite badges with a blue background, allowing him access to the entire West Wing and the Oval Office. Allowing him back into her life, where she wanted him.

Because she needed a friend she could trust.

Picking up the phone, she dialed the usher's office. "You may send someone to pick up the dinner tray," she said, then added, "and will you bring up the dog? Thanks."

She dropped the phone back into the cradle, wishing for a moment that Tyson were a toy poodle. She had grown to like the beast, even missed his company when he wasn't around. But one night of experimentation had taught her that Tyson couldn't do dinners, not even solitary ones. With no effort at all he could lift his head to the precise level of her dining table, and one flick of those mighty paws could topple a TV tray or yank a tablecloth, complete with a full dinner service, from a table. And if there was one thing Tyson enjoyed more than slumber, it was food.

She pulled the afghan closer as a sudden chill from the air conditioner made her shiver. The dog was a superb listener, but not exactly what she needed in a sounding board. Paul, however, might suit her perfectly . . . if he made it through the gauntlet.

Would the FBI report turn up the fact that she and Paul Santana had dated? Perhaps. They'd been a popular couple on the Yale campus. And for every ten people who knew they'd dated, there were bound to be three or four who had spied the tie hanging on Paul's apartment doorknob or noticed Daryn leading him out of her apartment at 8 A.M. Out of those three or four, one was bound to talk. But what of it? They had dated in '78 and '79, during an era when love was as casual as a block party and about as binding.

She batted away the annoying gnat of worry. No one at Yale, she was certain, had known about the complication in their relationship. In May of '79, with a year of law school to go, she'd discovered she was pregnant. Paul was shocked but supportive, offering to marry her as soon as he'd graduated and found a job, but she refused his offer. As much as she loved him—and she loved him with her heart and soul—she did not want to saddle him with a pregnant wife at the outset of his career.

The word *miscarriage* solved all their problems. A few days later, when Paul came for breakfast and she told him there would be no baby, she saw a shadow cross his darkly handsome features. "So God took the child," he said, reverting to his Catholic roots.

Those words shocked her down to her core. She had never heard him refer to a fetus as a *child,* never realized the word, used in that context, was part of his vocabulary. She couldn't have been more surprised if he'd stood up in a mock trial and begun to hurl invectives at the presiding judge. In debates, in class discussions, and in bed he had always been a feminist, as dedicated to a woman's right to reproductive freedom as she was . . .

But he had never before crashed into a woman's issue head-on.

In her kitchen that morning, tucked in the heavy warmth of her white terry-cloth robe, she had lifted her mug and refused to look at him. "Believe whatever you want to," she answered. And while Dionne

Warwick belted "I'll Never Love This Way Again" from the radio, Daryn had silently echoed the same words, knowing that Paul would never look at her again without thinking of the *baby* they'd created and lost.

In that moment, Daryn had known their love was hopeless. Paul was the most desirable man she'd ever met, generally open-minded and supportive of all the causes she endorsed, but in times of stress his religious superstitions surfaced like molten streams from a long-dormant volcano. He called himself a nonpracticing Catholic, like her, he prided himself on self-reliance, but occasionally the earth rumbled and streams of religion-induced guilt hissed and steamed and poured from some crevice deep in his soul . . .

She had no hidden geysers. Her parents had worshiped at the temple of prosperity, served the gods of positive thinking and power. The morals that mattered were the ones that helped you cope, and while all things were permissible, not all things were wise.

Earlier in the day she'd been grateful for her lack of religious conviction, for the pope himself had called to ask her to consider clemency for Michael Thomas Whittemore, the murdering anarchist scheduled for execution in six weeks. Without a moment's hesitation, she had calmly told the Holy Father that the American people and their courts had already decided the matter. Now she reflected that her lack of religion had served her well, bringing her from the red clay of Georgia to the gilded family quarters of the White House.

But she was alone, more solitary than any chief executive since the famous "bachelor president" James Buchanan. But though Buchanan never married, his niece and nephew lived with him in the mansion. And though Andrew Jackson entered the White House a widower with no children, through his late wife he had acquired two dozen nieces and nephews, many of whom lived with him at the president's house.

Daryn looked up, gazing at the crown molding, the tall windows, the shadow-dappled ceiling. The walls of this room had absorbed the laughter and squeals of families and children for generations . . . but now the sounds had stopped.

Dropping her head to her hand, she allowed herself a moment of melancholy. If she had married Paul, would she now be watching her own face on CNN? If she had carried her baby to term, would she be president?

She shook off the thought. Impossible to know, and useless to speculate about what might have been. Paul had found a career and taken a wife; apparently their family was happy and intact. And she had risen to a position she would never have dreamed of in her younger days.

She'd made a decision in 1979, committed an act that could not be undone. She would not waste time on regrets.

TEN

WITH HIS NERVES STRUNG TIGHTER THAN HIS new shoelaces, Paul drove through the traffic of Washington, D.C., and wondered if he'd just made the biggest mistake of his life. Around him, traffic jounced heavily through the streets while tourists crowded the sidewalks and occasionally spilled into his lane. A reeking fog of diesel and gasoline fumes lay upon the sunlit street, and jackhammer crews seemed to be on every corner, shredding sidewalks while summer tourists streamed mindlessly around them.

"Welcome to Washington," he murmured, slamming on the brakes as a laughing kid suddenly backed off the sidewalk. Paul's right bumper missed the boy by inches, but the young teenager darted back into the crowd, oblivious to his near-injury. Paul eased on the accelerator again, then stopped as the bus ahead of him shimmied and squealed to a stop.

Paul glanced at his watch. Nearly noon, so with any luck he'd be able to slip into his new office and find everyone else at lunch. He didn't want fanfare today; he wanted to creep in, drop off a few things, and scope out his surroundings. He'd spent the last two weeks trying to adjust to his new reality—he no longer worked for Lopez, Bentley, Kremkau, and Stock, but for the White House. The president.

Daryn.

Drawing a deep breath in an effort to settle the butterflies in his stomach, he turned from Seventeenth Street onto State Place, then rolled up to a checkpoint beside the Southwest Appointment Gate. With his foot on the brake, he pulled an envelope from the glove compartment, then scattered the contents over the empty passenger seat. A uniformed military guard stood outside the window, a patient look on his face.

Feeling helpless, Paul glanced at the guard, then indicated the clutter he'd just spilled: an official letter on White House stationery, a parking pass, an ID badge. "Good morning. Um—exactly which of these things do you want to see?"

The guard bent slightly, the shiny brim of his cap shading his eyes, then pointed to the badge. "May I see the ID, sir?"

Paul lifted the clip-on badge to the window, then exhaled in relief when the young man nodded. "Thank you, Mr. Santana. Now, sir, will you release the trunk?"

Startled, Paul automatically fumbled beneath the dash for a release switch, then remembered that the older model BMW didn't have one. "It's unlocked," he called over his shoulder. "Just press the button."

With both hands on the steering wheel, he watched in the rearview mirror as the guard picked up a mirror on a long pole, then slid the mirror beneath the car—checking for explosives, no doubt. After walking completely around the car, the man unlatched the trunk and rummaged through the luggage stowed there. Finally, he moved back to his original position and nodded. "All clear, sir. You may proceed."

Paul took his foot off the brake, then reconsidered. "Excuse me," he called, "but I wonder if you could tell me where to go from here."

The young man's stern expression relaxed into a slight smile. "You must be new."

Paul felt a flush burn the back of his neck. "As a matter of fact, I am."

Stepping forward, the guard turned and pointed toward an inner gate. "You're lucky—your parking permit will get you past that entry point. Swipe your ID badge at the turnstile, then proceed to the spot indicated on your parking pass. It's your slot—" his smile widened—"for as long as you last."

After nodding his thanks, Paul proceeded through the black iron fence surrounding the White House complex. He drove slowly, taking time to squint through the trees at his right to catch a glimpse of the fabled building. In the bright light of a summer morning, the mansion seemed to glow against the rich emerald lawn.

He couldn't help being impressed. Intentionally or not, Daryn had made her way to the top. At this moment she was the most powerful woman in the world, commander of the world's most advanced army, and mistress of this wedding cake mansion.

Two weeks ago he'd seen a news report on her first month in office, and the reviews had been favorable. Rumor held that she intended to nominate Lawrence Frey, governor of Texas and another moderate independent, to fill the office of vice president, and she had made headlines by being the first president to own a mastiff, supposedly the king of dogdom. The lead story had featured a video clip of Daryn playing fetch with an overgrown puppy that allegedly weighed 166 pounds at six months of age. The reporters were quick to point out that the ball she'd thrown to the energetic dog wasn't a tennis ball, but a *volleyball* . . .

Paul found himself driving on West Executive Avenue, a strip of asphalt located between the White House and the seven-story Old Executive Office Building. From his research he knew that the OEOB housed most of the people who worked for the president—the West Wing, after all, could accommodate only so many executives. But according to the folded letter on his leather seat, he would find his new office on the second floor of the West Wing, right next to the office of Alexander O'Leary, counsel for the president.

Though the lunch hour was rapidly approaching, he drove past rows of automobiles, most of them black and expensive, then spied an empty slot marked with a simple sign. Number twenty-three—the number on his parking pass.

He pulled the compact BMW into the slot, then turned the key and waited for the car—and his heart—to settle. A surprising wave of instantaneous and almost giddy relief washed over him.

He had arrived. He had made it to the land of white marble palaces—and this time he'd come not as a tourist, but as an insider. Soon he'd be walking through gleaming doors that remained closed to ordinary people, but they'd open for him because Daryn Austin would provide the key.

A thrill shivered through his senses. The barbed wire had finally fallen away from his memories, and on the silent drive he'd revisited far too many of them, almost, at times, forgetting that he now had a wife and daughter . . .

He'd made the drive to Washington alone, leaving Cristina and Maria to pack up the house and say their farewells to family and friends. Despite Cristina's enthusiasm for his new job, she didn't want to leave her Miami friends four weeks before she had to leave for college. Maria had been happy to remain in Miami with Cristina, assuring Paul she'd use the time to pack and oversee the movers once they arrived.

Maria had gaily waved him out of the driveway, and he suspected her reasons for wanting to remain in Miami had more to do with family than the movers. She wanted to savor every remaining moment with Cristina, and she didn't want to leave her widowed father. Paul understood wanting to stay with Cristina, but he had never understood Maria's childlike dependence upon Papa Lopez.

So his girls had wished him well, kissed him good-bye, and turned him toward Washington. He'd driven the distance in two days, stopping overnight at South of the Border in South Carolina. As he sat eating a mushroom omelet with vacationers and truckers, he looked at his fellow travelers and wondered what quirk of fate had set him apart. His parents had come from Cuba, he had no family or political connections to set him on this road, but a scholarship had taken him from Miami to Yale, and a chance meeting in a Laundromat had brought Daryn Austin into his life. And now, twenty-five years later, he was on his way to the White House while some of his boyhood friends were selling café cubana down in Miami's Little Havana . . .

Taking advantage of the solitude, he had given his thoughts and emotions free rein as the Beemer lapped up the miles. As he crossed into North Carolina, he couldn't help but notice the restless tapping of his left foot, a sure indicator of his rising anxiety. Though he'd never doubted his abilities as a lawyer, the practice of immigration and family law in Miami was a far cry from the debate of constitutional law in Washington. But surely every man needed to shake himself free from routine at the midpoint of his career. He had grown too comfortable within his family and community. Losing Elian Gonzalez had been difficult, but he'd had time to heal. Time enough to grow comfortable in the practice of *safe* law and the humdrum living of a *safe* life.

Daryn was offering him a job in a pressure cooker, as far from safe as man could get. On Monday he would begin to work under the scrutiny of lawyers and politicians who'd probably be just as happy to slit his throat as support him.

He couldn't wait to get to work.

And to see Daryn.

His anticipation had grown with every passing mile. Though he saw and heard her on television nearly every day, he longed to see her in the flesh, to look into her eyes as she saw *him.* He had not been able to formulate an answer to the perplexing question about why she had called him to Washington, but he knew he would read the answer on her face. He had always been able to read her eyes—as lovers, they had no secrets between them, and now he felt just sentimental enough to believe that kind of empathy could survive the tests of time and distance.

They would be friends—they had been friends before, so why should that change? She would be busy administrating the country, of course, and he had Maria and Cristina to consider, but if he were lucky enough to work with Daryn on even a weekly basis, there would surely be occasions when he could share his heart with her as he once had. Perhaps they would even find time to be alone, and he'd finally be able to ask why she had never given him the courtesy of a direct reply to his proposal of marriage . . .

His stomach shriveled at the thought of outright rejection. Perhaps it would be best to leave the past in the past and work on establishing a new and professional relationship. And she didn't hate him. She wouldn't have called him if she didn't at least respect him. He wouldn't be sitting in the West Wing parking lot if she didn't value him.

A new thought struck him as he opened the car door—to whom had parking spot number twenty-three belonged last week? And who had occupied his office? With West Wing real estate at a premium, it didn't take much thought to realize he'd displaced someone . . . perhaps someone who would hold a grudge.

He brushed the thought aside as he locked the car and shifted his briefcase from one hand to the other. Disappointment was part of life, and with all lofty positions came the inherent risk of falling. The man who rose one day could most certainly plummet the next, and mature people accepted those risks. Who could foretell the future? Not even Daryn could have known she'd be president one day, and that he'd be on his way to work for her.

Slipping his free hand into his pocket, Paul moved up the sidewalk toward the entrance to the West Wing. As he walked, he stared at the parked cars to his left and couldn't help noticing a discernable rise in their value as he moved closer to the West Wing entrance. In a week, when he knew what names went with what position in the pecking order, he'd be able to match cars to owners without a flow chart. Clearly, the closer a staffer parked to the double doors of the West Wing, the closer his or her standing to the hub of power.

He moved under an awning and passed through two sets of glass doors. Directly ahead, a uniformed Secret Service officer sat at a table and lifted his head as Paul approached. His eyes took in Paul's ID badge first, then studied his face. "Good morning," Paul offered. "I'd like to find my new office. I understand it's on the second floor."

"Straight ahead, Mr. Santana." The guard inclined his head toward an area behind a turnstile and an x-ray machine. "There's an elevator beyond the security checkpoint."

Paul dropped his briefcase to the x-ray conveyor—an automatic reflex that sprang from hundreds of jaunts through the Miami airport—but paused at the turnstile. A keypad waited there, with some sort of electric eye above it, but the keypad was blank.

Paul looked at the uniformed agent. "I'm afraid I wasn't given the daily password."

The agent didn't smile, but stepped forward, took Paul's ID badge, then pressed the badge to the electronic eye. Something within the badge—probably a computer chip—registered, a series of numbers flashed across the digital screen, and the machine beeped in approval.

The guard handed the badge back to Paul, who was suddenly grateful he had avoided the morning rush. "You may proceed, sir," the man said.

Paul moved ahead, picked up his x-rayed briefcase, and waited as yet another security guard approved the badge, then pressed a button beneath the edge of his desk. As Paul turned, an elevator door slid open. He stepped inside and waited until the doors closed, then leaned against the back wall and sighed in relief.

●

His office was smaller than he'd imagined, but every bit as plush as the office of his dreams. Burled walnut lined the walls, and the beige carpeting was either new or had just been cleaned.

He had entered quietly, only nodding at a man and woman he passed, and now he sank into the green leather chair and slid his briefcase onto the desk. After a quick look around—shelves behind him, a telephone and computer on the credenza to his left, the hulking desk bare but for a bronze lamp and a small silver gadget with a green screen he couldn't read without his glasses. Opening his briefcase, he lifted out a framed picture of his girls—Maria and Cristina at Cristina's high-school graduation.

"Santana?" He looked up as a deep voice commanded his attention. A tall, red-haired man stood in the doorway, with chilly blue eyes that seemed at odds with the faint freckles scattered across his cheeks. When Paul nodded, the man came forward, extending his hand. "Alexander O'Leary, White House counsel."

"Mr. O'Leary." Paul stood and came out from behind the desk. "Nice to finally meet you."

"You're early." O'Leary glanced around as if he expected to see boxes on the floor. "We didn't expect you until Monday."

"I know; I just pulled into town. I thought I'd come in and get a feel for the place."

"Good idea." O'Leary glanced at the mostly empty desk, then nodded toward the picture. "Your wife?"

"And daughter." Paul stepped back so the other man could draw closer. "Cristina will be a freshman at Harvard this fall."

"Congratulations." The lawyer's eyes narrowed for a moment, then he rubbed his hands together. "When your boxes arrive, we'll have someone bring them to your office. Briefings will arrive by special courier; staff meetings begin promptly at seven-thirty each weekday morning in the Roosevelt Room. Is there anything you'd be needing before I go?"

Paul shoved his hands into his pockets, then grinned. "I'm fine. Just a little overwhelmed at the moment."

O'Leary's gaze shifted and thawed slightly. "Sure, and don't I know. It's a little astonishing at first, especially with all the security. But you get used to it." He gestured toward the electronic gadget on the desk. "Figured that out yet?"

Frowning, Paul pulled his glasses from his pocket. "Haven't even looked at it."

"It's one of the handiest toys we have. Anytime you need to locate the president, just look at that lovely little screen."

Bending closer, Paul studied the palm-sized device. As white computer lettering glowed against a green background he read:

POTUS: Oval Office
VPOTUS: TBA

"President of the United States," he whispered, recognizing the common shorthand for the title. "And vice president?"

"Empty until the Senate gets around to approving the president's nomination," O'Leary said, shrugging. "When Parker was president we also kept tabs on the first lady, and before that, even Clinton's kid had a place on the thing. Not much on the screen now, but I hear the PPD—"

Paul lifted his hand. "I'm sorry, the what?"

"Presidential Protection Detail. The Secret Service guys who guard her. Anyway, they're thinking about typing in a listing for the First Dog."

Paul laughed. "He's for real, then? I was hoping that monster was a media invention."

O'Leary sighed. "Haven't I said the same thing? But he's real, he's a mess, and she has grown attached to the beastie. The agents like to joke that he makes things easier for them. If anyone tries to take a shot at her, the bullet will have to pass through fifty yards of sticky dog drool first."

Paul tried to laugh, but his short bark lacked humor. He wasn't ready to joke about assassins and bullets, especially when Daryn was the implied target. Reagan had been able to joke about being shot, and maybe Daryn had grown used to the threat, but Paul wasn't sure he would ever be able to laugh at danger.

He returned his gaze to the electronic device. "What do you call this thing?"

"Toaster, coaster, gizmo, gadget. Call it whatever you like. If you ask the Secret Service, they'll say the things don't actually exist."

Straightening, Paul drew a deep breath. "I thought Miami was dangerous, but all of this—" he waved his hand, indicating the surroundings—"is pretty intense."

"It is a high-pressured environment, but the president assures me you can handle it." Again, those cold blue eyes strafed him, then O'Leary smiled. "You know why they call this the most high-pressured workplace in the country?"

Paul fished around for an answer, but came up short. "Sorry."

O'Leary laughed. "Threat of biological attack. Engineers designed the air-conditioning systems so that the air pressure inside the White House is always higher than outside. If we're attacked with a germ or gas, the atmosphere will be sucked outward, away from the commander in chief." He grinned. "And, lucky for us, anyone who happens to be within the vicinity."

Paul forced a smile. If that comment was supposed to reassure him, it hadn't.

"You'll enjoy the work," O'Leary added, moving toward the heavily draped window. "Our job is primarily reactive, of course, but you'd be amazed what comes through the president's office. We inspect new legislation, research societal trends, investigate judicial nominees, whatever the president needs us to do. And with the election on the horizon, I think our work load will be doubling by spring."

Paul leaned back against the desk. "What's on her agenda now?"

"All the hot issues—slavery in the Sudan, fetal rights, the death sentence of that goon who bombed the federal building in San Francisco. The pope is pressuring her to pardon the guy."

"The pope?"

O'Leary's eyes narrowed. "Are you Catholic?"

"Yes—I mean no. In heritage, I suppose, but now I'm an agnostic."

O'Leary nodded. "Lapsed Catholic, then. Well, don't feel like the Lone Ranger." He took a step toward the doorway. "You ready?"

Paul blinked. "For—?"

"Your meeting with the president. She gave me strict instructions—the moment you arrive at the White House, I'm to escort you to the Oval." He glanced at his watch. "She's being entertained by some school kids from Virginia, but she said she'd make time for you."

A spasm of panic shot through Paul's body, making his heart knock against his rib cage, but somehow he managed a smile. "Lead on," he said, his voice sounding high and strained to his own ears. "I'm as ready as I'll ever be."

●

The president, Daryn had learned, spent 60 percent of his or her day enduring inescapable engagements—cabinet meetings, intelligence briefings, legislative and staff meetings. A variety of social functions invariably followed the business meetings—visits from foreign diplomats who called at the White House to present their credentials, national athletic champions who wanted to pose in the Rose Garden, and eager students who had worked all year raising money for a trip to Washington, D.C.

One group of third graders from Alexandria was beginning the third verse of "I'd Like to Teach the World to Sing" when Thrasher lifted his hand and discreetly waggled two fingers in Daryn's direction.

Thank heaven.

Standing, she moved toward one of the adoring parents and touched his sleeve. "I'm sorry," she said, smiling at the children who were now gaping at her instead of watching their director, "but something's come up. Before I go, however, I'd like you to know how wonderful these children are. I'm so proud of them."

Still singing, the children smiled, as she knew they would. And when the director turned and looked over her shoulder, her hands still pumping rhythmically, Daryn knew her words had reached the ears that counted. The kids who'd been too busy singing would hear them repeated a dozen times before sunset.

Smiling, she followed Thrasher out of the Diplomatic Reception Room and into the passageway that would take her back to the security of the West Wing.

"He arrived a few moments ago," Thrasher said, glancing at a folder in his hand. "The service cleared him at 12:08."

"And O'Leary?"

"The chief counsel is bringing Santana down. They should arrive at any moment."

"Give me five minutes, will you? Hold them in Ms. Park's office, then send them in."

"Will do. Wait—the dog's in the Oval. Want me to take him upstairs?"

Daryn tilted her head, then shook it. "Leave him." If conversation proved strained, Tyson would provide a nice diversion. The dog had already helped her ease into several difficult discussions with recalcitrant members of Congress. Neither the Republican nor the Democratic leadership had been pleased by her intention to nominate Lawrence Frey to fill the vice presidency, but moderate independents didn't exactly grow on trees. Frey, however, was just what she needed—loyal, flexible, and popular in a huge state—plus he had an extroverted wife, Patty, who would make an excellent second lady. Daryn fully intended to give both her vice president and his wife offices and full schedules.

Slipping into the office through the hallway door guarded by a Secret Service agent, Daryn passed through the open expanse of the Oval and entered the narrow hallway that led to the president's private office spaces. Her dining room lay straight ahead, her study to the left, her bathroom to the right.

Stepping into the washroom, she paused before the marble sink, studying her reflection. She and Paul had parted in '79, and the ensuing years had changed her. She was thicker than in the days when Paul loved her, and her hair was now a brighter blonde—a step necessary to cover the gray that had begun to sprout from her scalp after her thirtieth birthday. Her face carried the fine lines of a thousand stresses, but her skin had been creamed by the finest cosmetics money could buy, her complexion shielded from the sun. Her pale skin matched the pallid models currently parading over Manhattan runways, but Paul would neither know nor care about such things.

He'd look at her eyes first, and what would he see? Delicate lines at the corners, fragile skin beneath, creamed by a concealer. She squinted, trying to visualize her face through his eyes. He'd always said her eyes were her best feature, far more expressive than her hands or voice or body.

She blinked away the wetness that unexpectedly blurred her vision. This kind of foolish sentiment was unlike her, and unworthy of her present position. Paul was a married man with a child; he had probably discarded his memories of her along with his yearbooks and Farrah Fawcett poster. They were adults now, professional people at the top of their game. Neither one of them would have time for sentimental attachments.

Still—her heart warmed to know she'd soon be receiving a friend. Genuine friends were rare in the White House. The stateliness of the building, the hush of the halls, those somber portraits of past presidents all combined to reduce most former acquaintances to simpering idiots when they crossed the threshold.

But she had great hope for Paul Santana. Of all the men she'd known in her life, he was the least likely to be influenced by power or the trappings of prestige. Paul had always accepted people as they were, liking them for their congeniality, not caring if they had money or classy cars or blue blood . . .

Suddenly aware of the pending silence in the room beyond, she brushed her teeth, then patted her lips dry with a hand towel. As her heart thumped against her rib cage, she pulled a tube of lipstick from a pouch she kept hidden in an alcove behind the mirror, then painted a fresh coat of color over her lips. In the mirror, she saw that her hands were shaking.

She laughed, the sound a trembling waver in the small room. Why was she nervous? She was greeting a new political appointee, a man who happened to be an old friend. They would speak of nothing personal, for O'Leary would be present. She would welcome Paul to the White House, offer her help if he needed it, thank him for his contribution to the team. Very simple.

She twisted the lipstick back into the tube, slipped on the silver cap, and froze when she heard voices coming from beyond the hallway.

He had arrived.

She stared at her reflection, noticing that her eyes had grown huge. "Get a grip," she told herself, lifting her chin. "You are the president of the United States."

Opening the door, she stepped out to meet her newest employee.

ELEVEN

FOLLOWING O'LEARY'S EXAMPLE, PAUL SANTANA stood when Daryn Austin entered the room. He lifted his gaze slowly, taking in the leather pumps, the neat skirt and modest hemline, the tailored suit. The face, however, sent a shiver rippling through his limbs. The woman who wore that face was the woman he had known, kissed, and adored. It was impossible to look at that face and think of anything but the brilliant and determined girl he had once loved.

His heart, which had been battering his ribs for the last quarter-hour, slumped back into place like an unconscious boxer.

"Paul." She stepped forward and took his hand as any old friend might. "It's good to see you again. And I'm delighted you've decided to join our team."

Only a career of performing under pressure enabled him to speak. "Madam President," he began, the words catching in his throat. Couldn't she see that he couldn't *think* with his hand in hers? The words he wanted to say tangled with the memories her touch elicited, and if she didn't release him soon he'd be babbling like a two-year-old. "Madam President, it's nice—I mean, it's an honor—"

Despite his best attempt at seriousness, a smile tugged at the corners of his mouth. She saw the smile and laughed, then wrapped her arms around him in a friendly embrace. He found himself inhaling the luxurious scent of her perfume as he awkwardly patted her back. Daryn had always liked the rich perfumes, the subtle scents that lingered long into the night.

You look wonderful! he wanted to whisper, but didn't.

Stepping out of the embrace, Daryn looked at O'Leary. "You might as well know, Counselor," she said, "that Mr. Santana and I dated in law school."

A riffle of surprise passed across O'Leary's face, then vanished.

"I wanted you to hear it from me before you read it in the *Enquirer.*" Her voice dropped to a tone of wry humor. "And while I wouldn't add that tidbit to the press release about our latest appointee, I would also never deny it. If the subject comes up, feel free to confirm the truth."

Clasping his hands, O'Leary shrugged. "Fine. You dated. Anything else?"

Her eyes sparkled as though she wanted to say more, but wouldn't. "Nothing else," she said, resting her forearm on a marble bust of Lincoln as if it were of no more significance than a water cooler in Yale's Student Services Building. "Except that Paul is an excellent lawyer and a proud addition to our team. We expect great things of him."

Straightening, she folded her arms, and when she spoke again the words were for Paul alone. "Welcome, Counselor, and thank you for coming. I know I asked a lot of you."

He shifted his weight, resisting the urge to pinch himself. "I am honored to be here," he said, his voice flat in his ears. "And quite surprised that you thought of me."

Sinking to the sofa, she looked at him in amused wonder. "I've been following your career for years, and I want to surround myself with the best. I know you'll bring a lot to our administration." She gestured to the opposite sofa. "Please, gentlemen, have a seat."

Paul sat down, glancing for a moment at a framed calligraphy print on the coffee table. He recognized the Browning quote as one of Daryn's favorites: *Ah, but a man's reach should exceed his grasp, or what's a heaven for?*

Apparently she'd found her heaven. He couldn't imagine reaching higher than this.

"I wanted to tell you," he said, turning to face her, "that I was particularly impressed with the way you handled the pilot who went down in Iraq. That could have been tricky."

"It meant a couple of sleepless nights," she admitted, smiling. "But the good thing about being president is that I am surrounded by experts who know their jobs. I think that SEAL team was actually grateful for the chance to prove themselves."

"Well, they certainly did. And the episode didn't hurt you, either."

She looked at him, subtle amusement dancing in her eyes. "No. It didn't." She crossed her legs and leaned forward. "How's Maria? And your daughter?"

He blinked, momentarily surprised that she knew Maria's name. But she would have had access to all the files, reports, and questionnaires he'd had to complete before accepting the position. If she'd read the FBI background field report, she probably knew what his Miami neighbors six houses away thought of the Santana family.

"Maria's doing well," he said, not wanting to expand on what was probably only a polite inquiry. "She's excited about moving to Washington."

"Her illness? Is everything . . . all right?"

He eased back on the sofa, forcing himself to relax. "She's been cancer free for nearly three years. She's fine."

"That's good to hear." The light in Daryn's blue eyes did not diminish. "And your daughter?"

"Cristina starts classes at Harvard in a few weeks."

"Not Yale? I would have thought you'd want her to attend your alma mater."

"Cristina is her own person, always trying to be independent. She's like you in that way, and she adores you, because you've given her bona fide bragging rights in the dorm."

Daryn's laugh was deep, warm, and rich, a sound he hadn't realized he'd missed. Until now.

"Once she's settled, you'll have to invite her to the White House for the weekend," Daryn said, standing. He and O'Leary stood, too, then

Daryn gracefully slipped her arm through Paul's and led him toward the doorway, leaving O'Leary to trail in her wake.

"Would your daughter enjoy an invitation to one of the White House cultural events?"

He felt his anxiety melt away in a pool of relief. "She'd eat it up."

"We'll see to it, then." She glanced back over her shoulder. "Have you anything else for me, Alexander?"

"No, Madam President."

"Very good. Thank you for bringing Mr. Santana to see me."

With that gracious dismissal O'Leary slipped by them. Paul would have followed, but the president still clung to his arm, her gaze upon O'Leary's retreating back. An Asian woman, probably a secretary, watched from her desk, an impassive expression on her face.

When O'Leary had rounded the corner, Daryn released him. "Have you plans for dinner?"

He opened his mouth, but didn't speak quickly enough.

"Of course you don't; you've just arrived. Why don't you come to the White House and dine with us? I'm having dinner with a pair of senators who are determined to twist my arm around some bill I can't convince myself to like very much." The dimple in her cheek winked at him. "I could use someone in my corner. For moral support."

He shook his head. "Really, Madam President, I couldn't. My tux hasn't arrived."

She laughed again, and even the secretary cracked a half-smile. "It's not a state occasion, Counselor. It's a simple working dinner upstairs in the residence." She gave him a quick once-over and smiled with approval in her eyes. "What you're wearing is fine."

He glanced at the woman at the desk, whose expression now seemed to say *go for it.* He looked past her—two other women in the secretarial alcove were peeking over their computer monitors, waiting to hear his response.

Though he couldn't escape a sense of being caught up in a feminine conspiracy, how could he refuse? And a White House dinner was bound to taste better than the rubbery omelet he'd had last night.

"Since you put it that way—" he clasped his hands—"I suppose I must accept."

"Good." She nodded to the closest secretary. "Ms. Park, will you add Mr. Santana to the guest list for dinner tonight?" Reaching out, she smoothed the sleeve of his jacket. "Six o'clock, then. Just come through the West Wing and ask the agent on duty to escort you upstairs. You'll be on the list."

A quick smile, a flutter of her fingertips, and she was gone, vanishing through the curved door as completely as Alice had ever gone through the looking glass.

After nodding gamely at the secretary, Paul wandered down the hall, knowing he'd be gently and firmly escorted back to the proper path if he took a misstep.

One thought buzzed pleasantly in his brain: on his first night in Washington, he was going to have dinner with Daryn . . . who just happened to be president.

●

Daryn crossed the Oval in a dozen long strides, then entered her private study and shut the door. Tyson snoozed on the floor against the wall, taking up most of the available space, but he lifted his dark head as she approached.

"Oh, Ty," she whispered, sinking into the guest chair in front of the desk, "I thought he'd be pudgy and bald, but now he looks better than ever. He looks Andy Garcia good. Antonio Banderas good."

Warming to her voice, the puppy lifted his chest off the floor and inched toward her, his nose seeking the doggy treats she kept in a jar on the desk.

"Brother." Exhaling slowly, she uncorked the lid on the cookie jar, then placed a giant-sized biscuit in that gentle mouth. "What am I going to do?"

The dog chomped happily on his cookie, offering no help at all. Taking advantage of his new position, Daryn stood and stepped over him, then sank into the chair behind the desk. After sliding on her reading glasses, she picked up a file of letters to be signed. Letters from ordinary Americans were handled by the correspondence office and signed by an auto-pen; these letters required a personal signature.

"It's a good thing Ms. Park is dependable," she murmured as she scrawled her name at the bottom of each page after only a cursory glance at the content, "because right now I couldn't concentrate if the future of the free world depended upon it."

She stopped, realizing how foolish she sounded. She was a forty-eight-year-old woman, yet she was behaving like a teenager. Why?

Part of the reason might be that Paul was so amazingly handsome. He'd been good-looking before, but the passing of the years had matured him, brought shades of character to his face, his eyes. Since coming to Washington she had danced with Brad Pitt, lunched with Sean Connery, and had her photograph taken with Mel Gibson. She'd been pleased to meet the stars and flattered by their attention, but she wasn't fool enough to have her head turned by their sex appeal.

No—her pulse was racing because Paul's appeal had been magnified by twenty-five years of musing about what might have been. The two years she had shared with Paul had been so rich, it was only natural she'd look back on them with rose-colored glasses.

Surely that explained this emotional flight of foolishness—her intense feelings of nostalgia were mingling with an undeniable physical attraction and a pinch of *simpático*, the certainty that she and Paul had been cut of the same cloth, that they would always understand each other, no matter how time and distance had separated them.

She dropped her pen, then rested her forehead against her fingertips. Soon this feeling would pass, surely, and she'd be able to behave like the professional she had to be. After all, Paul was married and had a family, probably a dog, cat, and minivan as well. He was surely thinking about the family even now, yearning for one of his wife's casseroles, maybe, or thinking that he needed to call his daughter and ask about her day . . .

She waited, expecting this mental douse of cold reality to steady her heart, but her skin continued to tingle.

"Get over it," she told herself, driving her pen across the bottom of another letter. "What you're feeling is emotion run amuck. He's a married man, he's here to do a job, and so are you. You've always managed to put your personal feelings on a back burner, and this situation will be no exception. Keep your eyes on the prize, Daryn, and don't let yourself become distracted."

She flipped the letter over and stared at the next page in the stack, a thank-you note to the head of the "Reelect Austin" committee forming in Dallas, Texas.

"This is what you have to focus on," she reminded herself, positioning her pen for yet another signature. "Because if you can't hang on to the presidency, all your plans will vanish overnight."

At her feet, the dog snorted, moving his muzzle over the carpet in search of crumbs. Daryn finished signing the stack of letters without another thought of Paul Santana, then picked up the phone and punched Ms. Park's extension.

"Ms. Park," she said, slipping the signed letters into a folder, "will you call Senators Oliphant and Beatty? Please give them my regrets and ask if we can reschedule our meeting. I don't think I want to discuss the fetal rights bill over dinner."

"Yes, ma'am," the secretary answered. "And Mr. Santana?"

"Leave him on the schedule," Daryn answered, swiveling her chair to face the wall. "And arrange for dinner to be served in the residential dining room."

●

Hank Beatty accepted the news without batting an eyelash. He'd half-expected the president to cancel their dinner meeting; everyone knew she was trying her best to stall controversial issues until after the upcoming election.

"Thanks for the update, Justin," he said, motioning his aide out the door. "Guess I'll be free for dinner after all."

He leaned back in his chair, propping one leather shoe on the edge of a partially opened drawer, then looked across his desk. "She canceled our meeting tonight," he told Douglas Oliphant, the Democratic senator from Florida. "And I'd bet my bottom dollar she doesn't reschedule before the election."

Oliphant, the ranking member of the powerful Senate Health, Education, Labor, and Pensions Committee, made clucking noises with his tongue. "You shouldn't be surprised. Like me, she wants this to go away. She's afraid a fetal rights bill will take things a step further than the Unborn Victims of Violence Act."

"As it will." Beatty showed his teeth in an expression that was not a smile, the best he could manage for the man with whom his political disagreements were many and usually robust. "Guess our little showdown's been postponed. The president isn't willing to play referee as long as there's an election staring her in the face."

"You don't really believe—" Lines of concentration deepened along Oliphant's brows. "You don't really think she has a chance, do you? There's no consensus of independent voters."

"That's what they said last time, before Parker's movie star brother raised all that money and bought him a seat in the White House." Lowering his foot, Beatty straightened in his chair and gazed at the man who was now both his ally and his opponent. "Things are changin', Doug; we're lookin' at new players and new rules." He reached for his pipe, then nestled the curved bowl in the palm of his hand. The familiar touch brought him a measure of comfort.

Oliphant's mouth went tight with mutiny. "What if we don't like these new rules?"

"Learn to like them, my esteemed friend. It's like your mama said—you have to play nice with girls, but if you're sharp and think ahead, you can beat them, no matter what the game."

•

By five o'clock, Paul stood amid an ocean of empty cardboard boxes. His law books now filled the shelves behind his desk, photos of his family lined the credenza, and his favorite picture, a Norman Rockwell print called "Do Unto Others," dangled from a hook on the wall. The boxes had been delivered not long after he left the Oval Office, and Paul took their timely arrival as a good omen. His term of service in the White House just might be the highlight of his career.

O'Leary had stopped by on his way out, taking time to drop a heavy leather binder on Paul's desk. "Courtesy of the welcoming committee," he quipped, sliding the notebook toward Paul. "We were lucky—when we came in after Parker took office, we had two days of seminars to teach us how to handle this job. You'll be having to cover the material on your own."

Lifting the cover, Paul scanned the table of contents. "How Congressional Leadership Looks at the Policy Executive," he read. "Dealing with the Press. Standards of Conduct."

"I knew you'd be wanting something to fill your weekend," O'Leary joked. "That's guaranteed to put you to sleep, but it's important. This place can be a minefield, with everybody guarding their own little territory, so it might help you to know where you must tread carefully."

A rap on the door broke into his thoughts. He looked up to see a blonde woman standing in the doorway, a badge hanging from her neck and a leather portfolio in her hand.

"Mr. Santana?" She came forward with a confident step, beaming all the way. "I'm Mildred Lipps, with Georgetown Real Estate. I'm here to assist you."

Paul frowned as he took her hand. "I'm sorry, Ms. Lipps, but I don't recall setting an appointment for today. Did my wife call you?"

The real-estate agent laughed. "Goodness, no. Jacob Thrasher told me to stop by to see you."

As she dropped her portfolio to the desk, Paul searched his memory for Thrasher's name, then groaned when he found it. Thrasher was Daryn's chief of staff, and probably the most powerful man in the White House.

The real-estate agent pulled a stack of glossy brochures from her portfolio, then spread them as neatly as a dealer handling a stack of marked cards. "Mr. Thrasher, in fact, told me exactly what you'd be needing in a rental house. From our multiple listing service I've pulled up the following properties, and I'm sure we can arrange a few discreet inquiries."

Paul winced slightly—since when did the chief of staff know what sort of house he needed?—then gestured at the clutter around him. "I'm afraid I'll have to let my wife handle the house. I am planning to stay at a hotel until she arrives, and she won't leave Miami for at least another month or two."

Pulling her brochures together, the woman wrinkled her brow. "Should I fedex these brochures to her?"

"That might be best." He smiled as a picture of a particularly handsome house caught his eye. "That is a lovely home. But I understand property up here is expensive."

She laughed again, the sound trilling through the room. "Mr. Santana, you *are* new to the neighborhood, aren't you? Whatever you like can be arranged through, shall we say, *creative* financing. You have only to let us know what you like."

With that cryptic comment she tucked the brochures into her portfolio and left the office, waving as she went.

Creative financing? Something cautioned Paul not to press the matter, not yet. He wasn't sure how money flowed in the White House; he wasn't certain he wanted to plumb the intricate differences between soft money, hard money, campaign funds, and operating budgets. His job might require him to investigate these matters soon enough, and if it did, he'd apply himself to making sure the boundaries were never crossed.

He picked up an empty cardboard box and broke the bottom seal, then flattened it. Too bad he couldn't send these boxes back to Miami for reuse. Maria would need boxes to pack the house, and she didn't have the strength to scrounge outside grocery stores the way his parents did every time they moved. Maria would let the packers provide the boxes, and they'd charge her plenty for the convenience.

She teased him about his frugality, but she had grown up on Miami Beach, not Little Havana. Her father's law practice had provided the means to spoil his daughter from birth. To Maria's credit, she'd never been a whiny wife, but she expected things. Daryn, on the other hand, had always appreciated the little gifts he provided, but she hadn't expected them. Whether that was a testament to her generally accepting nature or her knowledge of his poverty, he couldn't say.

He continued working with the boxes, breaking and bending them until he had a neat stack piled beside the door. He could probably call someone and have the broken boxes hauled away, but he was trying to keep a low profile in the office, at least until Monday.

He had always preferred quiet work. And, unlike some of his former associates at the law firm, he didn't want to have money just to breed more money. As long as he had enough to provide clothing and shelter for his family, send his daughter to the college of her dreams, and care for his wife, he would be content. Even in Washington.

Paul sank into his chair, smiling as his bewilderment mingled with amusement. Jacob Thrasher wouldn't care if Paul lived in a hovel, but Daryn might. So maybe *she'd* sent the real-estate agent to his office, perhaps even suggesting half a dozen of the brochures in Ms. Lipps's tailored leather folio. After all, she knew his tastes, and maybe her heart had flip-flopped around in that strange little shimmy the way his had when she embraced him . . .

No. He shook off the thought. Daryn was POTUS, her every move tracked on dozens of desks in this office alone, and she had far more important things to do than investigate real-estate brochures for an old friend. She had probably told Thrasher to send someone, suggested a few ideas, and left it at that. If he allowed his fantasies to carry the scenario further, he'd be setting himself up for big trouble.

Still . . . his thoughts drifted toward the glossy photos. A Washington mansion had never been part of his dream, but if such a thing were ethically possible, he could handle living in an ivy-covered brownstone, even temporarily.

And Daryn would never ask him to do anything illegal—the risks were too great. Like him, she'd lived through Watergate, the Iran Contra hearings, and the Monica Lewinsky scandals. In law school, when they had worked together for the legal services organization, both of them had believed in winning by the rules. She would run a clean White House, and she knew he played fair.

Standing, he smoothed his shirt, then moved toward the hallway and the men's washroom. At dinner tonight, if he could find a private moment, he might ask her a few things about Washington real estate, if only to make certain his assumptions were still correct.

TWELVE

DARYN LAUGHED WHEN SHE OPENED THE DOOR AND saw Paul standing stiffly in the company of a Secret Service escort. "I hope you're not going to salute," she said, smiling her thanks to the agent. "You're expected. Come in."

She stepped back to let him enter, then suppressed a grin as his gaze traveled from the plush carpet to the crown molding.

"Nice digs." He folded his arms and moved further into the room. "And nice guards. For a moment there, I didn't think I was going to pass inspection."

"You'll never have any problem." She slid her stockinged feet into the brown loafers she'd kicked off beside the door. "That blue background on your ID badge will get you anywhere in the West Wing, and I've placed your name on the permanent admittance list for the residence. Anytime I'm in the residence and you need me, feel free to come and find me."

"I'll bet you say that to all your lawyers."

"No—just the ones who are old friends."

He didn't answer, but she saw color rise from the back of his neck. When he turned, however, his face seemed frozen in a permanent expression of preternatural composure. "Did I get the time wrong? I thought this was a business dinner."

"The senators had to cancel, but I thought it might be a good night for us to catch up." She moved to the carved door and opened it, then beckoned to him with a crook of her index finger. "First, how about a quick tour? I've got this great place, and I never get to show it off."

His brows flickered a little. "If you wanted a free night, perhaps I should go. I don't want to intrude if you want some time to yourself."

"Loosen up, Paul." She injected a teasing note into her voice. "Time I have; it's old friends I'm running short of. And don't be too impressed on my account. They only let me borrow this place."

If he'd had any misgivings, they vanished with her words. Grinning, he moved toward her with eagerness in his eyes. Pleased by his interest, she led him into the west sitting area, then pointed toward the grand hall beyond. "You want the economy tour or the works?"

"Whatever you want to show me." He gave her a bright-eyed glance, brimming with curiosity. "I'm new in town, remember? I haven't even had a tour of the Capitol yet."

She considered a moment, then smiled. "I'll show you the immediate vicinity. I haven't explored the place thoroughly myself, and there's no telling what sort of ghosts might be roaming the halls once the sun goes down."

"They've really reported ghosts?"

"Just part of the folklore, my friend. And the history. A positively frightening number of people have died here."

She pointed over her shoulder to the room they'd just left. "That room is part of the presidential suite. I use it for a living room, as did the Fords, the Carters, the Reagans, and the Clintons. JFK used it for his bedroom."

His brows rose. "Really?"

"Yeah. Professor Gifford—remember her?—she came to see me one weekend and slept in there. At least I *think* she slept. She might have spent all night caressing the wallpaper." Her heart warmed when he laughed. "Beyond that room is the master bedroom and a nice sitting room. From the sitting room window you can see the Oval Office."

Paul pressed his hand to the back of his neck. "Let me guess—for all those nights when the first ladies wanted to see if their husbands really were working late?"

"I imagine you're right." Lifting her hand, she gestured to the lavishly decorated area where they stood. "Meet the west sitting hall. It used to be formal and dark, with a staircase leading downstairs. This is an improvement, don't you think?"

She let her gaze rove over the airy space, accented with cream-colored carpeting and lined with bookcases. Paul would undoubtedly appreciate the elegant antiques. He had always had an eye for beauty, often dragging her through museums and forcing her to look at photographs in architectural magazines . . .

He nodded his agreement. "It's beautiful."

"Reagan used to have breakfast here." She ran her fingertips over a mahogany table near the entrance to the living room. "The residential kitchen is across the hall, along with what Jackie Kennedy dubbed 'the president's dining room.' It's for occasions like this—quiet dinners with friends."

She felt her heart lurch when he looked at her with the drowsy smile she used to adore, then lowered her gaze. He still possessed the power to make her stomach flutter; the years had concentrated him somehow, strengthening his appeal. Or maybe it was the idea of forbidden fruit that drew her, because he was married now, with a family—

Thankfully, he seemed unaware of the undercurrent that threatened to pull her under. He turned slowly, taking the place in, then gave her an incredulous smile. "It's really something, Daryn—but can you enjoy it? Don't you sometimes feel like you're living in a museum?"

She bit her lip as she considered the question. "Well . . . yes and no. I don't mind the museum aspect of it. The furnishings are beautiful, and I brought enough of my own things to help me feel at home. The Secret Service guys are always around, of course, but they don't track me in the residence, only at the exits. I suppose I think of it as living in a really nice apartment building attached to a museum and an office complex." She lifted one shoulder in a shrug, then snapped her fingers. "I nearly forgot the best part. This apartment comes with great amenities—fresh flowers every day and the best cook in the country, for whom nothing is too great a challenge."

"You didn't finish."

"What?"

"You told me what you don't mind. You didn't say what you *do* mind."

Looking away, she felt her flesh color. Why was he so perceptive? Why couldn't he be as dull and disinterested as most of the other men she'd dated?

She looked at him and knew from the gleam in his eyes that he would not let the subject drop. He had always been able to nail her with that look.

"What I don't like," she said softly, hauling her gaze from his face to some neutral object, "is the loneliness."

She looked up to find him watching her, his eyes searching her face as if he could reach into her thoughts—

No. She took three steps forward, then crooked her finger at him. "Come on, the chef should be ready. We're having *palomilla* and *yuca con mojo* for dinner."

Above a thoughtful smile, his eyes sparkled. "You have a Cuban chef?"

She grinned. "He's not Cuban, but he's one of the best in the country, and I hear he's been combing through Cuban cookbooks since noon. So why don't we go see what he's whipped up for us?"

His smile flashed, lighting his eyes. And as Daryn turned to lead the way into the president's dining room, she realized her heart felt lighter than it had in weeks.

●

Warmed by the wine and the memories, an hour later Daryn sat next to Paul on the sofa in her living room, an embroidered pillow squatting like a bollard between them and *The Goodbye Girl* playing on the television. Preferring to talk, they hadn't really watched the movie, but as Marsha Mason clutched Richard Dreyfuss's guitar and leaned out the window to tell him good-bye, Daryn curled one leg beneath her and propped her elbow on the back of the sofa.

"Do you remember the first time we saw this?" she asked, daring to break the silence that had crept over them. "It was 1978, in that little movie house downtown. I cried all through the ending."

"I remember." Easing into a smile, he shifted to face her. "You were wearing a little red sweater thing . . . and I thought I would die if you didn't kiss me good night."

Her eyes came up to study his face. "As I recall, you didn't die."

"No." With his left hand he began to trace the needlepoint pattern on the pillow between them. "And you didn't put up too much of a fight."

They looked at each other for a moment, then broke eye contact, their gazes drifting off to safer territory. The smoldering flame she had glimpsed in his eyes startled her, intensifying the pulse of the knot that had formed in her stomach when he walked through the doorway.

She had hoped that dinner, complete with mundane conversation about ordinary life, would dispel the romantic haze that had clouded her vision this afternoon. But the movie, the darkening room, and, above all, the powerful presence of the man next to her had awakened feelings she thought were dead and buried. Amazing, that these emotions could resurrect after a few hours, a shared conversation, and the exchange of a few "do you remembers." Amazing that she could still feel these emotions at all after forty-two days as the first American president who was scrupulously trying to avoid any and all references to gender.

She turned her face toward the television, pretending to watch the movie's ending. As the ache-in-the-heart theme song began to play, she found her voice. "Paul," she said, not daring to look directly at him, "I'm very glad you're here. Not only professionally, but personally. I don't have many friends, and there aren't many people I trust in Washington. Everyone I've met here is primarily concerned about what

I can do for them, and the people I passed over on my way to the White House aren't inclined to be supportive unless it suits their purposes."

Propping his head on his hand, he leaned toward her in mute acknowledgment of the bond they shared. "What about your father? I would think he'd be a valuable resource."

"Dad's eighty-eight now, Counselor. And though he'd love to think he was helping me, the truth is that I can't tell him anything of real significance. He's too proud of his political connections, and too apt to show off and speak out of turn." She managed a choking laugh. "Now I understand why Dad wore this sort of constipated look the entire time he was governor. I find myself wearing the same expression when I have to hold things in."

Paul's mouth quirked with humor. "I've heard that your chief of staff is loyal. And O'Leary certainly seems competent."

"O'Leary *is* competent; I'm not sure about loyal. Thrasher would walk through fire for me, but the man doesn't know how to take off his public face. We had dinner together once, and when I tried to talk about trivial things, Jacob looked at me like I'd lost my senses." Sighing, she lowered her gaze. "Washington is a company town. What you do all day is what you talk about in the evening, unless you're with a friend. It's hard to find a friend here, and harder still to keep one."

She looked up and found him watching her intently. "But I'm sure you understand these things."

"Actually, I'm glad you're telling me this. If I'm going to work here, it'll help if I understand the territory."

Relieved, she raked her hand through her hair. "It's hard to explain to an outsider. Because the unblinking eye of the media is usually focused on Washington, politicians tend to dehumanize themselves; they adopt public personas that evolve to fit the prevalent culture. Instead of being real people who sneeze and eat Doritos and watch TV, they become collections of positions on everything from irradiated food to arms control. After a few months of breathing the *Zeitgeist* of this crazy little world, the real person disappears."

His reaching fingers brushed hers as he thumped the pillow between them. "You haven't disappeared, Daryn. You're still here, and you haven't changed."

She laughed, the sound hollow in her ears. "I haven't been here that long."

"I don't think you'll change. You're too solid. Your public face *is* your private face—"

"You're wrong. It can't be." Her gaze clung to his, analyzing his reaction. "I'm going to have to develop two faces in order to survive. There's the public face people want to see, but I have to preserve a private face or I'll go crazy. I can't be perfect all the time, I can't live in a glass house; no one can."

"No one expects you to."

"Oh yes, they do. That's what the White House is, a big fishbowl where people can peek in and maybe catch a glimpse of the president. Half of them want to see her floating belly up."

The impulse to explode in hysterical laughter bubbled just below her skin, sparking in her blood like the wine they'd shared at dinner. "The other night, Paul, I had dinner with a senator and his wife, and I swear the guy was speaking to me in sound bites. When I made a comment about his reticence, he looked at me like I'd just fallen off a turnip truck. He deepened his voice in some kind of Charlton Heston–doing–Moses routine and said, 'I never say *anything* I wouldn't want to read in tomorrow's newspaper.'"

The corners of Paul's eyes crinkled. "You're kidding."

"I'm not. It makes me grateful I didn't drag a husband and kids into the White House. Having to be perfectly clothed in one's positions all the time, never wavering, never being able to speak freely, it's like—well, it's like never being able to change your clothes or get undressed."

She stiffened, momentarily embarrassed by her rush of words. Maybe it was the wine, or maybe the sight of Paul's brown eyes had loosened her tongue, but she had probably said far too much.

"It's okay." His voice was a rough whisper. "Don't worry."

She looked up, wondering if she should feel some guilt for the wave of gratitude breaking over her. Of course he understood; he had always understood her.

"You're the kind of friend I need," she said, daring to voice the thoughts that had been whirling in her brain for the last several hours. "That's why I wanted you to come to Washington. You're unchangeable. Though I know certain circumstances haven't been easy for you these last few years, I knew you'd come through the trouble with your integrity intact."

"Integrity," his voice thickened, "like beauty, lies in the eye of the beholder. Plenty of people in Miami think I must have sold out. They've never forgiven me for failing Elian Gonzalez."

She smiled, remembering again that Paul had never been the type to easily pocket praise. Reaching out, she covered his hand with her own. "I don't care what they think. I know you are a man of loyalty. And I desperately need a loyal friend."

His gaze traveled over her face while he seemed to weigh her words. "I want to help you," he finally said, as simply as if she'd asked for a ride to the airport. "I've always admired you, Daryn. Never more than now."

She squeezed his hand, resisting her overwhelming need to crawl into his sheltering arms. "You've had a long day. Do you have a place to sleep? There's the Lincoln Bedroom, just down the hall—"

"Thanks, but I have a hotel room. And I understand I have a ton of reading to do this weekend."

She smiled at him a moment, considering his answer, then unfolded her legs and stood. "I should say good night, then. I have an early cabinet meeting in the morning."

"On Saturday?"

"No rest for the wicked, I'm afraid."

He stood, too, and straightened his shoulders as if he'd suddenly remembered where he was. "Thank you, Madam President. It was kind of you—"

"Hush." Gently she placed a finger atop his lips. "That sort of thing is fine for the Oval Office, but up here you call me by name. This is where I wear my private face."

And then, before the mantle of formality could envelop him entirely, she rose on tiptoe, kissed his cheek, and pulled away.

●

Lost in a fog of impressions, desires, and anxieties, Paul took the elevator to the ground floor and made his way through the security checkpoints between the residence and the West Wing.

What in blazes was he doing? Ten minutes ago he'd been thinking about pulling another woman into his arms—

No. He'd been having a quiet conversation with the president of the United States, his new employer. She was also a friend—an old and dear friend—and they had always shared something special. Nothing inappropriate had happened tonight, nor would it.

She'd called him a man of integrity, and while the compliment warmed him, in the wake of his swirling emotions it also rankled. He had always tried to be a man who adhered to a high standard of morality. His standards might not be as rigorous as some, nor were they based in religion like Maria's, but his ethics were those approved and applauded by mainstream American society.

Surely there was nothing improper about his renewed relationship with Daryn. Other presidents had special friendships and managed to enjoy the White House without inviting undue media interference. Clinton had entertained a multitude of friends and relatives in the White House, and Nixon had partied there with his pal Bebe Robozo. Despite the private stories that did leak—of Nancy Reagan's astrologer, Kennedy's girlfriends, and Clinton's Monica—Paul knew there had to be scores of untold stories that had never been revealed.

Besides, meeting Daryn in the residence was not like meeting a mistress in a tawdry hotel, and as long as they were discreet their friendship would never be published on the front page of the *National Enquirer*.

This relationship would be protected by the Secret Service, by his own loyalty, and by the White House staff.

Not that there was anything that *needed* to be protected. Because nothing inappropriate was going to happen.

●

Paul reached the West Wing early on Monday morning, but he had no sooner dropped his briefcase on his desk than O'Leary slapped his hand against the door. "Come on, we're late," he said, without waiting for acknowledgment. Grabbing a notebook from his briefcase, Paul strode out the door and followed his new boss down the stairs and into the Roosevelt Room, a conference room only a few steps away from the Oval Office.

Thankfully, O'Leary motioned to a polished wooden chair as Paul entered the room. As he slid into it, he looked around the long table and tried to place names with faces. Most of the White House staff, he was amazed to realize, toiled in anonymity. He had never seen most of these people before.

"Listen up, I think I can only do this once," O'Leary said, bending low to speak into Paul's ear. "Starting at the head of the table, you've got the president, if she's available. The vice president, once he's confirmed, will be in on this meeting, too. Then there's the chief of staff—"

"Jacob Thrasher." Paul recognized Thrasher immediately. The man had been featured in several recent issues of *Newsweek* and *Time*, and for once, the coverage of a COS had been favorable.

"Right. Next to Thrasher you've got the cabinet secretary and staff secretary. Don't worry about their names for now, just know what they do and you'll be fine. Moving on around the table, you've got the assistant to the president for management and administration, the senior adviser for policy and strategy, the national security adviser, and me, counsel to the president."

Paul managed a weak smile. That title he recognized.

Leaning slightly forward, O'Leary looked past him. "Over there's the personnel security officer, the director of political affairs, and the directors of intergovernmental affairs, presidential personnel, communications, and the press secretary, the bodacious Natalie Morgan. Next to Morgan are the three stooges: the directors of public liaison, speechwriting, and presidential scheduling."

O'Leary paused, giving Paul a crooked smile. "You taking all this in?"

"Pretty well," Paul lied. "Is that, what, twenty-one titles?"

"If it is, I forgot a few." O'Leary stared around the rectangle. "Oh, yeah. That fuzzy-haired guy near the president's chair is Anson Quinn, director of the White House units of the Secret Service, and next to him is Templeman, the chief usher." His freckled face spread into a boyish smile. "And those are only the department heads."

The meeting began promptly at seven-thirty, when Daryn entered and wished everyone a cheery good morning. After a few perfunctory comments by the wunderkind chief of staff, O'Leary stood. "I'd like to introduce our new vice counsel to the president," he said, his hand moving to the back of Paul's chair. "Mr. Paul Santana, from Miami. I'm sure he will be a valuable addition to our staff."

Two dozen heads turned in Paul's direction, the same number of mouths twitching in pseudosmiles. Paul returned them, wondering at the thoughts behind those false fronts.

His musings were interrupted when Daryn cleared her throat. The ambient sounds of rustling paper and squeaking chairs suddenly ceased. "I'm sure you're all wondering why we brought Mr. Santana aboard," she said, flashing her smile around the room. "But I'm sure you're aware that it's time to begin serious planning for the upcoming election. I'm asking Mr. O'Leary to oversee the campaign, and I'm entrusting the running of the counsel's office to Mr. Santana." She paused, giving Paul a personal smile. "We'll give him a week or two to get his sea legs before giving him control of the ship. Then you'll see why I knew Paul Santana would be a great addition to our crew."

And that, Paul thought, watching as relief broke across several anxious faces, was why Daryn Austin handled the presidency so well. Like many women, she could sense the emotions of the people around her, and, unlike most male administrators, she would rather confront and explain than move on and hope trouble would go away.

"I'm sorry for the necessary evil of campaign tasks," Daryn continued, "but the future depends upon what we do in the next few months. The election won't be decided in November 2004—history tells us minds will be made up and the matter settled by next summer. So the foundation for our victory will be laid this coming January, in the State of the Union address. That speech will be a make-or-break opportunity, the ideal showcase for our administration and our message. The speech will also be the de facto declaration of our candidacy."

A thoughtful smile curved her mouth. "I'm sure you know there's no sense beating ourselves up to develop new programs and policies that are only going to be tossed out if another president takes office in eighteen months. So if we want today's efforts to matter tomorrow, we're going to have to divide our energies between the present and the future. We must begin to think seriously about the campaign."

Pulling his pen from his coat pocket, Paul prepared to take notes.

THIRTEEN

CURLED IN THE DESK CHAIR OF HER PRIVATE STUDY, Daryn absently rubbed Tyson's tummy with one stockinged foot while she and Thrasher critiqued her most recent speech on video. Two nights before, she had given the speech at a banquet for the Daughters of the American Revolution. Though she had never counted the conservative DAR among her supporters, her reception that night had been overwhelmingly enthusiastic. The usual protesters had gathered outside the hotel, but the women inside had radiated waves of pure love.

"Here," Thrasher said, pausing the video on a shot of a poster-carrying protester outside the security cordon. "Can you read that?"

Daryn squinted at the blurry image: "'More bitter than death is the woman who is a snare. The man who pleases God will escape her.'" She cocked an eyebrow at Thrasher. "What is *that* supposed to mean?"

"It's a verse from the book of Ecclesiastes. I looked it up." He leaned forward, peering at the wide-eyed man on the TV screen. "I also had Quinn and his guys take a look at this fellow. He didn't match anyone in the loony file."

Sighing, Daryn pressed her fingertips against her temple. The Secret Service maintained a "watch list" of nearly four hundred certifiably dangerous individuals who had made threats against the president; another thousand names were on a list of potential threats. On any given day, there was nothing to stop any one of them from hopping a bus or plane and coming to Washington to try his luck in a presidential shooting gallery . . .

Between the eyes, win a prize. Step right up, folks, put down your quarter and take your best shot.

Dropping her hand, she looked over at Thrasher. "Is someone checking this guy out?"

"The Secret Service has seen the video. His picture will be added to the file. If he shows up again, we'll have a match. Don't worry; if he's trouble, they'll nail him."

She sighed in relief when Thrasher punched the remote and the video rolled on. The cameras caught the motorcade turning into the hotel entrance, the crowds screaming out her name as the line of black sedans moved past the mob and drove toward the underground entrance.

"People think this life is glamorous," she said, giving Thrasher a wry smile. "I think I've walked through more hotel kitchens and back alleys in a month than most people will see in a lifetime."

"Tell me about it."

While the newscaster droned on about the historic significance of the evening—the nation's first female president addressing one of the nation's oldest female organizations in her first public speech as president—the camera shifted to the dais, where a matronly woman wearing an orchid the size of Cleveland was finishing her introduction. Daryn tilted her head as she saw her own image—a self-contained, neat, Barbie-doll-looking president—step out from behind a wall of red curtains.

"Why did it take us so long to get a woman president?" the matron asked, lifting one hand in a theatrical gesture. "Because—in this country, we have a tradition of saving the best for last!"

As a roar of approval swept the ballroom, Daryn watched the Barbie doll walk forward, embrace the plumpish matron, and exchange air kisses. Then she stepped onto the podium, gripped the bulletproof lectern her aides referred to as the "blue goose," and waited.

Even now, Daryn couldn't help but marvel at the sound. Waves of applause crested, broke, and crashed, only to crest again. Whistles, screams, and the rhythmic sounds of *WOOF, WOOF, WOOF* from a rowdy group of young women down front mixed with the pounding applause. She had heard such a welcome before, of course, at Parker's inauguration outside the Capitol Building, but that sound had floated free and drifted away. This was a gouging, ripping mayhem of noise that made the very building vibrate, and this time it was *for her.*

Too bad her dad hadn't been there to hear it.

"Ten minutes," Thrasher said, consulting his watch. "They didn't let up for ten minutes, and then you had to ask them to be quiet."

Daryn said nothing, but kept her eyes on the screen. The Barbie doll inclined her head graciously, lifted her hand, gave a few grateful smiles. Now she lifted both hands, signaling the need for quiet. When it finally came, a funereal stillness reigned, with nothing but a woman's amplified voice to disturb it.

"Thank you, men and *women* of America," she began, and the place erupted again. The tiny president smiled, acknowledging the support, then held up her hand for silence. "In 1987, Bella Abzug said, 'Is America less of a nation than Iceland? Is America less of a nation than Denmark? Is America less of a nation than England? If those countries are man enough to elect a woman, I think America can do so as well.'"

As the women in the seats leaped to their feet, she stepped back, smiling and nodding throughout the ovation.

"You know," Thrasher said in a wry tone, "if you get any more popular we're going to have to find another way to do your speeches. You can't seem to get a word out without being interrupted."

Daryn tossed him a look of faint reproach. "Trust me, I don't mind."

In truth, that night had felt like the apogee of a lifetime. All those years in the service of her father's politics, all the campaigns and elections and late nights and strategy sessions had finally borne fruit. As a willful teenager she may have ruined her father's opportunity to lead, but she had finally reached the place where she could make it up to him. As Daryn Austin, his daughter, his legacy, she had attained a position of real influence and, with the power of the people behind her, she intended to use it.

The president-as-Barbie gripped the blue goose again. "I have grown up," she said, her voice sounding tinny through the hotel speakers, "in a nation run by politicians who sent pilots to man bombers to kill babies to make the world safe for American children. This should not be! For the sake of our children, for the world's children, we must maintain a watchful peace. The stakes for women are too high for politics to be a spectator sport!"

Thrasher fast-forwarded through the crashing applause, then cut to Daryn lifting her hand. "I loved this part," he drawled.

"They say," the tinny voice continued, "that women talk too much. But if you've spent any time in Congress you can't help but notice that the filibuster was invented by *men!*"

"Uh-oh." Thrasher pointed to his watch, then punched the power off. "Three o'clock. My time's up."

Swiveling the chair to face the desk, Daryn stifled a yawn. "What's next on my schedule?"

"Your free time. Do whatever you like, Madam President, but I'll get out of your hair."

"Leave the video. I might finish watching it this afternoon." She paused for a moment, then lifted her index finger. "On your way out, will you ask Ms. Park to see if Paul Santana is available? I want to see how he enjoyed his first week in this madhouse."

Thrasher gathered his notes, then nodded. "No problem."

●

Within ten minutes Paul entered the Oval, a question in his brown eyes, and Daryn had to restrain herself when he crossed the threshold. She wanted to take his hands, pull him onto the sofa, and hear all about his week . . . but this was the Oval Office, the room where Ronald Reagan had refused to remove his coat and tie. Despite what subsequent presidents had done within these walls, she felt the office demanded a measure of dignity—and she'd wager Paul felt the same.

After welcoming him with a warm handshake, she sent her secretary in search of coffee, then gestured toward the sofa. As Paul sat, she took the wing chair at his right hand and leaned on the armrest. "How's it going upstairs?" she asked, searching his face for any signs of weariness. "Is O'Leary giving you the help you need?"

"He's been great," Paul said, shifting as Miss Park came in with a serving cart. "Very helpful. And those young legal eagles over in the OEOB are top notch."

Even if O'Leary had been less than cooperative, Daryn suspected Paul would be reluctant to tell her. He had always been a team player through and through.

As Miss Park poured the fragrant coffee, Daryn pressed on: "Did O'Leary lay out all the primary issues we're watching—crime, the slavery in Sudan, tax reform, and the need for a budget overhaul? I know he'll be keeping an eye on them with the campaign in mind, but we have to keep our finger on the national pulse during the months ahead. And we never know when the Supreme Court is going to drop a controversial decision on our heads."

"I think I have a handle on it."

Afraid she sounded like a nagging woman, she gave him an apologetic smile. "Did he explain the personnel procedures? We won't be adding much staff until after the election, but then I plan to commence with major housecleaning." Pressing her hands together, she leaned toward him. "The OPP will quietly begin to send you names in the fall, and you'll have to begin the vetting process. Only after we've won the election and the nominee has filled out all the forms will the information be sent to you for official review."

He gave her a conspiratorial wink as he accepted his coffee from the secretary. "It would help," he said, smiling, "if you could speak in full sentences without alphabet letters for a while. I think I'm beginning to catch on, but I still get my OPPs, my PASs, and my PAs confused."

"Office of Presidential Personnel," she supplied, thanking Miss Park with a smile. "Presidential Appointee requiring Senate confirmation, Presidential Appointee *not* requiring confirmation." As the secretary left, she dropped her head to the side of the wing chair and peeked at him around the edge. "Good grief, Santana, you're exhausting."

Leaning back, Paul snorted a laugh. "Yeah, right. Like you haven't been keeping me from sleep."

His words hung there, bold, brash, and possibly loaded with double meaning, yet she couldn't bring herself to touch them.

She shifted her gaze to the ceiling. "How's your family?" The question sprang more from politeness than curiosity. She'd have Paul's undivided attention only as long as his family remained in Miami . . .

"Cristina is getting ready to leave for Harvard, and Maria's helping her shop. The house in Miami hasn't been rented yet, but Maria doesn't seem to mind." A ripple of some negative emotion crossed his face, and Daryn wondered at its source. "I think right now she's more concerned about getting the baby bird out of the nest than renting the house. Once Cristina is settled in Cambridge, Maria will concentrate on the move."

"So you're still living at the hotel?"

"For at least another month, I'm afraid. Mrs. Lipps has found us a house in Georgetown, and the owner is willing to wait until we take care of the house in Miami. The moment it is rented, I'm vacating the hotel. After a while, the walls start to feel like they're closing in."

Daryn nodded. "Tell me about it. My last campaign was a two-year round of cookie-cutter hotel rooms topped off by a diet of rubber chicken and occasional humble pie."

As Paul laughed, Daryn sipped from her coffee cup, enjoying the companionable moment. In college they'd often stopped for coffee after classes, but in those days they'd sipped thick, boiled-down brews from plain foam cups at the diner . . .

"I've often thought—" she lowered her cup to the fine china saucer—

"that if Starbucks had been around when we were in school, we'd have accomplished a lot more. The coffee we drank was far too revolting for us to gain any real caffeine benefit."

He grinned. "I'd have gone broke if Starbucks had existed back then. There's one in Miami I visit every afternoon, but this brew can compete, no problem. And the company here is far more interesting."

She warmed to the comment, turning it over in her mind as she looked away. This was what she'd been missing for years, simple conversation with a caring friend who knew her as Daryn, not as Madam Politician.

"Your wife," she said, setting her cup and saucer on the table at her left, "I understand she was seriously ill."

Paul nodded. "Breast cancer. Found it three years go, then she underwent lumpectomy and radiation. She's currently in remission, and we hope, of course, that she's cured. But you have to get through five years before the doctors will agree to that."

"So she's good as new?"

"I wouldn't say that. The cancer frightened her terribly, and she seems a lot more . . . vulnerable. Her father has always treated her like some kind of porcelain doll, and the cancer seemed to amplify that tendency." He shot her a knowing look. "I can tell you this—if anyone *but* the White House had called, she wouldn't have left Miami."

Daryn crossed her arms. "Not even if the move were important to you?"

"Not even." He sat very still, his eyes narrow and focused on some interior field of vision. "That's why I turned you down at first—I'm assuming you know I turned you down."

"I knew."

"I never dreamed Maria would leave Miami. And something in me won't believe it until I see her in Washington."

Daryn felt the questions and assumptions bubbling up; she selected one off the top and tossed it at him. "So . . . are you two not soul mates?"

The look he gave her was bland; only a wary twitch of his eye indicated he knew she was treading on hazardous ground.

"We have never been of the same mind . . . at least, not like you and I were. Maria is a very traditional woman; all she's ever wanted is to care for her home and family. After Cristina was born we learned that Maria shouldn't have any more children, and that's been hard to accept. Her family is devoutly religious, you see."

Daryn nodded, understanding exactly what he meant. During her years as a volunteer at the legal services office she had encountered many devout Catholic families who did not believe in any sort of artificial birth control. Either they had babies every year, or husbands and wives learned to sleep apart. So if a couple shouldn't have children, their intimacy would decidedly suffer.

Paul looked away, a tide of color flooding his cheeks. "I'm sorry. I shouldn't have mentioned that. Maria is a very private person."

"It's all right; we've shared more private things than that." Daryn lowered her gaze, disturbed that he'd rushed to defend his wife, but strangely elated that he'd shared the confidence. She reached for her coffee. "So—you're not religious anymore?"

"No. Not since—well, not since we broke up." He spoke with light bitterness, and Daryn knew better than to prod him further. Sipping her coffee, she sat and thought while Paul did the same.

"No appointments this afternoon?" he said, finally breaking the silence.

She shook her head. "After three weeks of a nonstop schedule, I realized that even the president needs some downtime. Now the appointment office schedules a sacrosanct break for me every Friday. For two hours a week, I'm free to sit and twiddle my toes if that's all I want to do. Usually I take the time to catch up on my reading or phone calls, but today—" she smiled at him—"I wanted to catch up with you."

"Never thought I'd have to get an appointment to sit with my old girlfriend," he quipped, meeting her gaze.

"Never thought I'd have to command you to come see me." Her smile matched his as she returned her cup to the table. "Paul, I need your advice about several things. Are you available for dinner this evening?"

His brows lowered. "I'm not sure I should be the one advising you. Why not Thrasher or O'Leary?"

"Because you're my lawyer. Because you're the only completely *un*ambitious person I've ever known. And because I have a hunch that hotel room is looking pretty bleak these days."

He stared at her for a moment without expression, then slowly he nodded. "Yes," he said, the wariness melting from his eyes. "I'd love to."

FOURTEEN

WHILE A *SEINFELD* RERUN PLAYED ON TELEVISION, Paul and Daryn ate a gourmet Thai dinner on TV trays in the residence living room. Paul nearly managed to forget that he was dining with the commander in chief of the United States' military forces. Lively and good-humored, Daryn had shed her stiff dignity as easily as she kicked off her high-heeled pumps. Now, sitting crossed-legged on the sofa in jeans and a summer sweater, she ribbed him about refusing to eat his *pad woon sen* with chopsticks.

"Come on," she said, using the chopsticks as if she'd been born to them. "You've had enough Cuban food to last a lifetime. It's time you tried something different."

He stared at a piece of glazed meat he'd speared with a fork. "What did you say this was again?"

"Stir-fried chicken." Dramatically she popped a green something-or-other into her mouth, chewed for a moment, then swallowed and grinned. "Tastefully mixed with bean thread, eggs, pea pods, carrots, onion, broccoli, and at least a couple of other things I can't identify."

He tasted the meat and found it delicious. "Okay—you win. It's good."

"It's *great.* Remember where you are, bud. Only the best food makes it into my TV dinner."

"I hope your chef came up with a good dessert." He stabbed a brilliant bit of broccoli. "I've had a craving for something sweet all day."

"Sorry—no dessert with this dinner, but we might be able to scrounge up a piece of fruit or something. I've got to count my calories for a month or two. The *Post* did an article on my 'expanding waistline,' so I'm under strict orders from Jacob to cut back." She waved the chopsticks at his plate. "This entire dinner is less than 500 calories. I don't know how the chef does it, but he does."

Paul made a face. "Bet the *Post* wouldn't give a male president that kind of grief."

She shrugged. "I think the public is more attuned to a female executive's appearance, but they gave Clinton a hard time, too. Remember all those Big Mac jokes? I think that's why he had the jogging track built on the South Lawn."

"I've never heard a word about you using it."

"And you won't. I'm not going to give them the pleasure of knowing I even *heard* their criticism. If they think I care, they'll say a female president spends more time on her appearance than a male candidate. Leno will be doing Presidential Beauty Salon jokes, and Letterman will pay someone in a fat suit to come out and impersonate me." She shook her head. "I'll exercise, but I won't give them the satisfaction of letting them know about it. I especially won't let them know I care."

While Jerry, Elaine, and George stressed out over waiting for a table in a Chinese restaurant, Paul wondered how much Daryn had buried beneath her poised public facade. She'd always been a strong woman, realistic and logical, but she had a sensitive side, too—one she didn't often reveal.

Perhaps she was right about the necessity of having two faces.

"Speaking of food," he said, lowering his gaze to the relative safety of his plate, "I remember noticing you for the first time at a college banquet. You were surrounded by men, all of them buzzing around you like bees."

She laughed. "Those were the days when I played the Southern belle.

Everything I knew about attracting men I learned from reading *Gone With the Wind.*"

A smile tugged at his lips. "You're kidding."

"Serious as nuclear war. Scarlett O'Hara was my best teacher. I learned that smart girls should occasionally play dumb, that you can entice a man by laughing softly at him from across the room, and that walking pigeon-toed will make your hoop skirt sway attractively when viewed from the rear." She made a moue. "I never found much use for the hoop skirt thing. Walking pigeon-toed does *not* look attractive when one wears a miniskirt."

Lifting his water glass, he arched his brow. "You didn't have to play games to catch my attention. When we finally met in the Laundromat, I remember being astounded that you'd even speak to me."

A secretive smile softened her lips. "You underestimate yourself, Counselor. You always have."

Searching for a way to move the conversation back to safer territory, he prodded another piece of chicken with his fork. "So, tell me—how do you like your new job?"

She managed a small grin. "You mean, other than the fact I get fried if I wear a dress that makes me look a few pounds too heavy? It's peachy."

"I was being serious."

"So was I."

"Daryn." He spoke the word in a tone of rebuke, and after a moment she lowered her chopsticks.

"It's amazing," she said, pausing to press the linen napkin to her lips. "More pressure than I imagined. And my eyes have been opened. Within a week of moving into the Oval, I learned that Craig Parker never intended for me to be little more than a figurehead. I heard from a trusted source that he was hoping I'd pick up some of the duties that traditionally belong to the first lady, to spare his wife some of the stress that comes with the job. I had always suspected as much, but it was disconcerting to have my suspicions confirmed."

She shook her head. "Book signings and ribbon cuttings have nothing to do with my reasons for joining the ticket. I wanted to make real policy changes, but after taking office I learned that the vice president's role is pretty much limited to whatever the president wants it to be. Since Reagan, the VP has been a principal adviser to the president, but Parker didn't even want my opinion on women's issues."

"So—what are you going to do with *your* vice president?"

"As soon as Frey is nominated and confirmed, I'm going to work his tail off. This job is huge, and I need all the help I can get, especially with foreign relations." A flash of humor crossed her face. "Be careful, Santana—if for some reason Frey doesn't work out, I just might nominate you for the veep position."

A wave of genuine horror roiled through his stomach, then she winked. He released a sigh. "You can be downright scary, Austin."

"You haven't seen anything yet." Tossing her bangs out of her eyes, she stretched and extended her arm along the back of the sofa. When she spoke again, her voice had taken on a dreamy tone. "The morning after I took the oath of office I woke up and stared at the ceiling, a little overwhelmed by the job that had dropped into my lap. As president, I am to help govern 300 million people who can't agree on the best movie of the year, let alone what is best for their government. I'm working for 224 million non-Hispanic whites, nearly 35 million Hispanics, 34 million African-Americans, 10.5 million Asians, and 2.5 million Native Americans. I'm trying to safeguard 35 million citizens who are over sixty-five, and 70 million under eighteen. My policies will affect 17 million who live in families with a net worth of more than $100,000, and 36 million who live below the poverty line. Six hundred fifty-thousand of my constituents are Phi Beta Kappa members; while a quarter of Americans twenty-five years of age or older have less than a ninth grade education."

Her fingernail jabbed into his shoulder. "You tell me—how on earth am I supposed to achieve a consensus with those figures?"

"I don't think consensus is your job," Paul answered, shifting to face her. "You have to do what is best for the majority."

She snorted softly. "The majority is a pack of sheep led about by the media. The *Post* can print that I've gained weight, and the next thing you know, the *Times* will say I'm being lazy and derelict in my duties. They'll cite some failed congressional bill that I favored, then my approval rating will avalanche. Next thing you know, I'm out of a job and my administration becomes a mere footnote in the history books."

Paul propped his arm on the back of the sofa. "I don't think you'll ever be a *mere* anything. But, for the record, I think you're doing a fine job. The breadth and depth of the Executive Office is amazing, and you're guiding it with a firm hand."

She looked at him, and for a moment neither of them said anything. "I think it was Eisenhower who said that no easy problems come to the president, because if they were easy, someone would have solved them long before they reached the Oval Office." Her eyes softened. "Sometimes I find myself wishing for an easy problem just so I could know I've done something right . . . now it occurs to me that I have. I hired you."

He looked away, helpless to halt his embarrassment.

"I'm sorry," she whispered. "I know you don't like flowery praise. And I hope I haven't brought you into something you won't enjoy. Life in this place isn't always a bed of roses."

"I never expected roses." Turning to face her, he dropped his hand to her arm and squeezed her elbow, relishing the softness of her skin. "I'm just glad I can help."

"You are helping," she whispered, and the look in her eyes sent his blood surging through his veins. "Sending for you was the smartest thing I've ever done."

She leaned toward him, moving into the space beneath his arm, but Paul felt frozen in place. Daryn Austin was a beautiful and desirable woman, but she was also POTUS, the president, the nation's commander in chief . . . and he had a wife and daughter in Miami.

She didn't kiss him, but reached out, the tips of her short nails caressing his cheek. "It's all right, Counselor. There are no cameras, no tape recorders in this room, only a few discreet Secret Service agents down the hall . . . guys with conveniently unreliable memories."

He let out a short laugh. "I seem to recall that some of them have written books."

"Some of Clinton's guys were gossips, and that's how the public viewed them. Only the right-wingers took them seriously. But now—" her nails were now threading through his hair—"no one who knows you're here will say anything."

He caught her questing hand, held it fast as he lowered his forehead to hers. "Daryn, though my marriage isn't what it could be, it's still a marriage. And if you're concerned about your public image, perhaps we shouldn't let this—"

"My public image is one thing," she said, her eyes large and liquid. "And this is quite another. Even a president deserves to have a private life."

With that, her lips slowly ascended to meet his. For a moment he wavered, images of Maria and Cristina like stuttering home movies on the back of his eyelids as his brain struggled to overcome the sparking in his blood. But his lungs were breathing in the fragrance of lost love, and the enchanting woman in his arms was real this time, neither a memory nor a fantasy . . .

With an effort, he closed his mind to his obligations and surrendered to the moment . . . and the woman.

●

Lying between finespun sheets of the finest Egyptian cotton, Daryn reached through the darkness to touch the man beside her.

Still here. A miracle, after all these years. Paul Santana—at least part of him—still belonged to her.

Pulling the sheet closer to her chin she turned, then sighed in contentment at the sight of his shadowed form in what had been yawning emptiness. She closed her eyes, trapping a sudden rush of tears. By all that was holy, she adored him.

She drew a deep breath, hearing nothing but the quiet hiss of the air conditioning and the distant whine of an ambulance somewhere on the street. Here, in the very heart of the richest and most powerful capital on earth, she had found a private shelter.

Another miracle.

Her tired body cried out for sleep, but she refused to drift away. Some part of her feared surrender, lest Paul be gone when she awoke. Worse would be finding him in the living room with regret in his eyes.

Would he be sorry for this night? Would he avoid her on Monday? She might have ruined everything with that first kiss . . .

Opening her eyes, she studied the slope of his shoulders and the smooth line of his spine, lit by the dim security light that burned in the bathroom. Was he asleep? Paul had always been a restless sleeper; in the old days he woke every time she slipped out of bed to go to the bathroom or set the alarm clock. He could be sleeping, but something didn't feel right—

His breathing. She couldn't hear a sound, and Paul had always breathed deeply and regularly when he dozed. So he was awake now, and thinking, probably pondering the same questions that would not let her rest.

"Don't." The word shattered the stillness like a gunshot.

"What?" The pillow muffled his voice.

She sat up, propping her back against the pillows. "Don't lie there beating yourself up, Counselor. You haven't done anything millions of other Americans haven't done this same night. And you're safe. I'll protect you, the Secret Service will protect you, my entire staff will shield your privacy."

The sheets rustled as he rolled onto his back, the dim light lighting his profile. His eyes glowed fiercely in the dark. "If the word gets out, Daryn . . . with the election coming up, this could kill you."

"The word's not going to get out. Any time you like you can walk from the residence to the West Wing; from there you can log out and go home. Anyone who sees the records will think you worked late or fell asleep in your office."

"But some people will know."

"Very few. And those people are loyal. If they weren't, they'd be out in a heartbeat."

A ripple of annoyance crossed his face. "Shut up, Daryn, and listen for once. I'm your *ethics* officer! How in the world am I supposed to protect you from scandal if I'm committing adultery—with the president?"

Her lower lip trembled as she returned his stare. His harsh tone ripped through her, scraping across her strained nerves, but he had no idea of how things stood. He hadn't been in this place long enough to understand.

Lowering herself to his side, she laid her hand on the smooth skin of his chest. "You could never hurt me, Paul. How could you, when you're the one helping me maintain my sanity? And as for the adultery, surely your marriage ended a long time ago."

"It didn't end. We still have a daughter."

Daryn leaned closer. "Maybe the marriage didn't end, but I know you well enough to know it couldn't have come close to the relationship we shared." When he didn't argue, she pressed on. "I know you've kept things together for your daughter's sake, but let's face facts—Maria has not been a wife to you; she's been a homemaker. I can't be a homemaker, but I can be your soul mate. I always have been." She lowered her head to whisper in his ear, "The vast majority of Americans wouldn't blame either of us for this. They won't care, as long as we're discreet."

Her words must have taken hold, for he rolled to face her, then placed his hand in the curve of her waist, drawing her closer. "I'd forgotten," he said, brushing a kiss across her forehead, "how good we were together."

"Not a good thing to forget." She placed her hand upon his jaw, noticing how perfectly her palm fit that space. "I suppose I'll have to keep reminding you."

As he kissed the pulsing hollow at the base of her throat, she whispered, "It has always been you for me, Paul. No one else. Not ever."

FIFTEEN

SITTING ON ONE OF THE SOFAS IN THE OVAL OFFICE, Daryn propped her chin in her hand and absently watched the sunlight stream through the wide windows. Like Tyson in search of a cookie, it nosed her leather shoes, then her ankles, then warmed the middle of her calves. Soon it would reach the hem of her skirt, and they were no closer to this meeting's end than they had been at 10 A.M.

Sighing, she glanced from her chief of staff to her counsel, then to Paul. Winston Booker, director of the Office of Presidential Personnel, sat in a chair in front of the fireplace, his belly tugging at the bottom of his suit coat. It was his oral report that threatened to put her to sleep.

"So why in the heck can't we nominate Lawrence Frey to the office of the vice president?" Daryn interrupted, strafing the group with a stern glance. "Give me a reason in thirty words or less."

"Something came up in the FBI full-field investigation report," Booker said, dropping the printed pages from which he'd been reading. "In 1992 Frey divorced his wife and married his campaign manager."

Daryn closed her eyes. She did not need a problem at this point; she needed a partner. Not having a first lady to share the work load was hardship enough; not having a vice president was quickly becoming an embarrassment.

O'Leary took the conversational lead. "Surely 'tis not the end of the world. Who else is on the short list for the veep spot?"

Thrasher cleared his throat and gripped the armrests of his chair as if bracing for a storm. "There seems to be a shortage of qualified independents. Those who are affiliated with either the Republican or Democratic parties don't want to sacrifice those ties."

"Not even if we go into the primaries with great numbers?" Paul asked, shifting to face Thrasher. "They won't be sacrificing anything if they join this administration. The president is doing a fine job, and her approval ratings are high."

"The tide can change overnight, and they don't want to take the risk." Thrasher shrugged. "They're thinking long term, and most of them are betting on a Democratic resurgence in the 2004 election. They see Parker's victory as a fluke, and Daryn's accomplishment as nothing more than a honeymoon phase awarded to the first female president."

"Then we'll have to show them it's more than a honeymoon." Straightening, Daryn looked at Booker. "Let's go back to Lawrence Frey. So he divorced his wife and married another woman. What's so unforgivable about that?"

Booker blinked in confusion. "Um—his wife was in the hospital at the time. On the day he filed the papers."

"Did she contest the divorce?"

"No."

"Did he issue some kind of public apology?"

"Um . . . yes. He was a state senator at the time, he issued a statement saying his marriage had been over for a year, and he regretted the pain and suffering he'd caused."

Daryn thumped the sofa. "There you have it. The man came through a difficult situation; he faced his public; he married the woman he loved. End of story. Let's keep him."

Thrasher frowned. "Do you really want to run the risk of offending Middle America?"

"Middle America ought to be grateful we're being honest and not hypocritical," Daryn snapped. "We'll present Frey as a dedicated, hard-working independent who made a terrible mistake in the timing of his divorce, but quickly got his life back on course. And *because* he's been hurt, he now cares even more deeply for women and children and families." She stole a glance at Paul, who had slipped slightly lower in his seat. "Let's play up the Prince of Wales–Wallis Simpson angle—you know, forsaking everything for the woman he loved. Let's be up front about it. If we don't hide his past, anyone who slings mud on him will find that it just won't stick."

"Our duty, Madam President," O'Leary said, "is to warn you about the appearance of ethics violations. If Frey will hurt us in the upcoming campaign—"

"Your duty," Daryn interrupted, "is to make certain I don't make private use of public funds or use public knowledge for private gain. The American people care deeply about what officials do with their money—they don't care nearly as much about what political people do in the privacy of their bedrooms."

Paul's shoulders drooped noticeably.

Ignoring him, Daryn gestured to Winston Booker. "Run the reports once again and see if there's another candidate who would suit our purposes and is straight on the issues. If Frey still comes out on top, let's submit his name to the Senate. We need to fill that office."

As Booker nodded and scribbled on his notepad, Daryn turned to O'Leary. "What else do you have for me?"

He consulted a report in his hand. "There's a hot issue on the horizon—might be significant during the campaign, might not."

She leaned back, relaxing. Issues she could handle. "What is it?"

O'Leary glanced at Paul. "This one was yours, Santana. Why don't you present it?"

Straightening, Paul accepted the hand-off. "In June 2001, the North Dakota Supreme Court heard the case of *Maddox v. MKB Management Corporation dba Free Choice Women's Clinic.* The case had come up through the lower courts, with the plaintiff, a pro-life lawyer, alleging that the Free Choice Clinic misled women by giving prospective abortion clients a pamphlet stating that medical research does not support the assertion that having an abortion increases breast cancer risk."

"So what's the issue?" Daryn shrugged. "I've heard the same thing on TV a hundred times."

Paul hesitated. "Well, apparently the clinic's brochure was deceptive. Twenty-six out of thirty-two published medical studies *do* support the claim that induced abortion increases the risk of breast cancer."

Daryn stared at the carpet, a sense of unease slithering into her mood like a silent serpent.

Thrasher, however, waved off the news. "Thanks for the heads-up, Santana, but this won't be an issue in the campaign. We can't afford to be sidetracked by abortion, and neither can the other two parties."

Paul's eyes were abstracted, thinking, but they cleared as he looked up. "It's not exactly an abortion issue, Mr. Thrasher. The suit centered on a claim of false advertising. North Dakota law forbids placing before the public any assertions, representations, or statements of fact which are untrue, deceptive, or misleading."

Thrasher frowned. "So the clinic will pull the brochures. End of story."

"Not exactly. Given that the medical evidence supports the link between abortion and breast cancer, the plaintiff declared that withdrawing the false information was not enough. The clinic, she insisted, should give all prospective clients a report of the medical evidence along with a warning that abortion can cause breast cancer."

"Just like the warning on cigarette packages," O'Leary added. "Those were federally mandated."

"Even though for years the tobacco companies claimed there was no proof smoking caused cancer," Paul added. "Now a similar question lies before us—is the government required to warn women that abortion increases the risk of breast cancer?"

Catching Thrasher's eye, Daryn shook her head. "That will never happen. Public opinion wouldn't allow it. And I will not allow millions of women to be frightened out of their wits over the mere *possibility* of cancer."

"But public opinion can turn—as it turned against cigarette smoking," O'Leary pointed out. "And there are interesting precedents. In 1995, a suit against Planned Parenthood netted an $80,000 award for its plaintiff on the grounds of emotional distress after an abortion. Who knows what could happen if breast cancer patients began to sue the abortion clinics that provided their abortions."

"And if any of those clinics were federally funded . . ." Paul leaned back and let out a low whistle. "Batten down the hatches, 'cause we'd be in for a rough ride."

Groaning, Daryn propped her head on her hand. "What's the status of the case now?"

Paul consulted his report. "Free Choice lost, but they've said they will appeal to the Supreme Court based on the separation of powers principle. Their argument will be that the state legislature, not the courts, should be responsible for imposing warning labels on products or services. They also plan to challenge the provision in the North Dakota false advertising statute which confers standing on any person whatsoever to sue." He looked at Thrasher, who was following the conversation with a glazed expression. "In other words, they're going to say that Ms. Maddox, who had never had an abortion and was therefore not personally misled by the clinic's brochure, had no right to sue in the case."

Mentally envisioning a calendar, Daryn closed her eyes. "Any idea of the time line?"

"If the Supreme Court decides to hear it, the case might come before the Court by next fall." Paul's voice seemed to come from far away. "Not a very good time for you, campaign-wise."

"All depends upon which way the wind is blowing," Daryn muttered, lifting her eyelids. She stared at her advisers, then gave them a wry smile. "I suppose we just have to hope the Supreme Court denies certiorari. If they don't hear the case, it'll be dead in the water."

"What if they don't deny cert?" Ever the pessimist, O'Leary leaned forward. "We have a pro-life chief justice, and the Court's conservative bloc is strong. If they do agree to hear the case, the spotlight of public attention will be focused more tightly than ever on abortion. You won't be able to avoid the issue."

"If I didn't know better," Daryn drawled, wishing she could wave the news away, "I'd say the lawyer for the Free Choice clinic is playing both sides of the field. He's risking a lot by taking this national. Even if he wins, he will still have exposed the issue to the national press."

"The genie will be out of the bottle," Paul admitted, "but this news about a link has been available for years. Most of the media routinely ignores or debunks it, so it hasn't filtered into the national consciousness."

Daryn stared at him, her thoughts running at double speed. "It isn't true, is it?"

Paul spread his hands. "Depends upon who you talk to. The pro-life people cite the medical studies; the pro-choice people ignore them. But then you've got people like Dr. Janet Daling, a leading cancer epidemiologist and *pro-choice* advocate, who says the research is rock-solid and the data is accurate. The risk of breast cancer for women who've had an induced abortion is fifty percent higher than for other women."

Daryn shifted her gaze to O'Leary, derailing that disturbing train of thought. "Can you make it go away?"

Clearly knowing better than to say no, O'Leary pulled his digital recorder from his suit and whispered a reminder to himself.

SIXTEEN

THE HEATER SWITCHED ON, BLOWING A STREAM of warm air across the bed and rousing Paul from a shallow doze. Rising on one elbow, he kissed Daryn's bare shoulder, then climbed out of bed and dressed in the darkness. He glanced at the clock—1 A.M. Though most of the eastern seaboard slept now, the hour was not too late for a hard working West Winger to be still at work.

He *had* been working—for a while. At seven o'clock he and Daryn had heard the good news about Lawrence Frey's confirmation, then they had retired to the residence to celebrate. Frey's confirmation was more than a congressional victory; Daryn saw it as a validation of her political instincts.

Moving quietly, he slipped through the living room, picked up his briefcase, and paused to rub the curious dog's mammoth head. At nine months, the mastiff still had a lot of puppy in him, and Paul liked Tyson nearly as much as Daryn did. He couldn't help feeling a sort of kinship with the animal—they had arrived in Washington at about the same time, and they had both become emotionally attached to the president.

"The difference between us, fella," Paul whispered, turning the beast back toward the bedroom, "is that I've got to go home."

Five minutes later he was nodding to the somber pair of uniformed

Secret Service agents who guarded the elevator. They nodded back, and one of them called, "Good night, Mr. Santana."

Paul kept his head down, not wanting to look up lest he see a knowing gleam in the agent's eye. What did they think, these men and women who watched his comings and goings at odd hours? By now nearly everyone who worked in the White House or the West Wing knew that Paul and the president were old friends. But since Maria had moved to Washington four weeks ago, he'd been careful not to visit the residence more than two nights a week. And he'd been extremely careful never to address Daryn by her given name in public, or to touch her anywhere near the Oval Office.

She was like a drug, though, growing more and more necessary to his daily survival. It wasn't the power, he told himself as he followed the lush red carpeting toward the corridor leading to the West Wing. It was the woman he craved. Like fire and ice, they'd been designed to complement one another. His feeling for Maria paled in comparison to the white-hot passion Daryn could arouse in him by a simple quirk of her brow.

Of course, once he returned home, he had to cross the threshold into a cloud of guilt. Often, especially if he undressed in the dark and looked across to the narrow bed where Maria slept, he felt shriveled, dishonorable, and unworthy.

And absolutely elated.

He stepped out into a star-thick night, hurried past the white columns lining the Rose Garden, and felt the cool sting of an October wind against his face. Passing through the West Colonnade, he moved through the press office, then skirted the offices surrounding the Oval. Even at this hour, lights blazed from beneath closed doors and office machinery hummed. Though he heard no voices, the place pulsed with energy.

Ten minutes later he entered his own office, snapped on the light, and crossed to his desk. After slipping out of his suit coat and loosening his tie, he sank into his chair and rolled it forward. The ever-blinking message light on his phone caught his eye, but he ignored it and dialed his new house.

The phone rang four times, as he knew it would, then the answering machine picked up. Leaning back, he closed his eyes in relief. Maria would have gone to bed and turned off the ringer in their bedroom. He would leave a message and she'd find it in the morning. If she'd been annoyed at his absence at dinner, the message would take the edge off her irritation.

At the beep, he took a deep breath: "Hi, Maria, just called to say I'm working late. Sorry I missed dinner, but I'll see you in the morning. I'll try not to wake you when I come in—"

"Dad?"

He shot forward, the voice startling him out of his rote speech. "Cristina?"

"Yeah, who else would it be? Why are you calling so late?"

Alarm tightened his voice. "I'm working late—but . . . what are you doing home?"

She laughed. "A friend of mine drove me down from school, and we just walked in the door. Mom's outside talking to him now."

"Mom's awake?" Guilt twisted his gut. "I didn't know we were having company."

"I wanted to surprise you—so, surprise!" A pouting note filled her voice. "But you're not here."

"I'll be home in an hour or so. I'm working late."

"You said that already."

"I did? Well, I guess I'm tired."

"I doubt we'll be waiting up, Dad. Mom's getting the guest room ready for Jason and—"

"This is a boy? A *boy* drove you from Harvard?"

"He's a young man, Dad, and I think you'll like him. Besides, we're just friends. He's going to spend the weekend with us, then we'll go back Sunday night."

Uncertain what to say next, Paul clutched the phone. He had planned to work Saturday, making up for time spent with Daryn, but he couldn't miss this opportunity for time with his daughter . . .

His work would have to wait. "I'll see you tomorrow morning, then. *Te amo*, Cristina."

"*Te amo,* Dad."

Paul hung up, then pressed his hands to his face, suddenly overcome by the awful feeling that his daughter had just discovered him in the arms of another woman.

●

Across town, Maria listened to her daughter relay the phone conversation, then smiled and pointed toward the hall leading to the guest room. "Jason, I know you must be tired." She placed her hand in the center of the tall youth's back and guided him forward. "Thank you for bringing Cristina home. We will see you in the morning."

"It's okay, Mom." Cristina winked at her friend, then took Maria's arm. "You go on to bed. I'm going to fix Jason a sandwich, then we might watch a movie."

"You're not tired?"

"We're wound up, Mom, all that caffeine on the drive. But don't worry; we'll be fine."

Maria moved to the staircase and clung to the banister, watching with mixed emotions as her lovely daughter and the young stranger moved toward the kitchen. In her day, a young man and a young woman did not sit up at this hour unchaperoned. If he were here, her papa would plant himself in the family room until both young people were safely tucked into their individual beds . . .

But her papa was not here, and neither was Paul. And this was not Miami—it was not even the same century she'd grown up in. This was a strange place, an alien city, a cold and blustery world she could not adjust to . . .

After slowly climbing the stairs, she turned at the landing and moved to her bedroom, hers and Paul's, though Paul had spent very little time in it. His job kept him busy at all hours, filling his thoughts even when he came home.

The twin beds sat in the center of the room, looking for all the world like two cold, marble slabs despite the new floral comforters she'd bought last week. She had worried at first, afraid Paul would think the flowers too fussy, but he hadn't said a word about the new décor. Her bed dripped with lace pillows, an affectation he had revolted against years ago, and Maria now thought that the beds seemed to symbolize their Washington lives, but in reverse. Hers was the sterile life crowned by a solitary pillow; his the one crowded with laces and ribbons and crocheted flowers. He loved Washington; he seemed to thrive on his hectic schedule and many obligations, while she woke each morning and wondered what on earth she'd find to fill her day.

Moving to the bed, she tossed the pillows to the floor, then lifted the plump comforter and slipped between the bed linens. She dimmed the lamp on the nightstand to a soft glow, then glanced at the clock. One-thirty. Surely Paul was on his way home by now. She could stay awake to greet him.

Then again . . . perhaps she shouldn't. Paul would be tired when he came home; he'd want to go to sleep and might be irritated to discover that she'd waited up. He wouldn't want to talk. He seldom did. He had probably spent the entire day in conversation, and he'd want nothing more than to turn out the light and go to sleep.

She glanced down at her nightgown, then tugged on the ivory bed jacket, a satiny bit of fluff Cristina had bought her for Mother's Day. Maria had received many beautiful pieces of lingerie after her cancer treatments and she enjoyed feeling pretty in bed. Many times she had brushed her hair and sponged a bit of color on her cheeks, hoping Paul would look across the room and notice that she was trying to look nice for him, but these days he scarcely seemed to see her at all.

She felt the chasm between them like an open wound.

Leaning forward, she opened the drawer in the nightstand and removed her rosary beads. Saying the rosary had always brought her a measure of comfort, even during the cancer treatments. The steady cadence of her chanted prayers soothed her, as did the knowledge that God heard every word. So she offered her words in the hope that the heavenly Father would see that she was taking time for him, and desperately needed him to take time for her . . .

Holding the crucifix against her palm, she crossed herself and began to whisper the Our Father. As she recited the familiar words, her gaze shifted to a small ceramic statue Cristina had bought her years before, an adorable figurine of a young girl standing beneath a big umbrella. Though the little girl's eyes were big with apprehension, the artist had inscribed a phrase at the base of the figure: *Cast all your cares upon him; for he cares for you. 1 Peter 5:7.*

Maria halted in midbreath, struck by the phrase. First Peter? That was from the Bible. She bit her lip . . . if the Bible had other things to say about casting cares upon God, perhaps it'd do her good to read them.

Dropping her rosary, she swung her legs out of the bed, then bent by the nightstand. She didn't often read the Bible, but she knew she had a copy; she'd bought one shortly after Cristina was born.

She smiled when she pulled the leather volume from beneath a stack of magazines. *The Holy Bible.* Complete with the section called First Peter.

Curling back into her bed, Maria opened the book, scanned the table of contents, then flipped the pages and began to read.

SEVENTEEN

A BRUTAL WASHINGTON WINTER FADED INTO SPRING, and Daryn found her spirits rising with the brightening days. Considering Professor Gifford's Congress-as-college analogy, she thought many members of that illustrious establishment had been infected with spring fever—senators responded quickly and deferentially to her phone calls, representatives attended her appearances in their home states and posed for hundreds of pictures, her poll numbers began to rise as steadily as the hundreds of tulips breaking through the stubborn mulch to bloom on the South Lawn. Party leaders who had been predicting that she didn't stand a chance in the November election were now trying to find a way to run against her without appearing to strike at the woman who carried the banner for mothers and women across the nation.

On the campaign front, her stealth strategists had been at work for months. Tom Harris, Thrasher's deputy chief of staff and her campaign manager, had assembled a team to outrival anything in modern history: the best New York media consultant, the top numbers man and polltaker, a team of statisticians and demographers, a personal stylist, and a video producer fresh from the Emmy awards. The video man had already set to work filming quality moments: the president relating to schoolchildren of all races, Daryn Austin meeting with union leaders, the first executive playing checkers with senior adults. Harris had even made a visit to Atlanta, recording the first parents as they praised their daughter. One clip was already airing regularly: Daryn's mother telling the camera that she'd been accused of not supporting her daughter's political ambitions early enough. "What was I supposed to do?" She smiled, lifting her shoulders in a graceful shrug. "I didn't know she'd grow up to be *President* Austin."

Early polls taken after Daryn's January State of the Union address had revealed that the public gave Daryn high marks for poise and effectiveness but lower marks for decisiveness. After a series of appearances and a televised speech geared to counter those flaws, her numbers spiked upward. The surveys were integral to the campaign, not only to gauge voter attitudes, but to shape Daryn's slogans, TV commercials, and public appearances.

In the midst of Oval Office planning sessions, she often dropped her gaze to the small alabaster statue the professor had given her. The two faces of Janus—*her* two faces—seemed to grow more opposite with every passing day.

She wasn't the only politician with two faces. As her colleagues in the House and Senate prepared for elections back home, she compared their public statements with the people she'd come to know. More disturbing than the disparity between public and private was the oft-voiced belief that the world beyond Washington was infinitely less exciting, less rewarding, and less hectic—in other words, as boring as a biology lecture. She attended more than one retirement party where departing bureaucrats wore false V-shaped smiles and pretended to believe their colleagues' repeated assurances that there *was* life after Washington—a statement as patently false as compliments given to a woman with a bad dye job.

Though insiders considered nearly all work outside the Beltway insignificant, the beliefs of the uninitiated mattered immensely. Public opinion was the Sasquatch of American political life—rarely sighted or authenticated, but officials up for reelection did their best to feed it, hold its attention, and earn its adoration. Though something in her recoiled from such self-serving hypocrisy, Daryn steeled herself to play the same game.

On the morning of March 12, she sat in the Yellow Oval Room of the residence, enduring the weekly strategy session for members of her campaign team, including Jacob Thrasher and Alexander O'Leary. She had wanted to involve Paul, but some inner voice warned against bringing him in. Since Christmas he had occasionally seemed withdrawn during their times together, and she had to work to draw him out of his shell. Nothing had changed, he assured her—Maria seemed content in Washington, Cristina was doing fine in school and had found a young man to keep her company. And he was happy in his work, thrilled to be part of an administration that would make a real difference in Americans' lives.

"And me?" she had asked the last time they were together. "How do you feel about me?"

He had looked at her with something that looked like pain in his brown eyes. "God knows I love you more than ever."

She'd closed her eyes and silently clung to him, unable to find words to express her gratitude. The assurance of Paul's love buoyed her through a hundred daily frustrations and gave her the patience she needed to work within a stubborn and outdated system. But she didn't want to pressure him, so she took pains to keep him away from situations he'd find stressful. He meant too much to her; their relationship was too valuable to risk.

"The problem," Tom Harris was saying now, drawing her attention with a direct glance, "was that in the beginning you operated on a week-to-week basis. Being called up in midstream, as it were, you reacted instead of acting. The events of the week created the message of the week, which spawned the poll of the week, which birthed the speech and photo op of the week. Your people were not thinking long-term, and you must plan ahead if you want to win this election."

"That's why you're here," Daryn remarked, her voice dry. "So tell us—how *is* our long-term plan coming along?" She leaned forward, resting her elbow on her crossed knee in a most unpresidential posture. "I want ten years, Tom, and I'm trusting you to get them for me."

"We stick to the tried-and-true dictum," Harris said, his gaze moving around the circle. "We run hard to starboard in the primaries, shooting at all the front runners. When the dust has settled, we tack back to the center for the remaining months of the campaign. We avoid values talk because people see the word *values* as a code for abortion. Instead, we look at concerns that are common to most American families: trash on television, violence from Hollywood, drug abuse, kids who can't spell, racial unrest. Bash the trash, crush the Klan, and people will cheer. You can always make it up to the Hollywood set later."

"In other words," Daryn said, settling back in her chair, "we campaign in poetry and govern in prose." She glanced at Thrasher. "Who said that first? Mario Cuomo?"

Thrasher opened his mouth, but O'Leary cut him off. "I'm thinking we'll be needing to concentrate on defining our constituency. We know this president attracts a different group than Parker did. We're going to have to broaden her appeal if we want to keep the Parker independents and win."

Harris grinned, his eyes glinting from behind his glasses. "We've got that covered." He pulled a folder from his battered briefcase, then slid a sheet of paper from it. "We've been running telephone surveys for six weeks, and we know who our supporters are. If you look at the two voting groups by class and age, Parker and Austin come out about even. The difference is marital status—people with families preferred Parker to Austin by ten to fifteen points. The most prominent variable, the transformative event affecting people's view of politics, is the experience of having children."

"What?" Daryn glared at the pollster. "Parker didn't have any kids."

Harris shrugged. "Doesn't matter. People perceived him as having greater concern for parents. People see you as a swinging bachelorette."

"That's ridiculous."

"Oh, yeah? Well, it didn't help when you were photographed with Mel Gibson and plastered on the cover of *People.*" He pushed at the bridge of his glasses, then gripped the paper again. "Might help if you got married."

Daryn snorted. "Don't hold your breath."

"Well, it doesn't matter. There are other differences we can exploit. Austin supporters watch MTV; Parker supporters preferred Larry King. Austin people like rap, classical, and Top 40, watch sitcoms, and feel unsafe in their homes; Parker people own guns, watch *Nightline*, and listen to seventies stations. Austin people are intuitive types and tend to go with their emotions; Parker people are thinkers, not feelers. The kicker is this—most swing voters are thinkers, and that's why Parker pulled so many of them in the last election."

Lowering his sheet of statistics, he looked at Daryn. "If you're going to win this election, Madam President, you're going to have to pull all the swing voters from the left, the right, and the middle. You'll never get the die-hard Democrats or Republicans, but if you adjust your image a bit, you just might be able to pull it off."

"Short of getting married," Daryn drawled, "how do I manage this image adjustment?"

"Start talking about family values," Harris said. "Don't surrender those buzz words to the religious right. Find a niece or nephew, someone you can take out for public appearances."

"I don't have nieces or nephews," Daryn interrupted.

"Then borrow someone else's."

"You've got parents." Crossing his leg at the knee, Thrasher leaned into the conversation. "What about involving your parents more?"

Daryn lifted a warning finger. "Be careful with that idea. I owe them too much to risk their health in this campaign. Put out the word that my parents are too busy to travel—they'll love that—and let them do a few spots if they're up to it. But only if they're willing and able."

"Can we move on?" Harris flashed his brows, obviously annoyed by the interruption. "Forget trotting out the geezers—excuse me, the first parents—and hit family values in other ways. Talk more often about the dangers of smoking and drugs; start supporting flextime and family leave programs. Visit a maternity ward, cuddle a few babies. Go to church. Eat lunch at one of those pizza places where they hold kids' birthday parties and play games. Oh—and go to Atlanta, visit your folks, and take one of the Frey's granddaughters with you. People love the idea of a political dynasty. Daughter follows in famous father's footsteps, paves the way for future generations. That's the kind of family thing they'll eat up."

Thrasher interrupted with an uplifted hand. "I still think the president needs to focus on more serious themes. Her gender isn't an issue to most people, but if you start broadcasting video of her doing all these mommy things, people aren't going to take her seriously."

Harris cast a glance of well-mannered dislike in Thrasher's direction, then turned to Daryn. "Trust me. They will like you. Just look at the numbers we ran last week."

Daryn looked to her chief of staff. "What numbers?"

"The walk in the Rose Garden video," Thrasher answered, his voice scraping like sandpaper. "We shot it twice, remember? Once with the dog, and once without."

Harris pulled himself erect, his face shining. "The dog clip scored twenty points higher than the other." Tilting his head, he gave Daryn an apologetic smile. "I'm sorry, Madam President, but it's the truth. Issues are important, but image counts for more in an election. People buy into an image."

"The key, gentlemen," Daryn said, "is managing both sides of the equation." Sighing, she glanced over at Lorraine Nelson, director of the scheduling office. "It's going to be a busy summer."

As Lorraine began to outline the already-crowded presidential schedule, Daryn leaned back in her chair and pressed her hand to her eyes, effectively cutting herself out of the conversation. At this point they didn't need her. They would plan her life and her campaign, and, if all went well, they'd keep her in the Oval Office for another four years. They might exhaust her in the interim, but at least she'd be running the country from her hospital bed . . .

She exhaled slowly, her thoughts inexorably turning toward Paul. She needed him. At this moment she'd give almost anything to lean on his strength. When they were together, she could storm and weep and throw things if she felt like it, knowing he wouldn't think less of her. And when she had spent all her frustration and anger, he would pull her into his arms and help her feel like a woman instead of a president, pulling her away from her rigid edge to the soft side she had been forced to hide these last few years . . .

Harris's suggestion that she get married had struck a chord, though she could never admit it. Many times as she lay in Paul's arms she'd thought about how wonderful it would be if he could stay there, belong to her publicly . . . but that kind of freedom would come at a high price. Paul would have to sacrifice his family, and she'd have to surrender part of her independence.

The cost was simply too high.

Leaning back, she looked past Thrasher toward the phone. If these bozos would hurry up and leave, she could call just to hear Paul's voice. She would see him tonight at a state dinner for the prime minister of Canada, but there'd be no time for private conversation in a dining room set for two hundred people.

Straightening, she gazed wistfully out the door. Her living room was only a few steps away, with a secure phone by the sofa. If Harris would only stop talking about issues versus image, she could be on that telephone . . .

No one would know. She and Paul had been careful and discreet; no one could fault her for offending anyone's morals. They never exchanged e-mails, never talked on cell phones, and never met in the Oval Office except on official business . . .

She couldn't take another minute of this tedium.

Glancing at her watch, she cut into Harris's speech. "I'm sorry, gentlemen, but I do have another meeting this morning. If there's nothing else, can I leave things with you as they are?" She sent a smile winging across the room. "Thank you for your help."

When the last man had exited the residence, she crossed to her living room, closed the door, and dialed the number she'd memorized. "Paul?" she asked when he picked up the line. "About the dinner tonight—I know I told you to meet me in the residence at seven, but could you possibly come at six?" A smile slipped into her voice. "Five-thirty would be even better, if it's convenient for you."

A blush of pleasure rose to her cheeks when he said he would make it by five.

●

On Saturday morning, Paul rose from his desk and lifted his arms, relishing the stretch in his muscles. The dinner for the Canadians had lasted until eleven last night, then he'd spent another two hours with Daryn before driving home.

Home . . .

Despite the familiar furnishings, the big house didn't quite feel like home. Rented at a bargain price from a pro-Austin landlord who'd been willing to renew the lease on a yearly basis, the house appealed to Maria, who had promised to turn the sprawling Georgian into a showplace within a year. She filled her days with appointments and home tours, and Paul was grateful for the distraction. Sofas and *objets d'art* kept her mind off missing her father and daughter.

He moved to the French doors and flung them open, then stepped out onto the small balcony overlooking the rock garden. This upper room was his favorite, and he'd been pleased to no end when Maria said he could have it for a study. Like most Virginia homes, the builders of the old house had cut a cellar out of rock and clay, but because the house sprawled over a hilltop, Paul's wrought-iron balcony rose three full stories above the stony ground. Up here, at eye level with the upper reaches of the fir trees fringing the property, he could almost feel that he had escaped to a private place far away from the adrenaline of the pushy city.

A strong wind breathed through the evergreens, shivering his skin like the touch of a ghost. Running his hands over his arms, he took one last look at the sunlit stones below, then retreated into his study.

Last night he'd been pleased to discover a note from Maria telling him that Cristina had come home. This morning he had slept until nine, then quietly rose to look over some briefing papers he'd picked up before leaving the West Wing.

Now he looked forward to spending some time with his daughter. The scent of baking pastry had wafted up the stairs, and he could hear movement in the kitchen.

Padding downstairs in his robe and slippers, he crept over the terracotta tiles in the kitchen. Cristina stood at the sink, her hands in soapy dishwater, her head holding the cordless phone snug against her shoulder.

He tiptoed up behind her and poked her in the ribs with both index fingers. "Guess who?"

"Dad!" She might have turned to give him a hug, but her hands were wet and her attention diverted by the telephone. "You could scare me to death doing that!"

"I don't think so." Stepping around her, he went to the refrigerator and pulled a quart of orange juice from the top shelf. He glanced around the kitchen. "Your mom come down yet?"

Moving to the island in the center of the kitchen, Cristina murmured a good-bye, then clicked off the call. "Not yet," she said, dropping the phone to the counter.

"Not every day we get cookies for breakfast."

"They're oatmeal," she said, as if that ingredient qualified her offering as legitimate health food. She picked up a spatula and began to scrape cookies off the aluminum sheet.

Paul picked up one of Cristina's creations, then dropped it. *"Carumba!* It's hot."

"That's because it just came out of the oven." She grinned at him, then her smile faded. "Actually, Dad, I'm glad you're here. I wanted to ask you about something."

He broke off a small corner of the cookie, then popped it into his mouth. "Pretty good. Even for a philosophy major."

"Don't change the subject."

"I'm not." He assumed a look of feigned hurt. "What did you want to ask me about?"

"This." She pulled the front section of the *Washington Times* from the end of the island, then slid it toward him. He glanced at the picture above the centerfold—the photo was of Daryn in a striking white evening dress, on the Canadian ambassador's arm.

He kept smiling, though a cold knot had formed in his stomach. "What?"

"Don't you see yourself?"

Paul glanced more closely at the picture. Peter Chang had snapped the photo as the president's party came down the Grand Staircase, just before they entered the State Dining Room. Daryn and the prime minister, Edwin Blanchette, had led the way, of course, followed by Mrs. Blanchette and Paul.

He thumped the dark image on the page. "That's me? Behind the president?"

"Dad, you've got another woman on your arm."

He quelled the sudden urge to laugh by rubbing a finger hard over his lip. Mrs. Blanchette was sixty if she was a day, and even more matronly than Barbara Bush.

"Honey—" he lifted his head—"I don't even know Mrs. Blanchette. At least, I didn't know her when I was walking her down the stairs." He laughed. "I spent two hours trying to talk to her at dinner and I *still* don't know her."

Deftly wielding the spatula, Cristina sent him a reproving look. "How do you think Mom would feel if she saw that?"

"Saw what?"

Paul started at the sound of Maria's voice.

"Nothing, Mom." Cristina, he noticed, had the decency to blush. "We were just talking."

"About what?" Though her eyelids were still heavy with sleep, Maria was alert enough to sense a secret. She walked up to the island, dropped her hand onto Paul's shoulder, and peered at the newspaper. "Are you talking about this?" Her index finger tapped the front page.

"Yeah." Cristina unseated two cookies in one swipe, then dropped them onto the platter. "I was worried, that's all. You're home waiting for me while Dad's eating a White House dinner with some other woman. I just didn't want your feelings to be hurt."

"Honey—" a trace of laughter lined Maria's voice—"your father and

I have been married twenty-one years. If we couldn't trust each other, do you think we'd have stayed together this long?"

Paul felt his stomach tighten as Maria's dark eyes shifted to meet his. "Your father is just doing his job. He's a loyal employee, so if the president asks him to escort another woman, he is honored to do it. It doesn't mean anything."

"I just think it looks bad," Cristina grumbled, sliding the now-empty cookie sheet into the sink. "I mean, if Jason were out with some other girl and the paper printed *their* picture, I couldn't hold my head up."

"Jason?" Spying a way out, Paul lurched for it. "I thought you and Jason were just friends."

Maria pinched the trapezius muscle in his shoulder. "Hush, he's still asleep in the guest room."

"So are they friends or not?" Paul looked from his wife to his daughter. "As the man of the house, I think I have a right to know what's going on."

A thunderous scowl darkened his daughter's brow. "Mama, make him be quiet. I wasn't talking about Jason; I was talking about—"

"Daughter." Crossing the kitchen, Maria slipped an arm around Cristina's slender waist. "You don't have to worry about your papa. He's a good man. And things are different for professional people. When you're older, you'll understand."

Cristina shook her head. "I don't think so."

"Tell her, Pablo," Maria said, holding their daughter's beautiful face in her hands. "Tell her those things are only business meetings."

A surge of guilt caught him unaware, like a searing bolt of lightning through his chest and belly. He felt half-choked with it, but pushed the words out over the spreading numbness in his lungs and throat. "They are—" he whispered, lowering his hands beneath the counter so his wife and daughter would not see how they trembled—"only business. Now, if you two will excuse me, I have reports to read."

Before they could protest, he slipped from his chair and staggered out of the kitchen.

EIGHTEEN

SHOVING HIS HANDS INTO HIS POCKETS, CLIVE climbed from his pickup and trudged through the crusted snow toward his cabin. Moving through the air up here felt like pushing through gauzy curtains perfumed with an essence of pine, endless layers of pungent scent. Reaching the porch, he stomped on the planks, breaking loose the crusty clods of snow. Behind him, the sun was sinking beyond the mountains. Shadows on the porch pooled and thickened beside the water casks and stacked logs.

He turned, staring at a mountain landscape drained of all color. Nothing but snow and rocks and evergreens, all of them fading to black as the sun lowered behind the ridge. At this hour of the day the air seemed lifeless, the light melancholy and gray. "Nobody out there," he whispered, and the air was so cold his breath hung before his face like a frozen cartoon caption.

Satisfied that nothing but God's creatures moved in the gathering darkness, he stepped inside and latched the door. After building a new fire in the wood stove, he took the squirrel carcass from the icebox and quartered it with his hunting knife, then used the tip of the blade to flick away a few pieces of buckshot. After pulling a few greens and potatoes from the vegetable bin, he tossed them into a stew pot with the squirrel, then added water and set the pot on the stove.

An hour later, after his dinner, he moved to the desk by the window and lit the kerosene lamp. Gripping a pencil through a layer of protection offered by his lined leather gloves, Clive smoothed out a sheet of notebook paper and began another letter.

To the Whore of Babylon—

He scratched at his goatee, thinking back on the spy movie he'd seen at the Twin Cinema in Jackson Hole that weekend. Those good ol' boys at the FBI and CIA and Secret Service had all kinds of tricks up their sleeves, and he was doing his best to stay one step ahead of them. He'd worn the gloves every time he even touched a page, and he'd remembered to seal the envelopes with a swipe of a washcloth, not with his tongue. Every fool knew about DNA these days, and Clive's mother didn't raise no fool—at least not before she got herself killed driving drunk.

> *Your time is coming to a close. You think you are so high and mighty, but you will fall. Do not get comfortable in that house of sinners. Do not count on tomorrow. For what is your life? It is even a vapor that appears for a little time, then vanishes away.*

He hesitated, searching for words. Outside, the wind blew hard, pushing at a branch that knocked at the window of his room like an insistent gate-crasher.

That's what Daryn Austin was—a gate-crasher. Nobody invited her to the party; nobody had ever voted in a woman president. But there she was in the White House, acting like the queen of the world, pictured in the papers and magazines with all kinds of men hanging on her arm.

But she wouldn't stay in the White House. Sooner or later the right man would come along and knock her off her high horse.

He drew a serrated, eight-inch hunting knife from his drawer, deftly sharpened the tip of his pencil, and began to write again:

And he saith unto me, The waters which thou sawest, where the whore sitteth, are peoples, and multitudes, and nations, and tongues. And the ten horns which thou sawest upon the beast, these shall hate the whore, and shall make her desolate and naked, and shall eat her flesh, and burn her with fire. (Rev. 17:15–16)

For true and righteous are his judgments: for he hath judged the great whore, which did corrupt the earth with her fornication, and hath avenged the blood of his servants at her hand. (Rev. 19:2)

Beware of the day of the Lord. Beware of me, for I am Jehu, "God sees."

I see all and I know your time will soon come to an end.

●

On Sunday afternoon, while Daryn breathlessly pedaled her exercise bike in the same room that had housed the Reagans' gymnasium, a knock came at the door. Without having to look, she knew Thrasher stood outside the door. Only he and Paul had access to the residence without her prior approval, and Paul always spent Sunday with his family.

"Enter," she called.

Thrasher did not seem surprised to find her sweaty and in gym shorts. He himself wore polished leather shoes, khaki pants, and a designer shirt with a knitted collar—the professional beta male's idea of casual attire.

"I've just received a call from my cousin the law clerk." His eyes glowed as he sank onto the exercise bench and grinned at her. "He went golfing this morning."

Daryn pushed a hank of damp hair from her forehead. "I'm assuming there's a point to this."

"He went golfing with Justice Marshall Haynes."

Daryn cracked a smile. "That eighty-something-year-old man can still manage eighteen holes?"

Thrasher grinned. "Barely. But that's not the news—apparently the justice hinted that he wants to retire, but he doesn't want to leave before the election. He's afraid the vacancy will become an issue in the campaign."

Staring at her chief of staff, Daryn stopped peddling. "Of course it'd become an issue, but that's not the most important consideration. If the old man wants to go, he should vacate just before the Court's summer recess, not after the beginning of the new term. He may be waiting to spite us, but throwing the Court into disarray in the middle of a term is hardly a noble gesture."

Leaning forward, Thrasher clasped his hands. "Sure, but what can we do? The justices do their own thing. And they typically don't retire unless they're sick, exhausted, or in danger of impeachment."

Daryn shook her head. "That's not likely. No justice has ever been impeached."

She picked up a towel from the floor and wiped her brow. "Maybe . . ." She looked at her chief of staff. "Do you know of someone Justice Haynes trusts? Could we call in a favor, get someone to tell him that for the good of the country he should retire sooner rather than later?"

"You mean—"

"We should convince him to retire at the end of the term, a time line that will neither interrupt the Court nor allow the vacant seat to become an election issue. If he waits until fall, sure, the candidates will buzz about prospective nominees for the Court, but it will be just Cinderella talk. But if he retires in May or June I'll submit a nominee, perhaps even someone he approves of, and the matter will be settled before the fall debates."

Thrasher looked doubtful. "I hate to say this, but I got the impression you're one of the reasons he doesn't want to retire now. He doesn't trust you."

"Believe me, the feeling is mutual. But better the devil you know than the devil you don't." She stared off into space as thoughts whirled in her head. "What do you think he'd do if I paid him a visit?"

Thrasher squinted. "On the record, or off?"

Shrugging, she draped the towel around her neck. "Off would be best, I think. Maybe a private lunch . . . a cozy meeting between two lawyers."

Thrasher's mouth curved in a one-sided smile. "One of whom happens to be the president."

"And the other the head of the quiet and powerful third branch of government." She lifted her chin. "See if you can set something up. I know presidents don't usually meddle with the Court, so perhaps we should schedule the meeting on some unrelated pretext. Use your imagination and see what you can do. But let's do it quickly."

Thrasher's face was serious, but one corner of his mouth curled irrepressibly at the prospect of a diplomatic challenge. "I'll get right on it, Madam President."

●

On the third Monday in March, Daryn called O'Leary into the Oval Office. After a brief round of perfunctory chitchat, she folded her hands on her desk and looked her chief counsel in the eye. "I wanted you to know, Counselor, that I'm having lunch with Chief Justice Haynes this afternoon. I believe he's planning to announce his retirement, effective sometime in May or June."

Surprise siphoned the blood from O'Leary's ruddy face.

Accepting his speechlessness without comment, Daryn pressed on. "As president, of course, I have the right to nominate a successor for the Supreme Court and I intend to do so quickly, before either the Democrats or the Republicans have an opportunity to make an issue out of the Court vacancy."

However stunned he might have been, O'Leary made a quick recovery. "We've anticipated this, of course, since the last vacancy was in '91.

We've prepared a list of possible candidates, but we'll undoubtedly run into the same partisan difficulties we encountered in the Frey nomination. The same people who didn't want an independent for vice president won't want an independent for chief justice."

"I want to nominate Paul Santana."

O'Leary's eyes widened to the point that they appeared to be in danger of dropping out of their sockets.

"I've done the research," she continued, "and for a Supreme Court justice there is absolutely no requirement apart from the recommendation of the president."

"That's—that's untrue," O'Leary sputtered. "While there may be no written requirements, there are precedents, de facto norms of advancement you ignore at your own peril."

"What?" Daryn countered. "The justices have historically been lawyers, as is Paul Santana. Since 1943, every justice has formally graduated from an accredited law school, as has Paul Santana. Nearly all Supreme Court justices have had limited participation in politics, as has Paul Santana. Others have been governors, members of Congress, or high-level executives, as has Paul Santana."

"But he's working for you." O'Leary's face flushed. "And he has no judicial experience whatsoever."

"Judicial experience is not a prerequisite," Daryn answered. "And why not nominate a man I trust implicitly? You yourself have noted the difficulty of finding candidates who are not affiliated with either of the leading political parties. So why not appoint a man from my own staff?"

O'Leary shook his head slowly back and forth, like a bull stunned by the slaughterer's club. "He's a nobody in the political world. He's only been in Washington a few months—"

"He captured the public eye when he argued the Elian Gonzalez case, and today his public image is both sympathetic and admirable. He did a brave thing, defending a child against Communism, and he fought well. The country will accept him, I tell you. They will be eager to allow him to serve in a prominent position."

"Nobody remembers him."

"So we'll remind them. We'll get the press office to release video of Paul during the Elian situation. That, coupled with that terrible picture of the kid being taken away at gunpoint, should serve us well."

"So it's tit for tat? He gets beaten up by the previous administration's attorney general, so you make him part of the national arbitration committee?"

"And why not?" She leaned forward. "Think about it, Alexander. We are facing a divided Congress, and we are the minority. We would find it nearly impossible to get any candidate through on politics alone, but what patriotic senator could refuse to approve the man who fought for Elian? Paul Santana is our best choice for the Court on another level, too. Just over a hundred people have served on the Supreme Court in over two hundred years. All but two have been white, all but two have been men, and all but seven have been Christian. Paul Santana is Hispanic, an open agnostic, and he has movie-star appeal. He is exactly what we need."

Fire flashed in the lawyer's eyes. "I'll be wanting to speak honestly now."

"Please do."

"Paul Santana is an idiot's choice, Madam President. You cannot put a novice in the chief justice's chair."

She laughed. "Give me some credit, Alexander. I'm not going to make him chief. I'm going to move Justice Franklin to that position, and nominate Santana as a new associate justice." Smiling, she leaned back in her chair. "And not a single senator on the Judiciary Committee will be able to argue my choice. Paul Santana's public record is as clean as a New England kitchen. And his lack of judicial experience will be a plus. He has no recorded opinions on abortion, civil rights, gun control, or any of the other hot issues. In that regard he's a cipher and exactly what we need."

O'Leary stared at her, thought working in his eyes. After a moment, he looked at her with a calculating expression. "You are close to him." He leaned on the armrest of his chair, then glanced down at his hands.

"It suddenly strikes me that I'm lucky to have a job. If Santana wanted my position, you'd be replacing me in a heartbeat, wouldn't you now?"

"Don't be foolish," she snapped. "Paul has no ambition, and your job is the last thing on earth he wants. But I need two crack lawyers, and I need you on the campaign. Yet more than anything, in the coming year I'm going to need friends on the Supreme Court. Justice Franklin will be grateful for his promotion, and Santana . . . well, I trust him implicitly."

"I'm glad you do." His tone had cooled considerably.

"And I'm glad we understand each other." She nodded with a taut jerk of her head. "As you return to your office, will you tell Mr. Santana that I'd like to see him as soon as possible? And say nothing about my plans—I'd like to break the news myself."

She smothered a satisfied smile as O'Leary rose stiffly from his chair and left the Oval.

●

"She wants to see you."

The message, delivered without even the barest veneer of civility, sent a ripple of anxiety spurting through Paul's bloodstream. O'Leary stood in his doorway, a pensive shimmer in the shadow of his blue eyes.

Paul had been about to make a call; now he lowered the phone. From the look on O'Leary's face, he knew better than to ask who *she* was.

"Any idea what she wants?"

The chief counsel's face was smooth with secrets. "I'm operating under a gag order. But she wants to see you ASAP."

Paul nodded his thanks, then exhaled slowly as the lawyer left the office. O'Leary wasn't easily rattled, but something had upset him. Moreover, O'Leary probably knew, or at least suspected, the depth of the relationship between his deputy and the president.

Shoving the thought aside, Paul stood and lifted his coat from the back of his chair. Daryn probably wanted to see him about his report on the fetal rights issue. He'd written a full summation of the Fetal Rights

Bill pending in Congress, and he'd closed the report with his recommendation that she avoid the issue if at all possible. The legislation had garnered bipartisan support because the language avoided discussing the legal right to abortion. As long as Daryn avoided the matter, the issue couldn't hurt her campaign.

He shrugged into his coat, then picked up the folder with his report and made his way to the stairs. A few moments later he walked past the Secret Service guard at the door to the Oval. "I think I'm expected," he said, rapping with an ease he hadn't felt eight months before.

The guard nodded. "Yes sir, you are."

A moment later Paul stepped into the Oval, the golden carpet fibers spongy beneath his feet. He glanced around for Daryn. She wasn't in the actual office, so he peered down the private hallway. The bathroom door stood open, as did the door to the study . . .

"There you are." She stepped out from behind a corner of the small private dining room, then gestured to the table, which glistened with china and silver. "I've ordered lunch for three. I hope you're hungry."

Stepping into the private hallway, out of peephole range, he paused to breathe a kiss on her forehead, then pulled away and frowned at the third place setting. "Who's the third?"

"Chief Justice Marshall Haynes." She tilted her head slightly, examining his face with considerable absorption. "I hope you don't mind."

He shrugged to hide his confusion. "Of course not, it'd be an honor." He lifted the folder in his hand. "I thought you wanted to talk about the Fetal Rights Bill."

She laughed softly. "Why? I agree with you completely. We'll sidestep the issue unless we're forced to confront it. If someone holds my feet to the fire, I'll simply say that I trust the wisdom of my esteemed colleagues in the Congress."

Again, her eyes searched his face, then her voice softened. "You look tired. Are you sleeping?"

"Sure—when I get home." He chuckled. "I really have been working late these last few days."

She moved past him, exuding a soft cloud of fragrance that threatened to distract him from the business of politics.

"Come into the study, Counselor. I need to discuss something with you."

She stood beside the door to the private office; he passed her and took the guest chair as any White House staffer would. Then the door closed, and something in Paul's gut tightened at the click of the latch. The closed door removed them from view of the peepholes, the security monitors, and the listening devices. Behind the closed door, they were sheltered in complete privacy.

She moved to stand before him, then perched on the edge of her desk. Like some sort of protective guardian angel, she reached for the armrests of his chair and leaned over him.

"Do you trust me?" Her blue eyes were like searchlights above his face.

He lifted his chin to better meet her gaze. "Shouldn't I?"

"Of course you should." Smiling, she bent closer, until her lips were a scant two inches from his. "Do you know how much I love you?"

Unbidden, his hand rose to the bare skin of her neck. "I think I do," he whispered, his voice husky.

"Will you do something for me if I ask you to?" Before he could answer, she laughed softly. "I promise it's not illegal, unethical, or fattening. And it won't get you fired."

"If you're going through all this just to get me to accept your lunch invitation, it's overkill." He pulled her toward him for a quick kiss. "I'm hungry, Madam President."

"I wasn't thinking of lunch . . . exactly." Her breath fanned his face, then her lips feather-touched his with tantalizing persuasion. As she pulled away he tipped his head back to look at her. "Whatever you need, I'd do it even without the closed door," he said, firming his voice. "You don't have to bribe my cooperation."

Laughing, she straightened and stood, then walked toward the chair behind the presidential desk. "I'm glad to hear that, Counselor. Because a few days ago I had a brilliant idea, and today I plan to implement it. But I wanted to give you a heads-up."

Moving with the inherent grace that was part of her character, she lowered herself into the chair and smiled at him. He couldn't help but notice the body language—this favor she wanted apparently demanded that she assume a position of authority before asking.

She laced her hands together. "The chief justice is eighty-two years old, and we need him to retire before the term ends in June. I want to talk to him about retirement at lunch today. And when he agrees—"

"*If* he agrees," Paul interrupted, shifting lazily in his chair. "The executive branch has no power over the judicial."

A hint of scorn filtered into her voice as she continued: "*When* he agrees, I plan to move Justice Franklin to chief. That will leave a vacancy on the Court, which I'll be able to fill." She hesitated, distractedly clicking her nails. "With trouble brewing with the upcoming family values cases, why shouldn't I appoint someone who will reflect my viewpoint?"

Paul managed a laugh. "Presidents have been trying to replicate themselves in the Court since John Adams. Roosevelt went so far as to try to appoint a new justice every time one of the others reached the age of seventy and refused to step down. FDR's proposal failed, but if Chief Justice Haynes is willing to go—"

"I'm not sure he's willing. But it's time."

Considering the implications of her statement, Paul narrowed his gaze. "Well . . . if he goes, I should think you'd have no problem finding a pro-choice candidate who is also strong on women's issues. That should obviate the need for concern about these so-called family values."

"But my nominee will still have to get through the Senate Judiciary hearings. And not all judiciary members are pro-choice."

Relaxing, Paul brought his hand to his chin. "As long as you nominate someone who meets the basic criteria, I should think we'd have no problem. Congress knows abortion is a lightning rod issue—I think most of them will shy away from making it a litmus test."

She gave him a thoughtful smile. "What criteria, Counselor, would you suggest I use for evaluation?"

Paul began to tick off ideas on his fingertips. "You need a candidate of known and recognized integrity, someone with wide experience in government. Someone who's competent in the law, of course, and possibly with a national reputation. You can't place an unknown on the Court without offending the nation's leading jurists, and you can't risk nominating a well-known politician without offending his colleagues in Congress who will always feel they should have gotten the nod." He dropped his hand. "Fortunately, the Constitution gives you wide latitude in the matter."

Her smile deepened. "I agree completely, as always. And, after giving the matter a great deal of thought, I've come up with a candidate who fulfills all of your criteria."

"So soon?"

"He's perfect."

He stared at her in dazed exasperation. "Who?"

A smile lifted the corner of her mouth. "You."

Paul stared at her, completely baffled, then laughed.

"Oh, Daryn," he said, suddenly grateful for the closed door. He pressed his hand to his breastbone. "You should feel my heart. It's about to beat out of my chest."

Daryn laughed, too, as her eyes sparkled. "Can't you see yourself as one of those long-faced, black-robed guardians of the American way?"

"Heavens, no. A *Cubano* on the Supreme Court?" He chuckled in sheer relief. After seeing O'Leary he'd been worried about this meeting, but all she wanted to do was joke around. Probably wanted to relax before her meeting with the chief justice.

"Couldn't you just see it?" He wiped wetness from his eyes. "The Supreme Court refuses to hear an attorney's case about a little Cuban boy, so a few years later the lawyer packs up his books and storms those hallowed halls like a beachhead."

Daryn tilted her head. "Maybe those hallowed halls could do with a little storming."

Something in her tone rang an alarm bell, and when he focused on her face again, her eyes had gone dark and somber. He gaped at her. "You can't be serious."

"I am."

"But why me?"

"You're perfect for the job," she said, pressing her hands to the desktop as she leaned toward him. "You're loyal, you know my positions, and you can convey my goals to those stubborn conservatives on the Court. You're such a visionary you'll draw them to you, and then you'll charm them by your logic and intellect. Besides," her smile softened, "I love you, and what better gift could I give the man I love than a seat on the highest court in the land? You've always wanted your work to matter, Paul. Now it will matter for the ages."

Shock whipped his breath away. "Daryn, you can't do this. I'm not qualified—"

"I think I can. The Constitution seems to give me the authority."

"No—I mean, nominate anyone you please, but not me! I don't have any judicial experience. The press will eat you alive for this, and you'll invite all sorts of speculation about us."

"The press will report that I have made a wise decision. I will have moved a seasoned jurist into the position of chief; plus I will have given a voice to the thirty-five million Hispanics in this country. You have a fine legal mind, Paul, and an admirable public image. Every American who sees himself as an underdog will adopt you as his champion."

Cold, clear reality swept over him in a terrible wave. She honestly meant to do it.

"Daryn, this is madness. You'll destroy what we've worked so hard to regain. If I'm on the Court . . . I won't be *here.*"

Her brow wrinkled, and something moved in her eyes. "I know the situation between us will be altered somewhat, but I trust you. Only you. And I trust our love. If it could last twenty years while we were apart, surely it can last while we are separated by a few miles."

"I'll never see you again." He meant to utter the phrase in a matter-of-fact voice, but in the silence it sounded more like a threat.

"Yes, you will. The cloak surrounding our private lives will not be lifted."

The phone buzzed. Paul stared numbly as she picked it up, murmured into the receiver, then rose from her chair in one fluid movement. "The chief justice has arrived." She moved toward the hallway, and when he stood, she reached out to smooth a piece of lint from his shoulder.

"You look every inch a justice," she said, opening the door. "Never fear, Counselor. I know what I'm doing."

But as she walked out to greet her guest, Paul lingered in the doorway, bracing himself against the wall as his thoughts whirled. Supreme Court justices were appointed for life—and he had promised Maria they'd return to Miami once Daryn left the White House.

Unless he could change her mind, this president would pin him in a trap from which there'd be no escape.

NINETEEN

AT LUNCH IN THE PRIVATE DINING ROOM OFF THE Oval, Paul felt as though he were two separate people as he watched Daryn work. One of his selves sat stupidly in the chair, numb with her announcement and speechless with anxiety, while another self watched with frank amazement as she charmed the elderly chief justice into a state of trusting cooperation.

Paul's numbed tongue could not taste the delicious roasted chicken; it could do no more than murmur pleasantries and thank-yous when appropriate. His mind kept conjuring visions of Maria's face when he broke the news; his ears rang with her wail of distress . . . a cry that would be echoed, no doubt, by his daughter when she learned that her parents were getting a divorce. Because Maria would leave him. In the last several months she had endured his diffidence, his absence, and his near-constant distraction. She would not tolerate a permanent separation from her father in Miami.

His eyes watched Daryn smile and flatter and bend toward the old man with all the grace and poise the public expected of the first female president, then, just after the dessert had been served, her eyes went sharp and steely. As soon as the waiter closed the door, Daryn informed the chief justice that he needed to retire. "Late May or June would be best," she said, setting her chin in a stubborn line. "That will give us time to fill the spot and avoid confusion during the beginning of a new judicial term."

The venerable old man smiled at her, the parentheses around his mouth deepening into a look of firm resolve. "I'm afraid I'm not willing to leave so soon," he told her, tapping his fork upon the edge of an expensive piece of White House china. "My health is good; my family still supportive. Perhaps next year."

"Mr. Chief Justice, sir, I'm not sure you have thought the matter through." Daryn lifted her wineglass. "I think your reluctance to retire has more to do with the fact that you cannot imagine what you'll do with yourself once you no longer enjoy a position of authority. Perhaps you have grown to believe yourself indispensable, or perhaps your wife is afraid retirement will mean a loss of social standing."

Anger blossomed in the justice's lined face. "I beg your pardon."

Daryn didn't miss a beat. "If any of the things I've mentioned are even partially true, Mr. Chief Justice, I beg you to reconsider the idea of remaining on the Court. And may I speak frankly?"

He glared at her with burning, reproachful eyes. "I do believe I'd rather you not speak at all!"

The muscles in Daryn's lovely face tightened into a mask of anger. "I am the president of the United States, and I not only will speak, I must. Mr. Chief Justice—at eighty-two, you have few years remaining. Why not enjoy them in retirement? The country will benefit."

Haynes glanced at Paul as if seeking confirmation of the insult he'd just heard, then he turned back to the president. "Young lady, your insolence—"

"You should call me Madam President." Her face paled with wrath, though her voice remained calm and firm. "And don't call me insolent. Other presidents through the years have been known to explode and rant on occasion. If a woman exerts a little authority, however, why must she be immediately reminded of her gender?"

Sputtering, the justice interrupted. "Why, I never—it is not your place to tell me what to do. The judiciary remains outside the influence of the executive branch—"

"Calm down, sir." Daryn's mouth twisted in a slight smile. "I wouldn't want to aggravate your high blood pressure. People might assume that stress is taking its toll on your health."

Haynes turned to Paul, seeking support. Paul lowered his gaze as his blood pounded and his face grew hot with humiliation. He had not come to Washington to participate in this sort of behavior, but Daryn had been playing the game far longer than he had.

"My health is not suffering," the justice said, clenching his fist as he turned back to the president. "And even if I were only half-alive, I'd remain on the Court if *you're* in the White House. As long as I'm breathing, I can still cast a conservative vote."

"But the chief justice does so much more than vote," Daryn continued, her voice reasonable and matter-of-fact. "You are the permanent chairman of the nation's Judicial Conference, and you are the chairman of the Federal Judicial Center's governing board. You are manager of the Supreme Court Building and chancellor of the Smithsonian Institute. Most important, you preside over the Supreme Court conferences and direct the justices' discussions. And if you are half-dead, sir, you cannot handle all those responsibilities, so you should resign."

Leaning over a corner of the white linen tablecloth, Daryn focused her white-hot gaze upon the old man. "I have it on good authority that you haven't written an original opinion in three years. Your law clerks are writing for you, researching your cases, framing your opinions. You have been seen leaning heavily upon Justice Tolson's arm as you enter and exit the courtroom, and there's no telling what we'll learn when we speak to your physician."

"You'll learn nothing," Haynes said, his voice crisp and cool. "Medical records are private."

Shifting in her chair, Daryn shrugged. "Of course they are. But how will it look when CNN reports that your doctors refused to confirm or deny rumors of your poor health? Even if you are as healthy as a horse, which observations would seem to refute, your refusal to be forthcoming will hurt your cause."

She propped her elbow on her chair and tucked her index finger beneath her chin, a thoughtful pose. "Mr. Chief Justice—" she lowered her voice—"I do not want to see your wonderful record sullied in this election year. I would much prefer to see you retire in the glory you have earned than in the ignominy of those who stayed on the Court too long. I'm sure you recall what they always say about Justice William Douglas."

Haynes glowered across the table. "To which comment are you referring?"

Daryn turned to Paul. "Mr. Santana? Surely you remember the Douglas quote?"

Paul felt the tips of his ears burn. "Apparently," he said, hating to add fuel to the fire, "Chief Justice Burger told his clerks that Douglas was like an old firehouse dog—too old to run with the trucks, but every time he heard a siren, his ears pricked up just the same."

"Mr. Chief Justice—" Daryn whispered the words like a caress—"if you retire now, you need not fear being put out to pasture. You'll continue to receive your usual salary of nearly 200,000 dollars per year, and you'll stay as busy as you want to be if the new chief justice is willing to provide you with assignments. You'll still have an office in the Supreme Court Building and a staff. You will not lose your dignity."

The chief justice's face was now dead-white, sheened with a cold sweat that had soaked his thin white hair, but Paul could see calculation in his eyes. Daryn had made a simple but effective case—if he didn't retire, by a few well-placed innuendos she would drag his name and reputation through the sludge and make his remaining months a living hell.

Rubbing his hand over his face, Paul watched the old man and imagined the thoughts racing behind those clouded blue eyes. Marshall Haynes, who'd been a living legal legend at the time of his appointment in '78, might have defied Daryn in his younger years. Iron-willed and hard as nails, the man had ruled the Court for over a quarter of a century. But his confidence level had fallen in recent months, and Daryn's observations had obviously hit their mark. His strength was not what it had been, and public opinion was a fickle thing. If the media began to make an issue of his health, it would soon *be* an issue, one not even his understanding colleagues on the Court could ignore. Soon they'd be second-guessing his authority . . .

"The new chief justice." Haynes lifted his gaze to meet Daryn's. "Who did you have in mind?"

The president gave him a heartfelt smile. "Justice Tolson, with whom you've been allied for many years. I would not ask you to leave and appoint an opponent in your place."

Paul took a sharp breath, shocked by the outright lie. In the last few months he and the others had joked about the necessity of massaging statistics, bending the truth, and releasing the occasional harmless falsehood—all for the public good, of course—but he had never seen Daryn look a man in the eye, smile, and lie without flinching. When had she become so ruthless?

The old man grunted softly, then looked down at the tablecloth, tentatively pressing his fingertips to the linen. Veins squirmed across the backs of his hands like fat blue worms.

"I suppose, Madam President, that your offer makes a certain sense." He squinted up at her. "Though I think I now dislike you intensely. What you have done here today, Madam, is unprecedented and ignoble."

Stunned and shaken, Paul sat silently as Daryn inclined her head, conceding the point. "What you consider ignoble, sir, I view as sensible and expedient. I suppose it all depends upon one's perspective."

With that she stood, came around the table, and extended her hand to the older gentleman. "Thank you, Mr. Chief Justice, for agreeing to see me. I look forward to soon hearing the happy news of your resignation."

●

When the chief justice had gone, Daryn put out a hand and leaned against the wall. She'd battled her way through lunch on the strength of adrenaline, but that nervous energy was rapidly dissipating.

"Wow," she whispered, more to herself than Paul. "I wasn't sure we were going to pull that one off. I was half-afraid he'd call my bluff and speak to the press first."

"How'd you know?" he asked. "About the clerks writing his opinions?"

She straightened, tugging the hem of her jacket into place. "O'Leary has a friend whose daughter clerks for Justice Becket."

"Were you serious about nominating Tolson to fill the chief justice vacancy? Tolson's an archconservative."

She cast him a get-serious look. "I'm entitled to change my mind, aren't I?"

"Daryn." Rising from his chair, Paul came toward her, gripped her arm, and guided her into the study—rather forcefully, she noticed. When they were safely out of sight, he closed the door.

"Not me." He leaned against the closed door with one hand while he held a warning finger before her face. "I'll help you find a candidate; I'll go through the list myself until we find someone suitable. But don't nominate me."

Alarm rippled along her spine even as she offered him a small smile. "Why, Counselor! I thought you'd enjoy being a justice."

He stood there, tall and angry, while his brown eyes sparked with vehemence. "If you make me a justice, you'll destroy my family."

She leaned back against the door, momentarily confused. What did he mean? His marriage was a sham, and his daughter had already left the nest.

"I didn't know," she whispered, lobbing the words like carefully chosen stones, "that your family was so precious to you."

She knew she'd touched a nerve when a swift shadow crossed his face.

"It's Cristina," he finally said, dropping his hand. "She doesn't know that her mother and I are not . . . what we could be. She thinks we have a fairy-tale marriage."

"Oh?" Daryn glared at him, tempering her sudden anger with amusement. "So you play the role of Prince Charming when you're at home, do you?"

"Daryn, that's not fair." All the fire had gone out of his eyes. "If you had a daughter, maybe you'd understand."

"If you want fairness, Paul, take your case to the EEOC." She pulled herself off the door, her strength returning as her temper flared. "And as for having children, at least I am honest enough to admit that I can't be responsible for a child and the country at the same time. I stick to my priorities, whereas you continually waver between what you know is right and the remnants of your Catholic guilt!"

His face went pale, except for two deep red patches that appeared on his cheekbones. "You never could understand that part of me, could you?"

"I don't understand dogma or superstition, Paul. I'm too much of a realist. I see the truth, and I don't hide from it. And right now I see a man who says he's free from religion and family and marriage, but every time his boat is rocked by a wave he turns into a creature more dependent and hypocritical and traditional than—"

"Hush." He caught her shoulders and held her against the door, then lowered his head until their eyes were only inches apart. "Of all people, you should understand. There are no remnants of religion in my life; they all vanished with our baby. I decided then that any God worth worshiping wouldn't take an innocent child—"

"Shut up." Daryn closed her eyes, half-afraid he'd see into her soul.

"I'm sorry, I know you don't like to talk about the baby." His voice was lower now, repentant. "Daryn," he murmured, his hands fluttering over her arms and shoulders as if he were afraid to hold her too tightly, "I've given you my love and loyalty, and in return I ask this one thing—do not nominate me for the Court. Please, if you have any regard for me at all, do not do this thing."

Despite his pleading expression, his body language revealed his strength and determination. Daryn considered insisting, but now was not the time. He was upset. This had been a shock, but in time he could grow accustomed to the idea.

"All right, Counselor." She smiled up at him. "If this means more to you than I do . . ."

His arms went around her; his head dropped to her neck in a posture of grateful supplication. She patted his back, then placed her hands on his flaming cheeks and lifted his head. "I'll let you off the hook if I can find someone more suitable," she said, searching his eyes. "But if I can't, you already promised to help me. Remember?"

His tight expression relaxed into a smile. "Daryn, there are a thousand judges more qualified than I. I'm not at all worried."

"I am." Rising on tiptoe, she pressed her lips to his, then sighed. For a moment, she'd thought she might lose him again.

TWENTY

AS THE MIDDAY WEATHERMAN PROMISED SUNNY skies and a high of ninety-nine sweaty degrees, Maria Santana ripped the cellophane cover off a Lean Cuisine entrée, slid the dinner into the microwave, and set the timer. While the oven hummed, she moved to the tiny TV in the kitchen and increased the volume, then pulled a glass from the cupboard.

Though they'd been in Washington nearly a year, the Georgetown house still didn't feel like home. Sometimes she found herself staring at the cupboards and struggling to remember where she'd put the Tupperware. Of course, they'd lived in the Miami house for so long she could have found the tiniest Tupperware lid blindfolded.

She pulled a Diet Pepsi from the pantry, then popped the can and poured the soda over the ice in her glass. The midday news blared from the small television as a granite-faced reporter explained that a Beltway accident had claimed the lives of a young couple trying to change a flat in the breakdown lane.

She shook her head as the microwave beeped. Bad news all around, all the time. Miami had more than its share of crime, but Washington transgressions usually made national headlines. In the District petty crooks shared the spotlight with misbehaving congressional representatives, and scandal flourished like a fungus.

What was it with Washington people? In the revealing light of day they talked like angels; under cover of darkness they lived like the devil. No wonder Hollywood and Washington people got along so well; they were all actors. On Memorial Day Maria had watched video footage of Vice President Frey and his wife visiting a veterans' cemetery. While the cameras rolled, they wiped tears from their eyes and consoled one another as if this were a private, intimate setting, yet Maria knew they'd have to be as blind as moles not to see the hundreds of cameras pointed in their direction.

Thank goodness Cristina was in Massachusetts. She glanced at her watch. Cristina was probably breaking from her summer school classes and grabbing a bite to eat with Jason. Though she kept insisting the young man was just a friend, Maria had a hunch the friendship had deepened. During her phone calls, Cristina now routinely said *we* instead of *I,* and she seemed to spend every free minute with the tall boy from Wisconsin. If she hadn't come home so often, Maria might have resisted the idea of Cristina's staying in Cambridge over the summer, but Jason didn't seem to mind bringing her home for occasional weekend visits.

Humming softly, Maria removed the dinner from the microwave, then stirred the steaming entrée, mixing the Swedish meatballs into the gravy-covered noodles. Jason and Cristina would be a good match. After all, she'd fallen in love with Paul little by little, one day at a time. He'd been working for her father's law firm, and every time she met him Maria had walked away a little more impressed.

Smiling, she lifted a meatball and blew on it, scattering the steam. It hadn't hurt that Paul was the most handsome man she'd ever met . . . and one of the kindest. Her father assured her that Paul was a good lawyer and an honest one, and before too long she had successfully hinted for a first date. After six months of a sweet courtship, she'd gathered her courage and hinted that they ought to marry, and he'd had sense enough to agree. Cristina had arrived a year later, and even though the pregnancy had been difficult, Maria finally felt complete. God had given her everything she ever wanted—a handsome and successful husband, a beautiful daughter, and the support of a loving family.

The cancer had rocked her carefully ordered world. She had been shocked and horrified at the diagnosis, but the doctors had removed the tumor and reassured her through the radiation treatments. Each year, when she went for her blood tests and learned of good results, she picked up her rosary and offered prayers of thanksgiving.

In the last eight months, though, her prayers had changed. Since the night she picked up her Bible and read that God wanted to care for her, she'd begun her mornings reading the Scripture and ended her days with prayers from her heart. She still said the rosary, but now she often found herself talking to Jesus as she would talk to her papa or Cristina . . . and sometimes, when she least expected it, she thought she heard him answer. Occasionally as she read a section of scripture, her heart would leap with the certainty of recognition. Like a mother who could pinpoint her child's face amid a thousand baby pictures, she would know those words were for her, for that day or for that hour.

The dark fear that had shadowed her life ever since the cancer diagnosis began to recede. Color crept back into her world, brightening the lonely hours she would have found unbearable only a few months before. Like Moses, who had to spend time in the desert before he was ready to reenter Egypt, she became convinced that God had brought her to Washington in order to prepare her for a fuller life back home. He had saved her from cancer so she could be a model to younger women, an example of how a woman should raise a daughter and make a home for a husband.

She wanted to do more than keep house for her husband, but Paul didn't seem to require anything else from her, especially since they'd come to Washington. He cared for her in his reserved way and respected her wishes. But he did not often approach her bed on the days deemed safe for marital relations, nor did his eyes light up when she entered the room. If love had existed in his heart, time and familiarity had transformed it . . . into duty, perhaps.

Her gaze fell upon a framed picture on the window sill—a portrait of Paul and Cristina, their faces alight with smiles. Paul's love for Cristina was as obvious as sunshine. He smiled in her presence and stayed up late waiting for her to come in, even now. His pride in her was an almost tangible thing.

Sighing, Maria speared a forkful of noodles and took her first bite. She knew she ought to be grateful for a husband who didn't drink excessively or beat her. She ought to thank God that Paul loved their daughter and paid the bills without grumbling. She was grateful for his friendship, care, and commitment. And no matter how muted his feelings had become over the years, she knew he would never divorce her. Though he did not share her faith, he would live and die by the edicts of the Church as long as they meant something to her.

Still . . . sometimes she wished he would come home early and sweep her off her feet like the heroes in the romance novels she devoured. She would love to come home and find a rose on her pillow, or, better yet, candles burning in the bedroom.

But she was forty-nine and full-hipped, more a mother than a maiden. And Paul held an important job for the president of the United States, so it wasn't like he had time to indulge in silly games. So while it was fun to fantasize, her reality was far richer than that of most women she knew.

She put the fork to her mouth and tasted a meatball—not bad. As she ate, the television news shifted to a reporter standing outside a marble building. "We bring you this special report," the announcer said, then the man in the trench coat announced that due to failing health, the chief justice of the Supreme Court had just resigned. Maria stared at the tiny TV as the report cut to footage of an elderly gentleman moving away from a gaggle of reporters, his head bowed and his hand thrown up to block the photographers.

Maria stabbed another mouthful of noodles. Politics had never interested her, and the Supreme Court seemed a universe away.

"Moments after the chief justice's announcement," the reporter droned on, "a White House spokesman told reporters the president had already selected her nominee for the Court and would soon present the candidate to the Senate Judiciary Committee. Though some Court watchers are surprised at the speed of this declaration, the White House routinely maintains lists of possible nominees in the event of a sudden court vacancy. Washington insiders, however, note that while it is not imperative for the Senate to confirm the president's nominee immediately, the upcoming election has put pressure on the Austin administration. President Austin apparently hopes to see the matter concluded before she hits the campaign trail in midsummer."

Maria swallowed thoughtfully. If the president had already selected someone, did Paul know who it was? He had once told her that part of his job included checking on judicial nominees, but he hadn't mentioned investigating anyone for the Supreme Court. Then again, a couple of months ago the president had asked him to focus on campaign issues, so perhaps someone else in Paul's office was handling the Supreme Court nomination. Probably his boss, that Irish fellow . . .

A dart of despair entered Maria's heart, but she closed her mind to the sting. Paul told her very little about his work. He did not invite her to accompany him to cocktail parties or political meetings, and, in truth, she would not feel comfortable in a gathering of people she did not know. Still, it would have been nice for him to ask.

Her husband seemed to live in two worlds separated by a high-voltage fencing. He kept his briefcase locked, even when it rested on their own kitchen table. She'd wormed a few things out of him, but he did not enjoy discussing White House business at home. She knew he had to be discreet about his work, but what would it hurt to tell her? She had no political friends and no plans to make any, because as soon as Austin left the White House, she and Paul were going back to Miami.

She pressed her hand to her mouth as her mind ran backward, replaying the past weekend. Cristina had brought Jason home, so the family conversation had been light and impersonal. Paul had taken great pains not to mention Cristina's phone bill, her grades, or his work.

The weekend had been filled with smiles, laughter, and good food. Paul had seemed more relaxed than he had in ages, probably because the president was off on a campaign jaunt through the south. He had been working hard, but he'd been home by six on the night Cristina arrived, and he had not retreated immediately after dinner.

Maria picked up her iced tea glass and took a long swallow. From the television, a stentorian voice rang out: "We interrupt this broadcast for a special CBS report: A Court at the Crossroads."

Lowering her glass, Maria turned toward the tiny TV. The screen had filled with a shot of the empty Senate chamber, but within a moment it shifted to a view of an empty speaker's platform under balmy blue skies. The presidential seal had been affixed to a wooden lectern, behind which a man in a dark suit somberly proclaimed: "Ladies and gentlemen: the president of the United States."

As the assembled crowd stood, the camera zoomed in on the image of Daryn Austin, who walked with graceful dignity to the lectern. Gripping the edge, she gave the group a serious smile, then glanced down at her notes. "A few moments ago I was saddened to receive word of Chief Justice Haynes's intention to leave the Supreme Court. Understanding his situation, however, and agreeing with his reasoning, I hereby accept his resignation. Chief Justice Haynes's wisdom and eloquence will be sorely missed, but his opinions will benefit this nation for generations to come."

She paused as a plane shuddered in the air overhead, then acknowledged the interruption with a smile. "A good president is like a girl scout—her motto is 'be prepared.' And so my office will soon be sending two names to the Senate Judiciary Committee for confirmation to the Supreme Court."

Maria frowned at the screen. Two names? For one vacancy?

"The first name," the president continued, "is that of Justice Edward Franklin. Justice Franklin has served the Court admirably since 1978, and no one can deny that his role in shaping the complexion of the Court has been pivotal in a great many cases. So it is with great pleasure that I hereby nominate him to the position of chief justice."

"To fill the vacancy left by Justice Franklin, I hereby nominate a man from my own fine legal staff, a man you may remember from the earliest months of the year 2000. During that time, our nation became acquainted with a little boy, Elian Gonzalez, whose arrival in America was won by the sacrifice of his mother's life. One man spearheaded the legal charge to protect Elian from Communism, to keep him under the protection of this country. Unfortunately, the Supreme Court elected not to involve itself with Elian Gonzalez, but millions of Americans will remember the brave man who stepped forward to make a difference—Mr. Paul Santana."

Around Maria, the house fell silent, as if it, too, were listening in stunned disbelief.

"Today," the president continued, "I am pleased and proud to send the name of Paul Santana to the Senate Judiciary Committee. I believe our country needs more men of his caliber, and our Supreme Court will benefit from his passion and conviction." Smiling, she looked around the semicircle of reporters. "I'm sorry we have no time for questions today; I've a hospital to tour. But thank you for coming."

Maria pressed her hand to her face, staring through her fingers at the small screen where Daryn Austin walked among a crowd of men, her head and shoulders high. An unidentified voice from the television explained that the Senate Judiciary Committee would have to confirm the president's appointees, and the latter appointment might involve more controversy than usual. The Franklin nomination would probably pass with little debate, but few people outside Miami or the White House had ever heard of Paul Santana . . .

Maria stared at the television. Had Paul known? If so, why hadn't he told her? How could he have kept *this* secret?

The answer supplied itself: he didn't have the courage to tell her. He loved Washington, he wanted to stay, and he knew she wanted to leave as soon as possible. Her courageous husband, who could stand before judges and argue cases without once getting his thoughts in a knot, couldn't find the nerve to speak to her . . .

Because he'd fallen out of practice.

Because he no longer cared.

Because . . .

She shook her head. What did his reasons matter? He hadn't told her. He had known, surely he had known, so this was just another secret he shared with Daryn Austin.

Maria looked down, clenching her fists, as tears began to roll down her face, hot spurts of loss and fury.

She would go home. She'd pack her bags, write him a note, and go back to Miami. When the renters' lease ran out, she'd move back into her real home, and until then she could live with her father . . .

No, Maria. Since they are no longer two but one, let no one separate them, for God has joined them together.

"Dear God, no." She gulped hard, more tears slipping down her cheeks as the inner voice jolted her. "We *aren't* one. It's obvious Paul doesn't love me. He doesn't care."

Wait, daughter. Don't be impatient for the Lord to act! Travel steadily along his path. He will honor you. You will see the wicked destroyed.

Sniffling, she lowered her head to the countertop, then covered her head with her hands. At that moment she didn't particularly want to see the wicked destroyed; she couldn't even tell who the wicked *were.* All she wanted was a husband who loved her, a home that sheltered, and the sight of her loving papa's smile.

Lifting her head, she swiped tears from her cheeks and moved toward the phone. Her papa would know what to do. Even if he didn't, she would find the comfort she always found in hearing that he adored her—

No, child. Be silent . . . and know that I am God.

Maria paused, her heart beating hard enough, she was sure, to be audible a yard away. She had often heard the still, small voice like a nudging in her spirit, but never before had the words come so clearly and swiftly. She stared at the phone, wanting to pick it up, but knowing she shouldn't.

This was their battle, hers and God's, against . . . whatever the future held. And the Lord wanted her to wait in silence.

"I will be honored?" she asked after a long moment. "You promise?"

No answer this time, but a ray of sunlight streamed through the kitchen window, warming her clammy skin with its brilliance.

●

Sitting at his desk, his untasted lunch from the White House mess in a foam container before him, Paul watched the drama unfold from the television hanging in the corner of his office. His door stood open, and though no one had dared intrude upon his privacy, he could hear whispers coming from behind the wall.

He still couldn't believe what he'd heard.

He'd kept silent after that lunch with the chief justice back in March, trusting Daryn to find someone else for the position. As the weeks passed and she didn't mention the Court again, he believed his protests had convinced her to look elsewhere. He had continued with his work on her campaign, relating details to her in private nearly every evening, and things had been so *normal*, so blessedly routine, that he never dreamed she'd do this.

But she had. Without warning, she'd released his name before the entire nation, ambushing him while she was safely off in Tennessee and out of his reach.

Lowering his head into his hands, he muttered the vilest oath he could think of, then stared at the unappetizing mound of glutinous chicken à la king on his desk. He'd been hungry a moment ago, but Daryn's brazen announcement had snatched his appetite away.

"If you were here, Daryn, I'd—" He bit off the rest of the sentence. This wasn't the time for threats; she'd done what she wanted to do. What *he* had to do was figure a way out of the trouble and—

His thoughts came to an abrupt halt, his heart jumping in his chest. The sight of Maria and Cristina, safe in their sterling silver frame, sent a tremor scooting up the back of his neck. They knew. Maria—soon she'd be facing a pack of press. And Cristina, up at Harvard, would have no privacy, no warning. The press would soon be camped out around his family, if they weren't already.

He picked up the phone and punched in the first three digits of his home number, then dropped the receiver back into the cradle. He needed to explain this news in person.

As soon as possible.

Standing, he took his coat from the back of the chair and slid his arms into it. The White House Press Office would undoubtedly be preparing a press release congratulating Justice Haynes for his years of service as well as providing brief bios on Justice Franklin and Paul Santana. He'd be needed for interviews and questions, but first he'd have to talk to Maria. He would not do anything for anyone until he had faced her.

Annoyed by a series of shushings from the hall, he moved to the door, then nodded brusquely at a pair of red-faced interns. "Excuse me," he said politely, then closed the door and locked it behind him.

Striding through the West Wing, he considered other implications of Daryn's rash action. His nomination to the Supreme Court would not be good for staff morale. O'Leary's resentment at Paul's presence had simmered beneath the surface for nearly a year; this news might push him to the boiling point. Others who had labored for President Parker and planned to follow Daryn into her next term would be flabbergasted at Paul's sudden promotion—or worse, they'd be disdainful, particularly if they knew how much time the president and her deputy counsel spent together after hours. And while discretion was a key requirement for White House employment, sometimes resentment could overpower prudence . . .

"Hey, Counselor!" One of the agents at the security checkpoint waved for Paul's attention. "Congratulations!" Seeing him, Paul raised his chin in silent acknowledgement, then lengthened his stride. He needed out of the West Wing—*now.*

Five minutes later he sank into his car, locked the doors, and turned the key. As the air conditioner blew a refreshing cold stream, he held his hand to his forehead. Daryn had called the nomination an honor—and it was. But it was also a position held for life, and Paul was still a relatively young man. If Daryn persisted with this crazy notion, he'd be confirmed at fifty, a youngster compared to some of the other justices. His only escape would be death or retirement, and he couldn't retire until sixty-five if he wanted to receive his pension.

Which left him facing fifteen years on the highest bench in the land. While some lawyers might salivate at the prospect, Paul didn't think he'd particularly enjoy the daily grind. He had always enjoyed working with people, and Supreme Court justices had no clients, unless you counted the nebulous body of American law as a client. From what he knew, as a justice he'd spend his life surrounded by a handful of law clerks and eight other justices as sheltered and secluded as himself.

He put the car in reverse and backed out of the parking space, then roared toward the security checkpoint. No detailed inspection now, just a cursory glance, a nod, and the uniformed officer waved Paul through. Getting out of the White House was relatively easy, particularly if you were an insider. Getting out of the Supreme Court, though, might be his most difficult task yet.

He turned into the traffic and encountered a lunchtime bottleneck, typical for this time of day. Beating his hand against the steering wheel, he shot a wary glance toward the car phone, half-expecting it to ring. Surely someone wanted to scream at him—Maria, Cristina, Thrasher, or maybe O'Leary, for abandoning the office when his presence was most needed.

A wry smile twisted his face. Perhaps the solitude of the Court might prove to be his salvation. The austere halls of the Supreme Court would surely seem calm compared to the whirlpool of the West Wing.

In his short time as a Washington insider, he'd watched himself and others adapt to the fishbowl of public life. The interns and staffers who worked in the West Wing and OEOB had come from several different states and all walks of life, but they were gradually turning into cookie cutters—people who spoke in code, who wore a uniform (trench coat, navy or black suits with navy or red ties), cluttered their offices with neatly autographed "power pictures," and trained their thoughts to fit into the current presidential mold. Nearly all of them had created a public self, even within the small cloister of the West Wing, and the public self had little to do with the person behind the mask.

Had the man behind his mask changed? He wasn't sure. But Daryn certainly had, in ways both disturbing and alarming. Her Southern accent surfaced now only when they were alone, and the gracefulness that had wowed him in their college days had hardened into steel-tendoned poise. She had become fluent in doublespeak, and her intuition, always tuned to undercurrents and subtext, now seemed to pick up vibes from the other side of the Capitol. Such abilities were the tools of politics, and she had equipped herself like a pro.

The light changed, the car surged forward, then halted when the next block clogged with traffic. Paul changed lanes to avoid blocking the intersection and settled in to wait for another choking road to clear.

Glancing to his passenger seat, he picked up a book he'd bought at a nearby Barnes and Noble: *How to Survive in Washington*, subtitled *How to live at the center of political influence in the Capitol without losing your principles, detachment, or individual human qualities.*

Paul snorted softly as he tossed the book back into the empty seat. "Too little, too late," he whispered, voicing the thought that had been rattling in his brain for months.

When, exactly, had Daryn sold out?

His listless gaze focused on a bronze eagle sitting on the floor, a presidential gift he'd never bothered to take out of the car. Daryn had presented three of them as rewards for work done to correct the H-1B Visa Program, a quick INS fix that had brought in over 420,000 immigrants who specialized in computer science. American companies had benefited from their expertise, but at the conclusion of their six-year visas, the immigrants could not gain the green cards necessary to establish permanent residency. Paul and his staff had come up with a workable solution, the president presented it to the American people in her weekly radio address, and the INS experienced an abrupt change of heart. Last week, in an unusual gesture of appreciation, President Austin had held a small ceremony for White House staff in the Rose Garden, where she presented handsome statues of a soaring eagle to Paul and two of his assistants.

From the moment she placed the gift in his hand, Paul knew the award was a facade, and now he understood the reason behind it. She wanted to thank him publicly, to give him a tangible symbol of her appreciation and send him to the Supreme Court with something that would appear to validate their close working relationship. In her perfunctory speech she referred to Paul as her "right arm" and "close friend." He'd listened with his eyes lowered and his neck burning, knowing that if he looked up he would catch more than a few lifted brows and surreptitious winks among the assembled staffers.

She loved him. He knew it, Thrasher knew it, and there were probably two or three others who knew as well. Maybe a half-dozen staffers suspected that Paul and the president were sleeping together, and as many as fifty might be aware that the friendship between the president and her deputy counsel went deeper than that of chief executive and legal assistant.

Maybe all that awareness was making her nervous. He'd been uneasy ever since that first night in the residence, but she'd always seemed in total control. But now . . . faced with an election and the rigors of the campaign trail, perhaps she saw the Supreme Court as a safe place to stow her college sweetheart.

And install a puppet justice.

He tightened his jaw, biting down on the inside of his lip. For the first time since coming to Washington, he felt used. Daryn would expect him to render judgments favoring her positions, but since they usually agreed, he couldn't do otherwise without violating his own principles. As always, she'd weighed every aspect of her strategy. To vote against her out of spite would be a betrayal of his own conscience.

He blew out a deep breath, his blood boiling as his thoughts turned to her sneak attack. How *dare* she set him up this way? She knew he opposed the nomination. If she were any other woman he'd have put his foot down, but she was not just any woman. She was his president, his employer, and he'd promised to serve her in any way he could.

Even if that service meant the end of their affair . . . and the end of his marriage.

Heaviness centered in his chest as his thoughts returned to Maria. She must have been blindsided by this, and she didn't deserve to be. She'd been a good wife, a wonderful mother, and a faithful supporter of his dreams . . .

At his right hand, the phone buzzed. He stared out the window, letting it ring three times before picking it up. Soon Yi Park was on the line, asking if he could join the president in the residence at 9 P.M., after her return from Tennessee aboard Air Force One.

Nodding grimly, Paul promised to appear.

●

Maria's fingers hesitated upon the page as she heard the sound of a key in the front door. She glanced at the clock on the mantel. Paul was home at one-thirty in the afternoon? This was a day to remember.

Focusing upon the printed page, she kept her eyes upon the words: *The king's heart is like a stream of water directed by the Lord; he turns it wherever he pleases. People may think they are doing what is right, but the Lord examines the heart.*

She jumped when her husband called her name.

"Maria?"

Paul stood in the arched opening that led to the foyer, looking at her. Lines of distress were etched beside his mouth and eyes, thrown into darkness by the shadows of the unlit living room. Dropping his briefcase onto the carpeted floor, he sank to the love seat facing the sofa.

Slowly, reluctantly, she lowered her Bible.

"You know?"

She nodded. "I saw . . . I heard it on the news." She tilted her head as pain welled inside her chest. "Why didn't you tell me, Pablo?"

His head began a slow, slightly disgusted shake. "I didn't know. I don't expect you to believe me, but I was as shocked as you were."

"I can't believe that. Presidents don't nominate people for the Supreme Court without asking them about it first!"

He shuddered slightly, as though a cold wind had blown over him. "She said something about it months ago, back in March. But I told her I didn't want the position; I gave her a dozen good reasons why she shouldn't submit my name. I told her we were moving back to Miami; I told her I had no judicial experience; I told her I didn't want the job—"

"But she didn't listen." Maria pinched her lower lip between her teeth, then nodded slowly. "Will—will this thing go through?"

Paul took a wincing little breath. "I don't know. Probably, if she pushes it."

"Then it's okay." She looked down, hoping her bangs would hide the tears brimming in her eyes. He had no idea how much those words had cost her, but he would need to hear them.

"Okay?" He spoke the words in a flat voice, as if astonishment had wiped all expression from his vocal register.

"If you are placed on the Supreme Court, it will be God's will. I've been praying for an hour and a half; and I'm sure this is what God wants you to know. He is working here, Pablo. He controls the hearts of kings . . . and presidents."

Peering up from beneath the fringe of her bangs, Maria watched as her husband rose, picked up his briefcase, and walked out the door, looking for all the world like a man in a daze.

●

Paul dropped the magazine he'd been reading onto Daryn's coffee table as the door opened. Sighing, she stepped into the residence living room and gave him a weary smile. "I'm so glad you're here. After a long day like this, I could use some honest conversation."

He stood, steeling himself to face her. "I'm glad you feel that way. Because we have to talk."

She breezed past him, the silky swish of her slacks accenting every step. "Of course we do; that's why I invited you up. But first, will you help me with this zipper? This top is a veritable nightmare. I don't know what the designer was thinking."

He followed her from the living room into the bedroom, then pulled on the delicate zipper at her neckline. The slide moved easily over the curve of her back.

"Thank you, Counselor." She turned and pressed a kiss to his cheek, then moved toward the walk-in closet. "I think I was asked a hundred questions about you today. I stalled, of course. You need to speak for yourself."

"That was low, Daryn. You blindsided me with that announcement."

"Darling!" She whirled, her eyes widening in what he was sure was pretended surprise. "I couldn't help it! Haynes sprang his resignation on us, and with me in Tennessee, there wasn't time to contact you."

"You didn't have to say anything today." His voice coagulated with sarcasm as he sat on the edge of the bed. "Or maybe you did. You can't stand to let an opportunity pass by, can you?"

"Let's not insult each other, Counselor." Her voice came from the depths of the closet. "You knew I wanted you for the Court."

"I told you to find someone else."

"You told me to look for someone more suitable." Her head appeared around the corner. "I looked. There was no one on this green earth more perfect for the position."

"Then you didn't look hard enough."

"I looked under every rock in Washington, and quite a few in the real world. Then I decided—you're the one. Besides, you promised."

As she retreated into the closet again, Paul drew a long, harsh breath, struggling to master the anger that shook him. He couldn't stay mad at

Daryn for long; her pragmatism defeated his emotion at every turn. And now he couldn't even bring up Maria—against all odds and her own nature, this afternoon she'd freed him from the fear of losing his family. She had found comfort in God, her retreat of last resort . . .

At least she hadn't left him.

"I've already spoken with Thrasher and O'Leary," Daryn called above the rattling hangers. "They're going to work with you, get you ready for the gauntlet." She peeked out again, her mouth curving into a smile. "Think of it as cramming for a really important exam."

She stepped out of the closet, draped now in a filmy robe over lounging pajamas that must have come from one of the most exclusive stores in Georgetown. Without hesitation she walked over and sank to his side. "I apologize for catching you off guard. And I'll confess—I think I might have done it because I knew you'd kick and scream if I gave you warning. This way, I have the whole world urging you to accept the position."

He caught the hand she pressed to his thigh, then brought it up to his chest. "There's one more thing, Daryn, you should consider before you go ahead with this."

"And what would that be?" Her brows slanted the question.

"The press pool will investigate me," he said, his voice gruff with repressed frustration. "They may learn about us."

"As far as anyone from our past knows, that's ancient history."

"They may learn about the baby. They could get records from the hospital you visited when you had the miscarriage."

Abruptly, she pulled her hand free. "There are no records, Paul; give me credit for thinking that far ahead. I gave a false name at the hospital."

His stare drilled into her. "Why on earth—"

"I grew up as a governor's daughter, remember? I know the risks. I didn't go to the *dentist* under my own name, especially not in Georgia."

"But surely you went to your own doctor when you were losing the baby—"

She held up a hand to silence him, then spoke in a condescending tone that grated against his nerves. "I didn't have a doctor in New

Haven. The few times I needed medication, I went to the campus clinic." She dropped her head and released an audible sigh. "I'm sorry, but I don't like to revisit that particular memory."

Moved to sympathy by the thought of what she had endured, he slipped an arm around her shoulders. "Do you see my point? Any reporter who gets the urge can investigate our past. They'll find people who'll swear we were lovers, and then they'll track down others who'll say the same thing now. You can't survive the election with this kind of scandal hanging over your head."

"I'm not worried about what people think. Political Washington knows we're old friends, that we're *simpático*. And sophisticated people won't care about anything more than that." Her gaze lifted to meet his. "Two faces, Counselor, the public and private. Keep them separate, and you can accomplish almost anything."

Her eyes were soft and dreamy, cloudy as a summer sky. "In the last few hours, though," she said, her lashes dropping to cover those lovely eyes, "I've realized the truth of that old saying about cutting off your nose to spite your face. We're going to have to slow things down, Paul. For your sake, we're going to have to put the brakes on our relationship."

The words struck him like a slap across the cheek, but for some reason his facial muscles refused to absorb the news. He stared at her, his mouth still curved in the sympathetic smile he'd given her moments before. After a long moment, he managed a cynical laugh. "For *my* sake?"

"Yes. Because that oversensitive dinosaur conscience of yours won't let you enjoy what should be the best years of your life. And we're going to slow down for the country's sake. I truly believe you'll make a great justice. Together, with you on the Court and me in the White House, we can change the world."

The smile faded from Paul's face as a sudden fury flared in his soul. After all he had endured for her, was she turning him out? He flushed, momentarily seeing himself as a gawky teenager who'd just had his letter jacket returned from the head cheerleader.

"Don't think you can dismiss me," he said, his hand rising to tighten on the nape of her neck. "Not this time. If you think you can toss away all we've gone through—"

"Don't be a fool. I'm not tossing anything away, least of all you." Reaching out, she wrapped him in a close embrace. "If you love me, Counselor, you'll realize how much I need you to agree with me. Join the Court. Support me. We'll still see each other, but not as often."

Exhaling, he nestled his head into the fragrant softness of her neck and gritted his teeth. She demanded too much of him, but they had always asked a lot of each other. Their college relationship had been bordered by competition and drive, so why should he expect things to change?

He ran his hand over her spine, felt the tenseness in her neck. She was waiting for his reaction, already planning her next sentence if he did not agree with her decision. Capitulation had never come easily to him; he doubted it came easily to any man. So he could rant and rave for another half-hour—or he could swallow his disagreement and surrender to the will of his president.

"All right," he said finally. "I'll go through the confirmation hearings. But if the Senate doesn't approve me—"

"They will." She pulled away to look him in the eye, and he couldn't help but notice the relief in her face. "And this, my love, will be the last night we spend together for a while. Your rehearsals begin Monday."

TWENTY-ONE

By two on Monday afternoon, Paul had swallowed six cups of coffee and bitten back an entire week's worth of choice expletives. Thrasher and O'Leary had met him in the Roosevelt Room at 8 A.M., then proceeded to grill him on subjects ranging from affirmative action to Zambian immigrants' rights. With wry amusement he noticed that the dynamic duo spent an entire hour on issues dealing with the separation of powers—a situation that would undoubtedly arise if the Free Choice Clinic case found its way to the Supreme Court in the coming term. As Daryn's legal counsel, he had kept a careful eye on the case . . . ironic, now, that he might have a voice in deciding it.

"In the case of *Demetrio Rodriguez v. San Antonio*," O'Leary said, studying his legal pad of notes, "Justice Powell's opinion found substantial disparities in the funding of Texas school districts. This unequal approach forced poor children to attend poor schools. In your view, is the right to a quality education a fundamental responsibility of government, and should the states' power to fund schools be in any way rescinded?"

"I certainly believe in the power of education," Paul replied, idly rolling his pencil over the conference table. "But education is not among the rights afforded explicit protection under our Federal Constitution."

"The Constitution doesn't mention a fundamental right to abortion, either," O'Leary interrupted, "but Powell had no trouble finding *that* in the subtext."

Paul paused. "I believe I should study the matter further before offering a full opinion."

"If you haven't formed an opinion, *say* you haven't formed an opinion," O'Leary snapped for about the fifteenth time. His disapproval was palpable, even from across the room. "It's better to believe nothing than to pontificate on what you *might* think given a little more time. We need a *tabula rasa* for this court."

"My mind is not a blank slate," Paul answered. "And if I have an opinion, I'm going to share it."

"Share it at your own risk," O'Leary injected.

Paul gritted his teeth. "Trust me—I don't mind the risk."

"The president—" Thrasher jumped in, giving Paul the distinct impression that these two were tag teaming him in some sort of mental wrestling match—"means to change the country. As the opportunity arises, she will change the Court. And you, for God knows what reason, are her agent to lay the groundwork for change, so you'd better fall in line."

"I *am* in line." Paul clenched his fists as his temper spiked. These two had no idea how he'd agonized over the weekend, how desperately he'd tried to convince Daryn to choose someone else.

He turned the full heat of his glare upon O'Leary. "Save your speeches, Counselor, for someone who needs a pep talk. I know the president's positions, and I know how to articulate them. But if I go before the Senate Judiciary Committee, I'm going to articulate *my* thoughts. The job is for life, and I'm going to apply *my* life to it, not Daryn Austin's."

Duly rebuffed, O'Leary leaned back in his chair while Thrasher looked on in wide-eyed amusement. After a moment, Thrasher stood and picked up his briefcase, and Paul knew he'd go straight to Daryn and relate every relevant detail of the meeting.

"I think we're about done here." Thrasher tossed a quick grin in Paul's direction. "Thank you for your time, Counselor. We'll leave you now so you can take some time to prepare. Tomorrow we'll need your family in the Rose Garden at 10 A.M. That's where we'll make the official announcement."

As O'Leary filed out behind Thrasher, Paul closed his eyes and wished he'd been out of the office the day the White House called him in Miami.

●

The eighth of June dawned bright and blue, the rising sun swallowing up the wind that had howled at Paul's window all night. He slept until eight, then went downstairs to find his girls waiting in the kitchen, both of them bright-eyed and jittery in their summer dresses.

"Gee, Dad, some advance notice would have been nice," Cristina complained, coming over to brush nonexistent lint from his shoulders. "Jason and I drove all night, so I have industrial-strength bags under my eyes."

Paul glanced around the room. "Speaking of the devil, where is the boy?"

"Shhh, he's still asleep." Cristina pointed toward the small guest room tucked away at the front of the house. "He promised to wake up in time to watch us on TV, though."

"I'm surprised he didn't want to come along. Doesn't he consider himself one of the family?"

"Dad! Stop it."

Smothering the irritation that always arose within him when Jason entered the house, Paul turned to Maria, who kept tugging at the pearls around her neck. "They won't stay right," she said, her mouth twisting in exasperation. "I wanted them to look like Barbara Bush's, and the layers keep tangling—"

"Let me." Taking her hand, Paul lowered it to her side, then teased the strands of pearls into three separate lines. As he worked, Maria stood silently, her chin uplifted, her eyes wide, her hair soft and rippling with gentle waves. A wave of nostalgia threatened to engulf him, but he pushed it back. Today he had no time for sentiment or tears.

"Don't worry about a thing. You look lovely." He shot a quick grin in Cristina's direction. "Both of you look perfect."

Cristina made a face, then snatched up her purse and clumped toward the door on three-inch platform heels that brought her nearly to her father's height. Frowning, he pointed at the shoes, but Maria took his arm and pulled him toward the door.

"It's the style, dear. Just smile and say nothing."

He slipped his hand into his pocket and followed his wife. After twenty-one years of marriage, one would have thought he'd have smiling and saying nothing down to an art form.

But that technique didn't work with all women. It certainly wouldn't work with one who happened to be president.

●

Half an hour later, after passing through a set of security checkpoints outside the East Wing, Paul stood with his family inside the Diplomatic Reception Room and listened to Thrasher run down his list of preparations. The president would formally announce Justice Franklin's nomination to the position of chief justice later, but first she wanted to saturate the country with Paul Santana's name and image. The Press Office stood ready to release video and photos of Paul's illustrious law career, while groups who supported the president had already submitted endorsements of her nominees. Two minutes after the Rose Garden announcement, other Austin supporters stood poised to phone talk-radio shows, Larry King, anyone with an open mike. Hundreds of politicos, Paul realized, already knew his life story, although they'd undoubtedly heard a colorized, sanitized, improvised version.

At 9:58, President Daryn Austin breezed into the room, followed by the usual phalanx of Secret Service agents and the young aide, or "body man," who followed her everywhere in public. Thrasher and the aide stood to the side while Daryn warmly shook Maria's and Cristina's hands. "I know you're proud of your husband," she told Maria. "We are honored to be able to nominate him."

Moving on, Daryn took both of Cristina's hands in her own. "What a lovely girl," she called over her shoulder. Keeping her grip on Cristina, she gave the girl an intimate smile. "I see your father in you. You have his eyes."

While Cristina blushed and stammered her thanks, Daryn kissed her on the cheek, then moved to Paul. With a great show of formality, she pressed her palm against his, then gripped his elbow with her free hand. "I might have made you vice president," she said in a voice pitched to reach the edge of the family circle but not a breath beyond. "But you'll have more years to influence America in this position. Congratulations, Counselor."

A moment later, Paul followed the president and led his family into the Rose Garden, where Daryn stepped onto a platform draped with red, white, and blue bunting. A mantle of clouds had blown in to cover the sky, but shafts of bright sunlight dropped through the clouds like erstwhile spotlights. Daryn stood in one sunbeam, her blonde hair gleaming for the television cameras.

Before the platform, political dignitaries, White House staffers, and a veritable mob of writers, newspaper photographers, and television camera operators—pencils, stills, and sticks in White House parlance—crowded the garden. Boom microphones punctuated the crowd like dangling apostrophes, while a sea of reflective camera lenses winked up at Paul while the president spoke.

"During the past half-century," Daryn began, "Supreme Court appointments have become high-stakes political battles, with opposing parties using intelligent and qualified candidates as foot soldiers in the struggle for power. Intense special-interest groups, the media, and the Congress have all waged war in this arena. All of those participants have significantly constrained the degree to which a president may control the selection process."

She slipped a manicured hand into her suit pocket, then cast her blazing smile across the assembled group. "Ladies and gentlemen, distinguished guests, I am calling for an end to this partisan struggle. After accepting Chief Justice Haynes's resignation, I searched my heart to find the one individual who would best serve the country and the Court, and I believe I have found such a man. I have known him for years; he is a dear friend, but more important, he is a man of remarkable intellect, considerable candor, and resolute moral courage. You may remember him from the desperate days in which those of us who value freedom struggled to honor a mother's sacrifice by insuring that her son remained in the country for which she had risked her life. Or perhaps you know my friend from work he has done for you in Miami, or as a young law student in the legal services organization affiliated with Yale University. If you are lucky enough to know him, you know why I have not hesitated to submit his name for the Supreme Court. If you are not fortunate enough to have met my friend, let me introduce him to you now: Mr. Paul Santana."

Turning, Daryn lifted her hands in applause. As the crowd followed her example, Paul walked forward, shook her hand, and saw a hint of tears above her smile.

His heart beating heavily, he stood before the lectern and gazed at the sea of blinding lenses and curious faces. "Thank you, Madam President, and thank you, distinguished guests. This is not a position I would have chosen, nor is it one I accept lightly. I'll be honest—when I came to Washington, I looked forward to meeting new people and new challenges. I never expected to be standing here, for in all my years in the legal profession, I have never spent even an hour behind the bench. But I am committed to serving my country, and I count it a joy and honor to serve this president, Daryn Austin."

Fresh applause broke out, rising from the seated guests, punctuated by the whirring of cameras. Paul waited until the sound subsided, then finished: "I would also like to thank my family—my wife, Maria, and my daughter, Cristina—for allowing me to accept this opportunity. I look forward to appearing before the esteemed members of the Senate and answering any questions or concerns they might have."

Glancing down, he took a moment to clear his throat and rein in his galloping thoughts. "It has come to my attention," he looked up, "that some have reservations concerning my lack of judicial experience. But if you will study the backgrounds of the justices who served on the illustrious 1980–81 Supreme Court, you will find that of those nine, only six had served on lower courts, and in four of those six instances the justices served only for an average of five years. Rarely does a congressional session end without someone proposing that judicial experience be set as a requirement for service upon the Supreme Court, but time and time again the Congress—two-thirds of whom are lawyers—agrees that bench experience is not essential for service.

"In 1939 Melvin Tolson, father to our current Justice Kenneth Tolson, wrote, 'Putting a black robe on a man doesn't make him give just decisions any more than putting a suit on a monkey makes him a man.'"

A ripple of laughter followed this comment, and Paul smiled, relieved. Thrusting his hands behind his back, he lifted his chin and looked out upon the largest crowd he had addressed.

"Even so, in my opinion a clear head and a servant's heart are far more excellent indicators of whether an individual is qualified for a seat on the Supreme Court than the number of years he has served behind the bench. I'm looking forward to being examined by the Senate Judiciary Committee, which will have a crack at looking inside my head, but I trust the people will evaluate my heart."

Turning, he faced Daryn. "Thank you, Madam President, for your faith in me. I shall do my best to honor it."

•

That afternoon, under a relentless sun that made the air quiver and shimmy as it rose from the streets, Thrasher and O'Leary escorted Paul to the Richard B. Russell Senate Office Building. "Your ultimate task," Thrasher said, panting as they walked through the stifling heat, "is to convince ten out of eighteen senators on the Judiciary Committee to approve your nomination, then fifty-one out of the one hundred members of the Senate. We'd love to have 100 percent approval, but we'll take what we can get."

O'Leary, who flanked Paul's opposite side, kept a wary eye on the sidewalk as he dispensed advice. "I'll be wanting to remind you that today we're just here to make friends, Paul, so let them talk and have a look at you. They won't be tearing you up today—they'll save that for the televised hearings. They'll want to look tough for the folks back home."

Paul grimaced. "Is that supposed to reassure me?"

"That's how the game is played, Counselor." Thrasher's grin widened. "When the TV time comes, play along. Let them hammer you, smile, then stick to your guns and say only what you want printed in the next day's paper. Just keep bringing the topic back to the president's policies and you'll do fine. We've researched all the hot issues, and we know what will score points with the American people."

"You might want to mention your wife and daughter a wee bit," O'Leary added as they neared the ground floor entrance. "And have them in the audience, sitting right behind you. Since the president is single, we need to align her with a solid family man. You're perfect."

Sometimes perfection is an illusion.

Keeping his thoughts to himself, Paul felt the silent pressure of scores of curious eyes as they stepped into a line of men and women moving briskly into the building's security queue. No need to ask if any of these people had been watching TV this morning; most offices on the Hill had as many televisions as computers. Without a doubt, political Washingtonians now knew his face. The thought took some getting used to.

Thrasher led the way past the security checkpoint, then pushed the brass button on an elevator. "No need to worry, these are only preliminary visits." He stepped back and slipped his hand in his coat pocket, a forced posture of casualness. "Just wanting to give them a chance to meet you before the hearings start. Nothing formal here, nothing on the record."

Who was he trying to soothe?

"Nothing to be nervous about," Paul parroted, bringing his hand to his jaw to hide a sarcastic smile.

"Nothing at all," O'Leary echoed as the elevator opened.

Senator Hank Beatty, the Senate majority leader and an esteemed Republican from South Carolina, immediately asked to meet with Paul alone.

"It's not that I don't like you boys," he said, grinning at Thrasher and O'Leary. "I just want to see if Mr. Santana can put two words together for himself."

Paul smiled, mentally granting the bellicose senator two points for audacity.

With a tip of his head, he gestured toward the inner office door. "I would count it an honor to meet with you privately."

"That's the spirit." The senator slapped Paul's back, then pointed toward a leather sofa in his comfortable reception area. "You boys just make yourselves at home while Mr. Santana and I have ourselves a little chat."

The gregarious bonhomie evaporated the moment the door closed behind them. "Have a seat, Mr. Santana," Beatty said, slapping the padded guest chair as he lumbered by on his way to his desk. "This won't take long, and I promise not to bite."

Paul waited until Beatty lowered his bulk behind the desk, then accepted the offered seat. Staring at Paul with slightly hooded eyes, Beatty said, "Word is, Mr. Santana, that you and the president go way back."

"Yes, that's true. We went to law school together."

"Word is you were more than just friends, if you get my drift."

The man had good sources. Paul met the senator's gaze without flinching. "We were lovers, yes."

"Word is you might be lovers now."

Ripples of shock began to spread from an epicenter in Paul's stomach, tingling the crown of his head. He blinked slowly, concentrating on keeping his facial muscles under control. "I had no idea, Senator, that you listened to idle gossip."

"Then you deny that you are now sleeping with the president?"

Nodding through a vague sense of unreality, Paul folded his hands. "I deny that I am now sleeping with the president." He shot the senator a penetrating look. "Is this the sort of innuendo you intend to circulate in the next few weeks? If so, sir, I must protest. I have a wife and daughter."

Beatty shook his head, an easy smile playing at the corners of his mouth. "I hate dirty politics, Mr. Santana, but sometimes you've got to know how deep a manure pile lies in the path ahead. If you tell me you and the president aren't exchanging pillow talk, I'll believe you . . . unless I hear otherwise."

Paul ran his hands over his thighs as blood pounded thickly in his ears. The statement he'd made was true enough, if one were splitting hairs, for he and Daryn hadn't slept together in a couple of weeks. But if Beatty snooped in the right places and offered the right reward . . .

He forced a remote dignity into his voice. "I'd like to know where you heard such an inflammatory story."

Surprisingly, the senator laughed. "Come on, Santana, don't go getting your boxers in a knot. Rumors flow like water around here, or haven't you realized that? I know you've been a mite sheltered, spending all that time in the West Wing—"

"I've never enjoyed idle gossip. Particularly when it concerns people I care for."

Beatty's expression of good humor faded. "Well, sir, that's the rub, isn't it? If scandal didn't sting, there'd be no sport in pursuing it."

Standing, the portly senator took a moment to hitch up his belt, then he stepped from behind the desk and thrust out his hand. "Glad to meet you, Mr. Santana, and glad we got that little bit of gossip laid to rest. You don't have to fear me as long as you're honest. I reckon I can forgive about anything, 'cept a liar."

Paul stood, accepted the senator's meaty hand, then made his way toward the door. Beatty followed, extending boisterous apologies to Thrasher and Alexander as he crossed the room. Paul took advantage of their distracted attention to lean against the wall.

His initial nervousness had passed, but without it he felt empty.

TWENTY-TWO

"And now the Great Whore of Babylon has heaped another indignity upon our heads."

Straightening, Clive lifted his head and studied the speaker. Jimmy Griffin had sent e-mails to all his flock that afternoon, calling them forth for an emergency seven-thirty meeting of the True People.

Now Jimmy paced the rough wooden platform, the pearls of sweat on his forehead gleaming in the single overhead light.

"She has nominated a Communist to the sacred Supreme Court! She has struck another blow against the White Race, ignoring the thousands of qualified white men who could serve the nation, in order to uplift and exalt a Latino, a Cuban, a Miami espanol-o! And his name? Santana! Like the heathen rock group, like the religion that sacrifices chickens and works voodoo in the night, like Satan, the one who was cast down! Look at the letters in that name—S-A-T-A-N-A—and tell me she hasn't flaunted evil in our faces! And today she did it in the White House Rose Garden, parading him and his Cuban family in front of the entire nation!"

Clive felt his stomach sway. He'd worked at his cabin all day, running out only once for a burger he ate in his truck. He hadn't heard about this latest indecency.

Jimmy leaned over the wooden pulpit, slanting it toward the assembled membership. "Face the truth, brothers and sisters! The Whore of Babylon is planning to institute a one-world government with Jews and Cubans and Negroes at the helm. This infernal team will not be dedicated to the advancement of the White Race—it will seek to tear us down! Look at the results listed in Deuteronomy 32:24."

He picked up his battered Bible and flipped a few pages, then bowed his head and began to read. "'They shall be burnt with hunger, and devoured with burning heat, and with bitter destruction.'" His voice boomed like measured thunder. "'I will also send the teeth of beasts upon them, with the poison of serpents of the dust.'"

Jimmy paused, his blue eyes scanning the crowd with the intensity of a searchlight. Clive struggled to hold his head high—though he had not done all he could to keep America white, he'd certainly done his fair share. Not a week went by that he didn't drive to Wilson, Moose, or Moran to mail a letter to the White House. Once he'd even crossed the state line into Idaho to mail a letter from a dusty hole-in-the-wall where a sign proudly proclaimed "Welcome to Victor, Population 323." Let the feds figure that one out.

"God will make us hungry!" Jimmy roared, thumping his Bible to the stand. "Are you hungry for oil? For gasoline? Sure you are! This is a judgment of God!"

His vibrant voice drew groans and cries from the upturned faces. "God says he will devour us with heat!" Smiling, he wiped his dripping brow with a shirt sleeve. "Can any of you say you're not hot?"

Clive nodded, feeling a trickle of sweat course down his own spine. The sun had been hotter'n blazes today, especially when he went out to get his lunch. Seems like the weather got hotter every year, and he *knew* it had nothing to do with any hole in the ozone. That was a myth concocted by Washington bureaucrats.

"God says he will send bitter destruction upon us," Jimmy went on, moving to the front of the platform. He perched there, his toes jutting out from the edge, and tucked his thumbs beneath the lapels of his denim jacket. "Violence and crime have come to America through two-legged beasts who roam our streets and our countryside. Most of the crime in this country is committed by the aliens who dwell among us. Most of the crime is committed *against* white people *by* the minorities. The serpent who will come among us is Mystery Babylon, the Mother of Harlots, and she is living in the White House!"

Voices rose in the building, outraged tones in a deep, angry buzz, like bees from a disturbed hive. Hate beat a bitter rhythm in Clive's heart and set his blood to pounding in his ears.

"Brothers and sisters!" Jimmy raised his hand. "We cannot let this tide continue unabated! Will you join me in prayer for our nation? Will you do your part to preserve the White Race?"

"I will!"

"Yes!"

"Count on me!"

Energized by a common desire, the members of the True People stood, their hands uplifted. Clive leaped to his feet with the others, holding his hand high to be counted. He didn't know what he'd be called to do, but surely he'd be granted a special task. The War on Washington could not be postponed forever.

Until his way was clear, he'd continue writing his letters. When Judgment Day came, the woman in the White House could not deny she'd been warned aplenty.

●

"Counselor?"

With the phone to his ear, Paul lowered the case report he'd been reading and frowned. The voice was Daryn's, but she'd never called him at home.

"Madam President?"

She laughed softly. "Surprise. And don't worry, this is a secure line . . . as long as you're not on a cordless phone."

"I'm not." Still . . . he frowned, thinking of the telephone extensions. But there'd be a click on the line if Maria picked up—

"I miss you." Her words came out hoarse, as if forced through a tight throat.

He wanted to point out that *she'd* made the decision to exile him from the White House, then understanding dawned. She wasn't in Washington; Tom Harris had arranged a meet-and-greet somewhere out on the campaign trail.

He glanced out the open door, but nothing moved in the hallway outside his study. "Where are you?"

"The Beverly Wilshire." She managed a short laugh. "The presidential suite is palatial. Like the rooms you see in movies. And they're modern—not an antique in sight."

He knew she was waiting for some kind of romantic comment, but something in him resisted.

"The weather's hot here," he said, making an effort to keep the conversation on safe ground. Maria might come up the stairs at any minute . . .

"The weather?" Her voice cooled. "What's wrong, Counselor?"

"Nothing."

"Don't avoid the question; I know you too well. You don't talk about the weather unless you're preoccupied with something else."

He considered bluffing, then decided to be honest. "I've been making friendly little visits to members of the Senate Judiciary Committee the last couple of days."

"I know, that's why I called. How are things going?"

"Fine. I let them talk; I answer a few questions."

"So?"

"Yesterday I had a meeting with Senator Hank Beatty."

She exhaled softly into the phone. "And how is the senator these days?"

"Feeling pretty good, I think. Pretty powerful, at least. He must have some friends in high places, because he knew about our past. He also asked me about our *present* relationship."

"We are friends who respect one another. That's the public image."

"Beatty seemed to have a pretty good handle on the private picture. Nothing concrete, but I got the impression he wouldn't mind setting a couple of bloodhounds on our trail."

The line hummed in a short silence, then: "He can't prove a thing. None of my people will talk."

"What if they do?"

"If they *would*, they'd have already phoned Larry King. And Beatty would already be talking about a special prosecutor."

Rising up in his chair, Paul leaned forward to scan the hall for Maria's shadow. She had gone to bed early with a headache, but she might wake and wander down to the kitchen for a glass of water.

Silence flowed from the hallway, but Paul lowered his voice. "There will be no special prosecutor. You haven't done anything illegal. Immoral, maybe, but not illegal. After all, Clinton wasn't impeached for fooling around with his intern, but for lying about it. So unless you've given any sworn testimony lately—"

"I haven't."

"Neither have I." He thought a moment, remembering his conversation in Beatty's office. "I misled Beatty, though. And now I'm wondering if that will come back to haunt us."

She sighed heavily. "I don't want to debate the matter with you, Counselor. I'm tired, lonely, and not up to a wrestling match with your conscience." She hesitated, then: "So—what, exactly, did you tell him?"

"I told him we had been lovers in college. And I was not now sleeping with the president."

She laughed. "As in right this minute?"

"I applied a broader context to the word—as in the last couple of weeks. He seemed to accept it."

She fell silent for a moment, and when she spoke again he heard a smile in her voice. "The poll numbers are great, Paul. Approval ratings are at 60 percent, and they rise to 70 percent when your name is mentioned. The men approve of you, and the women think you're the hottest thing in shoe leather. The grandmothers want to bless your name for Elian's sake."

"Polls, unfortunately, don't hold much sway with the staid senators on the Judiciary Committee. I recently read that Senator Wardell believes Washington's absorption in reading polls is only slightly more advanced than our ancestors' fascination with reading the entrails of goats."

Daryn laughed. "Remember, Counselor, what politicians say and what they mean are two different things. We'll make sure every senator on that committee knows how popular you are with the home folks—especially those who are up for reelection. Just give us a couple more weeks. We'll have you seated on the Court by the beginning of the next term."

"You'd better hurry. There are some significant cases on the docket."

"Don't worry. I'm so certain you'll be approved that in my standard stump speech I'm citing your nomination as one of my most brilliant accomplishments. I wouldn't have nominated you if I thought you were a risk. If I can't get my candidate confirmed in the Senate, what would that say about my ability to pass legislation?"

"Not much," Paul murmured, playing along.

"Darn right." He could almost see her emphatic nod. "So do your best, and I'll support you every step of the way. Because what you do in the next few days will mean everything to the future of this nation." Her voice softened to a dreamy tone. "Think of the good we can do together, Paul—think of how we can impact history. We used to dream of making a difference, and now our hard work has resulted in more opportunities than we ever imagined."

Staring at the play of sunlight and shadow on the paneled wall of his study, Paul marveled at the woman's ability to sprinkle even a casual phone call with political fairy dust.

TWENTY-THREE

On Monday morning, June 28, Paul went before the Senate Judiciary Committee and the nation. The week before committee members had questioned him in a private session, a ritual that had been instituted after the difficult confirmation of Justice Kenneth Tolson in '91. During Tolson's televised confirmation hearings, liberal opposition to the conservative nominee had dredged up accusations ranging from drug abuse to wife beating. When none of those charges proved true, his opponents found an unhappy former coworker who testified that Kenneth Tolson had sexually harassed her. While the nation watched in mingled fascination and disgust, Tolson and his wife endured a seemingly endless succession of character assassins, each more tawdry than the last.

Paul's closed-door session had been exactly what he expected—someone mentioned rumors of an affair with the president, he denied them, the committee members leaned back in their chairs and chewed on their thoughts. Many of them were obviously uncomfortable with the close friendship between the president and the judicial nominee, but to make an issue of the relationship would carry the conversation into gender-based issues none of them wanted to risk. After all, other presidents had been friendly with the men they nominated for the Court . . .

Now Paul sat before the committee for the final time, exercising patience while they moved through questions designed more to prove to their constituents that they'd left no stone unturned than to uncover any useful information about the man now being called "Austin's stealth candidate."

While television cameras recorded every sigh and cautious smile, the assembled eighteen senators preened for the camera, swiped at their brows, and stared at him from over the tops of their reading glasses. They asked pointed questions about abortion, affirmative action, gun control, and civil rights while Paul repeatedly asserted that a judge was sworn to decide impartially and offer no forecasts of his opinions. "To do so," he said, staring into Senator Beatty's round face, "would show disregard not only for the particular case, but also for the entire judicial process."

"Would you," asked another senator, "see yourself as a Republican or Democrat?"

"My politics are not partisan," Paul answered. "Neither do I see myself as conservative or liberal. As a justice I would seek to uphold the rights granted in the Constitution, not to rewrite it. But—" he paused at a flurry of uplifted brows—"I believe it is important to realize we are not the same country we were when the Founding Fathers wrote the Constitution. In 1787 slaves were not citizens and women could not vote. Our society has changed, for the better, I believe, and I will do my best to write opinions that correctly interpret the principles of freedom without infringing the rights of any."

"So you believe in the nonoriginalist approach to constitutional interpretation?"

"When appropriate," Paul said, searching for the senator who had spoken. "It is impossible to plumb the understanding of men dead for two hundred years, so we cannot concentrate upon discerning the intent of our Constitution's framers. The nonoriginalist approach, which recognizes that speech in the Constitution is deliberately and often purposefully vague, allows our national law to evolve over time. This approach, gentlemen, guarantees that our Constitution will stand for centuries without being amended to accommodate every ideological quibble of the moment."

The senator from Massachusetts, whose heavy cheeks fell in worried folds over his collar, gripped his microphone. "You have been affiliated with the president for nearly a year," he said, his voice flat and accusatory. "You left the practice of law to work for the executive branch, so how can we believe you will serve the judicial—"

"My time in the White House was spent interpreting legal situations for the president," Paul interrupted. "Besides, while it is true that a justice naturally draws on his or her own values and perspectives in approaching cases, most justices act not as politicians but as adjudicators. They must work within the constraints of legal precedent to give judicial answers to problems that come to the Court. They do not seek cases; they represent no clients. As such they are not engaging in politics, but in something higher."

"This *something higher—"* Senator Warren Wardell, a Republican from Florida, gripped his microphone—"do you follow the principles of a particular religious creed?"

Obeying one of Thrasher's most insistent orders—*If religion comes up, be pleasant*—Paul gave the senator his most engaging smile. "I believe, Senator Wardell, that religion is a private matter, with no place in a man's public life."

Wardell's brows drew together. "You think religion has no bearing at all? Do you not recall that this country was founded by men who prayed? That an image of Moses and the Ten Commandments decorates the hallowed courtroom to which you now aspire?"

For a long moment Paul studied the flushing senator, then leaned into the microphone on the shiny dark desk. From the corner of his eye, he saw a video cameraman waddle closer, the unblinking lens turning silently as it devoured his image.

"I believe," he said, choosing his words with the precision of a sculptor, "that all religions affect the country by affecting the individuals who adhere to them. As for myself, I choose to follow principles that require me to treat my fellow men and women fairly, kindly, and with integrity. I have learned, however, not to cling to broad rules, for if I speak too broadly, if I advocate too open a solution, I may bind myself down the road. There are always exceptions to the rule."

Wardell seemed about to choke on something. "Indeed?"

"You will find," Paul added, his wedding ring clunking against the mike as he gripped it, "that I'm not afraid of hard work or independent judgment. I am wary, however, of absolutes."

With an officious rustling of papers, Senator Beatty took charge of the questioning. "Some of our colleagues—" he peered at Paul over a pair of horn-rims—"have expressed concern about your close working relationship with President Austin."

Aware of the cameras, Paul forced a smile. "President Austin is an old and dear friend of mine, just as she's a friend to many of you. But we are not cut of identical cloth."

He exhaled in relief when Beatty nodded, apparently satisfied. "Well, Mr. Santana," the senator said, glancing left and right at his colleagues, "I must say I am delighted by your openness and your answers. It has been a pleasure to sit on a panel where inquiry rather than injury motivates our queries. Your pleasantness has made congeniality prevail over confrontation, and we are pleased to be entering a new era of bipartisan cooperation. I think I can confidently say that your ability, character, intellect, and temperament to serve on the Supreme Court are not in question. Our primary concerns have to do with relationship and experience—"

"Which," Paul said, daring to interrupt the senator's speech, "I hope I've answered clearly. I bring twenty-five years' experience in the practice of law to the Court. And as a junior justice, I will gain the experience I lack while being guided by eight of the finest legal minds in this country."

"No one is denying your legal experience, Mr. Santana." This from Senator Lombard, a stalwart conservative from Michigan. "Nor your sincerity."

The hearing broke up shortly after Beatty's final speech, and the next day, after a Judiciary Committee vote of twelve to six, his name was submitted to the Senate for approval along with Franklin's.

●

On July 2, the final workday before the Senate's July fourth recess, the Senate met to vote upon President Austin's judicial nominees.

Watching C-SPAN from his study at home, Paul reclined with his feet propped atop his desk as the Senate voted to confirm Edward Franklin as chief justice of the Supreme Court. The vote passed with little comment; Franklin had long ago proven his competence.

Paul told himself his own confirmation didn't matter. He hadn't wanted the job. If for some reason a majority of the Senate couldn't accept a Hispanic lawyer with no judicial experience, he'd be content with their decision.

Pressing his hand to his mouth, he stared at the television screen. He could lie to a lot of people, but never to himself. Daryn had injected him with a taste of real power, and like a junkie, he now yearned for more.

After a round of applause for the new chief justice, the vice president, Lawrence Frey, called on each senator to register his or her vote on the matter of the nomination of Paul Santana for associate justice. After a tedious and time-consuming oral vote, during which Paul filled three pages of his legal pad with doodling, the verdict was tallied: by a vote of sixty-four to thirty-six, the Senate had consented to the nomination of Paul Santana for the position of Supreme Court associate justice.

Paul exhaled in a long sigh, then grinned at Maria as she ran into the room. Bending, she wrapped her arms about his shoulders. "I watched from the bedroom," she whispered, breathing into his ear. "Congratulations, Pablo. God has brought you to this place, and now he will use you."

Clapping his hands on her arms, Paul stared at the image of Lawrence Frey, who was giving the camera an enthusiastic thumbs-up.

God, of course, had nothing to do with it. The day's victory belonged solely to Daryn Austin.

●

"Madam President, thank you for seeing me on such short notice."

Daryn blew out a breath. "What is so urgent, Mr. Quinn?" She had four meetings scheduled, two briefings, and a session with the White House photographer, but Quinn had convinced Thrasher to squeeze him into her schedule. Both men sat across from her desk now, and Quinn wore the expression of a man on an unpleasant duty.

"It's this, ma'am." Quinn slid a file across her desk. "For some time we've been receiving letters from a man—at least we're pretty sure it's a man—who calls himself *Jehu*. We don't think it's much of a threat, but since you're traveling out west this month—"

"He lives out west?"

"Wyoming, probably. Or even Idaho. He's been careful to mail the letters from different towns, but the towns aren't spaced far enough apart for him to be a truckdriver or other long-distance operator. So we're sure he's being deliberately deceptive."

She gave him a questioning look. "So he probably lives in—?"

"In or around Jackson. It's the largest town within the circle of the postmarks. But if you're coming within a couple of days driving distance, he could show up."

She flipped the file open, then read the letter at the top of the stack: "'Dear Whore of Babylon . . .' Good grief, he's a religious nut. Don't you have a special file for those?"

"The Protective Research Division keeps tabs on all these cases—they've got a file on Jehu that grows with each letter. From our profilers we've determined that he's probably single, eighteen to twenty-five, and a high-school graduate, no college. He's zealous, committed, and a racist. In his letters you'll note several references to the white nation."

Daryn crinkled her nose as she read another line. "Ye shall make her desolate and naked, and shall eat her flesh, and burn her with fire?" She frowned at Quinn. "What kind of raving idiocy is this?"

"It's, um, Scripture, Madam President. And a lot of people take Scripture seriously."

"The mainstream religious groups don't take that stuff literally,"

Thrasher was quick to add. "This guy's obviously on the fringe. But his consistency bothers us. We've been getting an average of a letter a week since you took office, and Jehu's tone is escalating in intensity."

Shaking her head, Daryn snapped the folder closed. "Agent Quinn, I respect you and your men completely. You don't have to show this stuff to me; I'd go nuts if I dwelt on it. You tell me when to duck, and I'll do it."

Quinn shot Thrasher a sharp look. "Well, ma'am . . ."

"It's like this, Madam President." Thrasher folded his arms. "You wanted to walk a rope line in Denver. No can do. It's only four hundred miles from Jehu's territory."

Daryn scowled. "Are you telling me that the president of the United States can't get out and shake a few hands if she wants to?"

"Not in Denver, ma'am." Quinn's frown matched her own. "This man is certifiably dangerous."

"Oh, come on!" Daryn leaned back in her chair. "With all the manpower we have at our disposal—"

"Too many variables, ma'am. Denver is a no-go for the rope line. You can shake hands within the perimeter inside the building."

"Why would I want to shake hands with two hundred people who are already supporters?" She raked her nails through her hair. "They'll be paying five hundred bucks a plate; their votes are already committed! I need to be out where the undecideds are, out among the crowd!"

Quinn looked at her in patient amusement, but didn't speak. Thrasher shook his head. "No."

"Well—" Daryn dropped her hands into her lap—"if you two are going to tell me what we can and cannot do, I suppose there's a little problem here. I seem to recall that one of my titles is commander in chief, and if I can't command the Secret Service, what in the heck am I doing here?"

Quinn lifted a finger. "May I remind you, ma'am, that the law prohibits you from declining Secret Service protection?"

Daryn's mood veered sharply to anger. "I'm not declining; I'm *modifying.* If I want to meet-and-greet or walk a rope line, you need to find a way it can be done."

Folding his hands, Thrasher adopted a more relaxed posture. "The service routinely tracks people on their watch list whenever the president is in the vicinity. The problem with Denver is that they haven't yet identified this Jehu character. So there's no way to sit on him for the duration of your visit—"

"Madam President—" Quinn tipped his head back—"pardon the interruption, but as you may know, my wife works in the correspondence department."

Daryn stared at him, stupefied. What was she supposed to do, congratulate him?

"Anyway, the other day Gayle told me an interesting story. Seems that in 1939 President Franklin Roosevelt got a letter that almost went straight to the kook file—it was filled with misspellings and cross-outs, and it had been typed on a rickety typewriter. Worse yet, the author said he had developed a theory that could lead to an explosive device that might one day destroy the world."

He paused, looking to Thrasher, who silently nodded.

Quinn lifted one shoulder in a shrug. "Today we'd probably send that letter to the Protective Research Division and forget about it unless the guy wrote again, but a correspondence clerk in 1939 had the perspicacity to forward the letter to the president. It was from a man no one had heard of at the time: Albert Einstein."

Daryn froze into blankness as Quinn leaned closer.

"So you see, ma'am, we take every letter seriously. And we strongly recommend that you do your utmost to cooperate with us in Denver. You can shake hands till the sun goes down, but we'd like you to shake the hands of people we know. All right?"

She nodded in mute agreement.

●

Two weeks after the Senate vote, Daryn sat on the edge of the bed in the Denver Hilton presidential suite and pressed the volume control on the remote. On the other side of the country, where it was 4 P.M. and late enough to give the networks a good feed for their evening news, Paul Santana stood with his wife and daughter in the East Room of the White House, preparing to take the oath of office.

Daryn felt her eyes sting as she stared at the image of Paul, erect, somber, grave. She would have given anything to stand beside him, but O'Leary had wisely suggested that it might be more appropriate if she stayed away. After reading transcripts of the Senate Judiciary hearings, she had to agree. Her appearance would only add fuel to the speculation about her relationship with her first Supreme Court nominee, and at this point in the campaign she couldn't afford speculation.

The camera zoomed in on Lawrence Frey, who appeared tall and statuesque behind the blue goose and the presidential seal. Frey had all the personality of a dishtowel, but he'd tested well with the focus groups, who saw his sturdy silhouette as a complement to her slender, more feminine form. His politics were traditional, his charisma only average, but he knew what she expected of him and he didn't seem to mind his role as permanent stand-in and international ambassador.

Besides, she was treating him with far more respect than Parker had treated her. She'd given Frey the responsibility for foreign relations, explaining that her primary concerns were domestic. So while Frey worked to ease slavery in the Sudan and jaunted around the globe, she allowed his wife to oversee White House social functions and thrill the political ladies-who-lunched. The partnership wasn't particularly dynamic, but it worked.

The crowd noise hushed, the CNN announcer lowered his voice to a golf tournament whisper, and the camera zoomed in on Frey's dark head. "Thank you," he said, flashing a smile around the room. "The president asked me to share a few words from her heart, since she cannot be here on this important occasion."

Daryn moved closer to the television. The speech would hold no surprises—it had come from her best speechwriter and she'd approved every word—but she wanted to be sure Frey delivered it well.

"Welcome to the White House," he began, looking only a little less robotic as he shone a smile at the camera. He proceeded to welcome members of Congress, the Supreme Court, and members of the Santana family, many of whom had flown in from Miami.

"American citizens from the southern tip of Florida to the northernmost point of Alaska have written us in support of Paul Santana. What prompted them is what brought you here today—the desire to honor a man who symbolizes the American ideals, the values of faith and family, of freedom and hard work. Paul Santana has given his life in service to the concept that all men are created equal, with an equal right to protection under the law. When we ask our justices to uphold the Constitution, we entrust to them the laws that give life to our American principles. Paul Santana now joins the ranks of the distinguished jurists to whom we entrust this sacred task, who, in the stark and simple words of Chief Justice John Marshall, will tell us 'what the law is.'"

Daryn blew out her cheeks, then shifted her gaze from Frey to Paul. She couldn't see his face in this camera shot, but from the way his leg jiggled below his clasped hands, she could tell he was suffering from a case of the jitters.

"Paul Santana," Frey continued, "did not travel the usual road to service in the nation's highest court. The son of refugees from Cuba, he grew up appreciating the freedoms and fairness under the law most Americans take for granted. His intellect earned him a place at Yale University, and his academic prowess took him to the very top of his class. Yet, though he could have served in any law firm in this nation, he chose to return home, to serve his people and others who sought the same freedom and fairness he'd come to value in America."

Daryn nodded in approval. She'd inserted that bit about *his people* specifically to please Hispanic voters.

"Paul Santana has known the love of friends and family—his wife and daughter stand with him today. His rise to prominence demonstrates that America does value integrity and perseverance, and his concern for the common man will serve him well on the nation's highest tribunal."

Daryn studied the wife and daughter. The girl was lovely, dark and exotic looking like her father, but the wife looked like a little plump wren.

"Do not be overawed by the solemnity of this moment." Frey lifted his gaze to smile, then lowered it back to his paper. Daryn resisted a chuckle. She could almost hear him giving the smile a three-count.

"Celebrate today," Frey finished. "Celebrate this son of America, this friend of the family. America is honored to have a man of this character seated upon its highest court."

As the spectators applauded and the camera shifted, Daryn leaned closer and studied Paul's face. His half-smile might be called abashed, even humble, by those who watched on television, but she suspected the speech had stirred his mostly latent religious guilt. Paul had never warmed to the spotlight, and this kind of attention, if prolonged, would make him miserable.

The vice president turned. "If Mr. Chief Justice Franklin, Mr. Santana, and Mrs. Santana would step forward."

Turning slightly, Frey extended his hand toward Paul, a gesture that seemed stiff and practiced. Paul stepped forward, shadowed by the chief justice and Maria Santana.

The new chief justice administered the oath of office. As Paul began to recite the words, Daryn pressed her hand to her throat and fought back tears.

"I, Paul Santana, do solemnly swear that I will administer justice without respect to persons, and do equal right to the poor and to the rich, and that I will faithfully and impartially discharge and perform all the duties incumbent upon me as an associate justice of the Supreme Court under the Constitution and laws of the United States. So help me, God."

Daryn gulped back a sob as the small crowd in the East Room applauded. This was *her* moment—hers and Paul's—and only the petty spitefulness of public opinion had kept them apart. But she could still enjoy it. And if they never shared another private minute for as long as she remained in the White House, she would know she'd sacrificed his companionship for a noble cause.

As the camera followed Paul's movements down the line of dignitaries, she pressed her hand to the television screen. Upon reaching the lectern, he stopped and faced the crowd. "Thank you, Mr. Vice

President," he said, his voice strong and sure. "Thank you, Mr. Chief Justice. And thank you, every one of you, who have come today."

He smiled the drowsy smile she loved, then gripped the blue goose with both hands. "I'm grateful to President Austin for appointing me to a position of such responsibility. I appreciate the personal time and attention she gave to the selection process, and I'm grateful for the able work of the White House staff."

"I am especially thankful to the Senate Judiciary Committee and its capable chairman, Senator Hank Beatty. That committee has a central role in preserving our democracy and defending the rule of law. So I thank the committee and the full Senate for their decision to confirm me, and I will do my best as a member of the Supreme Court to justify the confidence President Austin and the Senate have placed in me."

"I must not, however, neglect to thank my wife and daughter, both of whom have endured twenty-two and a half hours of public confirmation hearings. Just as they sat behind me during the confirmation process, they have stood behind me in life, encouraging me all the way. I can honestly say I would not have come to Washington without their support; nor would I be standing before you today."

Daryn felt the corner of her mouth droop. The wife and daughter had nothing to do with his success . . . still, such public praise was necessary and expected. The image of a doting wife and adoring daughter would help dispel rumors about the president and her handsome Supreme Court nominee.

The campaign was on track, and this successful day had propelled her miles down the line. Within three months the campaign would be over and she could get down to the serious business of changing government as usual. First on the agenda would be sweeping out the remaining Parker appointees, along with the stubborn fools who had insisted on maintaining the man's so-called legacy. She'd have dozens of appointments to make in the appeals courts, new heads of agencies to employ, *and* a persuasive associate justice in place with the Supremes . . .

She sank to the carpet and wrapped her arms around her bent knees, engulfed in a bittersweet tide of mingled triumph and despair.

TWENTY-FOUR

FOR PAUL, THE FOLLOWING DAYS FELL LIKE AUTUMN leaves from a maple tree, one after the other, almost indistinguishable. While Daryn campaigned energetically through the month of July, he stayed in his home office, working in bare feet, gym shorts, and a T-shirt. While the world of the West Wing whirled on without him, he studied constitutional law and devoured everything he could find about his new colleagues. Packages from the Court arrived almost daily, with petitions to be reviewed and motions to be considered.

In August, as the Republicans and Democrats rallied at noisy national conventions and named their official candidates (Howard Reynolds and Chad Foster, respectively), he took Maria and Cristina on a two-week tour of the Peruvian rain forest, enjoying the opportunity to relax in a country that spoke his native tongue. As the moist night settled around him and the sound of cicadas and native birds lulled him to sleep, he could almost forget he lived in a white marble city.

In September, he sent Cristina back to Harvard as a sophomore. Maria moped around the house, dabbing at her leaky eyes, and Paul decided that the time had come to move into the Supreme Court. Though the term would not begin for another month, he wanted to set up his office, meet his secretary and law clerks, and get a feel for the place.

Once settled into his quarters, a plush paneled suite overlooking the marble steps and the Capitol Building, he spent his days preparing for cases scheduled for argument in the fall.

On the first Monday in October, while Maria watched from the visitors' chairs and Daryn campaigned in California, Paul took his seat at the boomerang-shaped bench and looked out upon a sea of anxious faces. An almost sacred atmosphere filled the courtroom, and everyone who entered, from the attorneys to the observers, seemed in awe of the place.

As the junior justice, Paul sat farthest to the right on the bench and in the annual photo; he also served as doorkeeper and messenger during the Court's private conferences. For two weeks the Court sat in public sessions, hearing oral arguments and delivering opinions. Those two weeks were followed by two private weeks of recess, used for conferences and writing opinions. Each week more than 130 petitions crossed his desk, each of which had to be carefully evaluated as to whether or not it should be heard by the full court.

Sometimes Paul felt that his life had become a never-ending cycle of reading, writing, and deliberating. He enjoyed the work, but the endless hours in his office proved tedious, for his thoughts inevitably turned to Daryn, then soured in frustration. The world thought they were friends and mutually supportive. Maria thought he was grateful for his position on the Court; everyone assured him that the president had given him a plum position other lawyers would sell their souls to claim.

But while part of him accepted that truth, even believed Daryn's claim that she'd put him on the Court because she loved him, he couldn't forget the way she had manipulated the former chief justice with a lie and a smile.

A niggling voice inside Paul's head insisted she had manipulated him as well . . . but with a kiss.

●

Alone in the sitting room off the presidential bedroom, Daryn stood at the window and watched fireworks cascade over the Washington Monument.

At midnight, Eastern Standard Time, CNN had proclaimed the election of the first female president. Against all odds, a woman running as an independent had defeated the Republican and Democratic candidates. She accepted concession speeches from her newly humbled opponents, then celebrated with her staff. As cameras clicked and video cameras whirred, she raised a glass of champagne, then promptly spilled the bubbly as dozens of carefully screened campaign workers—none of whom really knew her—embraced their new president in a frenzy of delight.

Within the hour, the talking heads took to the airwaves. The leadership of both the Republican and Democratic parties licked their wounds, pointedly worrying about the rise of a new "feminist" party.

"How can we oppose her? It's like firing a woman over forty," left-leaning columnist Brad Hershey proclaimed on a late-night call-in talk show. "You can't do it without getting slapped for age discrimination *and* sex discrimination. No, the best thing we Democrats can do is let Daryn Austin have her run and find another female candidate to carry our party banner in 2008."

On the other side of the debate, the congressional representatives who would have to work with Daryn during the next four years took turns praising her, using words like *unflappable* and *resolute*. Hank Beatty, who couldn't quite seem to bring himself to congratulate his newly elected president, reminded the national television audience that in '69 Richard Nixon had said, 'Certainly in the next fifty years we shall see a woman president . . . a woman can and should be able to do any political job a man can do.'"

Daryn had beaten Tricky Dick's deadline by fourteen years, and all of America apparently stayed up to celebrate. Now, as the hands of her watch edged toward 2 A.M., she sat in the darkened sitting room and idly scratched Tyson's velvety ears. The dog, lost in the delicious pleasure of his master's loving touch, exhaled deeply.

A light zipped across the sky, then flowered into a starburst of white and yellow, reminding her of the daisies Paul used to bring her back in New Haven. He didn't dare bring flowers now . . .

In fact, he might never send her flowers again.

This should have been the happiest night of her life, but what good was victory without someone to share it? Her father, for whom she had done all this, had not called. He had probably watched the news on television, then turned over to go to sleep. And Paul, who should have been by her side through the entire day and night, had retreated into the marble sanctuary to which she had exalted him.

She released a choked, desperate laugh, then reached for the glass of scotch on the table by her love seat. As she sipped, Tyson lifted his head, seeking the warmth of her caress, and something in the sight of his adoring dark eyes unraveled the strings of her composure. Daryn dropped the glass to the sofa, covered her face with trembling hands, and gave vent to the agony of her loss.

●

Since moving to the Court, Paul rarely spoke to the president, but he knew she'd been delighted by the election's outcome. Now she had a mandate, de facto permission from the people to change the status quo. Without waiting for the inauguration, she cleaned house as she'd promised, accepting the resignations of every Parker appointee who had not warmed to her leadership, and announced her new cabinet within two weeks of the election.

Every night Paul turned on the evening news and caught a glimpse of her day. In one single December week he saw video clips of Daryn conferring with Amir Jabir al-Ahman of Kuwait, signing a bill to continue appropriations for the next fiscal year, and nominating Michael G. Konig to be United States Ambassador to the Republic of El Salvador. In that week she also issued proclamations establishing National Disability Employment Awareness Month, National Women in Space Week, and National Elementary School Teachers Day.

She was, Paul had to admit, doing good things.

Just before Christmas, as snow dusted the streets of Washington and bright splashes of red appeared amid the marble, a national tabloid broke the story of Daryn's college relationship with Paul. The White House press secretary promptly responded with a statement acknowledging a youthful affair, and John Q. Public reacted with a sustained yawn.

At home, however, Paul tiptoed around the topic. He could pinpoint the day Maria first heard of the story by the strained look that appeared around her eyes, but despite the headlines that leered from every grocery store checkout stand, she refused to broach the subject. Paul suspected she had also warned Cristina against bringing it up. His daughter's phone calls remained newsy and Jason-centered, while Maria sang falsely cheerful carols around the house, made plans for Cristina's holiday homecoming, and shopped with more focus and determination than usual.

When Barbara Walters called, however, Paul knew the family could no longer ignore the story. Walters wanted to speak to *Mrs.* Justice Santana, and Paul urged Maria to refuse Walters's request. But Maria responded with a rare display of stubbornness, and in the televised Christmas Eve interview she proclaimed Paul the best husband any woman could want. Looking Walters directly in the eye, she told the country that the past was past, and if her husband had spent hours at the White House, it was because he was a hard worker and devoted to America.

"You don't know my Pablo," she told Walters, her dark eyes flashing. "I do. And I trust him with my heart."

Watching the special at home, with Maria seated at his side, Paul felt his wife gently squeeze his thigh. He knew he ought to take her hand, to say something, but he couldn't manage the right gesture or find the right words. Instead of whispering his thanks or slipping his arm around her shoulder, either of which would have been better than what he did do, he bolted from the sofa and strode to the kitchen, murmuring something about celebrations requiring a drink . . .

After the holiday recess, Paul's colleagues on the Court were kind enough to refrain from commenting on the TV special and the tabloid reports. They were a dignified group, as settled in their habits as they were in their custom-fitted seats around the angled bench. Through their silences, discreet glances, and pronounced propriety he learned that the Court considered itself above publicity, rumor, and political maneuvering. His fellow justices rarely spoke to members of the press, preferring to allow the public information officer to handle questions from the public and members of the media.

A mantle of dignity and secrecy surrounded the Court, and though Paul had been aware of it, he had no concept of its depth until he found himself beneath it. In a very short time, however, he grew to appreciate the invisible barrier that kept the justices above the fray. Cameras were not allowed in the courtroom, nor were tape recorders or notepads. And while members of Congress and the White House staff were often overcome with verbosity as they defended certain actions, the justices possessed neither the desire nor the inclination to explain themselves.

At a holiday cocktail party, Paul overheard a lawyer ask the chief justice about a recently issued opinion. Franklin smiled, then said, "I think I said it as well as I could in the opinion. If I could have been clearer, I would have."

After only a few weeks of working with his fellow justices, or "brethren," as they referred to themselves, females included, Paul learned to admire each of them. Lorne Crispin, Harold Woodward, and Kenneth Tolson comprised the conservative block, with whom Carolyn Cookson, the Court's first female justice, occasionally voted. Cookson and Charles Becket were considered the Court's moderate members, though Becket usually leaned toward the more liberal mind-sets of Edward Franklin, Teresa Richards, and James Layton. Paul knew Daryn expected him to be the fifth member of this liberal block, and, after taking his measure of his colleagues, he saw no reason to disappoint her.

"Yes," Justice Tolson told him one morning before a conference, "the Court is quiet. But it is the quiet one finds at the eye of a storm."

TWENTY-FIVE

BLINKING IN THE STING OF A JANUARY WIND, CLIVE stepped out of the Triple-A Clean Sweep van and shoved his hands in the pockets of his coveralls. Around him, the three other crew members were griping about missing Friday night down at Danny's Bar and Grill, where the drinks were half-price and the women half-dressed.

Clive hunkered deeper into his jacket, wishing they'd shut up and grow up. Even in the darkness he could see that one of them, Charles somebody-or-other, had blue eyes and skin the color of a cocoa bean. If he wasn't descended from a jig, he'd been spending way too much time in a tanning machine. Either way, the man was a waste of skin.

"I want to get this place done in three hours." Hank Whitlow, the crew supervisor, slid out of the driver's seat and settled his white AAA cap on his bald head. "Clive, you take the library and halls. Tom, you and Jonsey cover the classrooms, and don't forget that they have dry erase boards, not the old-fashioned kind. You'll need that special spray to get 'em really clean."

Clive squinted up at the well-lit sign before the low, sprawling building. They were working at the Mildred Hill Elementary School, where the marquee proudly proclaimed that the place was "A Presidential Honor School, recognized for academic excellence and ethnic diversity."

He snorted softly. The witch in Washington had brainwashed even this community.

He moved to the back of the van, where Whitlow opened the double doors. After grabbing a bucket of cleaning supplies, Clive ducked his head into the wind and strode through the darkness.

The library wasn't too bad—the place was even kind of cute. A flick of the light switch had revealed rows of little-kid tables and thousands of picture books, including a gigantic selection of Dr. Seuss. Clive sprayed the tops of the shelves with lemon polish, then ran his cleaning rag between the upright books on display. The dozens of colorful covers drew his eye, and many rang a bell of memory—*Blueberries for Sal, Mike Mulligan and His Steam Shovel, Caps for Sale.* There were other books he didn't recognize—*Heather Has Two Mommies, Nappy Hair,* and *The Snowy Day,* which featured a decidedly black boy on the cover.

A shiver of revulsion rose from his core. Jimmy Griffin would have a fit if he saw this evidence of the white race's undeniable demise.

Shuddering, he plucked the offending books from the top of the shelves and carried them to the waste can, then pitched them in, one at a time. *Swish,* two points each. Trash belonged in the garbage.

He wheeled the industrial-sized waste can to the librarian's desk, then dumped her trash as well—her can, plus a paperback copy of *Uncle Tom's Cabin* that had been sitting in the center of her desk. How could anyone expect young Americans to grow up properly if the guardians of the books let their guard down?

The librarian's computer sat off to the side, triggering an idea. But no . . . the woman's computer wouldn't work. Better to use one from the long line of anonymous cubicles that edged the rectangular room.

Glancing out the window in the door to be sure none of his idiot co-workers was lazing about, he sat in one of the kiddy chairs and punched the power on. The screen sprang to life with a colorful image of a wizard, then settled into the typical Windows desktop. Clicking the e-mail icon on the taskbar, he opened up a window and held his fingers over the keys. Should he? Why not? Hundreds of people moved through this place every day. And even if they did trace this message to Triple-A Clean Sweep, he'd be long gone. He was only working tonight because his cousin Joe needed the night off to celebrate his anniversary.

He tabbed to the address line and typed president@whitehouse.gov. Moving to the text field, he tapped out another short message, then signed his special name.

Crossing his arms, he pressed his spine against the back of the tiny chair to reread the note. It would do. Let her know he hadn't forgotten her. In fact, since the election she'd been more on his mind than ever. He couldn't *believe* a majority of his fellow Americans had actually voted for the witch, but the election result only proved Jimmy Griffin's point: America was failing fast, suffering from her own blindness and the alien invasion. Only a miracle could keep her from the abyss.

He smiled as another thought occurred: perhaps the witch knew him by now. He wasn't naive enough to think she'd actually received all of his letters, but the feds kept an eye on these things. They'd be surprised to get an e-mail.

Closing the message, he watched as it appeared in the message program's outbox, then he shut down the computer. He wouldn't even send it. This note would sit in the computer until some bright-eyed second grader switched on the power Monday morning. His face split into a grin. The kid who launched the message might even be one of Jackson's proud cultural minorities.

Feeling relaxed and invincible, Clive stood, pulled his headphones from his coveralls pocket, and punched the play button on his Walkman. Shimmying to the beat of an all-white band, he grabbed his rolling trash can and danced his way through the little-less-multicultural Mildred Hill media center.

●

Anson Quinn shivered in the blustery cold as he stepped off the jet at the Jackson airport. Agents from the Wyoming division of the Secret Service were scheduled to meet him, and as he left the tarmac and entered the gate he spied them at once—two men in sunglasses and dark trench coats, hands folded, feet spaced shoulder width apart. GI Joes without the fatigues.

He approached and lifted his chin in a silent hello. "Have you informed the school?"

"Not yet. We were told to keep it close until you arrived."

"Then let's go."

Twenty minutes later they pulled off snowy Highway 191 and into the parking lot of a brick school that reminded Anson of the one he'd attended back in Beaver Falls. The flat building sprawled over the better part of two acres, with a snowy playground taking up fully half the available space. Why did they even have a playground? They were probably able to use it only a couple of months in the year . . .

They parked their dark sedan in a parking lot brimming with new Beetles and Hondas, then Quinn led the way to the glass doors at the front. The blousy-haired receptionist at the counter widened her eyes as they entered, then back-stepped to an inner office without so much as a how-do-you-do.

Anson glanced behind him. Sure enough, GI and Joe were still at attention, still in the sunglasses. No wonder the woman had freaked.

"M-Mrs. Hawley," she said, sliding back around the corner, "is our principal. Did you want to see her?"

Anson pointedly pocketed his own shades and forced a smile. "Please."

Turning, the woman tossed a scared-rabbit reply over her shoulder. "This way."

Leaving the agents in the receiving area (and knowing they would not avail themselves of the empty vinyl chairs), Anson walked into the principal's office. "Mrs. Hawley?"

"It's *Dr.* Hawley. Sadie." A tall woman in a boxy suit stood as he entered. As he shook her hand, Anson thought the principal of the Mildred Hill Elementary School seemed harmless enough. Her graying, shoulder-length hair had been pinched back in a wide barrette, and her face seemed open and elastic—the sort that might stretch at any given moment with a disproportionate smile or frown.

She tilted her head and gave Anson a how-can-I-help-you look.

"I'm Anson Quinn, ma'am, with the Secret Service." Anson fished a card from his pocket and placed it in her hand.

The eyes widened, the mouth pursed into a perfect *O*.

"I'm afraid we've had a little trouble from your school."

The woman shook her head. "I don't understand. What have we to do with the Secret Service?"

Anson folded his hands. "On Monday morning, ma'am, the White House received a threatening e-mail from a man we've been tracking for months. That e-mail was sent from this school."

Sadie Hawley sank into her chair with a soft *thoosh*. "That's impossible," she said, one hand coming up to cover her mouth. "This is an elementary school, Mr. Quinn. These are children."

"If I may, ma'am, I'd like to see all your computers. I have a team of agents with me, and we'd like to look around."

The woman frowned off into space, her fingers tapping her lips, her brow furrowed. "Do you think," she whispered, "it was a prank? I'd hate to think it possible of any of our children, but sometimes their imaginations do run wild. They see so much violence on TV."

"We don't think it's a prank, ma'am. Every threat against the president is taken seriously, and we have evidence that this is the work of a man we've heard from before."

Her squint tightened. "A man?"

"We'll need a complete list of your staff members—and I'd like you to indicate anyone who would have access to a school computer."

She rose from her chair, blinking rapidly. "Yes, of course. I don't understand how such a thing could be possible, but you're welcome to investigate. But could you do it quietly? I don't want to alarm the children."

Anson slipped his hand into his coat pocket. "The students won't know we're here. We don't want to tip off whoever wrote the note."

He and his companions spent the morning secluded in the office, scanning the list of school employees and searching for names of known malcontents in the area. While he sipped coffee and watched his agents fax names and social security numbers to the Washington office, he overheard Dr. Hawley telling her staff that the men in suits were education officials from the capital—wasn't it wonderful, Mildred Hill might be named a presidential honor school for two years in a row!

Quinn didn't care what she told her people. He cared only about trapping Jehu, who might have slipped up this time. Ordinarily they'd have allowed the local agents to check out the situation, but Quinn had asked for special permission to visit Wyoming. Jehu had been haunting him ever since he found that letter in the correspondence office, and lately the messages had become more intense. The creep had also made his professional life decidedly difficult. Daryn Austin didn't like hearing *no* from her Presidential Protection Detail.

"No matches," one of the GI Joes reported at one o'clock. "None of the school employees are in our files."

"Check for part-time employees, support staff, even the landscapers," Quinn snapped, pulling his organizer from his pocket. "Check anybody and everybody who walked into the building this week. Wait—" he clicked his pen, thinking—"better make that *last* week."

"Got it."

While the agent asked the timid secretary for more information, Quinn slid a folded copy of the e-mail from a pocket in his organizer. *You will die,* the kook had written, *before you take the oath. Then they shall bring out the damsel to the door of her father's house, and the men of her city shall stone her with stones that she die: because she hath wrought folly in the land, to play the whore in her father's house: so shalt thou put evil away from among you.*

"I'd like to put *you* away," Quinn muttered, scowling at the page. They had not shown this note to the president. With the inauguration only two days away, she had enough on her mind. But the thought of Austin walking behind a bulletproof limo upon a street lined with protesters sent a cold panic down his spine. No agency could prepare for everything.

At two-fifteen, when the last screaming youngster had left the building, Quinn and his men strode to the media center, where the only other computers with telephone access were located. The two agents set about dusting the three modem-equipped desktops for fingerprints while Quinn walked around the room, his eyes alert.

Had Jehu sat in this room? How could anyone walk through this room of storybooks and kid-sized furniture and still be filled with hate?

He turned when the librarian, an unstylish, soft little woman, tiptoed past him. "Excuse me." She shrank back from Quinn's gaze. "I just have to get my purse."

"Ma'am?"

"Yes?"

"Did you notice anything odd about the library when you came in Monday morning? Anything out of place? Anything missing?"

Quivering, the woman pressed her lips together and dropped her gaze, then abruptly looked up at him. "I haven't had time to do a complete inventory, but I did notice that my copy of *Uncle Tom's Cabin* disappeared. I was sure I left it on my desk before leaving Friday, because I read a chapter to the fifth graders every Monday morning. But last Monday, it wasn't there. I looked everywhere and finally decided I had misplaced it."

Her bright, birdlike eyes met his. "I thought I was, you know, getting a little absent-minded."

Quinn gave her a smile. "Thank you, ma'am. That's very helpful." Sure—they already knew the guy was a racist. But what would he have done with the book? Stolen it? Not likely. He'd be more apt to . . .

Quinn stepped to the tall trash can near a pillar and peered inside. Wads of paper, a soda can, a stack of mimeograph material, the inky scent rising up to tickle his nose. No books of any kind.

After the librarian had retrieved her purse, he caught one of the Joe's attention and pointed to her desk. "Dust that for prints, too, okay?"

"Got it," the agent said, setting to work.

TWENTY-SIX

Surrounded by stacked volumes of *United States Reports*, Paul answered the rap on his door without lifting his eyes from his reading. "Enter!"

"Excuse the interruption, Mr. Justice Santana."

Startled by the voice, Paul looked up to see Justice Lorne Crispin, an apologetic smile on his face, standing in the doorway.

Paul stood immediately. "Mr. Justice Crispin—what a pleasant surprise. I didn't expect you."

"No one ever does." He smiled, his sagging cheeks gathering up like curtains. "Do you have a moment to spare for a colleague?"

"Of course." Stepping out from behind his cluttered desk, Paul gestured to two leather chairs against the paneled wall. "Please have a seat. I'm honored you'd take the time to stop by."

"Not exactly flooded with visitors, are you?"

"Not exactly." Grinning, Paul sank into the soft leather chair, then pressed his fingertips together. "I was beginning to think it was bad form for justices to visit one another in chambers."

"Bah." The elder justice waved Paul's concern away. "It's not that we're not friendly; it's just that we're not exactly friends. And we do spend altogether too much time at close quarters in the conference room."

Paul smiled. The eight justices were pleasant enough in conference, and their determined politeness went far to bridge philosophical differences. After three full months on the job, he had to admit that genuine cordiality prevailed in the Supreme Court Building, both on and off the bench.

Looking at his visitor, he allowed his curiosity to show on his face. "What brings you to my chambers, Mr. Justice Crispin? I hope you don't want my opinion on the Wexler case. I haven't quite thought the matter through yet."

"My reason for coming has nothing to do with any case." The justice pressed his hands together in a thoughtful pose, but his long legs shifted back and forth, touching and parting like the knees of an energetic teenage boy. "I came because something you said at lunch yesterday intrigued me."

Paul shook his head slightly. "I'm sorry, I don't remember what we talked about."

"You referred to your wife."

"Maria?"

"Yes." The justice's faded blue eyes cut to a photo of Maria and Cristina on the coffee table. "Is this your wife? And your daughter, I suppose."

"Maria and Cristina." As the man extended his hand and lifted his brows, silently asking permission, Paul nodded. "Please, be my guest."

Crispin held the photo at arm's length, a smile spreading over his face. "Lovely ladies, both of them. Your daughter favors you."

Paul shrugged aside the compliment. "I'm not sure she'd be pleased to hear it."

"Of course she would. I saw her at your confirmation hearing, and anyone could see her pride in you. Your wife, too, seems very supportive."

"She is. Though I think she feels a bit lonely in Washington. She misses her family in Miami."

"But you are her family."

Paul laughed. "I'm not enough."

Crispin returned the photo to the table, carefully setting it in its original position. "You mentioned your wife's loneliness at lunch, and that's why I'm here. I, too, have a lovely wife, who has been blessed, shall we say, with a gift for hospitality. I know she'd love to take your Maria to lunch, perhaps followed by a bit of shopping. Do you think your wife would be agreeable to an invitation?"

Paul smiled, as charmed by the thought as by the justice's old world manners. "Maria would be delighted. She is an outgoing woman, but she doesn't care for politics so hasn't hooked up with a strong circle of friends here. Sometimes I worry about her. She's a cancer survivor, you know, and though she's been in remission nearly four years I can't help worrying about her lack of a support system."

"Then you'll have to give me her number so Elaine can call. I'm sorry to hear about the cancer. We've lost several friends to that terrible disease, but I don't suppose those statistics are surprising at our age." The justice rubbed his chin. "Tell me—is your wife a person of faith?"

Paul blinked at the question. "Yes, I suppose she is. She constantly carries her rosary, and lately I've been coming home to find her asleep with her Bible open on her bed."

"That's good." The justice's long, narrow face furrowed with concern. "I don't mean to pry, Mr. Justice Santana, so forgive me if I seem intrusive. But when you've lived as many years as I have, you learn not to waste time skirting the issues when a direct approach will be more effective. When it comes to matters of faith, my wife and I have learned that directness is often the best way to approach the subject."

Smiling, Paul acknowledged his colleague's straightforward style. Crispin, a Reagan appointee, had a reputation for tough talk on the bench. More than once Paul had seen attorneys at the courtroom lectern wither in the heat of Crispin's stare. At seventy-two, the man possessed one of the sharpest and most experienced legal minds in the country, but now his face seemed soft with concern.

"I have no use for religion, but I don't think my wife would mind the question," he said, doing his best to sidestep the issue. "And I think she'd enjoy a lunch with Mrs. Crispin. By all means, let's get them together. It's kind of you to think of Maria."

"Wonderful." Crispin's sparkling blue eyes sank into nets of wrinkles as he smiled. "I learned long ago not to try to predict the workings of a woman's mind, but I hope this is the beginning of a long and prosperous friendship."

"That would be nice."

The justice lowered his gaze to a copy of *An Essay Concerning Human Understanding* on the coffee table. "I admire John Locke," he said, bending to pick up the book. "Have you read his *Reasonableness of Christianity: As Delivered in the Scriptures?*"

"I can't say that I have."

"A remarkable work, really." Crispin flipped through the pages of the book. "I have to agree with Locke—law ought to be based on the will of God as revealed in Scripture. His concepts of natural law are, after all, the foundation upon which our government rests."

Leaning his elbow on the chair, Paul smiled. "I'm afraid most modern men would disagree with you."

"How so? Even Jefferson and his deists held that natural law was self-evident."

"Yes, but they ascertained law through the exercise of intuition and reason rather than through recorded religious revelation."

Crispin smiled, a faint light twinkling in the depths of his intelligent blue eyes. "They feared what they could not accept, but still they were forced to acknowledge the truth—God's laws are the best principles for guaranteeing a society's liberty, protection, and justice. After all, who is more qualified than the Creator to provide guidelines for human life?"

Not wanting to argue with his first visitor, Paul spread his hands. "I'll have to read the other Locke book. I'm not familiar with it."

"I think you'll find it fascinating."

As Crispin stood and offered his hand, Paul rose to accept it. "I look forward to serving with you, Mr. Justice Crispin."

"And I with you, Mr. Justice Santana." Walking slowly, his hips swaying beneath his belt, the older justice gestured toward the window, where the Capitol Building gleamed in the late afternoon sun. "Are you attending the inauguration tomorrow?"

"In the good seats, I hope," Paul joked, sliding his hands into his pockets. "I don't want to keep Maria out in the cold any longer than I have to."

"Good idea. I appreciate the president's intentions, but I think Elaine and I will watch from home. Mr. Chief Justice Franklin is the only one whose presence is required."

Paul's smile deepened into laughter. "He won't mind a little chill. It's clear he owes the president a favor."

"Do you?" Crispin turned, his eyes searching Paul's face. "Owe her something?"

Paul rocked back on his heels as a flush burned his face. "I didn't ask to be put on the Court. In fact, I resisted at first."

"But in the end, you agreed. No man would go through that trial by fire without a good reason."

Swallowing hard, Paul met the old man's gaze. "I had a reason."

The blue eyes searched his face, probing for an answer, then the spiky brows flickered. "I'm sure you did; forgive me for asking. I warned you that my directness gets me into trouble—especially with my wife."

"It's all right."

"And it occurs to me that God might have a reason for bringing you here. Are you familiar with the story of Esther?"

Stifling the urge to sigh, Paul shrugged. "Vaguely."

"She wasn't happy to be caught in the national leader's scheme, either. But when a crisis arose, one of her advisers said, 'Who knows? Perhaps you have been elevated to the palace for just such a time as this.'"

Taking a step toward the door, Justice Crispin waved. "I'll leave you with that thought, Mr. Justice Santana. Thank you for your time. I can't wait to see what will happen now that we've received an infusion of young blood."

With that, he smiled, turned, and left. Paul waited until the door closed, then moved back to his desk and picked up the book he'd been reading. But his eyes remained clouded with the vision of Crispin's smile, and his heart retained a glow from the man's warmth.

They might well be ideological opponents on the bench, but the man had his charms. He'd been the first to speak to Paul as a person since his ascension to the Court.

●

From the VIP grandstand erected outside the Capitol Building, Maria Santana hunched into her coat and tried not to shiver. Though the day had dawned bright and blue, the crisp wind nipped at her exposed ears. Her legs, bare except for a pair of Hanes pantyhose, felt like stubby pillars of ice.

Beside her, Paul kept his face turned toward the dais where the chief justice was administering the oath of office. Since there was no first lady to hold the traditional Bible, Craig Parker's widow had been selected to stand in the spouse's spot.

Mrs. Parker, Maria noticed, had aged ten years in the last two. The animation had vanished from her face, the color from her cheeks. Her hair, which had been a warm shade of strawberry blonde, had gone as white as the ashes of a spent fire.

What had changed? The need to maintain an image, or the desire for it?

Time had not, on the other hand, diminished Daryn Austin one iota. Though many presidents showed signs of physical change from one term to the next, Austin seemed as poised, polished, and professional as ever.

Maria lifted her chin and scanned the crowd. Where were the president's parents? No one in the VIP section resembled the tall, gaunt governor Maria had seen in news magazines, but the man and his wife had to be pushing ninety, and this weather would not be kind to geriatrics.

The wind gusted over the spectators, whipping the flags around the platform and contracting the crowd as people instinctively huddled together. Maria moved closer to Paul, seeking his warmth, but the wool of his coat felt nearly as cold as the expression on his face.

For some inexplicable reason he was not happy with Daryn Austin. He seemed to enjoy his work at the Supreme Court, and he spoke highly of his fellow justices, even those whose views made him flush with frustration. The work was challenging, the hours long, but predictable—nothing like the schedule he'd kept at the White House. And though he'd publicly thanked Daryn Austin a half-dozen times for the honor of placing him on the nation's highest court, Maria knew something had come between him and his old friend. One had only to watch him watch *her* . . .

Was it the tabloid story? Surely not. Though he had not wanted Maria to do the Barbara Walters interview, he'd complimented her afterward. And the interview couldn't have upset the president; the issue had nothing to do with her, not really. Walters had tried to imply that Maria ought to be jealous of the relationship between her husband and the president just because they'd dated in college, but how realistic was *that?* If Hollywood people were rendered dysfunctional by past relationships, no movies would ever get made. Everybody dated everybody out there, and Washington didn't seem much different.

But still . . . Stealing another glance at her husband's face, she noted the set of his jaw, the glimmer of steely resolve mingling with pain in his eyes. This was not the face of a man happy for an old friend. This was the look Mel Gibson had worn in *Braveheart* when the Scottish prince betrayed him in battle.

The roar of applause broke into her thoughts. Daryn Austin had finished the oath. She embraced Mrs. Parker—who seemed as stiff as a corpse—then turned to shake her vice president's hand.

Maria looked up at Paul. A muscle moved at his jaw, and though she knew he had to see her questioning expression from the corner of his eye, he did not look down.

Shivering, she folded her arms and stomped her feet as the navy band played a rousing chorus. This was only the beginning of a long day, with the lunch, the parade, and the inaugural balls still to come . . .

President Daryn Austin moved to the microphone, her smile beaming like the television lights mounted around the platform. "Chief Justice

Franklin," she began, "Vice President Frey, Honorable Representatives, Reverend Clergy, friends, and my fellow Americans: There are no words to express the honor you have bestowed upon me by asking me to continue as your president. I will do my best to be worthy of your confidence and trust as we move this nation toward a future where no woman, no man, and no child has to do without the basic privileges of a civilized nation. We must cast off the outdated shackles of tradition and move forward into a bright future."

Frowning, Maria looked around the crowd. Inaugural addresses usually celebrated tradition and history, so Austin's tone was unusual . . .

"In the last two years," the president went on, "I have continued the programs of my predecessor, President Craig Parker, because the American people voted him into office. And now that you have heard *my* plans and validated *my* programs, we shall move forward with a new agenda. *You* went to the polls, *you* cast your vote, and the Congress heard your wish: let's move *full steam ahead!*"

Maria pressed her gloved hand to her forehead and rubbed her temple. Something in the strident cadences and pounding rhythms of political speeches always gave her a headache.

"The Constitution's basic requirement," Austin continued, "is that every person must be accorded the dignity he or she deserves as a human being. All people must be treated fairly and equally under the law, without discrimination because of any characteristic they inherited or have chosen to express their identity—their race, religion, nationality, gender, sexual orientation, politics, or disability. No matter who you are, if you are an American citizen, we embrace *all* your qualities!"

Maria brought her hand to her forehead, ostensibly shading her eyes but actually cutting off her view of Daryn Austin. Despite her assurances to a national television audience, she had never been able to shed an uneasy jealousy of the woman. Though she'd laughed at Barbara Walters's question about whether or not she envied the president, she had lied. God would forgive her.

With her free hand she fingered the rosary in her pocket, running her gloved thumb over the beads. Whenever she felt a jealous pang, she turned her thoughts heavenward. God wanted her to cast her cares upon him, for he cared for her. In the last few months she had begun to cling to him more tightly than she had ever clung to her papa, but God had proven himself faithful.

Despite the creeping uneasiness at the bottom of Maria's heart, all the events of the last few months boiled down to one truth: Daryn Austin had moved her husband to a position that enabled him to spend most of his nights at home. Though they might not return to Miami until after Paul's retirement, Maria was certain the trade-off would be worth the sacrifice.

TWENTY-SEVEN

ONE WEEK AFTER THE INAUGURATION, DARYN HOSTED a dinner for her primary staff in the East Room of the White House. Every detail had been artfully arranged by Mrs. Patty Frey, the nation's official "second lady," and Daryn couldn't have been more pleased with the result. At one point during the afternoon she'd returned from taking Tyson for a walk and cut through the East Room, then stared at the sight of uniformed florists holding hair dryers over the rose bouquets. When she asked what they were doing, one woman demonstrated how the closed roses were teased open by a stream of warm air. Every bouquet in the room would be picture perfect when they had finished.

"You do this for every banquet?" Daryn asked.

"Of course not," the woman had answered, laughing. "Only for the banquets with rose bouquets."

Now Daryn sat at a perfect table with Lawrence and Patty Frey, Alexander and Jan O'Leary, Paul and Maria Santana, and Thrasher, whom Daryn had asked to be her escort.

She smiled graciously at Patty Frey as she took her seat. "Patty, the menu is wonderful. Everything is just as it should be."

Ever the hostess, Patty beamed. "It *is* nice, isn't it? I'm learning as I go and was grateful to have a few months to plan this."

Patty was probably already planning how she'd change things when she lived in the White House, Daryn realized, but she brushed the uncharitable thought aside and sipped her champagne. No one would care about wooden Larry Frey once Daryn left office, so bubbly Patty had better grab all the limelight she could.

The mood was light, the conversation casual even though Daryn was aware of an uncomfortable silence emanating from where the Santanas sat. Paul seemed preoccupied; even Thrasher remarked upon his unusual reticence. Paul replied with an offhand remark about how Supreme Court justices were supposed to be meditative, and Daryn exhaled in relief when the clock chimed ten. She stood to go upstairs, effectively ending the party, but pointed at Paul before taking her leave. "Mr. Justice Santana—" she gave him a smile—"could I see you upstairs for a moment before you go? I have a little something for you."

Like the perfect assistant, Thrasher turned to Maria. "Have you seen the Vermeil Room, Mrs. Santana? We've recently installed some new art I think you'd enjoy."

While Maria watched, as wide-eyed as a teenage actress in a horror flick, Daryn stood and led the woman's husband toward the stairs.

●

The moment she heard the door close behind him, Daryn turned and drew Paul into her arms, starving for the taste of him. The calm aloofness that had surrounded him all night seemed to thaw with the hunger of her kiss. His arms slipped around her, pressing her to him for the barest instant, then he relaxed his grip and looked away.

"I've missed you terribly," she whispered, brushing her lips against the smooth, musky skin of his jaw. "I thought I'd go mad, sitting with you across the table. So many times I wanted to say something about how much I've missed you."

"You could have said as much in a phone call." His voice was thick, but as she wrapped her arms around his neck he groaned and pulled out of the embrace. "Good grief, Daryn—are you drunk?"

"Of *course* not." Straightening, she spat the words at him. "In public I always drink in moderation."

"But how much did you have up here, before dinner?"

She covered her hurt with a frosty shrug. "That's none of your business, is it?"

"Apparently not." Stepping back, he slipped his hands into his pockets. "I was only wondering if this is wise. Don't you think this little private conference will add fuel to the rumor mill? Presidents and Supreme Court justices don't usually have business together. And Maria is downstairs—"

"Don't worry." Laughing softly, she stepped away from his warmth and moved toward the small gift box she'd left on the sofa table. "I only wanted to give you a token of my gratitude for all your help during the last administration."

"You already gave me a bronze eagle."

"So I needed an excuse to get you alone. But I'll only keep you a moment."

His brow lifted at that, and she shook her head. "No time for more than a kiss, I'm afraid. And a quick conversation about the Court."

Nodding thoughtfully, Paul leaned over the back of a wing chair. "Are you planning on pressuring another justice to retire?"

"Of course not. The right players are in place, but I need to be certain they know their parts." She moved toward him again, lifting her hand to the place where his neatly edged haircut brushed the fold of his collar. Massaging the tense muscles of his neck, she murmured, "The Free Choice case—how close are you to deciding whether or not to hear it?"

He had lowered his head, now he lifted it sharply. "The petitions for cert are still circulating. I can't say how long it will be."

She smiled, sliding her hand to the middle of his back, where she applied a firm and even pressure. "I've heard that Cookson and Becket may be leaning toward a hearing, and I know Crispin, Woodward, and

Tolson will vote in a block. You have to make sure that Cookson and Becket understand the implications of that case. If people get the idea abortion isn't safe, reproductive freedoms will vanish." With her free hand, she squeezed his forearm. "That case is a Trojan horse. People think it's about state statutes and false advertising, but a world of danger lies in its underbelly. If the Court grants cert, you'll bring all sorts of trouble to the surface. And if, heaven forbid, the Court hears the case and rules against the petitioner, our nation will take a gigantic step backward."

He stared downward, his long lashes shuttering his eyes. "I'll do my best to make my colleagues aware of the risks. It's a complicated situation—"

"No more complicated than anything else that comes before the Court. You are persuasive, Counselor, that's why I put you on the bench." She stood on tiptoe to breathe in his ear. "That's why I sacrificed our happiness. Because as much as I want you near me, the country needs you on the Court."

He straightened then, his gaze shifting to the small box on the table. "That's my alibi?"

"Yes." She walked over and picked it up, then presented it to him with a half-smile. "I actually picked it out—a Mont Blanc pen, with the presidential seal, of course."

"Thank you."

He turned and kissed her cheek much as a brother might, holding the narrow silver box like a barrier between them. Something about the prim exchange made her want to call him back as he moved toward the door, but his wife and a crowd of onlookers waited below.

She watched him go, heard the door close with a definitive click. Then she moved into the bedroom, snapped off the lights, and began to undress in the darkness, feeling more alone than she had in weeks.

●

Maria held the silver box in her lap on the drive home. Paul had come downstairs and handed it to her without comment, then gestured toward the exit and asked, "Ready to go?" Without being told, Maria knew his visit to the residence had nothing to do with the gift box in her hand.

Though he had turned on the radio and occasionally hummed along with the tunes on the seventies station, Maria sensed that her husband's thoughts were focused on a faraway mental horizon he visited often and about which she could only guess.

"The dinner was lovely," she said, desperately trying to draw him back. "And Mr. Thrasher is a very nice man, don't you think? A good escort for the president, even though he is probably ten years younger." She hesitated. "I wonder if anything's going on between them? After all, they work together every day—"

"Don't be ridiculous."

Maria blinked, caught off guard by the sudden sharpness of his tone. Her rambling remarks must have struck home, which could only mean he was thinking about Thrasher or the president or his former position at the White House. He had liked that job; he'd felt his work was important.

But his work at the Court was important, too. And she was praying he'd find his purpose there, and discover the plan God had foreordained.

Carefully she smoothed her skirt. "I got a call yesterday from Elaine Crispin. She seemed very nice and invited us to their home for dinner on Saturday night."

Paul's eyes clouded. "Elaine Crispin?"

"Your colleague's wife," Maria gently reminded him. "Mr. Justice Lorne Crispin."

"Oh." He flushed. "Sorry. I wasn't thinking."

"At least you don't forget to think very often." She kept her voice light, not wanting to offend. "Anyway, I accepted for us because I didn't think you'd mind. Elaine said you'd given her husband our home number."

Keeping his eyes on the road, Paul nodded. "I did, but I was under the impression Elaine wanted to take you to lunch. I thought it was a nice gesture, that maybe she'd help you get to know some of the other justices' wives."

"Apparently Mr. Justice Crispin would like to get to know you, too."

She sighed when he shot her a look of bewilderment. "Don't be nervous, Pablo, I'm sure they don't bite. You can come out of your cave long enough for dinner and drinks, can't you?"

"I can only hope," he said, turning into their drive, "that it's not an Amway meeting."

"Not Amway, but Elaine did mention there'd be a time of prayer." Before he could glare at her, she turned her face toward the window. "Because, you see, I've been to the doctor. We've found another lump."

Sitting in the darkness of his study, Paul lifted another glass of scotch to his lips and swallowed. Maria's announcement in the car, delivered with the carelessness of a weather forecast, still echoed in the recesses of his guilty mind.

The cancer had returned. While he was fooling around with another woman and selfishly focusing on his own desires, cancer had invaded his wife's body. While she had been telling him that God would take care of them, God had allowed the enemy to establish another beachhead in Maria's body.

He took another swallow of the scotch as a thousand accusatory thoughts whirled through his head. Maria had been unhappy in Washington, and unhappiness caused one's defenses to drop. Perhaps her unhappiness had affected her immune system to the point that the cancer had awakened from dormancy . . .

The idea was impossible to prove, he knew, and probably the result of too much guilt and too many drinks. But in the cosmic scheme of things, where the mind and body intermeshed and one's life influenced every other life with which it was entwined, how could he deny that he had hurt Maria? And would continue to hurt her as long as he continued his association with Daryn Austin?

Drowning in waves of guilt, he made a decision. His relationship with Daryn must end, but how? If there were a routine to change, he would change it. If Daryn were a coworker he saw every day, he'd find a way to avoid meeting her. But how did a man end a connection that had existed his entire adult life? Since his move to the Court, Daryn had called a halt to their late-night rendezvous, and he thought he could resist any future invitations. But how could he stop the mere mention of her name from setting his blood afire? The heart did not always want to obey the will . . .

He tossed the last of the scotch down his throat, then set the glass on the armrest of the chair and watched as it teetered for a moment before settling on the buttery leather. How long had Maria known about the lump? At least a day, perhaps two. She had worried in silence for hours without breathing a word.

The realization struck him—the old Maria would never have been able to hide her panic. Sick with worry and fear, she'd have taken to her bed calling for her father, for Cristina, for Paul.

He frowned. Who had Maria called for this time?

He massaged his forehead, unable to find the answer. He must have been preoccupied; he had missed the signs of anxiety. One thing, though, was clear—Maria's fear had compelled her to accept Elaine Crispin's invitation for dinner and prayers.

"Not dinner and drinks," he whispered, lightly running his finger around the rim of his empty glass. "Not if Crispin's wife is a born-again. We'll probably have grape juice and bread for dinner, with kneeling pillows provided after dessert."

He closed his eyes. In his entire life he'd known few genuinely religious people. Maria, of course, seemed to take honest comfort from her prayers and Bible reading, but she'd never let those things interfere with their normal family life. She didn't faint when he cursed or deny him an occasional bottle of scotch, nor did she try to shove her prayers down his throat. Maria's religion had never been a bother . . . though, on occasion, it did perplex him.

Daryn, on the other hand, believed steadfastly in nothing. For a few months in college she'd attended outdoor meetings with women who wore long white dresses and worshiped the mother goddess—or, as Paul called her, Queen of the Earth and Everlasting Hooey—but in the end

Daryn had come to believe those women were misguided. Humankind created its own gods, she told Paul, and people with ambition, skill, and a little luck rose to the top of the power structure. If you wanted to tap into power—which, she believed, was what religious people really wanted—then why not seek that power yourself?

At the time Daryn's views had seemed heretical to a staunch Catholic who'd been taught never to question the Church. But later, after she lost the baby, he'd begun to wonder why he had ever believed God loved, guided, or even cared. Then, though Daryn continually accused him of clinging to his religious guilt, he discovered that casting off his religion was as simple as not caring in return.

After that, every time he brushed up against a self-proclaimed Christian, he found himself repelled like a negative ion that had suddenly encountered one of its own kind.

Strange . . . except for the moment when Crispin had praised Locke's devotion to natural law, Paul hadn't sensed any negative vibes from the older justice. Crispin seemed a thoughtful and reasonable fellow, though given to moments of rigidity. He never explored a legal solution without putting faces upon participants in a possible future complication, and he had a habit of wearing his heart on his sleeve—unusual for an avowed Republican. On occasion he could be brilliant—a quality Paul did not associate with any religious folk of his acquaintance—and he frequently affirmed his colleagues' courage and convictions . . . as long as those convictions matched his own.

No, as much as he respected Lorne Crispin, he did not want to attend a prayer meeting at his house. But Maria, despite her brave front, had to be frightened, and prayer would comfort her. Hadn't medical studies proven that prayer helped the recovery of sick people who believed in it? As long as Elaine Crispin was not one of those who prayed with raised hands and in a babbling tongue, the act of prayer might even give Maria the boost her immune system needed. Given a little time, prayer might help her.

Why not give her that gift? Why not be selfless for once, and allow the woman he'd married to inject hope into her life? Cristina needed her mother, and Maria needed to believe God would heal her. She probably needed to be reassured that Paul wanted her healing . . . so he had to go with Maria to the Crispins' for dinner and prayers.

Opening his eyes, he watched the dancing shadow of a moonlit oak glide over the wall. Apart from his wife, he had known only one other truly spiritual person. His grandmother had been raised Catholic in Cuba, but stopped attending Mass after Castro rose to power. After the family's escape to Florida, however, a desire for directions to the grocery store sent her into a nondenominational, Spanish-speaking church in Little Havana. After that, she'd hurried to the building every time the doors opened.

As an adult, Paul visited his *abuela* at his mother's house. She'd sit in a chaise on the lanai, resting in the shade, her dark brown complexion as cracked as a lake bed after summers of intense drought. At ninety-two, her spine curved in a dangerous hook while her hands resembled the knotty roots of a live oak, but her button black eyes snapped with joy even on the most pain-filled of days. "Ah, Pablo," she'd call, spying him through the sliding glass doors. *"Déjeme cantarle de Jesús."*

Let me sing to you of Jesus.

He'd gone to her, of course, because to do otherwise would be disrespectful. He would sit in the folding chair next to her chaise and let her rest her gnarled hand upon his arm, her eyes closing as she blissfully sang songs he'd never heard about a relationship he'd never wanted.

She died the year he turned forty, and as he stood at her graveside listening to an a cappella choir from her little church, he realized she had found a joy that had thus far eluded him.

A siren wailed in the night, bringing him back to the present. Like all parents, Paul took a moment to remind himself that his daughter was not on the road but safe in Cambridge, then he pushed himself out of the chair, knocking the glass to the floor.

He stood and looked for it, then spied a solid crystal shimmer against the dark carpet.

He was surprised it hadn't broken. Lately he seemed to ruin everything he touched.

To Paul's surprise, dinner at the Crispins' included wine, ham, and a chocolate cheesecake that would have shamed the White House pastry chef. He told Elaine Crispin so, then felt Maria gratefully squeeze his hand when Elaine blushed and stood. "If you like, you can carry your coffee into the living room," their hostess said, gesturing toward the large space they'd walked by on their way to dinner.

The other guests—two other couples, Sharon and Bill, John and Kathy, none of whom seemed to be affiliated with the government in any way—moved into the living room, the women stopping by Elaine's side to offer help in clearing the table. The men gravitated to Lorne Crispin, who slapped them on the back and urged them to make themselves at home.

The Crispin home was not exactly what Paul had expected. The spacious colonial befitted a man of the justice's age and position, but among the elegant furnishings were the marks of a family man—ceramic clumps of clay marked with tiny handprints, framed photographs of young adults with babies in their arms, a bright plastic box of toddler toys tucked beneath a cherry end table.

Paul sank onto a plush sofa, joined a moment later by his wife. Elaine, who'd left the dishes on the table, sat next to Maria, while Justice Crispin stood behind a wing chair positioned at the center of the room. The other two couples—Paul kept wanting to call them Bob and Ted and Carol and Alice—squeezed onto the opposite couch while exchanging friendly banter.

"We've brought you all together," Crispin said, glancing at his wife with a smile, "because Maria Santana has an urgent need we can meet." His gaze shifted to the other two couples. "Elaine and I know you are committed to intercessory prayer, and we'd like to ask you to pray for Maria."

A sludge of nausea roiled in Paul's belly. In his years of law practice he'd been in many situations where he felt threatened, including the hideaway of a Colombian drug lord whose mother couldn't get a visa, but never had he quite felt as uneasy as in this million-dollar home surrounded by religious fanatics. He leaned forward, about to stand, but the touch of Maria's hand stopped him.

"I asked Elaine to pray for me," she said, speaking loud enough for the group to hear though she looked only at him. "I need God's help for this."

Though her voice was soft, he heard a faint trace of accusation in her tone. Was she saying she needed help from the Almighty because she hadn't received any support from her husband?

Shamed into stillness, Paul stared at the Oriental carpet.

"Maria's doctor has discovered a lump," Justice Crispin said, resting his hands on the back of the empty chair, "and she's battled breast cancer before. So we need to pray she will find the strength to confront what lies ahead."

The niggling part of Paul's brain that delighted in a good round of devil's advocate launched a question: "Wouldn't it make more sense to pray the lump is benign?"

A corner of the justice's mouth rose in a half-smile. "We're just beginning to pray, Paul, and we'll have to seek God's face to know his will in this situation. But this much I do know—God wants Maria to be strong and to believe he is working for her good no matter what the future holds."

Elaine Crispin reached out and took Maria's free hand. "I've spent some time on the phone with Maria." She looked across the polished cherry coffee table toward the other couples. "And I'm convinced she knows Jesus in a personal way. Experience has taught her to place her faith in Christ alone."

Like some sort of priestly jury, the two couples on the sofa inclined their heads in silent understanding, then Bill leaned forward and braced his elbows on his knees. "Let's pray, then." He smiled at Maria. "Jesus assured us that if two or three agree on anything on earth, it will be done in heaven. But first we'll seek the Father's will, to know exactly what we should agree on."

Paul watched, his mind spinning, as the three other strangers shifted positions and bowed their heads. Bill slipped from the sofa to the carpeted floor in order to pray on his knees. John went to the floor, too, and rested his tented hands upon the sofa as if it were the railing at a kneeling bench. Elaine Crispin pressed her fingertips to her forehead and closed her eyes, while her free hand clutched Maria's. And Justice Crispin still stood behind the chair, his eyes closed, his face turned upward, his palms lifted toward the ceiling.

Paul felt the serpent of anxiety wrapped around his heart slither lower, to writhe in his guts. *Catholics*, he wanted to whisper in his wife's ear, *do not pray like this! And intelligent, reasonable people do not seek anyone's* face *about anything. If they do pray, they are logical about it, telling God what they need and when they need it . . .*

A few feet away, Elaine Crispin began to sing a soft song about praise and adoration . . .

Across the room, Kathy and Sharon sang, too, while John punctuated the melody with heartfelt exclamations: "Yes, Lord. I love you, Jesus."

Shuddering faintly, Paul resisted the twisting of his bowels as long as he could, then stood. Carefully stepping over Maria's and Elaine's shoes, he left the living room and moved into the hallway.

Justice Crispin intercepted him before he found the room he sought.

"Are you all right?" the justice asked, concern furrowing his brows.

"Fine." Paul smoothed his tie. "Just looking for the rest room."

The justice pointed toward a door off a side hallway, then smiled. "Thank you for understanding, Paul. I realize this is probably outside the realm of your experience."

And your comfort zone. He didn't say the latter words, but Paul read them in the older man's eyes.

"It's all right." He took a step toward the bathroom. "If this sort of thing helps Maria—"

"God will help Maria—" Crispin gave Paul the sort of smile you'd give a slow child—"because she is his and she asked for help. But who, Paul, is going to help you?"

Paul tugged on his tie, then forced himself to meet Crispin's earnest gaze. "I appreciate the concern, Mr. Justice Crispin, but I don't need help."

The older man opened his mouth as if to speak, then bit his lip and cast Paul a knowing look. "When you do," he said, turning, "don't be shy about asking for it."

TWENTY-EIGHT

AT FIVE O'CLOCK DARYN STRODE THROUGH THE Oval Office doors and went to the kennel, released Tyson, then led him into the elevator. When she was safely inside the residence, she unhooked his leash and dropped it into some former first lady's antique water pitcher, then kicked off her pumps and fell onto the sofa.

Exhausted, that's what she was—not physically, for she'd done little to tax her body, but mentally and emotionally. During the campaign she'd felt alive down to the tips of her toes, but now she felt enervated. Being in the White House didn't help, for the feeling of emptiness worsened when she saw the portraits of her predecessors, men who had come away from the inauguration with zeal and high hopes.

Winning the election had been wonderfully gratifying, but the victorious feeling had faded within a week after the inauguration. By the first of February she realized there'd be no surprises waiting for her, no new perks for the presidency.

The thrill of riding in Air Force One had dissipated, she had wearied of watching movies alone in the White House movie theater, and she could die happy without ever riding in another helicopter or presidential motorcade. The only good thing about travel in her bullet- and bombproof tank of a limo was accessibility—when the president was on the move, all other traffic in the vicinity ground to a halt.

This third day of February had begun with a prayer breakfast to which she'd been invited as a figurehead. At 6:30 A.M., while she sat at the head table and pretended interest, a long-winded clergyman from an African-American church in D.C. prayed for the sins of the nation, particularly those of the White House. Daryn wasn't certain what sins he attributed to her, nor did she really care. But the press perked up its collective ears during the prayer, and afterward she'd been forced to ignore the staccato attack of pointed questions as she walked from the service entrance to the waiting limo.

She'd hurried back to the White House for a meeting in the Roosevelt Room only to discover that none of her newly appointed cabinet members wanted to agree with one another. Daryn's right temple began to pound when Ann Evans, Secretary of the Interior, openly contradicted Diane Martinez, Secretary of Energy. As Daryn pasted on a patient smile, she found herself thinking that it might be a good idea to fire the entire lot and start afresh. She had happily accepted resignations from Parker's cabinet officials, but those people, at least, had learned how to cooperate. This crew, all freshly approved Austin appointees from various corporate firms and political organizations, apparently got through elementary school without learning how to play nicely in the sandbox.

She lunched with Thrasher and O'Leary, both of whom were as nervous as mice about her judicial appointees. They had just sent her list of a dozen appellate court nominees to the Senate, where Republicans and Democrats alike were taking aim at anyone who smelled like opposition.

"'Tis a terrible thing, but I'm thinking we just can't win," O'Leary mumbled between bites of a turkey sandwich from the White House mess. "You are the first truly bipartisan president in generations, but no one can identify with you."

"They identified with me in the election," Daryn pointed out. *"Both* women and men."

Thrasher lifted his water glass. "That was different. Senators aren't the public. They're trained to aim at the enemy, and with a two-party system in Congress, everyone on your judicial list is someone's sworn enemy."

"Every other president has managed to get most of his judges appointed."

"Every other president has been able to offer party favors in exchange for support. Face it, Madam President, you don't have partisan skirts for them to hide behind. There just aren't enough independents in Congress."

"I don't need skirts." Daryn tamped down her rising irritation. "I selected judges who have outstanding records on civil liberties. If Congress gives my people grief, I might find it expedient to publicly point out the illogic of opposition to constitutionally protected freedoms."

She'd been in a bad mood by the time the meeting ended, and O'Leary and Thrasher left the dining room with identical frowns on their faces. After lunch, Daryn had three hours of what she called "presidential busyness." She edited a draft of her message to the Congress deferring sanctions against Iran, approved a statement announcing yet another Middle East Peace Conference, and skimmed the final draft of remarks she would give when she presented her judicial nominees at a press conference later in the week. She approved one presidential proclamation establishing National Consumers Week and another marking May 2 as United Nations Day.

At four o'clock she painted on a bright red smile and stepped out to welcome the Cleveland Browns, Super Bowl champions, to the White House. In the East Room she posed for pictures with hulking fullbacks while Peter Chang blandly snapped shots that would soon be hanging in the coach's office. At four-fifteen she met with Mrs. Frey, who wanted to ask Daryn's opinion about redecorating the White House Map Room (certainly, go ahead), and at four-thirty she participated in a three-way telephone conference with the newly elected president of Russia and the English prime minister. That call had ended five minutes ago, and Daryn had fled for the shelter of the residence.

Lumbering to the sofa, Tyson placed his huge head next to hers and sniffed vigorously. "Oh, Ty." She crinkled her nose. "You smell like wet dog."

Tyson sniffed again, his huge muzzle leaving a trail of saliva and dog hair over her jacket. Groaning, she sat up. In two hours she had to appear at a reception honoring President Jorgé Martinez of Guatemala, and it wouldn't do to appear before another head of state in a slimed suit.

She pushed herself off the sofa, then moved toward the bedroom. As she lingered in the doorway, her eyes fell upon an embroidered wall hanging she'd been given at a recent visit to an all-girls school in Nantucket. The words upon the sampler were from an old ditty once sung by Nantucket whalers' wives:

Then I'll haste to wed a sailor, and send him off to sea,
For a life of independence is the pleasant life for me.
But every now and then I shall like to see his face,
For it always seems to me to beam with manly grace,
With his brow so nobly open, and his dark and kindly eye,
Oh my heart beats fondly towards him whenever he is nigh.
But when he says "Good-bye my love, I'm off across the sea,"
First I cry for his departure, then I laugh because I'm free.

She had loved the gift, seeing it as a clever way to represent the roles of both married and independent women, but in the last few weeks it had come to symbolize something altogether different—her relationship with Paul.

She leaned against the doorframe, mentally envisioning Paul on the edge of her bed, where she'd so often seen him. "First I cry," she whispered, "then I laugh."

But she would not laugh tonight, for she missed him desperately. Every meeting in the Oval seemed colored with his presence, every corner of her study shadowed with a memory. She had to work twice as hard to focus on the task before her, and in unguarded moments her thoughts turned to him as surely as night followed day.

She had thought she'd be able to cope with not seeing him every day—after all, they'd been separated for twenty years when he lived in

Miami. But finding him again, learning to lean upon his strength, had changed her in ways she didn't want to consider.

Paul wasn't making things easier. He'd been edgy the last time they were alone, his kiss more restrained than passionate. Necessity had demanded that they separate when the media vultures were swarming, but he didn't have to stay away now. If he missed her as badly as she missed him, he could find a way to be with her. They'd have to work around the Worker and Visitor Entrance System, of course, since WAVES recorded the entrance and exit of every visiting nonemployee, but if the records were questioned, they could always say he was handling some detail of his former work . . . or only visiting an old friend.

She moved toward the bulletproof glass at the window, then pressed her hand to the ice-cold pane. The White House might be one of the most beautiful residences in the nation, but it was still a gilded prison. If she were any other woman, she'd get in the car and drive to meet her beloved, no matter where he was or how long it took to reach him. But her days of freedom and anonymity had been traded away.

Driven by an urge she could no longer repress, she moved to the phone and punched in Paul's cellular number. Turning, she caught her mirrored reflection as the phone rang once, twice, then an automated greeting cut in, an anonymous voice asking her to leave a message.

She dropped the phone back into its cradle. The president of the United States did not leave messages for anyone.

Lifting her chin, she turned toward the mirror and began to unbutton her soiled suit.

●

Peering at his watch, Paul followed the red carpet through the private corridors to the justices' robing room. In less than ten minutes the marshal of the Court, clothed in a traditional formal morning coat, would pound his gavel and announce "the Honorable, the Chief Justice, and the Associate Justices of the Supreme Court of the United States." As Paul and his colleagues filed into the courtroom through an almost sacred silence, the marshal would cry, "Oyez, oyez, oyez. All persons having business before the Honorable, the Supreme Court of the United States, are admonished to draw near and give their attention, for the Court is now sitting. God save the United States and this Honorable Court."

No matter what worries pressed at Paul's mind, a thrill ran up his spine each time he heard the traditional salutation. To him the Capitol always seemed to bustle, the West Wing to hum. In contrast, an almost holy hush permeated the Supreme Court, no matter how many people filled the grand hallway, the courtroom, or the wide piazza beyond the marble stairs.

"Good morning, Mr. Justice Santana." Teresa Richards and Carolyn Cookson stood in the robing room, already dressed in the simple black robes designed to give the impression of uniformity among the so-called "priestly tribe." The uniform was supposed to give the impression that judges attained their wisdom from a single superhuman source, so their individual attitudes did not affect their decisions. That idea, of course, was ludicrous, for individual attitudes colored every thought and act of each person on the planet.

The women seemed eager to get back to whatever conversation Paul's approach had interrupted, so he nodded his greeting and went straight to the narrow cubicle that held his robe. Breathing deeply as he shrugged out of his coat, he inhaled the scent of furniture polish—the entire building smelled of lemons after a night visit by the cleaning crew.

Hanging his jacket on a padded hanger, he looked up to greet Justices Franklin, Layton, and Becket, who entered en masse. Harold Woodward came in a moment later, his forehead dotted with beads of perspiration, and Paul smothered a smile as he wondered whether the justice had been caught in traffic or in a nap. At seventy-nine, the man had a tendency to doze off, even in the courtroom.

Justice Crispin was the last to arrive. After nodding to his colleagues, he pulled his robe from his compartment, then caught Paul's eye. "I've been thinking about you, Mr. Justice Santana," he called, adhering to the rule of respect that governed every aspect of decorum within these hallowed halls. "How is your lovely wife?"

Paul took a moment to fasten the hook at the top of his robe, then walked over and put out a hand to hold Crispin's coat. "She's doing as well as can be expected, Mr. Justice Crispin. She had a biopsy on Tuesday. The tumor was malignant, so they removed it immediately. She'll begin drug therapy next week to see if they can halt the formation of any additional tumors, but they're waiting for more detailed lab reports."

Crispin nodded thoughtfully as he slipped out of his tweed sport coat. "My wife and I have felt led to pray that your wife will feel a miraculous touch from God—something to convince you he is more than the air up there."

Justice Becket thrust his head into the conversation. "Watch out, Mr. Justice Santana. If he gets his hooks into you—"

Paul forced a laugh. "Don't worry, I'm not nibbling at that bait."

Crispin smiled, but his eyes remained serious. "Prayer does work, my friend. Don't you want your wife to be healed?"

"Of course. But I'm not willing to surrender who I am to participate in some sort of spiritual charade. I can't change my beliefs without compromising my own identity, and without that—" he shrugged. "Well, I wouldn't be the man Maria married, would I?"

Crispin gave him an appraising look as he pulled his robe from the hanger. "You're utilizing human reasoning when this is something you need to consider in light of the supernatural. 'He who loses his life shall find it.' Does that quote ring a bell?"

The corner of Paul's mouth twisted. "That would be 'Who is Jesus Christ, Mr. Trebeck.'"

"Touché." Pausing to fasten the zipper that ran the length of his robe, Crispin added, "I wouldn't urge you to consider anything I haven't tried myself. I was about your age when I realized there had to be more to life than man's efforts to perfect his world. For all of man's striving, the world around us keeps getting worse . . . and then I understood. The world, and our view of it, will never change until we do. And the only way we can change is through the power of God. He wants our lives. He wants to make us into vessels shaped for his purpose."

Shifting his gaze, Paul shook his head. "I'm afraid God would have no use for me. I've too much—well, the Catholic word is *sin.*"

Crispin laughed. "I know the word all too well, having experienced a fair amount of it myself."

Aware of the time, Paul looked to the chief justice, who bore the responsibility of initiating the opening handshake, the traditional gesture of goodwill preceding every meeting of the justices. With two minutes to spare, Chief Justice Franklin shook Justice Tolson's hand, setting the process in motion.

Paul took Crispin's hand. "You don't know me well."

"You've come through a Senate confirmation hearing, son. What could remain on your conscience after that trial?"

"Something, frankly, that I don't want to discuss." Paul tugged on his hand, but Crispin's iron grip held tight.

"We all have things we'd rather keep hidden," the elder justice said, his blue eyes burning. "But those are the things we need to face. We scatter parts of our souls when we sin, and if we don't stop, soon we will find our souls empty."

An electronic warning bell chimed. Crispin released Paul's hand, freeing him to greet the others before walking through the legendary red curtains.

TWENTY-NINE

ON THE FIRST MONDAY IN MARCH, DARYN SAT in the privacy of the Oval Office study with her reading glasses perched on the end of her nose. Her contacts had been giving her trouble, and though she never wore her reading glasses in public, necessity demanded she wear them now. Her eyes had been burning, a condition aggravated by a lack of sleep and mental ennui . . .

She glanced up when O'Leary rapped on the open door. The man was five minutes late for his appointment, not an unforgivable sin, but irritating nonetheless. His brows were a brooding knot over his blue eyes, and his usually pleasant face was drawn.

"You all right?" she asked.

"Sorry I'm a wee bit late," he said, entering the room. "But sometimes life can put a fellow in a desperate bad humor."

She hesitated. "Something we need to talk about?"

"Not yet," O'Leary answered. "No sense getting our knickers in a knot about blarney."

Knowing better than to borrow trouble, she opened the leather folder O'Leary handed her, then yawned and pointed to the guest chair in front of the desk. "Have a seat," she said when the yawn had played out. "And let's see what the Supremes will be handing us in the next quarter."

This quarterly review of pending Supreme Court cases had been part of her routine for the last two years, but never had Daryn looked forward to it as much as today. Paul had now been in place six months, and she felt certain he'd developed a sure and influential presence. As the fifth member of a liberal voting bloc, the Court's decisions would finally begin to fall in line with her vision for the nation.

O'Leary sat, his right foot on his left knee, and for a moment she lost her focus. Paul used to sit in that posture, in that same chair. She shielded her eyes with her hand, distracted by the sudden mental comparison of her chief counsel's stout legs with Paul's trimmer physique.

"Okay," she murmured, scanning the document in her hand. "Let's see what the brethren are up to."

She scanned the list of cases on the Court docket, pausing occasionally as her weary brain refused to summon facts related to the case.

"This one." She tapped her fingernail on the page. "*Handyman Roofing, Inc. v. Citizen Band of Pequot Tribe of Connecticut.* What's this about?"

O'Leary pointed toward the folder. "There's a full summation on the following page."

She glared at her chief counsel. "If I wanted to read the summation, I would. Didn't you review these?"

"The relevant ones, sure. And I don't think that case will be coming anywhere near our issues. It involves an Indian tribe and a roofing company—some flap about contractual obligations."

Daryn flipped the page. "What about this one—*Florida v. Gregory?*"

"That one will bear watching. Outside Orlando, police officers acted on a tip that Thomas Gregory had marijuana hidden in his home. They were in the process of getting a search warrant when Gregory showed up at the house. The cops prevented him from going in until the warrant arrived two hours later. Once they went inside they found drug paraphernalia and marijuana, then arrested Mr. Gregory. His lawyer moved to suppress the evidence on the grounds of an unlawful seizure."

Daryn rubbed her temple. "The history?"

"The Florida trial court granted the motion to suppress, and the state appellate court affirmed."

She peered at him through her splayed fingers. "What position should we take?"

He shrugged. "As a proponent of civil liberties you might be tempted to take the defendant's side, but I'd be careful. Public opinion is leery of criminals' rights, and the public has lost its tolerance for drugs and guns. I'm thinking the Court will deny the suppression of evidence and say the police action was reasonable under the Fourth Amendment."

Sighing, Daryn turned another page. "All right. Civil liberties are supportable unless they impinge upon the public good. That will sell."

She skimmed the next list, fitting memories to names on the docket, then halted at an unfamiliar case. *"Bainbridge v. City of Tyler?"*

"Again, a civil liberties case, and this time the public good isn't an issue. Texas law makes it a misdemeanor, punishable only by a fine, for a front-seat passenger in a car not to wear a seat belt or for the driver not to secure a small child in front. The warrantless arrest of anyone violating the law is authorized by statute, but the police may issue citations in lieu of arrest. Seems this Mrs. Bainbridge was driving in Tyler, Texas, with her small children in the front, and none of them was wearing a seat belt. A Tyler cop pulled them over, observed the seat-belt violations, verbally chewed her out, then handcuffed her and placed her in his squad car." O'Leary grinned. "I'm thinking the petitioner wasn't exactly cooperative during all that dither, because after she arrived at the police station, she was forced to remove her shoes, jewelry, and eyeglasses. Officers took her mug shot and placed her in jail for about an hour, then she was taken before a magistrate and released on bond."

Daryn gave him a look of disbelief. "They're tough in Texas, aren't they?"

"Sure, don't I know it? Mrs. Bainbridge paid the fine, then she and her husband filed suit alleging that the actions of the city had violated her Fourth Amendment right to be free from unreasonable seizure. The District Court ruled her claim meritless; the Fifth Circuit Court affirmed."

Daryn shook her head. "We'll not touch that one. If we side with the city, we're antiwoman; if we side with the woman, we're saying people can toss babies into the car like grocery sacks."

Her mouth tightened when she saw a familiar name on the list. *"MKB Management doing business as Free Choice Women's Clinic v. Maddox?"* She lowered the paper and looked at her counsel. "I thought we had managed to stop that one at the gate."

O'Leary hooked his locked hands over his bent knee. "Well, they only needed four votes to schedule a case for review."

"But the odds!" Daryn bit her lip. Most cases that reached the Supreme Court on appeal made the discuss list, but few petitions for certiorari did. "Can you guess which justices voted to hear this thing?" She dropped the pages, ticking off the names on her fingertips. "Tolson, for sure, and Woodward, Crispin—but who's the fourth?"

"Probably Cookson," O'Leary answered. "Because she's a woman."

Daryn narrowed her eyes, thinking. "Did she vote to review it because she's a woman concerned about breast cancer . . . or does she want to confirm a woman's right to reproductive freedom?"

"No way to know, Madam President. Unless you can glean some information from our friend on the Court."

Sighing, Daryn picked up the report again. "I'll see what I can do. But I'm not worried. When this thing comes up, Paul will come through for us." She turned the page with an air of nonchalance she didn't feel, then looked up when Soon Yi Park cleared her throat.

"A message for Mr. O'Leary," she said, handing him a folded slip of paper.

O'Leary took the paper, read the note, then slowly folded it. Daryn watched as a muscle flicked at his jaw.

"Not a lot of blarney then," she said. "Real trouble afoot?"

"Could be." O'Leary spoke in the slow voice he always adopted when he wanted to bring up a difficult subject. "I've heard something from an aide in Senator Beatty's office. The esteemed senator from South Carolina has been busy lately."

"Doing what?"

"Following up those tabloid reports that surfaced during the campaign."

She released a humorless laugh. "The American people are tired of hearing about me and Paul Santana as college sweethearts."

"Beatty thinks he's discovered a new twist—and it might be a good thing he learned about it before the *National Enquirer* did."

Something in his tone set off an internal alarm. "What are you talking about?"

The lawyer uncrossed his legs and leaned closer. "Apparently Beatty's people found a nurse in Connecticut who remembers you visiting an abortion clinic in '79. I hear there's a sworn affidavit."

Daryn pressed her hand to the pearls at her throat as the room began to swirl before her eyes. "She's mistaken."

"She says she's not. According to our source, she says she never forgets a face, and yours was an especially pretty one."

"Then let her prove I was there."

O'Leary leaned back in his chair. "She can't. There are no records of a patient named Daryn Austin, no paper trail—believe me, Beatty's people have looked. But there is an eyewitness, and in a court of law, a witness can get you into all kinds of trouble."

"I'm *not* in trouble!" Daryn threw the words at him, then reminded herself to maintain control. She was tired and stressed, so it was doubly important for her to remain calm.

She drew a deep breath. "If this woman swore out an affidavit because she *thinks* she remembers seeing me, we're off the hook. People can't always remember meeting someone they met five minutes ago, so there's not a court in the country that would accept a twenty-six-year-old eyewitness testimony. Even if they did, abortion was perfectly legal in '79."

O'Leary lifted his hand, acknowledging her point. "Still—do you want to go down in history as the first American president who's had an abortion? This is not a good thing to bring before the public. There is still a strong conservative element in this country, and if they think you had an abortion of convenience—"

"Be quiet a minute, will you?" Lowering her head, Daryn pressed her hand to her pounding temple. She didn't fear the American public; they could usually be led like sheep. But if Paul heard the story . . .

A chill struck her in the pit of her stomach. Paul, who abounded with deep-rooted guilt and an equally deep-rooted disapproval of abortion. The man who loved children, and had only one . . .

She glanced up. "Is Beatty going to go public with this little tidbit?"

He shrugged. "If it suits his purposes, probably. Though he may wait until he needs a favor."

"What, a new bridge in South Carolina? A thousand new government jobs? We could arrange it, I suppose, but I have neither the time nor the patience for a game of political blackmail."

"I don't think Beatty cares much for jobs and such—his constituents have been receiving the benefits of his finagling for years. I think he'll wait for a sign of weakness before he strikes." He leaned closer. "Make no mistake, Madam President, Beatty is wanting your head—and probably your job. When he thinks you're most vulnerable, he'll close in for the strike. This information could be the dagger in his hand."

Daryn exhaled softly. Ambition, she reminded herself, could creep as well as soar. Beatty could hold the story for as long as he wanted.

She glanced up at Thrasher. "Does he know we know?"

"I doubt it. The guy who passed it to us was as nervous as a cat. But he's an Austin supporter."

"Can we trust your contact to take care of this?"

"What did you have in mind?"

She pressed her lips together, then shrugged. "I don't know . . . but I'm sure we can do a little digging, find out what would make this nurse happy. A better job at a VA hospital? A new car? You know people, O'Leary; you can think of something. Nothing major and nothing traceable, just whatever it takes to change her story from 'I know' to 'I can't be sure.'"

O'Leary looked away, then nodded. "I can check into it. I think our contact in Beatty's office might be persuaded to help us out."

"As soon as it's handled, let's get him out of there and into the West Wing. Then we'll all sleep better."

The lawyer stood. "If there's nothing else then, I'll get busy."

Daryn closed the folder on her desk. "There's nothing else. Nothing as important, anyway."

THIRTY

"DAD!" CRISTINA THREW A CHUNK OF HER FORTUNE cookie across the kitchen table, striking Paul on the jaw. He ducked, too late, and his head struck the tray of lemonade in Maria's arms. Only Jason's quick grab saved them from a sticky mess on the floor.

"See what you nearly made me do?" Paul said, laughing.

"I *warned* you." Cristina broke into a wide, open smile. "The dinner table is not the proper place for your terrible jokes."

Paul gestured to the empty boxes of Chinese takeout. "But we're nearly finished with dinner. Isn't there some sort of deadline for my joke prohibition?"

His daughter gave him a look of abject horror. "Are you kidding? No joke telling at all while Jason's here. I don't want him to know what a truly twisted sense of humor you have."

"I've always thought I had a good sense of humor." Paul glanced at Maria. "Don't you think so, hon? You've always laughed at my jokes."

Maria didn't crack a smile as she set the tray on the table. "I only laugh to make you feel good, Pablo. Your jokes are not that funny."

Paul dropped his jaw in pretended amazement, then pressed his hand to his heart. "I'm crushed."

"Save the theatrics, Dad. You're not a good actor, either." After accepting her lemonade from her mother, Cristina looked at Jason and jerked her thumb toward the den. "Wanna watch something?"

"Sure." Ever the conversationalist—what *did* they talk about at school?—Jason stood and ambled toward the den, following Cristina like a devoted puppy.

Maria sighed as she sank into her chair. "That Jason is a nice boy," she whispered. "I think they may get married."

Paul's heart sank. "You do?"

Maria nodded. "He cares for her; I can see it in his eyes. And look how he brings her home so often. A man who loves a woman will do things like that—" She stopped and lowered her gaze, a rich blush staining her pale cheeks.

Paul looked away, understanding why she'd suddenly bitten her tongue. A man who loved a woman would take her home to her family, to Miami, especially when she was afraid of the cancer that had reappeared in her life.

But Paul did not want to leave while the Court was in session, especially with several crucial cases slated for review. Maria hadn't asked him to take her home, but still . . .

He made a mental note to call Papa Lopez. Perhaps Maria's father could come up for an extended visit. They could give him the guest room, and if Jason brought Cristina home again, the boy could sleep on the sofa.

He looked at his wife, about to suggest that they invite her father to Washington, but something in her appearance made him catch his breath. The six weeks of drug therapy had been hard on her, but last time uncertainty and fear had drained her far worse than any treatment. Now, however, her eyes glowed with contentment. Where did it come from? Maria had been far stronger in the last six weeks than she'd been years before when the prognosis had been decidedly more optimistic.

He brought his hand to his chin, studying her. What had made the difference?

"I think I'll clear the table now." Maria stood, about to lift the tray again, but Paul caught her arm. "Let Cristina and Jason handle it. You and I provided the dinner—let the young ones clean up."

She looked at him, her eyes widening, then she gave him a tentative smile. "All right."

"Besides, I have some cases to review. I'll be working late tonight."

The smile that had risen at the edges of her mouth died, so Paul paused to kiss her cheek before leaving the kitchen. He climbed the stairs to his study, then moved to the French doors. A chilly drizzle had begun to fall during dinner, an April rain that slicked the cobblestones of the garden path thirty feet beneath his balcony. From out of the eastern sky a bolt of lightning lit the night, then faded as a thunderclap exploded and shook the room. As its grumble faded into the distance, Paul sank into his leather chair, turned on the desk lamp, and plucked a petition from the top of the waiting stack.

He tried to read. His eyes floated over the words, but exhaustion and emotion blocked them from his brain. He kept thinking of his wife, his lover, his family. If he were suffering from a terminal disease, would Maria's thoughts be centering on a man she'd known in another life?

The thought was so absurd he actually began to laugh, though he felt a long way from genuine humor. Perhaps he was being too hard on himself—after all, he hadn't been with Daryn in months, he had comforted Maria as best he could, and he had tried to protect her from the harsh truth about his relationship with the president.

On the other hand, he'd tried to be fair to Daryn, too. He had been keeping tabs on her programs, going so far as to publicly praise her Violence Against Women initiative due to be unveiled later in the week. He was doing his best to be faithful to his president and his wife, not an easy thing for a man to do . . .

"Paul?"

He stiffened at something jagged and sharp in Maria's voice. She thrust her head into the doorway of his office, and on her face he saw a strangled expression. "I think you'd better turn on the TV. Channel two."

Frowning, he picked up the remote and powered on the small television nestled in his bookcase. The screen filled with the images of two local television anchors, their eyes wide and focused upon the TelePrompTers.

"Entertainment Television has retracted the story," the helmet-haired blond reporter was saying, his mouth set in a serious expression, "and the witness has refused all further interviews."

Paul glanced toward the doorway, hoping Maria would explain, but she had vanished. He pressed the remote, surfing to another local channel, and hit another reporter, this one in front of the White House, a bank of blooming cheery trees behind her.

"Entertainment Television broke the story this morning," the woman said, clinging to an umbrella as the wind whipped hair across her face. "This afternoon that network retracted the report, claiming that the woman who provided the information has recanted her version of events. Even so, political pundits have to wonder whether this will affect Daryn Austin's popularity, particularly on the eve of the president's presentation of her 'hit a woman—go to jail' legislation. The woman who could do no wrong is suddenly looking all too human, and the political vultures have begun to circle. Polls show Daryn Austin still riding high on a crest of political favor, but the country remains divided over the matter of abortion."

Abortion? The word hit Paul like a slug in the chest. What were they talking about?

Another flurry of channels brought him to CBS, where Natalie Morgan, the White House Press Secretary, was speaking to Steve Dasher. "It's inconceivable that anyone would bring this sort of unfounded rumor into play," Morgan said, her eyes flashing. "But the president is aware of her political rivals and their tendency to engage in scandal mongering. She is particularly concerned because several crucial pieces of legislation are now before Congress, including the Violence Against Women bill she supports. She deeply regrets that her philosophical opponents have stooped to slandering her with false rumor and baseless innuendo."

Paul cursed softly as he pressed buttons. Finally, on CNN, a reporter provided the information he sought: "This morning Entertainment

Television broke the story of a Connecticut nurse who last month offered a sworn affidavit testifying that she was on duty in 1979 when Daryn Austin, apparently using a false name, entered the New Haven Women's Clinic to have an abortion. Later today, however, the nurse made a statement saying she has withdrawn her affidavit and is prepared to face the penalties for perjury if necessary—"

Paul clicked off the power as the words, disjointed and nonsensical, ticked in his brain. The truth, when it stuck, exploded into his consciousness like a bomb.

In 1979 Daryn had been pregnant with his child.

A miscarriage, she'd said. She'd lost their baby in a miscarriage, so they didn't have to hurry to get married. Waiting would be better for both of them.

He pressed his hand to his forehead, massaging it as though he could rub out the painful memories. After learning about Daryn's pregnancy he'd been ready, even eager, to marry her and provide his child with a home and a father. Once the initial shock had worn off, he'd been unable to hide his excitement about the baby, but Daryn had never shared that thrill. The pregnancy meant an end to her dreams and ambitions . . . and she'd been unable to hide the relief in her eyes when she told him about the miscarriage.

He saw the truth now. He should have seen it then, but love had blinded him. He'd wanted to believe her, wanted to believe they loved the same things . . . but now he knew the truth. She had loved her ambition most of all. The ruthlessness he had observed in her conversation with Justice Haynes was not a new development; it had resided in her character all along.

Disappointment struck him like a blow in the gut, forcing him to choke back the bitter bile that rose in his throat. Daryn had had an *abortion.* She'd aborted their child and lied about it because she knew he wanted the baby. Though Paul had supported a woman's right to choose, she'd known him well enough to know he could never willingly abort *his* child. His sense of family ran too deep, and that Catholic conscience she was always griping about had been real and alive in him then . . .

So she had lied. And rather than risk her future again, she had gone home to Georgia and begun a life apart from the one they'd planned.

He lifted his gaze to the window, where the rain made long, wavering runnels down the windowpanes. He was such a fool! Love had blinded him in '79; lust had blinded him in the last year. He'd excused Daryn's little lies, accepted her assurances that what one did in one's private life didn't count, but it did. Concealed corruption had a nasty habit of creeping to the surface like underground oil . . .

He remembered what the newscaster said, how the nurse had changed her story. How had Daryn managed that? Someone must have tipped her off about the Entertainment Television report, then Daryn or Thrasher dispatched someone else to take care of the nurse. Someone high in the power pyramid, no doubt, who could charmingly convince the woman that she could find a faulty memory more profitable than a clear one.

Outside the window, a wet wind moved in the trees. Paul pressed his hand to his face as grief rose up from within him and became a presence so overwhelming and palpable it was like another body in the room—a threatening, accusing presence. How could he have been so foolish?

When she'd told him about losing the baby, he had blamed God for taking the child. In her kitchen he had tried to comfort her, but in the privacy of his apartment he had stormed and railed and broken things in the heat of his anger. God was heartless, he had decided, uncaring and unconcerned. He had confessed his sin of fornication when Daryn told him she was pregnant, he had promised to marry her and be the best father he could be, yet God had stolen the child away—

But he hadn't.

Daryn had destroyed their baby. Swept it from her womb, just as she had swept him from the heart of his family and then from the White House.

His years of indifference, cynicism, and blame—all the result of a lie.

A lie that was now public knowledge. The White House would deny the story, of course, and millions of Americans had probably already dismissed it. Daryn's enemies would trumpet the original affidavit, seeing the nurse as the equivalent of Clinton's Paula Jones, but Ms. Jones had never recanted. His fellow justices would hear the report, and a few might even believe it, but they'd never want to become involved in a presidential scandal. They had outlasted rascals in the White House before, and they would outlast them again.

But what about Cristina? She'd hear the news and put the pieces together. If she didn't, a thousand and one reporters would be willing to paint the picture for her. She might be hounded at school, while Maria—

A new flash of grief stabbed at him. Even now the truth had to be seeping into her bones like cold on a winter's morning. From the wintry voice of a reporter, she had learned that her husband had not only created a baby with another woman, but that he had kept secrets from her for over twenty years. And with one look at Paul's face, she would recognize the bitter reality.

"O God!" Paul felt the astringent sting of tears. "What have I done?"

Slipping from his chair, he crumpled to the floor and felt the well of untapped emotions within him rise and erupt in a scalding geyser of regret.

He wasn't certain how long he wept, but when a deep voice rumbled through the silence, he was ready to listen.

"Your wife called me," Justice Crispin said, standing in the doorway, a look of incomparable compassion on his face. "Don't you think it's time we talked?"

Looking up, Paul shriveled at the sight of concern he didn't deserve. Then, wordlessly, he nodded.

THIRTY-ONE

DRIVEN BY A BARELY TAMPED FIRE THAT RAGED within him, Clive sat at a table in the Sassy Moose Inn and fired off another letter to the president. He'd heard the news this morning when he'd come into town for supplies, and the way everybody at the inn was giggling about it, nothing at all had changed in Washington. The president was still doing wrong and getting away with it. Didn't matter if it was a man or woman in the White House, things were business as usual in politics. These people were still walking down the path of sin and tempting others to do the same, then lying and trying to cover it all up.

Well, this time the Washington witch had gone too far. Abortion was a troublesome thing, even though Jimmy Griffin often pointed out its advantage (keeping minority births to a bearable minimum), but a white woman who'd abort a (presumably) white baby—well, that was an affront to the whole flea-flickin' world.

You, the Witch of Washington—

He took a deep breath to calm his racing heart. He couldn't get sloppy now, couldn't let himself slip up. This paper was fine, just a blank second sheet from the Sassy Moose, and the ballpoint was one of about ten thousand for sale at the Jackson General Market. He was wearing his gloves (the April chill made this unremarkable, even to the locals), and for all the folks drinking coffee at the bar knew, he was writing out his grocery list. No sir, no one would pick up on this, no one at all.

Do not prostitute thy daughter, to cause her to be a whore; lest the land fall to whoredom, and the land become full of wickedness. And the daughter of any priest, if she profane herself by playing the whore, she profaneth her father: she shall be burnt with fire. (Lev. 19:29; 21:9)

You, Witch of Washington, have profaned the memory of our White forefathers. You have slept with wickedness; you have committed murder; you have tried to cover up your sin. And he that covers sin shall not prosper! You shall not only not prosper, but you shall die in your sin, and many people shall see the sight, and shall know what you have done.

Jehu

Trembling, Clive finished the letter, then pulled a napkin from beneath a set of silverware. The silverware clattered and fell to the floor as he dipped the napkin into his water glass.

"You okay over there, Clive?" Susie, the round waitress, lifted her chin in his direction. "You want some coffee?"

He swiped the wet napkin over the adhesive on the envelope. "Not today, Susie. I got somewhere to go."

"A little coffee would help keep you awake."

"I'm plenty awake, thank you." He paused to give her a deliberate smile. If anyone asked, the folks at the Sassy Moose would say he'd been happy as a lark on the morning of April ninth. A man without a care in the world.

"Okay, then." Susie turned and slid her coffeepot back onto the burner. "You drive careful now, you hear?"

"I will." Clive slid the envelope into his coat, then stood and flipped a couple of quarters on the table even though he'd had nothing but water. Susie would remember that, and tell anyone who asked that Clive was the nicest, most generous, and most reasonable white man in all Wyoming.

Satisfied with his preparations, he shoved his hands into his jacket pockets and strode out the door.

●

One of the nicest perks awarded to the chief justice was the chief justice's office—a huge three-room suite, with an inner office large enough to hold a conference table and nine matching leather chairs. On days when the Court did not sit, the justices were most often in conference, a term Paul considered a misnomer. They didn't often *confer* about the cases on the docket, but rather shared their already-formed opinions. In order, by seniority, Chief Justice Franklin would call upon the others to offer any comment they wished to make, and all justices were given the chance to speak before anyone could assume the floor again. As a result, the conferences were often long, dry, and repetitive.

As the junior justice, Paul sat closest to the paneled door because to him fell the task of calling for reports, pens, and occasional pitchers of water. When the Supremes were in conference, no one else, not even a secretary, could enter the room.

The justices' conference began with the traditional shaking of hands, then the brethren took their seats around the large table. Paul nodded at his fellow justices and wondered if his smile showed any frayed edges. The weekend had been long and draining, and he still felt a bit like a volcano on the verge of erupting. Justice Crispin's visit had given him a new lease on life, but he still had to deal with the vestiges of the old one . . .

Maria had said nothing further about the president's alleged abortion, and none of the clerks in Paul's office had mentioned the weekend brouhaha. But a trophy fish had been spotted in the river of the press pool's imagination, and only if bigger game came along would they stop trying to reel in the details . . .

"We'll begin by revisiting our discussions on *MKB Management Corporation dba Free Choice Women's Clinic v. Maddox*," Chief Justice Franklin announced, pulling out the leather folio holding his papers. "As usual, we'll comment in order of seniority, then open the floor for further comment."

Harold Woodward, as the most senior member of the Court, began by rambling through a series of similar cases involving health warnings. After twenty minutes of rehearsing details they had all already uncovered, he summed up his position: "If the government," he pulled back his shoulders and lifted his granite jaw, "requires health warnings on packages of cigarettes, women should certainly be notified of an increased cancer risk resulting from an elective abortion. The First Amendment not only guarantees freedom of speech, I believe it sometimes necessitates speech. So we must uphold the North Dakota court decision."

Paul lowered his eyes and pretended to scan his own notes. Without hearing the others' arguments, he could already predict that Woodward, Crispin, and Tolson would side with Maddox, while Franklin, Richards, and Layton would side with the Free Choice Women's Clinic, the petitioner. Becket and Cookson would cast the deciding votes, and the pressure would fall upon him if they split.

The discussion continued around the table, with the debate moving to the legal authority of states versus the rights of women, then swinging toward issues of free speech and the separation of powers. Franklin criticized the reliability of the medical research, but Crispin, speaking in turn, pointed out the fallacies in studies claiming to disprove the connection between abortion and breast cancer. Becket added little to the conversation, saying he preferred to wait until he'd heard his colleagues' remarks, then Cookson flatly stated that while she was concerned about women's health issues, she would hate to be a part of any judgment that might cast a pall over a woman's right to privacy and the inherent right to abortion. "Furthermore," she added, her nostrils flaring slightly, "I can't believe we're hearing this case. The Tenth Amendment requires jurisdictional matters such as this to be referred back to the state."

"Thank you, Justice Cookson," the chief justice said, his voice dry. "But since a majority of us believe this concerns a broader constitutional picture, we are hearing it."

Finally the table looked at Paul. "Mr. Justice Santana." Chief Justice Franklin moved his head slightly to improve his perspective. "May I ask if you have considered recusing yourself from this case? I understand your wife is a breast-cancer patient."

Paul lifted his chin. "I'm sorry, Mr. Chief Justice, but I fail to see why I should recuse myself. My wife does have breast cancer, but she has never had an abortion. *Free Choice Women's Clinic v. Maddox* has nothing to do with my personal situation."

The chief justice nodded. "Then may we have your thoughts on this matter?"

Taking pains not to look at Justice Crispin, Paul spread his hands. "I'm afraid I have nothing further to add. The disadvantage of speaking last, of course, is that many of you have already voiced my opinions. And so, in an effort to save time, I'll return the discussion to you, Mr. Chief Justice Franklin."

Franklin's brows flickered slightly, but then he turned to Woodward and asked if there were any issues the most senior justice would like to revisit.

●

Daryn had just completed a meeting with the new Russian president when Anson Quinn burst into the Oval Office and jerked her away from the window.

"What?" She stumbled forward, then caught herself on the edge of the guest chair.

"A gunman at the property perimeter," Quinn said, his weapon extended. He stared out the French doors, his eyes focused. Almost instantly, two other agents came through the other doors, each with their weapons drawn.

Daryn sank into the chair. She was fine, perfectly safe, but the thought of gunplay sent terror snaking down her backbone.

She forced herself to breathe deeply. "President Varvarinski—is he safely away?"

"Affirmative." Quinn still would not look at her. "He's secure at Blair House."

She acknowledged this with a nod. "So he wasn't the target?"

"Negative."

Then she heard it—the muffled report of distant gunshots, dry, thin sounds like sticks snapping underfoot. She brought her hand to her chest as her heart rate increased.

The agents at the windows tensed, then Quinn murmured something into the radio microphone at his sleeve. After a moment woven of eternity, all three agents relaxed and returned their weapons to their holsters.

Thrasher burst into the room, perspiration shining on his forehead. "Madam President! You're all right?"

"Of course." She straightened in her chair, determined that not even he should see her anxiety. "No one could get in here with a gun."

"Well, we didn't know how many there were, or exactly what was happening—"

"I'd like to know, exactly." Daryn looked at Quinn. "A full report as soon as possible, please."

●

The call rang into Paul's chambers at two that afternoon. He marked his place in the book he was reading, then picked up the phone. "Yes?"

"Did you hear? Someone just tried to kill me."

The voice was Daryn's, and a faint thread of hysteria ran through it. Despite his intention to face her calmly, Paul felt a breath of fear blow down the back of his neck.

"Are you all right?"

"Of course, it was only a single shooter. He didn't get past the gate."

"Thank God."

"Thank the Secret Service, you mean." Now he heard a smile in her voice. "Listen, Counselor, that's not why I'm calling."

Paul stirred uneasily in his chair. "Go on, then."

"Don't let them recuse you from the Free Choice Clinic case," she said, her voice going taut with energy. "I'm not too late, am I?"

Frowning, he turned to see if any of his clerks stood near the open doorway, then lowered his voice. "How did you know we would be discussing that case today?"

"Come now, Paul, surely you don't think everyone who works in that place has taken a vow of silence? Besides, it wasn't hard to guess. Maria's condition is common knowledge around here, and I knew the case was on the docket. I'm a little mystified, though, about *why* it made it this far."

For an instant anger singed his control. She was accusing him of disloyalty? He ought to confront her about the abortion, about his belief that the rumors were true. But he could not talk about that over the phone. She might not have respected their life together, but he did, and he would confront her face to face.

"I need to see you," he said, his breath burning in his throat. "Soon."

"Well." Her voice went husky. "I want to see you, too. But I'm leaving this afternoon for a little R and R at Camp David, then flying to Brussels. I won't be back to Washington for at least eight days."

He searched his memory for news of an international trip and found nothing. How quickly had Thrasher arranged this little junket? He had probably worked a miracle to pull things together so quickly. He'd do anything to get Daryn out of town and turn the press toward something more interesting than an abortion scandal.

"When you return, then. Will you let me know a good time?"

"Perhaps." Her voice was light, lilting. "First I need you to promise you won't recuse yourself from the Free Choice case. I need your vote, and I need you to convince Becket and Cookson." She paused. "But maybe you already know how the others will vote."

"I don't." Paul felt a twinge of conscience at this, but at least two other justices had been noncommittal. "I'm sure the others will vote their own minds."

"I need to know I can depend on you."

He swallowed a surge of bitter laughter, then rebellious words tumbled over the barricades of his earnest intentions. "I need to know something, too. Did you abort our child?"

He heard the hiss of the phone line, followed a moment later by a forced three-note laugh. "Why, Counselor! I can't believe you listen to gossip television."

Paul bit back an oath. "Have a good trip, Madam President. I'll be waiting to hear from you."

Before she could respond, he dropped the phone back into its cradle, then covered his face with his hand.

A new life, Justice Crispin had said. A life complete with forgiveness, peace, and goodness. The Spirit would act as his guide, Crispin had promised, and the Scripture would lead him. Like all things, he'd start out as a baby, digesting spiritual truths one bite at a time . . .

Lifting his head, Paul blew out his breath and ran his hand over his shirt, smoothing his tie. One day at a time.

In his dark hours with Crispin, he'd come to understand that all his beliefs were false. Until last Friday night he had believed himself a fair and kind man, a man of integrity, if not honor. But Daryn's deception, and his part in it, made him see himself for what he was—a selfish man who was slowly destroying his wife and daughter, a judge who could not rule his own desires.

And there, on his knees in his study, he confessed all his wrongs to Justice Crispin . . . and to God. And after the confession came sweet release, along with the promise of new life. "You told me once that I didn't really know you," Justice Crispin whispered in the stillness of Paul's study. "But I don't have to. The One who died for you knows you better than you know yourself. And he loves you, Paul. He stands ready to forgive."

"It doesn't seem fair," Paul countered. "I've wounded my innocent wife and daughter. I have committed adultery. People look to me for justice, and I'm the biggest hypocrite on earth. It doesn't seem fair that I should be able to wipe all that away simply by saying that I'm sorry."

"Fairness is based on the changing whims of society," Crispin answered. "Justice is founded upon the immutable principles of God's Word. God is just, Paul, but he is also merciful. To those who affirm his righteous standards and confess their failure to achieve them, he grants mercy, undeserved though it may be."

And in that moment, Paul stretched forth his hands and embraced with his heart the love he had never been able to comprehend with his mind. Supported by Justice Crispin, he rose to his feet with a feeling of hope.

"It won't be easy," Justice Crispin had said. "But you will have people praying for you, and you will have the Lord by your side. Do not fear, Paul. Just walk the path Jesus places before you; take it one step at a time."

One foot in front of the other.

There was no turning back now.

●

Twenty minutes later, Quinn and Thrasher sat before Daryn. She felt drained by the experience with the shooter and her conversation with Paul, but Quinn seemed energized. There was a quickness to his movements, a vivacity she hadn't seen in a long time.

"He was a single shooter, apparently acting alone," Quinn said, consulting a notebook. "We found his hotel room and his vehicle—a pickup loaded with enough ammunition to blow the White House to kingdom come. Apparently he was scoping the place out, got caught by the barricades, and was spooked by the guards on bikes. As one of them approached, he pulled a gun, and that's when we got the alert."

She nodded, fascinated and repulsed at the same time. "And then?"

"He kept shouting nonsense, then he pointed at one of the officers and fired. That's when they mortally wounded him."

"The officer?"

"He's fine. Either the shooter wasn't a marksman or he intended to commit suicide by cop. He's dead; the officer is alive and well. End of story—almost."

Daryn raised a brow. "Keep talking, Agent Quinn."

A satisfied light filled his eyes. "We found his wallet and ID in his vehicle. His name was John Hudson, from Rexburg, Idaho."

She shot a confused glance at Thrasher. "Have I done something to offend Idahoans?"

"Don't you see?" Quinn leaned forward. "John Hudson, JH. Jehu. We may have just snagged our nut case. Jackson, Wyoming is only fifty-seven miles from Rexburg."

She leaned back in her chair. "I thought you had a good lead on that guy—didn't you find an e-mail?"

"That lead went nowhere, so the PRD guys assumed Jehu somehow hacked into the school's computer system. But we'll do the background work on this John Hudson guy, and I'd bet my bottom dollar that they find something that ties him to a computer."

"Isn't it odd," Thrasher drawled, "that a hacker would send only *one* e-mail?"

Quinn lifted his hands. "Hey, if there's one thing we've learned in profiling presidential stalkers, it's that they can't be predicted. I think they're crazy, pure and simple."

Daryn pressed her hand to her head as a wave of relief washed over her. The Secret Service still had a long list of potential assassins, but tonight, at least, the list would be one name shorter.

"Thanks, Quinn. I hope you're right."

Taking her comment as a dismissal, Agent Quinn stood and left the room. Thrasher edged forward on his seat, too, but Daryn stopped him with an uplifted hand. When the door closed behind Quinn, she shot her chief of staff a piercing look.

"Who is your source at the Court?"

"Why?" Thrasher's voice was curt. "Did I give you bad information?"

"Not exactly. But Paul said he couldn't tell what the Free Choice vote would be."

"He's hedging his bets." Thrasher leaned back in his chair, his eyes darkening dangerously. "I have it on good authority that they discussed the Free Choice vote in conference today. My source pulled all the documents together."

"So—who's your source? I'd like a name."

Unable to ignore the direct question, Thrasher smiled. "Charles Brogan. One of Santana's own clerks."

Daryn brought the tips of her fingers together. "And how will we repay Mr. Brogan for his help?"

Thrasher shrugged. "A spot in the White House counsel's office would be satisfactory, I'm sure. But he knows he has to pay his dues. I figure he's good for at least a year at the Court."

Daryn nodded. "That's fine. Just be sure he plays straight with us. I want to know what's happening in Santana's office, and I want to know as soon as possible."

THIRTY-TWO

DARYN KNEW THE TRIP TO CAMP DAVID WAS A RUSE, the state visit to Brussels only a media distraction, but she welcomed an opportunity to leave Washington. She needed time to relax and center herself. Since the election she'd been so busy trying to keep campaign promises to special-interest groups and maintain peace among her warring cabinet members that she'd lost sight of her personal goals.

From the presidential retreat in the Catoctin Mountains she phoned Octavia Gifford to bounce a few ideas off her old professor; then she called home to chat with her parents. Her father was not strong, her mother said, but the doctor was adjusting his blood pressure medication so things should be fine soon.

When her father came on the line, she wrapped the phone cord around her wrist as the old insecurities rose in her chest. "Hi, Dad." She glanced out the window. "How's the weather there? Nice and sunny here—"

"Daryn, what's this ridiculous gossip we're hearing?" His voice quavered with age and indignation. "Don't let those right-wingers get you in their sights. You keep moving, you hear? Don't take them seriously for a minute, and nobody else will, either."

"I know, Daddy."

"It's all a bunch of bull malarkey. Nobody who knows you would believe it for a minute." He cackled a laugh. "Abortion! That's almost funny, considering how you were raised. You give 'em guff right back, you hear? Don't let them get ahead of you."

Daryn closed her eyes and exhaled slowly. Her father was as out of touch with her life now as he had been in her early years. Despite all the trouble she'd caused as a teenager, he persisted in seeing her as some kind of virginal princess . . .

"I won't, Dad. And hey—I hear the Atlanta mayor has decided to dedicate a downtown statue to you. That's really something."

As if she'd flipped a switch, his mood shifted from indignation to pride. "Yeah, that *is* something, isn't it? You need to come down here, maybe put in an appearance at the dedication?"

"I'll try, Dad. I'll run it past the scheduling office."

After chatting a few more moments about everything in general and nothing in particular, Daryn hung up the phone, poured herself a stiff shot of bourbon, and stared at the rough hewn walls. Except for Tyson, who slumbered at her feet, and the agents who surrounded the perimeter of the camp, she was completely alone.

And she missed Paul. Even though their relationship had been rocky of late, and though she suspected he hadn't forgiven her for sending him to the Supreme Court, she still needed him. He'd been the friend who accepted the woman beneath the public image, the only man in the White House who didn't think of himself first. He had always been honest with her, even when she didn't want to hear the truth, and he was one of the few men who weren't intimidated by meeting a woman with brains and power.

Bored, she picked up the remote and pressed the power button, then clicked through channels until the image of her own face stopped her cold. A&E was replaying a biography feature they'd put together last fall—a good piece, Thrasher said, that had probably helped them win the election.

Amused by the idea of watching the special from the opposite side of the campaign, she dropped the remote and settled into the sofa cushions with her drink. On the screen, the Daryn image passed through a dozen different metamorphoses—Daryn as campaigner, complete with straw hat sporting red, white, and blue campaign buttons on the crown; Daryn as executive; Daryn as socialite. In the last few frames the camera had caught her at a state dinner dancing with the king of Spain.

"By the fall of 2004 the American people had realized that women do make good presidents," the announcer whispered in a confident voice-over. "Daryn Austin has demonstrated that she can handle an unruly cabinet meeting, command a tank crew, and dance a divine waltz. Perhaps we erred in always giving the presidential nod to men. Perhaps we erred in waiting too long for a woman like Daryn Austin."

Daryn slowly closed her eyes as the warmth of the drink crept into her bones. Paul was still angry with her—that much had been evident in their last phone conversation—but their relationship had always been marked by great passion, and anger could easily flame into desire if given the right opportunity.

He knew about the abortion now, which was unfortunate. Of course, no one would ever prove the nurse's allegation, but Paul knew Daryn too well to accept another lie. He knew the truth about the baby, but surely he could see that it had all worked out for the best. If they'd had that child, they would probably be married—or married and already divorced—and living in Miami or Georgia. Neither one of them would be in Washington. Neither one of them would have made history, either, but because she'd had a little foresight and ambition, now both of them would.

The TV image faded to a shot of Daryn and Tyson gamboling on the South Lawn of the White House. "President Daryn Austin," the narrator said. "Confident, quick, and firmly in command. One of the new breed of female executives who stand ready to lead our nation in the twenty-first century. We can only hope she'll be given every opportunity to do so."

So. She tossed back the rest of her drink, then dropped the glass to the varnished pine table. When she returned to Washington, she'd have to face Paul, bear his anger, and then point out that she'd been right all along. For he seemed to be enjoying his new work, and from the looks of things he would have a far longer career at the Court than she could ever have at the White House. The history books would glow with praise for Supreme Court Justice Paul Santana, and historians would forever link their names in cross references.

Turning, she tucked her knee under her and smiled at a songbird who watched her from a branch outside the window. "Do you know, little bird," she whispered, "who you're watching?"

The bird stared at her another moment, its bright black eyes shining, then flew away. Daryn reached for the bottle and poured herself another drink—one of the advantages of a private presidential retreat was that she could drink all she wanted and no one would care or notice. There was no one here to remark upon her manner, her speech, no one to snap her picture or record her most casual words . . .

Freedom. And loneliness. Just a day in the life of an exemplary commander in chief.

●

On the nineteenth of April, Daryn landed on the South Lawn in the presidential chopper. As she stepped out from *Marine One*, she waved to the members of the press in their cordoned area within the black iron fence, then paused to clap her hands for Tyson's attention. The bulky mastiff, who had weighed 250 pounds at his last checkup, lumbered down the steps, then jogged toward his mistress with a goofy grin on his face.

Daryn stood upright and smiled, well-aware of the rhythm of the clicking cameras to her right. After a moment of silence for pictures, she caught Tyson's collar and walked over to the press cordon, knowing that the smart reporters had remembered to bring dog biscuits.

"Madam President!"

"Isn't he handsome?" She glanced at the reporters en masse. "I missed him while I was in Europe."

"Madam President, have you any comment about the abortion story?"

"What happened to the Entertainment Television report?"

"Whose baby did you abort?"

Steadfastly ignoring the questions she did not want to answer, Daryn met the gaze of a reporter with a doggy treat in his hand. "You must have a dog of your own."

"Indeed, I do." The man straightened, a blush brightening his pale skin. "Nigel Thompson, ma'am, of the British Press."

"Nice to meet you, Nigel."

Nigel, apparently no fool, knew how to play the game. "Did you accomplish your goals in Brussels?"

Daryn gave him a friendly smile. "Indeed, I believe I made a start. I spoke at the European Union's Commission on Women, an audience of over five hundred international female delegates. My topic was female circumcision, a terrible problem in many countries including our own. Female genital mutilation, as it ought to be called, has been performed on over one hundred million women. As African immigrants move to this country, bringing their customs with them, we are seeing more American girls mutilated every year."

"How's the dog, Madam President?" Another reporter waved his hand, but Daryn looked at Nigel Thompson.

"Any other questions?"

"Um, just one." He squinted up at her through a pair of black-rimmed glasses. "Since women's issues are one of your favorite causes, can you confirm the alleged abortion?"

Daryn turned on her heel, leaving Nigel and his cohorts behind the roped-off area. Tyson lumbered at her side as a stream of questions flowed into the afternoon silence.

"Did you know this nurse?"

"Who were you sleeping with in 1979?"

"Has this any connection to Justice Paul Santana?"

That one stung, but she pressed her lips together and kept walking.

●

Once inside the Oval Office, Daryn embraced the three secretaries who seemed genuinely glad to see her, then picked up a stack of phone messages Miss Park considered vital. She had received packets of briefings while on the road, but a new stack of leather-bound reports had already appeared on her desk. She riffled through them, then hesitated when her gaze fell upon a copy of a Supreme Court decision dated April 19: *MKB Management Corporation dba Free Choice Women's Clinic v. Maddox.*

"Miss Park," she called, picking up the folder. "When did this decision release?"

The secretary stepped into the Oval. "It was announced in the courtroom this morning, Madam President. The printed report arrived a few hours ago."

Sinking into her chair, Daryn opened the folder and began to read. The reporter of decisions had added a headnote summarizing the decision at the beginning of the opinion, and Daryn eagerly skimmed it. The Court had ruled against the petitioner by a six-three vote . . . and Paul Santana authored the majority opinion.

With rising horror, she read the Court document. Not only did the justices uphold Ms. Maddox's right to sue for false advertising, but Santana urged states to consider displaying printed warnings in hospitals, abortion clinics, and gynecologists' offices . . .

She drew in a quick breath, seething with mounting rage. Paul had not only voted against her, he had come out from anonymity to tell the world why he disagreed with his president.

Though she could have easily roared with anger, she punched the button on her intercom to address Miss Park. "Send Thrasher in immediately, please. And tell him to bring any clips he has on the Free Choice decision."

Five minutes later Thrasher entered through the hallway door, his face cherry-colored and his tie askew. Without a word, he dropped a handful of printed wire reports on her desk, then dropped into the empty guest chair.

"If there is a bright side to this," he said, both brows lifting, "It's that now no one is calling Santana your puppet."

She picked up a copy of an editorial cartoon. In the picture, a man in a black robe stood on the White House lawn, his thumbs in his ears, fingers a-twiddling, and his tongue thrust out. The caption: "Bleah!"

She resisted the surge of fury that murmured in her ear. "They don't waste any time, do they?"

"No. They don't."

"Then let's get Santana over here."

Thrasher shook his head. "I don't think that would be politic. The press would see him coming in, and you'd stir up the relationship rumors we've been trying to stamp out."

Raking her hand through her hair, she frowned, then looked up and met his gaze. "Then call for my car. I'm going out."

Thrasher bit his lip. "I'm thinking there's not time to arrange for the full motorcade. Quinn will need at least a couple of hours, and you have that dinner with Senator Howard tonight—"

"I don't want a motorcade. I want one car, nondescript, and Quinn can throw in a backup if he wants. But I *am* going out and I'm going out now."

His face darkened with unreadable emotions. "Are you sure that's wise?"

"You bet it is. I've got to contain the damage before Paul gets out of hand."

●

Just after three o'clock, as Paul was walking to his office from the Supreme Court library, two athletic-looking men in dark coats appeared at his side. He recognized one of them as Wayne Sovocol, a member of Daryn's Presidential Protection Detail. "Mr. Justice Santana," Sovocol said, gesturing toward the elevator. "The president would like to have a word with you."

Paul halted, his body tingling in shock. "She's here?"

"Come. She's waiting."

Staring at his companions, Paul shifted his briefcase from one hand to the other, then stepped into the elevator. Though these guys looked like they meant business, Sovocol might have been recruited for some kind of joke. Presidents didn't pop across town to visit congressional representatives or justices, and for Daryn to drop her busy schedule—

Unless she'd read the court opinion. They had announced it in session that morning, and she would have received a copy this afternoon.

"Gentlemen," Paul said, trying not to let his exasperation show on his face, "I'm afraid I'm a little out of the loop these days. Would one of you care to enlighten me about the nature of this meeting?"

Neither of them answered, but he didn't really expect them to. He had known this meeting was inevitable, and perhaps it was best that she had come to him—he would feel like a rookie ballplayer being trashed by the manager if she had summoned him to the Oval Office. But where were they going?

He glanced at the elevator panel and saw that the round button marked *B* was lit. *B* for basement, where the Supreme Court had hidden its parking garage.

The elevator stopped. From force of habit Paul stepped out and turned toward the right, where he parked every morning, but one of the agents gripped his elbow—a little roughly, Paul thought—and propelled him toward the left, where the shadows gathered in deep pools.

The car parked there, he saw as they approached, was not the new presidential limo that drew attention like dead men draw flies. This was a smaller sedan, almost ordinary in its design, and the windows had been tinted to complete opaqueness. One of the agents stopped at the front bumper, while Sovocol escorted Paul to the back and opened the door. Stooping, he saw the sheen of blonde hair reflecting in the dome light.

"Madam President?"

"Get in."

He slid in. The door slammed, and Sovocol walked forward to stand with his partner, both of them facing the expanse of the garage beyond. Paul glanced at the front. No driver.

"Isn't this a lapse in security?" He gestured toward the empty front seat. "Only two Secret Service guys?"

A faint smile played at the corners of her mouth. "There's a car full of agents at the entrance."

Turning, he waited for his eyes to adjust to the deep gloom. Daryn looked as lovely as ever, though deep lines bracketed the sides of her mouth. He didn't need the overhead light to see determination in the jut of her chin.

"What—" her voice was like chilled steel—"did you think you were doing? I've just read the Free Choice opinion."

Paul forced a smile. "I'm honored you took the time to read my first majority decision."

"Have you completely lost your mind, Paul? I sent you to the Court to preserve women's rights, to uphold all we've won over the last few years! I gave you every lawyer's dream job, and you've used it to slice my throat!"

His mind filled with sour thoughts. "Perhaps you forgot to read the job requirements. A Supreme Court justice is to render decisions to the best of his ability. And that's exactly what I've done."

"Without me, you'd still be working immigration cases in Miami!"

"Without you, dear Daryn, I'd be living near my family, close to the people I know and love." Struggling to control his frustration, he softened his tone. "Strange, isn't it? I never realized how much I loved Miami until you guaranteed I could never return there."

Her face twisted as if someone had suddenly struck her, then her blue eyes trained on him. "This is about the baby, isn't it? You heard about the abortion and you wanted to strike back at me."

"What abortion?" He said the words slowly, allowing them to hang in the empty space between them. "You *miscarried.* That's what you said, and I thought I could believe you."

A car passed in the garage, rippling light and shadows over Daryn's expressionless face. "I gave you the truth you wanted to hear," she finally said. "I knew you couldn't handle anything else. For all your talk about women's rights and freedom of choice, I knew you wouldn't accept my decision to terminate the pregnancy. You'd rather I terminate my dreams and my career. For all your posturing and preening, I knew a machismo Latino lived beneath that charming facade, eager to father sons—"

"You're being unfair. I was committed to your career, too."

She laughed softly. "I don't think so. Any woman who takes time off to bear children will never catch up to her male peers in the workplace; any fool knows that. Besides—" she leaned closer, her eyes large and challenging before him—"I had to hide the truth from you. Even if I could have convinced you of the sense in it, your inbred Catholic guilt would have made you miserable. You would have destroyed us."

"So you destroyed our baby."

"Don't use archaic and inflammatory language with me! It was a fetus, a blob of *tissue.*"

"It was a preborn baby, just as the young woman I loved was a pre-elected president!"

She glared at him. "Now you're being fatuous."

"I'm being logical. You killed our baby, and then you killed us. You went to Georgia, you followed your dreams, or should I say you followed your father's—"

"I never stopped loving you." Her words were warm, but her eyes flashed like cold steel. "I loved you, Counselor, but I couldn't trust you to do the right thing. And now I see nothing's changed. The moment I leave the country, you make a point of doing the one thing that will most upset my constituents—"

"I would have done it no matter where you were. I would have voted as I did no matter who sent me to the Court. Logic demanded my vote, and concern for women—"

She snorted.

He grabbed her arm and held her tight. "Yes, my concern for women, for you! Have you never considered that having an abortion has put you at a greater risk for breast cancer?"

"That's a lie." Her eyes glittered with accusation. "I've seen those studies; they're pure poppycock. None of the leading American medical societies will support them."

"They're frightened, that's all, the same way hospitals in the early days were afraid to admit that smoking causes cancer. You have let your ambition blind you, Daryn; you're so eager to do the politically profitable thing that you no longer have any idea what the right thing is."

Without warning she spat at him, the cold wetness blasting his cheek. His grip on her arm tightened as violence bubbled beneath the surface of his skin, then, with an effort, he willed his fingers to release her.

"I don't expect you to understand," he said when he could speak in a controlled tone. He reached for the handkerchief in his pocket. "But when I heard about the abortion, all the pieces fell into place. And then I realized that your miscarriage was the pivotal event that caused me to turn my back on God so many years ago. I blamed him for everything that had happened, but he had nothing to do with it."

Her lips went thin. "So—now I'm the devil?"

Carefully he wiped the spittle from his cheek. "You were confused and selfish, Daryn, as was I. But now I see things clearly and I know God is not my enemy. He's been waiting for me all this time, ready to forgive, ready to help me out of the mess I've made. And now when I consider the world, I find that my viewpoint has changed. I expect many of my positions to change as well."

The line of her mouth tightened a fraction more. "So now you've joined the religious right?"

He chuckled. "I wouldn't say that, but I am beginning to see things differently." He paused, searching for words she would understand. "It's hard to explain, but I've met God on a personal level. It's profound. The warp and woof of my life has been subtly altered."

He hesitated as someone stepped from the elevator and began to walk through the parking lot. The Secret Service agents tensed, their heads following the man's movement, and as the fellow moved into a beam of sunlight, Paul recognized him—Charles Brogan, one of his own law clerks.

When he looked at Daryn again, he saw that disappointment and frustration had brought a hard frown and a glint of temper to her face. "Does your *wife* approve of this change?"

He lowered his gaze, unable to look at Daryn while his brain replaced her image with the gloomily colored memory of Maria in the hour he had confessed all his failures. She'd been hurt, wounded in heart and soul, but after a time of weeping her arms had reached out to draw him close and whisper words of forgiveness. She had offered him love at a time when she needed it far more than he had, and her forgiveness, paid for with his own shame, had begun to dissolve the burning rock of guilt in the pit of his gut.

"Maria," he said, his thoughts bittersweet, "is stronger than either of us. I told her everything, and she forgave me."

Daryn's eyes were as hard as iron; her mouth drawn up into a knot. "You are worthless to me, Paul. I wish I'd never called you from Miami."

He dropped the soiled handkerchief to the leather upholstery. "I'd agree with you, but then I would never have learned the truth. And the truth, as they say, has set me free."

Shifting, he reached for the door. "Maria, too, has changed," he said, realization beginning to bloom in his brain. "She's a different woman now and a hundred times stronger. If she were here, she'd probably thank you."

Daryn's fingertips brushed his sleeve. "Paul," she whispered, her voice breaking, "I'm sorry for the things I said. I'm sorry for the past and how I lied to you. I'll do anything to make up for it, but don't leave like this. And don't turn against me on the Court."

Turning, he saw that from this distance she looked pitiful and small against the voluminous leather seat cushions. The tracks of tears shone upon her cheeks, while mascara smudged the rims of her eyes.

He could feel her loneliness creeping through the car like a fog . . . and this, too, was his fault. By allowing himself to love her, he had grievously wronged two women.

Floundering in an agonizing maelstrom of despair, he lowered his head to meet her gaze. "I'm sorry, Daryn, that I allowed you to depend upon emotional support that was not rightfully mine to give. I know this is hard to hear, but I hope you can eventually forgive me for the pain I've caused you."

"Paul!" She wept in earnest now, extending her arm toward him as he stood outside the car. Her face filled with anguished pleading. "Paul, don't leave me!"

Aching with an inner pain he dared not express, he closed his eyes to block the sight of her tears. "Good-bye, Madam President."

The Secret Service agents didn't even flinch when Paul closed the door and moved away.

●

For three days Daryn couldn't stop trembling. Even though she kept her hands calm and still in her lap during the state dinner on Friday night, a trembling rose from inside her and spilled unexpectedly from her voice, her knees, her eyes. During the meal she had to lower her gaze as the Canadian prime minister addressed her, lest he see the twitching of her lashes and wonder at her distress.

In those moments when her guests expected her to perform, she pressed on a plastic smile and rose to the occasion, letting the rehearsed words of her speech flow while her thoughts revolved around a man who might as well be a world removed.

Her heart squeezed in anguish as she recalled the note of finality she'd heard in Paul's voice the last time they met, a note she'd never heard before. And his hot Latin temper—a temper she'd succeeded in evoking a hundred times before—had vanished, even after she insulted him in the most impolite way. Had this religion business really changed him? If so, he would now be more dangerous as a foe than he'd ever been as a secret lover.

As she smiled at the prime minister, even her lips felt cold. Paul's betrayal had torn a gash in the heart she'd protected and toughened and fortified against everything life could throw at her. Her distant father had wanted a son, so Daryn had done everything she could to excel in areas where the Austin son might have been expected to excel. Her teachers had wanted her to shine, and so she'd shimmered like a meteor, rocketing far out of an ordinary orbit to command awards and attention. The state of Georgia had wanted a star as governor, and so she had done her best to make the governor's mansion a showplace, to advance the Peach State in education, transportation, standards of living . . .

Paul had wanted an intellectual equal, a beautiful woman to fill his bed, and a wife—and she couldn't be all three.

The evening's entertainment, a young Asian cellist, took center stage and bowed first to her, then to the Canadian prime minister. Daryn led the applause, grateful for the noise. Perhaps it would cover the pounding of her anxious heart.

As the young virtuoso began to wield his bow, she focused her gaze on him as her thoughts played leapfrog amid the flowing melodic passages. For years to come, Paul Santana would continue to wreak havoc on the Supreme Court. Lorne Crispin was a known Bible-thumper, and, according to rumor, Carolyn Cookson had begun to attend an evening Bible study at the Crispin home. Crispin himself was almost a moot point, for years of right-wing decisions had resulted in a reputation for intolerance and extreme conservatism. Besides, his advanced age would limit his years on the bench.

Paul, however, could serve another twenty to thirty years on the Court. Why should he have thirty years when she, who had been *elected* by the American people, could only have another eight at most? He had profited from her ambition and hard work, and then he had betrayed her, publicly thumbing his nose at the woman who had given him the world.

She caught the eye of a waiter, then tapped the stem of her empty wineglass. As he hastened to fill it, she refocused on the cellist and applied a fresh smile.

Something would have to be done with Paul Santana, and soon, before he had another opportunity to communicate his altered viewpoint to the nation. He had stabbed her in the back on *Free Choice v. Maddox*; if she didn't do something he could slice her throat on even larger issues.

Quietly, Daryn reached out and tugged on Thrasher's sleeve. As he leaned toward her, she whispered, "Find Samuel Tomlin, and have him meet me in the Oval ASAP. I'll be going there as soon as the concert concludes." Without saying a word, Thrasher nodded, then stood and hurried away, his shoulders hunched with the urgency he'd heard in her tone.

Daryn sipped her wine, aware that dozens of curious faces had turned in her direction. She kept her eyes on the cellist, nodding her head slightly to the gentle rhythm of the music.

She'd let them wonder.

●

Tomlin had not arrived by the time she returned to the Oval Office, so she wandered into her private study and poured herself a drink from the bottle of scotch hidden in the bottom cupboard. She'd had three glasses of wine at dinner, but they paled in comparison to the power of the scotch. Its warmth seemed to trickle through her veins and arm her with courage.

Falling into the chair behind the desk, she stretched out her long legs and studied the way her calf peeked through the slit in her beaded gown. Paul had always liked her legs. But apparently God no longer approved of his liking.

"Madam President?" The door opened a crack and she caught a glimpse of Thrasher's blue eyes.

"Come in." Pushing herself up out of the chair, she stood to shake Tomlin's hand. "Thank you for coming, Director Tomlin. I'm sorry to bring you out at such a late hour."

Any other government official might have been curious, but Tomlin, executive director of the CIA, merely shook her hand. When he released her, he pointed to the closest of the leather chairs in the study. "Should I sit here?"

"Please. Jacob—" she sank into her chair—"I'd like you to stay, too."

When both men had settled themselves, she picked up a pen and idly tapped it against the desk. "I've made a mistake, gentlemen." She let her head fall against the leather headrest on her chair. "I trusted Paul Santana, and this week he betrayed us." She blinked in Tomlin's direction. "Have you read the Supreme Court decision in the Free Choice Clinic case?"

The man's expression did not change. "I did not, Madam President."

She lifted both brows, then placed a hand to her chest to stifle a small belch. "Doesn't matter. Santana has opened the lid of Pandora's box, and all sorts of evils are about to swarm over us. As the decision now stands, family planning clinics cannot tell women that abortion is safe. In his decision Santana went so far as to suggest that Congress pass *laws* requiring warnings to be posted in all family planning clinics! He wants women to be terrified not only of an unwanted pregnancy, but of the slim chance of breast cancer, too. He has become a tool of the religious right, and this—" she leaned forward to look Tomlin in the eye—"does not bode well for the future."

She shifted her gaze to Thrasher, who rubbed at his temple, then said, "Could we find him guilty of some crime? We could have him impeached."

"An impeachment could drag on for months, even a year." Daryn dropped the pen and picked up her scotch, not caring if these two saw her drinking. Both of them worked at her pleasure, and both of them would be *gone* if she wanted them out.

Glancing down at her desk, she picked up her train of thought. "The Senate would be involved in an impeachment process, and we'd have to deal with one hundred curious voices. The procedure would be messy . . . and difficult. I doubt we'd be able to find anything to make Paul Santana appear guilty of a crime." She turned her gaze upon the CIA director. "Even if you found something, you'd have trouble making it stick. Santana is now a choirboy." She laughed, amused by the image. "He's gone from boy scout to choirboy—why am I surprised?"

Thrasher cleared his throat. "Could we convince him to retire?"

"At fifty-one? Not likely. He hasn't served fifteen years, so he couldn't draw a pension. I suppose we could suggest that he go back to Miami, but I suspect he's grown attached to his new position . . . and the power."

She shook her head slightly. "No, gentlemen, I don't think either impeachment or retirement are options for Paul Santana, but we have to do something. So if you should happen to come up with an answer I haven't considered, I trust you'll do your best to make our problem go away."

Silence fell over the room, a quiet so thick the only sound was the soft rhythmic whistle of Thrasher's breathing.

Daryn closed her eyes, then pressed her hand to her chest. "Thank you for coming, gentlemen, but you'll have to excuse me now. I'm really not feeling well."

THIRTY-THREE

MARIA BREATHED IN THE OVERPOWERING SCENT of carnations, then opened her eyes and saw a swirl of plaster above her head. Where—? Home. She was home, and the pinching pressure at her side came from the bandages.

She'd come home from the hospital a few hours ago, after surgery and a week of supervised recovery. Despite the drug therapy, another obviously aggressive tumor had begun to grow in her breast tissue. After a long discussion with Paul and her doctors, she decided to have a modified radical mastectomy. The operation, followed by yet another round of radiation or chemotherapy, would give her the best chance of survival.

With an effort, she lifted her head. The bedroom was dark, lit only by a dim bulb in the table lamp. The bedside clock said the time was 9 P.M., but the TV was uncharacteristically silent for such an early hour.

A hank of brown hair spilled over the top of the chair facing the TV. "Cristina," she whispered, groggily forcing words over her parched throat. A pitcher and plastic cup stood on the nightstand, but she didn't think she could sit up without help. "Cristina?"

The hair moved, but the face that turned to greet her was Paul's.

"Hi," he said, his swollen eyelids lifting. "Sorry, I must have fallen asleep. What can I get you, honey?"

Maria forced a swallow even as her brain absorbed an unlikely fact: Paul had fallen asleep watching over her.

"Where—" she pushed the words out—"is the nurse?"

"I sent her home." Paul walked to the side of the bed, rubbed his eyes, then gave her a weary smile. "I thought I could handle taking care of you at night. That's a husband's job, isn't it?"

Maria closed her eyes, thinking she might burst from the sudden swell of happiness his words elicited. A tear slipped from beneath her lashes, but she let it fall, afraid to draw attention to it by reaching up to swipe it away.

"Maria, are you all right?" She felt a sinking at the side of the bed, then the touch of a finger upon her cheek.

"I'm fine." She forced her eyes open and blinked another wave of tears away. "It's only—I never expected—"

Paul took her hand. "I know. There are many things you never expected, but should have received. More of my attention. More of my love. And my complete faithfulness."

Swallowing the sob that rose in her throat, she clung to his hand. "I knew I wasn't what you wanted, Pablo. Yet you were kind to marry me—"

"I was a fool to take you for granted. You have been faithfulness and light to me, and I've done you a great wrong." Pressing her hand to his heart, he leaned over her and looked earnestly into her eyes. "I can't remove the misery and hurt I know I've caused, but I can promise you that from this day forward I will try to be the husband I should have been all this time. I only ask that you'll be patient with me. I feel like a child who grew up in Cuba but has forgotten every word of Spanish. Can you, will you, help me be a Christian husband?"

She closed her eyes, her heart aching with joy. "I know you by heart, Pablo," she whispered. "And I trust you, so together we will help each other."

He kissed her then, tenderly and gently, taking care not to press upon the bandages stuck to her chest. As she smiled up at the man she had adored for years, he slipped his arm around her and lifted her head, helping her to drink from the cup. When she had swallowed all she needed, he settled her back onto the pillow and adjusted the blanket.

"The nurse will be here in the morning," he said, smoothing a stray strand of hair from her forehead. "Cristina's coming home, too. I'll try to stay out of their way, but I'm not going back to the Court until you're on your feet. I can work at home, and if the court sits for a case, six judges constitute a quorum." He smiled. "I'm pretty sure they can get by without me."

She opened her mouth to protest, but he pressed a finger across her lips. "Sleep now, *mi amor*," he whispered. "I'll see you in the morning."

●

"Señor Santana?"

Paul jerked instantly upright at the sound of a man's voice. He had fallen asleep in the chair by Maria's bed, but who was this speaking to him? A clutter of thoughts ran through his mind—the day nurse, Cristina, her boyfriend, Jason—but the man pushing the bedroom door open with one gloved hand was none of those people.

Paul lowered his gaze and blinked as his swimming eyes focused upon the glint of a weapon. A gun. And while he didn't know anything about weapons, this gun seemed particularly large and dangerous.

"Señor Santana?" The man's voice was low, almost seductive, and softly accented. "We don't want to wake your wife, do we? So please step out into the hall where we can talk."

For a frantic instant Paul considered diving for the phone on the nightstand, but the intruder discerned his thoughts. "Please, sir—" a note of reproach lined his smooth voice—"we have no time for theatrics. If you want your wife to continue sleeping peacefully, I suggest you come out into the hallway."

Paul stood, pausing only a moment to study Maria's face in the rectangle of light from the doorway. The man made a clicking sound with his tongue, urging Paul forward.

"Te amo," Paul whispered, brushing Maria's hand with his own as he stepped toward the door.

In the hall, he stood tense and quivering, but he kept his voice calm as he met the stranger's steady gaze. "You're not here for money, are you?"

The man smiled, his teeth white and large in a tanned face. "You are clever, Señor Santana. Perhaps this is why they made you a judge, no?"

Speaking with an eerie sense of detachment that sprang from an awareness of impending disaster, Paul took a step toward his study. "Are you going to explain why you're here?"

The man nodded, his dark hair gleaming in the overhead light. "I suspect my reasons will become obvious in a moment. Now we are going into your study, where you will write what I dictate. If you do as I say, no harm will come to your wife."

Paul nodded, alternately amazed and frightened by this new evidence of Daryn's ruthlessness. Walking on legs that felt like wooden stumps, he moved into his study, then sat behind his desk.

"Any particular kind of paper you want me to use for this note?"

"Whatever you have on hand."

Paul pulled a sheet from the drawer, then uncapped his favorite pen. For about ten seconds he considered the idea of rushing the stranger like some sort of hyped-up Rambo, but the man's plan A could easily become plan B, a staged home invasion in which a man and his wife were killed in their beds . . .

No. For Maria's sake, he would not try to be a hero.

Leaning against the bookcase, the man waved the gun from side to side as he dictated a memorized message in a clipped monotone. Paul wrote quickly, hurrying to keep up, and by the time he had filled the page with words he understood everything.

When the stranger finished, he gave Paul another smile, wider than the first. "Sign your name, please, in your usual handwriting."

His hand trembling, Paul obeyed as best he could.

"Now it is time."

Paul grimaced as his stomach churned and tightened into a knot. Beneath his damp hair, his scalp tingled.

Justice Crispin had said the just should live by faith. Did they die by faith, as well?

He glanced up, but apparently the man did not intend to shoot him here. Standing, he stepped out from behind the desk. "Will you give me a moment to make my peace with God?"

The assassin's unending smile dimmed slightly. "One moment only."

Paul dropped to his knees by the side of the desk, then found that his brain was too flooded with fear to form words. Justice Crispin's Bible studies had not yet covered how a Christian man should die . . .

In the interior silence, a voice answered the wordless cry of his soul: *Even when you walk through the dark valley of death, do not be afraid, for I am close beside you.*

He knelt for a moment woven of eternity, then felt the cold kiss of metal at the back of his neck.

"Up." The smile had vanished from the man's voice. "Time to finish."

Paul rose upon trembling legs, then turned slowly, his hands uplifted. "You will not harm my wife?"

"Not as long as you do this right."

"Then tell me exactly what to do."

The man waved the gun toward the French doors. "Open the doors, Mr. Santana, and face the street."

I am close beside you. Even in the dark valley of death.

As the Spirit of God enfolded him, Paul swallowed his fears and moved toward the balcony.

●

Maria drifted in a hazy, drug-influenced sleep where the only sounds were the echoes of her heartbeat and the quiet rumble of the heater as it poured warm air into the room. Occasionally she skated close to wakefulness and pain, then remembered that Paul was keeping watch.

She could sleep in peace.

She drifted on, luxuriating in the healing power of slumber, until a sudden sound cut through the haze like a knife. Burdened with the certainty that something had changed, she swam up through the fog between sleeping and waking, knowing that the situation in the house had somehow been altered.

Her own room, the real world, slowly invaded her consciousness. A chilly breeze caressed her cheek as her eyes opened. A draft? From where? In April, the windows should still be closed.

"Paul?" she called.

She waited, but could see no sign of him in the chair. Though the night-light still burned, no one else breathed in the room. She fell silent but for the pounding of her heart, then pulled herself upright. The world shifted dizzily for a moment, then she swung her legs out of bed and lowered her toes to the rough texture of the Berber carpet.

"Paul?" No answer, though someone creaked the stairs. She knew that familiar sound, knew the second step made that distinctive creak.

She strained her ears, then heard the quiet beep of the alarm system and the soft closing of the front door.

She glanced at the clock—4:15 A.M. Too early for the nurse, but perhaps Cristina had arrived from Cambridge. Paul could have heard her knock and gone down to welcome her. He was probably outside in the driveway now, helping Cristina unload her suitcase.

More awake than asleep now, Maria eased herself off the bed and took tentative steps toward her bedroom door. The door stood partially open, so she caught the edge and leaned against it, pausing to catch her breath. She wasn't supposed to take the stairs so soon after surgery, but she could call out and let Cristina know she could come up. There'd be plenty of time for sleeping tomorrow.

"Cristina?" Clinging to the banister, Maria peered into the darkness of the foyer below. "Honey, is that you?"

No answer, but a fresh breeze blew across the landing. Shivering, she turned, following it to Paul's study. A light burned at his desk, a handwritten page lay upon the blotter, and the French doors stood open, letting a stream of cold air into the room.

"Paul?" For no reason she could name, the sight of the gaping doors sent ghost spiders creeping down her spine. She trembled in the thin material of her gown. "Paul, are you on the balcony?"

She moved closer to peer outside. The terrace looked empty, occupied only by the wicker chair and fern stand she'd placed there months ago. The wind whistled through the trees around the house, sending a remnant of last winter's dead leaves skittering across the tiled terrace.

Her bowels tumbled as she inched forward, the wind strumming another shiver from her weakened frame. She sighed in relief as she stepped onto the balcony, then reached for the brass doorknobs. Despite the cool breeze, the night seemed heavy and ominous, with little star shine or moonlight to brighten the sky.

Hoping to catch a glance of Cristina's car in the drive, she moved closer to the railing. Her trembling hands caught the wrought iron and felt the sting of its frosty touch, then her gaze fell to the driveway. Nothing. Her eyes wandered to the doctor's house across the street, then her attention was distracted by an odd shape in the garden three stories below.

There, outlined by the dim glow of the garden lighting, lay an unmistakable silhouette. Paul lay face down among the sprouting tulips and daffodils, his arms bent at an unnatural angle, his face pressed into the garden outlined by stone borders.

For an instant Maria felt as though she would faint, then her adrenal glands hastened to remedy the situation, dumping such a dose of adrenaline into her bloodstream that her heart contracted like a squeezed fist. Clutching the rail with both hands, she began to scream.

THIRTY-FOUR

"MADAM PRESIDENT?"

Hearing the voice as if it came from far away, Daryn automatically reached for the bedside phone.

"Daryn, it's Jacob. You need to wake up."

Awareness hit her like a slap in the face. Amazed at both the message and the messenger in her bedroom, Daryn's eyes flew open. "What on *earth* has happened?"

Dressed in khakis and a sweater, the most casual she'd ever seen him, Thrasher nodded toward the television as he switched it on with the remote. "The news will hit in a few moments, but I thought you should get a heads-up."

She pulled herself to one elbow and raked her hand through her tousled hair. Not a national emergency, then, but something personal. And important enough that Thrasher had been able to convince Quinn that he needed immediate access to the residence.

She peered at him with bleary eyes. "What is so important that you need to wake me—" she glanced at the clock—"at 6 A.M.?"

Thrasher sank to the edge of the bed. Pushing his fingers through his hair, he released an audible sigh.

Daryn's heart thudded. "Did something happen to one of my parents?"

Thrasher shook his head. "Paul Santana died last night. His wife found him just after four this morning, and the police agree it's a clear case of suicide. He left a note on his desk before jumping."

Her mind, numb from exhaustion, exploded into sharp awareness. "Paul *jumped?* From where?"

"His own balcony. Apparently his home office was three stories up and situated above a rock garden." He grimaced. "High enough to do the job."

Daryn looked away as a dozen different emotions collided. Paul, suicidal? The idea was ridiculous . . . yet he had been unhappy with her, and lately he'd been caught up in that spiritual mumbo jumbo. From the clerk Brogan she'd also heard that Maria's condition had deteriorated—she'd had major surgery just last week, and Paul had gone so far as to take an indefinite leave of absence from the Court. But would those things drive him to suicide?

Sitting up, she lowered her head into her hands, not wanting Thrasher to read the emotions on her face. Could Paul have regretted their last encounter as much as she did? Had he begun to regret the Free Choice decision, the treachery that had driven them apart?

Bending her legs beneath the sheets, she hugged her knees and managed to whisper, "Have they released a copy of the suicide note?"

"Not to the public," Thrasher answered, "but the police faxed me a copy. I received it just before I came to wake you."

In the dim light of the television she saw the folded sheet of paper on the nightstand. She reached for it, then waited while Thrasher turned on the bedside lamp. The brightness hurt her eyes, forcing her to shield her face while Thrasher moved back to the television and searched for an early morning news program. When she could bear the brightness, she unfolded the page and squinted at the words written there in bold black ink.

The note was simple and straightforward, nothing they couldn't eventually make public. Paul wrote that he felt burdened by his new responsibility and inadequate for the job he'd been selected to perform. His wife was suffering with terminal cancer; his daughter would be better off without him. After much consideration, he had decided to escape the suffering of this life and hoped his wife would soon join him in eternity.

The words were the ramblings of a confused, heartsick individual, and though the handwriting undoubtedly belonged to Paul, Daryn couldn't imagine him writing one word of it. He would have to be drunk, temporarily insane, or suffocating in a manic depression to write such things.

She lowered the note to the nightstand. "Did they find anything else?"

"An empty bottle of vodka," Thrasher answered, sinking to the foot of her king-sized bed. "And an empty glass. Apparently he got pretty plastered before taking the leap."

An unformed thought teased her brain as she watched the morning shadows play across the room. Drunkenness could well account for the unfamiliar verbiage, but something still didn't fit. Drunks and children always told the truth, or so she'd been told, and Paul would never believe his daughter would be better off without him. In their years together he had seen how Daryn suffered from an absentee father; he would not have said that about Cristina.

She fixed Thrasher in a don't-patronize-me stare. "What does Maria Santana have to say about this?"

A muscle moved in his jaw, and he looked away before he answered. "I'm told she was hysterical when the police arrived. She kept saying her daughter was in the house, but the police found no sign of anyone else. But Maria is recovering from surgery, it was her first day home, so they think she might have been all doped up and imagining things. She's been sedated. A nurse is with her now, and the daughter is expected to come home today."

In a dark, virgin territory of her mind Daryn stumbled upon another possibility. "Jacob," she asked, tendrils of fear creeping through her, "a few nights ago I asked Samuel Tomlin for help with Paul Santana."

She let her words hang in the silence, then spread her hands. "Is this—did that conversation have anything to do with this?"

Thrasher turned back to the television, punching the volume button as the six o'clock morning news credits rolled across the screen. "Don't be crazy, Daryn. The CIA has nothing to do with law enforcement."

"Don't speak to me in riddles! Did the CIA have anything to do with Paul Santana's death?"

He turned to her then, his features distorted by the shadows in the room. "Of course not, Madam President. Tomlin would have wanted someone to speak to Justice Santana, perhaps apply a little political pressure. But murder is not his style."

Sighing in relief, Daryn sank back against her pillows, then bit her thumbnail as the newscaster announced the morning's top story: Paul Santana, the newest Supreme Court justice, had committed suicide.

As Paul's image filled the screen, she trembled at a sudden realization: her only friend wasn't merely out of touch, he no longer existed.

Feeling as though her foundation stone had suddenly dissolved, she lowered her head into her pillow and wept.

●

The sound of weeping came through the doorway, thrumming against Maria's sodden nerves. Because the house had begun to fill with relatives within hours of the announcement, her doctor had given her tranquilizers in addition to her pain pills. The combination left her feeling as though someone had encased her brain in cotton. Words and sounds and facts penetrated, but without the sharp edges.

Cristina hovered over her, dear Cristina, who had come home to find the house filled with police and well-meaning strangers. She had not seen her father's body in the rock garden. For that, at least, Maria was grateful.

The police investigators told her it was certainly a suicide. They showed her the note, written in Paul's hand, but she knew her husband could not have written those things of his own free will. She remembered Paul in the darkness, kissing her forehead and promising that life would be different. The man who had kissed her good night would not have leaped from that balcony.

Before the drugs took effect, she had overheard the police investigators talking among themselves in Paul's study. "Quite a risk," one of them said, his careless voice drifting down the hall to her bedroom. "Three floors is not such a great height. He could easily have survived with a dozen broken bones."

"He coulda been paralyzed," another added. "Not exactly the way I'd have chosen to go out, especially when there are dozens of other places to leap."

"Me, I'd off myself in the Potomac," the first answered. "Swift current, lots of bridges—they wouldn't find the body for a week."

"Mama? You okay?" Cristina's youthful voice sliced through the fog of memory, and Maria slowly turned her head. Her daughter stood beside her, a cup of water in one hand and two pills on an open palm.

Maria shook her head. "No more pills."

"Please, Mama. They'll help you."

"No pills."

The policemen attributed Maria's memories to the pills. They said she was groggy, that's why she'd heard the creaking stair and the opening door. When they arrived they said no one had been in the house, no one at all. There was no sign of either forced entry or Cristina; they found only Maria huddled on the staircase and Paul in the rock garden.

But someone *had* been in the house. She had not been dreaming or sleepwalking.

She lifted her eyes to the television mounted in the bookcases to the left of her bed.

"Cristina, turn on the TV."

"Mama, I don't think—"

"Turn it on!" The forceful words hurt her throat, but they elicited the desired effect. Cristina turned to obey, and a moment later the screen flooded with images of the exterior of their home.

Maria heard a whimpering sound rise from her own throat.

"Washington was stunned today by news of the apparent suicide of the nation's most junior Supreme Court justice, Paul Santana. Santana, who filled a vacancy left by Justice Franklin when he became Chief Justice, was said to be despondent over his wife's terminal illness—"

"Mama, you shouldn't watch this." Cristina stepped directly into Maria's field of vision, blocking her view of the TV. "You need your rest."

"You must let me watch." Maria leaned forward, trying to see around her daughter.

"No, Mama." Moving toward the television, Cristina lifted her hand.

"He did not kill himself! You must let me watch!"

The words, pulled from a reservoir of energy Maria didn't know she possessed, echoed in the quiet room. Cristina turned, surprise written into every inch of her face.

Maria lifted her hand, then lowered herself back to the pillows, the bandages pulling painfully at her skin. "Cristina, watch with me. Help me see. There has to be an answer."

For an instant the girl wavered and Maria feared she had lost the argument, then Cristina sank onto the end of the mattress. Together they watched the news report, which was followed by a hastily edited video clip highlighting Paul's career. The last shot featured the White House swearing-in ceremony, when Vice President Frey administered the oath of office and assured Paul that President Austin wished she had been able to attend the event.

Cristina folded her arms. "*She's* responsible."

Maria stared at her daughter. "What are you saying?"

The thin line of Cristina's mouth clamped tight for a moment, and her slender throat bobbed as she swallowed. "If he had never known Daryn Austin, none of this would have happened."

Maria said nothing as grief and despair tore at her heart. Cristina had been away at college, far from the Washington rumor mills, but national gossip traveled at the speed of light. How much had she heard about her father and Daryn Austin? More important, how much had she *believed?*

"Cristina, mi amor." Maria lifted her hand toward her daughter. "You can't believe everything you read."

"I don't, Mama. But you can't deny this much is true—if she had never brought Daddy to Washington, he'd still be alive. And happy. He was almost always happy in Miami. I don't think he's ever been happy here."

"That's not true." Lowering her hand, Maria met her daughter's dark gaze. "A few weeks ago, he began to change. He found joy . . . with God."

Cristina snorted softly. "What sort of God makes a man jump out the window? What sort of joy leads a man to abandon his family?"

"That's why I know he did not do it. He did not kill himself."

Cristina stared at her with wide, disbelieving eyes, and Maria realized her story would never be credible. She opened her mouth, about to explain the definite sounds she'd heard, but the television news coverage suddenly switched to the White House Briefing Room.

"There she is!" Cristina's hiss broke the silence. "Look at her! How can she even face the camera?"

In an uncommon silence, President Austin walked to the lectern emblazoned with the presidential seal, but Maria noticed that the woman's usual air of confidence had evaporated. She wore a trim black suit, a white collar providing the only spot of brightness, and in the unforgiving television lights her face appeared puffy.

Maria felt her own eyes fill with tears as she watched the woman her husband had loved.

The president gripped the lectern, cleared her throat, and looked down as if searching for her notes.

When she finally spoke, her voice wavered. "Ladies and gentlemen," she said, her voice more subdued than Maria had ever heard it, "it is with great sadness and regret that we announce the death of Supreme Court Justice Paul Santana. We at the White House, the vice president and his family, all the staff, and I, extend our deepest sympathies to Justice Santana's wife, daughter, and extended family. He was a truly remarkable man, and this is a great loss not only for the Supreme Court, but for the American people. A life full of promise has been cut short, and we shall undoubtedly suffer for his absence. I know I already miss him."

As the president nodded and took a half step back, Maria clenched her hand until her nails entered her palm. She had not been confronted with the woman's image since Paul's confession. Though she'd been able to accept the apology of a broken man, staring at an unrepentant woman stirred up malignant feelings she did not want to forget.

A reporter in the front row shouted out a question: "Who will be nominated to fill the Santana vacancy?"

Daryn Austin scowled at the man, her brows knitting together. "I haven't even considered the matter, nor will I at this point. Let us first give respect and honor to the deceased."

With that the president turned and exited, followed by her retinue, and the broadcast shifted back to the newsroom. Maria looked away, her misery like a steel weight in her soul. The woman's grief had looked real; her condolences sounded genuine. Then again, her public image had never even borne the sheen of tarnish.

"I hate her," Cristina said, the corners of her mouth tight with distress. "I hope someone takes her out—"

"Hush." Maria exhaled the words on a tide of exhaustion. "Your father admired her."

"Mom! You know what they're saying about them—"

"I know what your father said, and that's all I need to know. He loved us, Cristina. You can believe that forever."

She smiled at her daughter, then closed her eyes, her concentration dissipating in a mist of fatigue.

●

Daryn forced a smile as she shook the hand of the last eighth grader to troop through the Rose Garden. She'd been greeting Eighth Grade Academic All-Stars for an hour, and though the program was one of her own, now she was ready to tell every last fresh-faced youngster in Washington to get on the bus and go back to wherever they'd come from.

"Thank you, Madam President." The last group of thirty chorused a good-bye. Daryn gave them a final wave, then turned and tossed the bouquet they'd given her into the arms of her body man. "Get rid of those, will you? And get Tyson a drink of water. The sun is killing him."

The young aide, her third this year, ducked and mumbled something, then ran to fetch the dog. Daryn stalked over the colonnade, then slipped through the French doors into the blessed coolness of the Oval. The last week of April had brought unseasonably warm weather, and today the sun seemed intent upon beating her down to a pool of perspiration . . .

She had no sooner slumped into her chair and pressed her hand to her forehead than the French door opened again. "Madam President? I need a word, if you please."

She opened one eye and peered through her fingers. Anson Quinn stood in the doorway. "Can't it wait, Agent Quinn?"

"No, ma'am. It's about the graveside service tomorrow."

Daryn drew a deep breath. Paul Santana would be buried at Arlington tomorrow, and security arrangements would be tight. Not only was Arlington a public place, but the cemetery was situated on a hill and filled with trees, delightful cover for a sniper.

"Come in, Quinn."

Quinn wasted no time in coming to the point. "Madam President, we don't think you should attend."

She lowered her hand. "Forget that idea, Agent. I am going. I know Arlington is a challenging environment, but I have every confidence in you."

"There's more, ma'am." He leaned toward her, his eyes sharp and direct. "It's Jehu. We found him. Positive ID."

Despite her exhaustion, she felt a spark of interest. They'd all been disappointed when another Jehu letter arrived after John Hudson died outside the White House gates. "Well, that's good news. Who is he?"

"Clive Wilton, of Jackson, Wyoming. We traced him through the e-mail sent from the elementary school—seems he was hired as a temp for one night, and took that opportunity to send you a note from the school computer. The principal knew nothing about him, of course, but eventually the cleaning crew supervisor put two and two together."

Daryn gave him an honest smile. "Congratulations, Quinn. So—why can't I go to the graveside?"

"Because Clive Wilton is no longer in Jackson. We sent a pair of agents to pick him up and found that he left town on April ninth. Nobody from Jackson has heard from him since."

Daryn turned the thought over in her mind. The abortion story broke on April eighth, and even though they'd tried to cover it quickly, apparently they hadn't been quick enough. It had apparently rung this nut's bell.

"Anybody there have any idea where Clive was heading?"

Quinn looked at her with lethal calmness in his eyes. "Everybody there knew what Clive was up to—seems he was one of the True People, a white supremacist group famous for taking Scripture and twisting all the logic out of it. They're on record for hating about everybody—African-Americans, Jews, homosexuals, Hispanics, American Indians."

"Women who step out of line." Daryn whistled softly. "Sounds like a roll call of my cabinet members. And that's why he hates me."

"That's about right."

"So where is he now?"

Quinn's eyes almost disappeared in his taut, bony cheeks. "He's in Washington, Madam President. And this is his latest letter to you."

Leaning forward, he slid a sheet of paper toward her. Reluctantly, Daryn picked it up. This letter had been handwritten on stationery from the Federal Hotel . . . in D.C.

She looked at Quinn with an uplifted brow. "I'm assuming you sent someone to this hotel?"

Quinn nodded. "He was gone. But we got a pretty good description from the hotel clerk. He's young, probably in his early twenties, with short brown hair, pale skin, and a goatee. He's about six-two, one hundred seventy pounds."

Daryn began to read:

Whore of Babylon:

Draw near hither, ye sons of the sorceress, the seed of the adulterer and the whore.

Daryn looked up at Quinn. "He heard the abortion story. He left Wyoming after the story broke."

"Maybe," Quinn said, shrugging. "The guys in the profiling division are working on that angle. But if that's valid, then he's probably more aggravated than he was before."

She kept reading:

> *And there came one of the seven angels which had the seven vials, and talked with me, saying unto me, Come hither; I will shew unto thee the judgment of the great whore that sitteth upon many waters. She shall be burned with fire!*

She dropped the page to the desk, then placed her hand under her chin and stared at Quinn. "I understand your concern." She kept her voice firm. "And I appreciate it, I really do. But I have to attend this service tomorrow. You can close the cemetery; you can close the interstate if you have to. But I'm not going to allow Jehu to keep me from doing what I have to do."

"He'll be watching," Quinn said, his countenance immobile. "We believe he's tracking you, waiting for the right moment to make his move. And this is a guy who lives in the woods, so he's likely to be a crack shot."

"Then do your job, Agent Quinn." Pushing herself up out of her chair, Daryn stood. "Take a bullet for me if you have to, but I'm not going to hide in the White House." She forced a lopsided smile. "Besides, according to his letters, he won't use a gun. He's more likely to use a flamethrower."

THIRTY-FIVE

FRIDAY MORNING DAWNED GRAY AND DARK. LOOKING out the Oval Office windows toward the Washington Monument, Daryn saw the heavy sky, swollen with unspent rain, sagging toward the earth. She ground her teeth in irritation. The Secret Service guys would be tenser in weather like this, the mourners more melancholy. The graveside service would be hard enough without all the added pressures . . .

The scene at Arlington National Cemetery reinforced her suspicions. The Secret Service closed the interstate and the approaching exits, and only reporters with approved White House press credentials were allowed through the roadblocks and into the special roped-off area near the gravesite. Paul's family, including several dozen relatives who had flown up from Miami, had to show identification before they could pass into the cemetery. Though in years to come they would be proud to remark that the president had attended his burial, Daryn knew today they were probably cursing her under the brims of their black hats. She, after all, was the woman who lured him away from Miami . . .

As the hour of the service drew near, Daryn stood on the grassy hillside slightly apart from a knot of men and women in black. Flanked by a dozen agents in sunglasses and dark suits, she placed her hand on her heart as the bugle played a slow and somber version of "Amazing Grace," then lowered her head as the cameras began their not-so-furtive clicking. As the bugle played, she shifted her gaze until she could see Maria and Cristina Santana, who stood to her left.

The widow clung to the arm of a handsome man in a black suit, and from the look of him Daryn assumed he was one of Paul's Miami relatives, possibly a cousin or uncle. A chorus of weeping women in black dresses and lace veils crowded behind Maria and dabbed at their eyes with handkerchiefs. Cristina, hatless, wide-eyed, and hollow-cheeked, kept her eyes on the flag-draped casket, with only the quiver of her chin to indicate a turbulent wellspring of emotion below the surface.

Daryn had lobbied for a burial site off Sheridan Drive, near the grave of Oliver Wendell Holmes Jr., Civil War veteran and Supreme Court justice. She had personally applied pressure for the choice spot; land was at a premium in Arlington, and prime plots nearly impossible to obtain. Sheridan Drive was near the entrance, however, and far enough from the popular graves of John and Jacqueline Kennedy that she could visit, if she liked, in relative obscurity.

The honor guard that had accompanied the coffin snapped to attention at the conclusion of the hymn, then a rifle squad fired three shots while the bugler blew the slow and stately "Taps." As a final gesture, the guard lifted the American flag from the coffin, folded it in ritual movement, and solemnly presented it to Maria Santana.

Daryn stiffened at the sight. She had been weeping for days; she had arranged for the military burial. Though the family had planned a private funeral service, Daryn had been the one to order a magnificent marble headstone, as fine as any in the national cemetery, to adorn Paul's final resting place. Yet Maria carried the flag; Maria was now centered in the photographers' lenses. But Daryn could change that . . .

She stepped toward the widow, waking the press people from their momentary lethargy. "Mrs. Santana—" she forced a note of polite dignity into her voice—"let me tell you how very sorry I am."

Maria Santana's dark eyes were shadowed with loss, but she lifted her soft chin at Daryn's words. "Madam President," she said, her accent thicker than Daryn remembered, "I have something for you."

Daryn tensed as Maria slipped her hand into her purse. Paul had said Maria knew about the affair, that she knew everything. And in the madness of grief, a bereaved and wronged widow might do anything . . .

The PPD agents around Daryn stiffened as the widow reached into her handbag, one going so far as to reach into his coat, but the object Maria withdrew was a simple white envelope.

"The police report." She pressed the envelope into Daryn's hand without looking up. "I want you to read it. But first you should know that my husband did not jump from the balcony. Only a fool would do such a thing, and my Paul was no fool."

My Paul.

Aware of the sudden whirring of the cameras, Daryn took the envelope and dropped it to her side. The reporters would ask what she'd received from the widow, and she'd either have to come up with an answer or think of some way to evade the question gracefully.

She sighed. Why didn't people think before bothering her?

She extended the envelope behind her back and waited until her body man took it before giving Maria a polite smile. "How can you be so certain about this, Maria? Paul was upset about many things."

The woman lowered her voice to a whisper. "Because Paul had given his life to God. Paul knew he was obliged to accept life gratefully and preserve it for God's honor. He saw himself as a steward, not an owner, of the life God entrusted to him. His life was not his to dispose of."

Daryn lowered her voice, matching the woman's conspiratorial whisper. "What is that, catechism 101?" She managed a twisted smile. "I'm sorry, Maria, but all men have their breaking point. I believe these things happen when the pain in a man's life outweighs his resources for coping with the pain." Catching Maria's wrist, she leaned closer to whisper in the woman's ear. "Paul was in agony. Your illness—well, it wore him down. He told me so. He told me many things about you."

She stepped back, noticing that the cameras had begun to whir again.

Tomorrow the headlines would read *President Consoles Justice's Widow* and her poll ratings for sensitivity would vault upward.

Maria Santana simply stood there, her brown eyes glazing in the most extraordinary expression of pain, and Daryn felt a small sense of satisfaction in knowing she'd hurt the woman who had caused her so much agony. In the last few days she had begun to believe that Paul killed himself because his newly awakened sense of religious guilt drove him to despair. If Maria's cancer hadn't reappeared, if he hadn't fallen under the spell of the Bible-thumpers, things would have been different. He would have adjusted to his role in the Supreme Court. He would have written decisions to promote the policies of the Austin administration for years to come. And he would have returned to Daryn's arms.

But, as dear as he was, Paul had never had her strength. And that was why he was dead, and she slept in the White House.

Turning on the ball of her foot, Daryn led her entourage away from the graveside as a rising wind shook the trees and howled in the face of the approaching storm.

●

After the funeral, Maria went home and slept for two days. For another two days she wandered around the house in a fog, occasionally peering at the floral arrangements that seemed to have sprouted like mushrooms in the most unlikely places—the guest room, the den, and the foyer. A stately green vine—philodendron, she thought they called it—sprawled over the back of the toilet in her bathroom, and she had no idea who placed it there. One of the relatives, probably, perhaps Aunt Carmelita.

Satisfied that she was ambulatory and in her right mind, the relatives departed for Miami on Monday morning, but not before reminding the drop-in nurse to keep an extra careful eye on Maria. "She's never been strong," Maria overhead Carmelita telling the nurse. "In Miami, she was afraid to even spend the night by herself."

Now Maria pulled the collar of her robe closer to her neck and studied the steam rising from her coffee cup. The relatives needn't have worried. She had learned many things in Washington, including how to depend on someone other than Paul or her papa. She had learned to lean on God as a living being, not some entity in the sky, and though every muscle in her body felt as though it had been battered, she knew his loving hand supported her every moment.

Upstairs, a door slammed, and Maria's subconscious informed her that Paul was up and moving around. No—not right. Paul was gone and Cristina was home from school. Day Seven without Paul, and her brain still hadn't broken free from its old thought patterns. How long would it take her to stop listening for his car in the garage, his tread on the stairs? When Cristina left, she would be rambling around in this big house all alone but for her memories . . .

She felt a tear trickle down her cheek, but she didn't lift her hand to wipe it away. Her skin must have tracks in it by now, for lately she wept without even realizing it. But what did they say? After forty, a woman had the face she deserved, the one she'd earned through life. And Maria had earned every track, every laugh line.

"Mama?" Cristina came into the kitchen, her brows knotted in worry. "You okay?"

Maria managed a smile. "I'm fine. Do you want breakfast?"

"No—too close to lunchtime." Turning, she peered out into the den. "Did the aunts and uncles leave?"

"All of them left this morning. Carmelita and José were the last, and they said to tell you good-bye."

As Cristina moved back into the kitchen, Maria sipped from her coffee, marveling over the fact that conversation after a death could come easily. She'd done well prior to the funeral, too, almost as if an exterior Maria had taken over and seen to the greetings, thank-yous, and matters of hospitality. But even in those busy days when the police and government people kept her on her toes, occasionally an unexpected wave would crash over her, driving her to the bathroom where she buried her face in a towel to muffle her cries.

She shook her head slightly as she lowered her coffee cup. As a child she'd lost her mother, and more recently she'd developed cancer, but the grief that surrounded those events was nothing like this. She'd been frightened on those other occasions, scared to death of losing herself, but fear held no sway over her heart now. She had met her greatest fear and endured the greatest cruelty of her life, yet neither could drive her to despair.

"Perfect love casts out fear," she whispered, smiling as she remembered the Bible verse. "And I am loved."

Lifting the coffeepot, Cristina arched a brow and looked across the room. "Did you say something, Mom?"

Maria smiled. "Just thinking of something I read the other day. And realizing that we're going to be all right."

The hand on the pot trembled as Cristina sloshed the fragrant coffee into a mug. "You think so?"

"I know so." Leaving her cup on the table, Maria stood and walked to her daughter, then placed her hands on her shoulders. "Your father did not kill himself, but he was prepared to die. I know that." She reached up to push a hank of dark hair out of Cristina's face, then tucked the strand behind her daughter's ear. "Death is not the worst thing in life, dear one. Living alone is."

"But you're going to be alone now, Mama!" Cristina looked up, her red-rimmed eyes bordered with fresh tears. "When I go back to school—"

Drawing her daughter into her arms, Maria whispered, "I'm not alone, darling. I am living now with Jesus, just as your father was. And as long as we have him, we have all that matters in this life."

Sniffling, Cristina pulled out of the embrace, then drew a tissue from her pocket. "Whatever," she said, her voice flat. "Now—" she moved toward the pantry in an obvious attempt to escape—"what do you have to eat around here?"

Leaning back against the counter, Maria pressed the fingers of one hand to her lips. Cristina did not understand . . . not yet. But in the coming months, she'd see the difference Christ made in a life.

"There are a dozen casseroles in the fridge," Maria offered gently. "Brought by the people from our prayer group."

Yes, in time she would understand.

●

Daryn walked in the central hall, her feet bare upon the red carpet but obscured by a moving mist that swirled around her ankles. From her right and left, portraits of previous presidents—Carter, Ford, Clinton, and Reagan—gazed down upon her, derision in the curl of their lips and the depths of their eyes. The older presidents did not smile, but sat stern-faced in mute appraisal, their eyes accusing and condemnatory.

She reached the end of the hallway and stood beneath the portrait of a gaunt Lincoln, then heard Mary Todd's wailing for her dead son and husband. Death filled the White House, having been home to William Henry Harrison, Abraham Lincoln, Chester Arthur, James Garfield, Letitia Tyler, Zachary Taylor, Willie Lincoln, Caroline Harrison, Ellen Wilson, Warren Harding, Calvin Coolidge Jr., Franklin D. Roosevelt, and John F. Kennedy when they died. By all rights, Daryn thought, the list should also include Paul Santana, who had occupied her heart.

Sometimes, in the quiet of the night, Daryn thought the residence seemed to echo with the voices of the dead, creaking with their sighs and whispers, dreams and disappointments. Paul had joined them, and though his portrait would never grace the walls of the visitor's center, Daryn would never look across her living room without seeing his lanky form sprawled in her wing chair, never look up from her bed without remembering him by the sink in the bathroom, a toothbrush in his hand and a gleam in his eye . . .

She blinked the images away and looked up at the Lincoln portrait, replacing Lincoln's brown eyes with Paul's, exchanging the wavy hair with Paul's straighter, longer style. Mentally she softened the chin and erased a few of the facial lines, until Paul looked down upon her, his expression both loving and regretful.

"Daryn." His voice echoed through the hall. "You have lost yourself in this place."

A sudden chill climbed the ladder of her spine. This could not be happening, portraits did not talk even in the White House, and mist should not be swirling around her feet. She looked down, feeling the clammy tendrils of fog, and saw that they had gone from gray to red, the color of alarm and blood and war—

"Jehu!" She sat up, clutching at the damp sheets beneath her palms. Instinctively she pounded the panic button by her bed, and before she could count to five, the agent on duty kicked the door open, then shoved his gun into the empty space.

"Madam President?" She could not see him, but the light from the living room revealed his shadow. Feeling foolish, she reached for the bedside lamp, then turned it on. She was completely alone.

"It's all right." She pulled the sheets to her chest. "I'm alone."

Now the agent advanced into the room, his gun still drawn, his face a study in concentration. "May I have the pass code please?"

"I'm all right." She pressed her hand to her forehead and felt the dampness there. Even though the room was cool, she'd been perspiring like a field hand.

"All the same, ma'am, I'd appreciate the pass code."

She closed her eyes, trying to remember the phrase for this week. "Yellowstone."

The agent holstered his gun. "Do you want me to call the physician? You look a little pale."

She opened her mouth to reply, but at that moment Anson Quinn burst into the room, his gun extended. "We received the alarm signal, Madam President. Is there a problem?"

Weakly, she fluttered her fingers at him. "Can't you see I'm alone in here? No one has a gun to my head."

Quinn glanced at the other agent. "Pass code?"

"Given."

Apparently satisfied, Quinn put his gun away. "Sorry for the disturbance, ma'am."

Daryn ran her hand through her damp hair and forced a laugh. Only in the White House could you rouse men from their positions in the dead of night, scare them to death, and then receive an apology for it. "I'm the one who should apologize. I had a nightmare. Not a very presidential thing to do, I'm afraid."

The shadow of a smile flitted across Quinn's face. "I wouldn't be too sure about that. This isn't the first time I've been called up here because somebody had a bad dream."

She smoothed the comforter over her legs and gave the agents a calm smile. "Thank you, gentlemen, for rushing to my rescue." She frowned at Quinn. "Don't you ever go home?"

"Putting in some overtime," he quipped, pulling the door closed behind him. "Don't worry about it."

Overtime? Her mind supplied the answer. Because of Jehu.

They left her wondering which other recent White House occupants had been plagued with nightmares. Carter, during the hostage crisis? Reagan, after the attempted assassination? Clinton, during the impeachment imbroglio? Every president endured some sort of trial, and daily life in the political cauldron was enough to inspire nightmares in anyone.

Yet she had a personal ghost. Paul had been dead a full week, yet still he seemed as close as her shadow.

Feeling suddenly restless and irritable, she threw off the heavy comforter and paced before the window. Somewhere out in the night, Clive Wilton waited for her, but if he stepped onto the White House property seismic detectors in the grass would detect his footfall. He'd have to pass through a gamma radiation detector, a magnetometer, and at least three checkpoints before he could enter the White House, and now all the security guards had copies of the artist's sketch with his likeness. Amid such security, how could anyone be afraid?

But she was. Faceless fears had dogged her sleep every night since Paul's death. The specters did not vanish with the daylight, but lay dormant in her subconscious, ready to rise and assert themselves at the oddest moments. She could turn a corner in the West Wing and visualize Paul leaning against the wall; she seemed to catch whiffs of his cologne in the pillow he'd reclined against as he read through briefs and news reports. In some ways he seemed more real to her now than he had after she moved him to the Court.

She shook her head in a vain effort to cast his memories aside, then spied the folio of briefings on her nightstand. She'd scarcely bothered to look at them before going to bed, but perhaps their claim on her attention lay behind her restless sleep. After all, as Truman said, either a president stayed on top of things, or she'd soon find that things were on top of her . . .

She skimmed a series of reports from several cabinet members, then paused to peruse a memo from the Office of Communications. The president traditionally presented the annual budget message in early February, but Daryn had requested such a financial overhaul that only now were her people comfortable with releasing details to Congress. The Office of Communications was suggesting that the particulars be released over the next week, rather than in one news cycle, so they could seize every opportunity for airtime between the present and Daryn's scheduled speech, still eight days away.

Daryn pulled a pencil from the nightstand drawer and wrote *YES!* in the margin. Aside from the January State of the Union message, the budget presentation would be her most important public moment this year.

Satisfied that she'd be able to sleep, she was about to shove the remaining briefings aside, but a single page note from the White House counsel's office caught her eye. O'Leary had written a memo to inform her that Senator Hank Beatty had called for a special prosecutor to investigate the death of Justice Paul Santana. The motion, made in the Senate, had been seconded by Democratic Senator Douglas Oliphant.

She drew in a breath, the audacity of Beatty's ambition staggering her. What did he expect to gain from such a gesture? More moments in the spotlight? Did he hope to paint himself as the crusader for a widow who could not accept her husband's final desperate action? Or was he simply trying to drive Daryn from the White House by portraying her as some sort of immoral woman who should be condemned by Republicans and Democrats alike?

"Call Jehu," she muttered, pulling the pencil from behind her ear. "You two would make a good team."

She scrawled a note at the bottom of the memo: *O'Leary—see me ASAP.*

Thrusting the memo back into the folio, she tossed the entire mess onto the nightstand, then fell back upon her pillows and stared at the ceiling. A Senate investigation might steal most of her energy, but several of her predecessors had endured special prosecutors and triumphed in the end.

If they wanted to play hardball, she'd play along. But she would play to win.

●

Eager to meet with O'Leary the next morning, Daryn blanched when she learned that Lincoln Walker, director of the FBI, had requested a private meeting.

"He said it was urgent," Miss Park added, handing Daryn the request form from the Office of Presidential Scheduling.

"Walker?" Daryn struggled to place a face with the name. She knew the head of the FBI by reputation because he'd been a Parker nominee, easily confirmed by the Senate in 2002. But she couldn't recall meeting the man.

"He says it's confidential," Thrasher said, glancing at his notes. "But I was thinking I should sit in on the meeting—in case you need something."

Daryn resisted the temptation to glare at her chief of staff. Thrasher seemed anxious these days, thinner and twitchier than usual. Still, she didn't know what she'd do without him.

"I'll see Mr. Walker first, then," she said, moving to the chair behind the historic Oval Office desk. "Let's get him in and out, because I need to meet with O'Leary."

Lincoln Walker, tall, thin, and dark-haired, came squinting into the room like a schoolboy who'd been summoned to the principal's office. His hair lay in greased waves upon his head, and his eyes seemed hooded behind his glasses. He did not smile, but took Daryn's hand when she offered it.

"A pleasure to see you again, Madam President," he said, diplomatically reminding her that they had met before. "I'm only sorry I have to meet you again during such a sad situation."

"What situation would that be, Mr. Walker?" Daryn pointed to the guest chair, then took her seat behind the desk.

"I'm referring to Justice Santana's death, of course."

She noticed that he didn't use the word *suicide.*

Lowering her tone, she said, "A terrible tragedy."

"Yes." He looked down at his lap, then squinted up at her. "Can you think of any reason why a CIA operative would be at Paul Santana's house the night of his death?"

The direct question caught her off guard, and a quick glance at Thrasher proved he was just as startled.

"The CIA?" She took an audible breath of astonishment. "Why . . . no. Paul had nothing to do with the CIA."

"I was hoping you'd know. Because we have discovered this."

He pulled a grainy black-and-white photograph from his briefcase, then handed it to her. Without being invited, Thrasher rose from his chair and stood behind her, leaning on the desk as she studied the shadowy images.

"I'm sorry, Mr. Walker, but I have no idea what this is."

"It's a still shot from a security camera belonging to Justice Santana's neighbor. The video camera is triggered by a motion detector—when it senses movement, it begins to pan, capturing any image in the surrounding area."

Daryn stared at the picture. "I'm sorry, I still don't see—"

"This—" Walker stood and pointed to a light area of the photograph—"is the Santanas' house. And this darker area is the balcony railing. And this—" he tapped the cap of his pen against a blurred shadow—"is an image of two men, one appearing to support the other."

Daryn sat perfectly still as a wave of shock slapped at her.

Walker pulled another photo from his briefcase. "This is a video frame taken one second later. Here you see one man on the balcony, his hands on the railing, and another man—" he tapped the picture again—"in midair. The second man, of course, was Santana."

Daryn looked up, her tongue momentarily paralyzed.

"These are only blurs and shadows." Thrasher took the photos from Daryn's hand and gave them back to Walker. "How can you be sure what you're seeing?"

"We have digital reconstruction techniques that would amaze you," Walker replied. "We can furnish pictures of the pores on each man's face, if that would help convince you. I brought these because I wanted you to see the images in context."

Daryn managed to whisper a single word: *"Who?"*

Walker set his jaw. "The other man has been identified as Carlos Montoya, a Colombian who regularly works for the CIA in South America. Of course we have no idea why he would be in Washington, and no clue why he'd show up at Santana's house. But the Supremes are sometimes controversial, and their opinions tick people off. This Santana, being the newest, might have been the easiest target. He was the most popular, anyway, and the only one who doesn't already have one foot in the grave. We think someone might have been trying to send the brethren a message by striking at their strongest member."

As the image of murder filled her brain, Daryn gasped. "I can't believe it."

Thrasher picked up the conversation. "Do you have any idea who could have done this? Surely there are organized groups who might do something like this for publicity."

"That's just it—no one's said a word. When this kind of thing happens as an act of terrorism, usually it's splashed all over the news and milked for publicity. But someone wanted this to look like an accident, or else they wanted to send a quiet message. We think the most likely scenario is that someone wanted Santana dead. The man must have stepped on some pretty powerful toes."

"Excuse me." Pressing her hand to her mouth, Daryn stood and hurried toward the rest room. As she ran, she heard Thrasher say, "You've given her quite a shock. They were close friends, you know. She's not over it yet."

●

Daryn sat at the desk in her private study, her hands upon the blotter, her eyes staring at the old-fashioned pocket watch a group of schoolchildren had given her. The minute hand of the dangling clock seemed to have become stuck in the space between one black stroke on the dial's perimeter and another. Time had stopped—and with it, Daryn's ability to think.

Paul had been murdered. By someone who worked hand in hand with the CIA. While she, only a few nights before, had stood in this very office, high on drink and self-importance, and asked two of her closest associates to please do *something* about that troublesome Justice Santana . . .

Ignoring the headache beginning to blaze a trail behind her weeping eyes, she reached into the center drawer. A leather book occupied the center space, a gift from Justice Crispin, who had handed her the volume as she left the cemetery after Paul's service. "I think you should have this," the aged justice had said, his eyes narrowing as he studied her. "Paul began to write in it during a Bible study at my house. I believe he saw it as a journal of his new life in Christ."

"Perhaps, Mr. Justice Crispin," she answered, mindful of the listening ears around them, "Mrs. Santana should have it."

"No, Madam President." A smile lit the old man's weather-beaten face. "Mrs. Santana does not need it."

Now she stared at the book, a simple brown leather volume with no inscription or title. But on the inside, Paul's bold handwriting flowed like water over the pages.

The first entry was Sunday, April ninth.

For the first time since my boyhood in Miami, I have gone to church. How familiar the setting seemed to me, though I have never been in a Protestant church in my life! Maria seems to like this group, too, which does not adhere to any particular denomination, but rather claims faith in Jesus Christ as the link that binds its members together. Justice Crispin says the Church is a living body, united by the Spirit throughout the world, and I began to feel that unity today. Being with those people, singing the songs, and hearing their words of praise, I am beginning to understand how we could be united not by a creed or custom, but by a Spirit—

How little I knew until I turned to Christ! I thought I had it all, but I had nothing. Nothing! Now I am like a baby, but Justice Crispin assures me I will grow . . .

Frustrated, Daryn flipped through several more pages. Paul had written about his delight in studying the Bible with Justice Crispin, about his experiences with prayer, about his hunger to grow deeper in the spiritual life. He wrote of hours spent in study (of the Bible? When he should have been studying the law?) and time spent in meditation upon the things of God.

Lowering the book, Daryn closed her eyes. This was not the man she knew. The writer of this book might have occupied Paul's body, but the mind and character were not the same.

She flipped a few more pages, about to give up, then saw her name.

Last night I confessed everything to Maria—my past relationship with Daryn and my involvement with the president since coming to

Washington. I hurt Maria deeply, I could see pain in her eyes, and yet she has changed, too. The events of recent weeks have drawn her into a new dependence upon the Lord, and she is willing to forgive.

May heaven help me if I ever hurt my wife again. May God have mercy upon my soul for the pain I have already caused my wife and daughter. And may God have mercy upon Daryn Austin, who remains on the path I was so blithely following, the road that leads to destruction and heartache and utter pain. How I wish she would realize the truth of the Scripture, "The king's heart is like a stream of water directed by the Lord; he turns it wherever he pleases." God is turning her, using her for his purposes. I can only pray she will one day understand.

Daryn's breath caught in her lungs. If Justice Crispin had read this, he knew more about her private life than she wanted anyone outside the Oval to know. And yet he had calmly handed her this book—why? Political blackmail? A warning? Was he going to take her story public, or carry it only as far as Maria Santana's house?

She closed the book, dropped it back into its hiding place, then slammed the drawer. Too many things were happening at once, and she could not allow these pressures to destroy her composure. She was the president, capable of wielding war in scores of ways, and she had a host of advisers to help her out of private and public predicaments. Moreover, she had power.

She picked up the phone and punched in Miss Park's extension, then asked the secretary to summon Jacob Thrasher and Samuel Tomlin. Thrasher had the foresight to wait in his office until Tomlin arrived, then they entered Daryn's study together.

When both men were seated across from her, she folded her arms and fixed them in a direct gaze. "I want to know—" she took pains to keep her voice steady—"exactly what happened to Paul Santana."

Tomlin didn't blink. "Madam President—" he casually crossed his legs—"you don't want to know. You can't commit perjury if you don't know, and now that Beatty has appointed a special prosecutor, people will be asking questions you shouldn't answer."

"You have nothing to worry about," Thrasher added. "As of now you know no details, and that's how it should be. No one can tie the Colombian to the CIA—"

"Walker could. He did."

"Carlos Montoya works for many nations," Tomlin said. "He's a professional freelancer. There is no evidence to tie him to us, to you, to anything. Other than what you've learned from the press and the police report, you know nothing about Paul Santana's death. Let's keep it that way."

But she did know. She knew the truth as surely as she knew the sun would rise the next morning. She had needed Paul as a friend, a colleague, and a lover. He needed her, too, until he changed. She didn't lose him when he moved to the Court; she lost him when he moved to God. Then, in a drunken fit of pique, she had wished him dead. And in the morning, like the heroine of nearly every fairy tale, she had awakened to discover that for the granting of her wish she'd pay a horrific price.

"Say nothing," Thrasher's voice droned beneath her thoughts. "You've called us in, but let this be the last time we three meet alone in this office. You'll be the one committing suicide—political suicide—if you ask anything else. Play along, keep quiet, and everything will be okay."

Doggedly, she shifted her gaze to Sam Tomlin. "How involved in this are you?"

The man shrugged. "I never spoke to Montoya, if that's what you mean. There are no phone records, no payments from my office, nothing to trace. They can investigate me until Judgment Day, and they'll come up empty."

"Thank you, Mr. Tomlin. You may go." She closed her eyes as the CIA director rose and left the room. Perhaps she could get away with it. After all, ambition had brought her this far, and she'd had to bend the rules on a few other occasions. If she stayed the course, she'd have another eight years to win victories for American women. And the first female American president had to be the *best* American president . . .

A quote from her favorite campaign speech came back on a rush of memory. "Women who seek to be equal to men," she'd assured America, "lack ambition."

Opening her eyes, she found Thrasher watching her, his eyes dark with anxiety. "Are you going to be okay?"

"I'll be fine." She waved at him, but her hands trembled. "Can you get me some time away? A weekend at Camp David would be nice. I could take the dog—"

"You can't blow this, Daryn." Thrasher's voice was low and taut with anger. "Don't get weak-kneed on me. You'll sink the entire ship."

"But I loved him!"

"You *used* him!"

"I did not!" The cry rose from within her, erupting in a spray of noisy tears. "I don't expect you to understand; you're married to this outrageous job—"

"Stop right there." Sliding to the edge of his chair, Thrasher leaned forward until his burning eyes were only inches from hers. "Get a hold of yourself and do it now. You can't afford the luxury of emotion, not today. There is no looking back, Daryn, no time for regret."

"But—"

"You did what had to be done. Santana was becoming a problem, and I personally think you handled things with a great deal of wisdom. Now you can nominate someone else to the Court, a candidate who has been supportive of your administration from the first day. Fate has smiled on you, Madam President, and it's time you realized it."

Trembling with unspent emotion, she lifted her gaze to meet his.

"If you don't continue to steer the ship, Captain," he whispered, his tone bordering on mockery, "you'll find yourself alone while the crew mutinies. I'll go to the special prosecutor myself and tell them all they need to know . . . and a great deal more, if that's what it takes to get out of here unscathed."

She sat there, blank, amazed, and shaken, as Thrasher stood and assumed his normal posture. "If there's nothing else, Madam President, I have some matters to attend to."

He meant it. Looking into his eyes, she saw that he would destroy her if she surrendered.

He waited, one blond brow upraised, while she gathered the raveling strings of her courage. With an effort, she met his accusing eyes without flinching. "Don't worry about me, Thrasher. Janus has two faces, remember? I'm sorry you had to glimpse so much of the private one, but you can trust the public persona."

The corner of his mouth drooped slightly. "That sounds more like you, Madam President."

"Don't worry," she repeated, crossing her arms. "I'm not going anywhere."

THIRTY-SIX

RELUCTANTLY, DARYN SURRENDERED THE THOUGHT of Camp David. Rattled by Thrasher's display of defiance, she decided to remain in Washington and regather the reins of control. But first she wanted information and she wanted to get it without leaving a trace—a task easier imagined than accomplished, especially when living in the White House.

She considered sending an aide to the Library of Congress, but even that was too public. Phone calls were traceable, and Thrasher had access to her private records. So at midnight of the day following Lincoln Walker's visit, she slipped on a jogging suit and took Tyson down to the Oval Office, jokingly telling the agents on duty that she needed to cram for a test. Once inside the windowless walls of her study, she powered up her computer and logged onto the Library of Congress's Web site.

An hour later she was still at the computer, her reading glasses perched on the end of her nose, a pencil between her teeth, and Tyson slumbering in the hallway. She had done a search for CIA documents, then followed a link that led her to a paper on assassination methods. The pencil dropped out of her mouth when she read the following excerpt from a CIA manual declassified in 1997:

The most efficient accident, in simple assassination, is a fall of seventy-five feet or more onto a hard surface. Elevator shafts, stairwells, unscreened windows, and bridges will serve . . . The act may be executed by sudden, vigorous [excised] of the ankles, tipping the subject over the edge.

The manual went on to recommend a blow to the temple in order to stun the subject first.

Her blood was suddenly swimming in adrenaline. Paul hadn't been dropped seventy-five feet, but few people would survive a hit on the head *and* a skull-first dive into a collection of stones.

All the events of the last several days collided in her head like bits of glass in a kaleidoscope. Paul's murder had been a by-the-book assassination. If she could find this, so could the FBI. So could Beatty's special prosecutor. So could Matthew Drudge or Rush Limbaugh or any eighth grader with a computer . . .

Her presidency was doomed.

Feeling suddenly claustrophobic, she shoved her chair back and stepped out into the hallway, taking deep gulps of air. The Oval Office beyond lay wreathed in shadows, the graceful Austin desk a thin mockery of all she'd dreamed it could symbolize. Her administration was about to be relegated to the hall of shame, along with Nixon's, and Clinton's, and Warren G. Harding's . . . unless she could do something to stop the destruction.

What? Nixon had resigned, but his accomplishments remained tainted. Clinton had denied everything and remained in office, maintaining high approval ratings even when DNA on a certain blue dress proved every word of Monica Lewinsky's testimony—but lewd acts in the Oval Office bathroom were a far cry from the assassination of a Supreme Court justice.

She pressed her hands to the wall as her breath caught in her lungs. Could she convince a grand jury of her innocence? In her current frame of mind she couldn't even convince herself! And there were reputable people who, if called to testify, could bring Paul's own words to support the prosecution's inevitable claims. Beatty and his cronies would say she'd had Paul killed because he spurned her; they'd say she used the power of the presidency to avenge herself. They would forget every good thing she had done for children and families and women, and her name would go down in the history books as . . .

The Whore of Babylon.

A tide of shivers rippled up each arm and raced across her shoulders, colliding at the base of her neck. Jehu, the Scripture-quoting white supremacist, had prophesied her judgment almost from the first day of her administration. He and the other religious rabble-rousers had been waiting, probably *praying,* for her destruction, and either fate or divine intervention had used Paul to bring her down.

"You want me out, God?" She lifted her gaze to the ceiling. "Paul thought you were directing me, but I've gotta tell you, I don't see it. If you're directing me, prove it! Do something good for a change! Because you and your people haven't impressed me one whit so far. "

Her voice echoed in the emptiness, bounced back from the shadows. From the corner of her eye she saw movement outside the wide windows. Her yells had alerted the agents who'd moved to surround the Oval when she left the residence, but she didn't care. She probably wasn't the first chief executive to fill this office with a roar of rage.

"God!" With her fist uplifted, she walked into the center of the empty space and stood on the eagle emblazoned on the presidential carpet. "You stole my only friend! He was the only person I could trust, the one who kept me sane!" She hesitated, her fist slowly sinking. "Why would a God who cared do that?"

No answers came, no sounds at all but the steady shush of the air handlers that kept the air pressure consistently higher than the world outside the white walls.

Exhaling softly, Daryn nudged the sleeping dog with her foot. She hadn't expected a miracle, a voice, or even a lightning flash. But the thought that God had made himself real to Paul while hiding from the president of the United States—

"Frankly," she told the dog, "I find that extremely irritating."

THIRTY-SEVEN

SENATOR HANK BEATTY NARROWED HIS EYES AT the young man who sat on the sofa in his office. Charles Brogan, former law clerk to the late Supreme Court Justice Paul Santana, had called the senator's office a week earlier, hinting that he had valuable information. Now, nearly two weeks after the justice's death, Beatty wondered if they were chasing the same rabbit.

Brogan, who sat in his crested navy blazer and khaki slacks with the self-satisfaction of a TV lawyer, crossed one long, loafer-clad leg and gave Beatty a smile that seemed a little worn around the edges.

"Let me get this straight, son," Beatty said, shifting in his chair. "You clerked for Santana how long?"

"Nearly seven months," Brogan answered, a blush beginning to glow on his cheekbones. "Ever since he came to the Court."

"And in seven months, you think you learned some deep, dark secret?"

The flush deepened. "I know I saw things . . . that people probably didn't want me to see. And I know Jacob Thrasher, Austin's chief of staff, asked me for confidential information. I'm assuming he passed my reports on to the president."

Beatty considered this in silence. There was no hard and fast law requiring the Supreme Court to operate in utter secrecy, but the

Constitution proclaimed that the three main branches of government were to be separate and equal. Therefore, Austin's meddling in the Court's business—or attempted meddling—might be serious, but only if they could prove she'd been interfering. So far this young man had only proven that a lowly legal clerk could be swayed by a persuasive White House staffer who may or may not have passed confidential information to his boss.

Beatty glanced at his aide, Justin Grieco, who sat with pen and steno pad in hand. Justin had made a few notes, but so far they'd learned nothing earth-shattering.

The senator tried again. "What sort of information did you pass on to the White House?"

"Um, mostly stuff about *Free Choice Women's Clinic v. Maddox*. That's what Thrasher asked about."

"And what did you tell him?"

Brogan shrugged. "That Mr. Justice Santana was still considering the matter. I know for a fact that when the case came up in conference, he hadn't made up his mind."

Beatty nodded, as patient as a scholar with a slow pupil. "And how did you learn these things? Do justices usually share their opinions with their clerks?"

The young man swiped at his bangs, where drops of moisture now clung to his damp forehead. "Mr. Justice Santana was very open. Some of the justices are fairly closemouthed, but he liked to hear our opinions about the cases. Sometimes he'd bring lunch from home—something his wife had cooked up—and we'd sit down and talk about the petitions while we ate."

"He ran a casual office, then."

"Yeah, but he was thorough. He'd require us to write extensive memorandums about the case before we could even begin the discussion. And if we didn't have the work done, we couldn't eat." The tip of the clerk's nose went pink. "We, um, all wanted to eat. Mrs. Santana made really good Cuban food."

Sighing, Beatty rubbed the back of his neck with his hand. The fact that the White House had been checking up on Santana was interesting and possibly inflammatory, but probably not illegal.

"Anything else, Mr. Brogan?"

"Just one thing." The clerk cut a look from the senator to the door, then lowered his gaze. "Um, on April 19, the day the Court released the Free Choice opinion, I got a call from the White House."

"From Mr. Thrasher?"

"Yeah. Yes. He wanted to know if Mr. Justice Santana was still in the building."

Beatty glanced at his aide. "Go on."

"I said he was, Thrasher said okay, then hung up. And not fifteen minutes later, these two security types came into the office and asked for Santana. I told them he'd gone up to the library."

Beatty pressed his lips together. "What happened next?"

"These two guys—they looked like Secret Service types, you know, with the earpieces? Anyway, a few minutes later I see them walk by with Mr. Justice Santana. They take him down to the basement—I know, because I watched the elevator after they got in. A few minutes later, when I go down and pretend to get something from my car, there's a black sedan guarded by the two guys."

"Could you see who was in the car?"

"No. But I could hear muffled yelling. A man and a woman, and they were going at it."

Beatty felt the corner of his lip rise in a half-smile. He looked at his aide. "A lover's quarrel, do you think?"

Brogan shook his head. "I couldn't tell what they were saying, and the windows were completely dark. But I sat in my car for a minute, and then I saw Mr. Justice Santana step out. Then I heard a woman scream, clear as day, 'Paul! Don't leave me!'"

He shrugged. "That was it. Mr. Justice Santana went back to the elevator, the guards got in, and then the car peeled out. After a while, I went back upstairs."

Pressing his hand to his chin, Beatty studied the young man before him. "What do you think happened that day?"

"I don't know." Brogan's eyes flicked away, as though afraid to rest very long on Beatty's face, but he'd been direct enough when he told his story.

"Would you be willing to tell the special prosecutor what you just told me?" Beatty lowered his hand. "I'm not sure when or if we'll need you, but there's always a possibility."

An odd mingling of wariness and amusement filled Brogan's darting brown eyes. "I'm always happy to tell the truth."

Beatty nodded. "Good. And I suppose a young man like you has plans for the future?"

Smoothing his slacks, Brogan flashed a smile. "I'm open right now. Since Mr. Justice Santana's passing, I've been doing grunt work at the Court, waiting for something to open up."

"We'll keep you in mind," Beatty answered, cutting to the chase. "I have a feeling, Mr. Brogan, you'll soon be going places."

He stood and waited until the leggy young man shook his hand and left the office. As the door closed, Beatty turned to his aide. "Justin, get Lincoln Walker on the horn for me, will you? That fella and I need to talk."

Justin nodded, then gestured toward the door. "You want me to find this kid a job?"

"Heavens no," Beatty answered, reaching for his pipe. "The last thing we need around here is another turncoat."

●

Daryn was just concluding a meeting with Lawrence Frey when Miss Park stepped into the Oval Office. She waited until Daryn looked her way before speaking.

"Madam President, I'm sorry, but the Office of Presidential Scheduling has informed me that Senator Beatty needs to see you ASAP. Can you squeeze him in, or should I have him try later?"

Daryn looked at her vice president, who'd just returned from a goodwill trip to South Korea. "Are we done here, Lawrence?"

"I think we are, Madam President." Ever the gentleman, he stood and shook her hand. "Thank you for taking the time to see me."

"The pleasure's all mine, sir." She stepped to the edge of the desk and smiled him out of the room, then nodded at her secretary. "I'll see the Senator . . . but ask Mr. Thrasher to step into the meeting, too. No, wait—on second thought, I'll see him alone. You may show him right in."

As the secretary left, Daryn retreated to the privacy of her study to pull her thoughts together. Beatty could not be bringing good news, and his timing was disastrous. She was scheduled to give her budget speech before both houses of Congress tomorrow night, so Beatty was probably coming to proffer some sort of threat or ultimatum . . . but which?

She heard the soft opening of the door, the approach of male and female voices, then Miss Park's melodic offer of coffee or tea.

"No, thank you, ma'am, I don't need anything," Beatty replied, his voice more robust than Daryn had ever heard it. "I'll just make myself at home until the president is ready to see me."

Daryn clenched her fist. The senator's plan, whatever it was, had apparently filled him with confidence.

Straightening, she checked her reflection in the small mirror behind the door, then slapped on a smile and strode into the room, offering her hand to the Senator as though he were her most ardent supporter. After a mindless exchange of pleasantries, she purposefully made her way to her desk, pointedly ignoring the more comfortable and friendly sofas.

Sliding into her chair, she crossed her legs with a zip of static from her pantyhose. As the senator creaked his seat, she regarded him with a level gaze. "How may I help you, Senator?"

"Madam President," he began, bending his head to study his hands, "lately we've become aware of some troubling particulars involving the death of Justice Paul Santana."

"Really?"

"Sad but true, Madam President." His chair groaned as he settled into it. "We have information tying a CIA operative to Justice Santana's death. We have visitor logs linking this office to the CIA, and specifically linking you to Mr. Santana. We also have sworn testimony that puts you and Mr. Justice Santana in the Supreme Court Building on April 19, only one week before Santana's death. Our witness claims he heard you two having a quarrel." One of the senator's stiff brows quirked. "An . . . *intimate* quarrel, perhaps?"

She pretended not to understand the implication beneath his smirk. "Paul and I were old friends. Sometimes friends disagree."

The senator's expression changed, the polite and respectful veneer peeling back to reveal the ravenous ambition underneath. "Let's get to the point, shall we, Madam President? A few weeks ago your people managed to convince another witness that she shouldn't recall a few pertinent details relevant to your past relationship with Santana. But seein' as how I predict a major shift in the political winds, I'm thinkin' we could convince her to regain her memory."

Daryn merely looked at him from behind her mask of presidential indifference. "This is all very interesting, Senator, but I'm afraid I don't have time to deal with matters of speculation and supposition right now. As a matter of courtesy I allowed you to visit without an appointment, but now I must ask that you respect my more pressing engagements. I've a speech to deliver to the nation tomorrow night—"

Wearing an expression of remarkable malignity, Beatty cut her off with an uplifted hand. "I don't think you should give that speech."

Daryn allowed her lips to part in a gentle gasp of indignation. "I beg your pardon?"

"No, ma'am, I don't think that speech is a good idea a-tall. Oh, I'm not begrudgin' a single minute of your prime TV time, but I was thinkin' tomorrow night would be a good opportunity for you to resign on account of personal reasons. Cite concern for your aging parents, if you like, or say you're sick—"

"I'm perfectly healthy."

Beatty grinned. "Well, the public doesn't *know* that, do they? Say you're anxious, menopausal, diabetic—heck, I don't care *what* you say, but give the American people a good reason and then get out of this office. Because you don't belong here, Ms. Austin, and I'm beginning to think you never did."

Numb with increasing rage and shock, Daryn glared at him. "Senator Beatty, I would never lie to the American people."

"Madam President, I think lying is just the beginning of what you've already done. We have evidence suggestin' that you have attempted to interfere with the working of the Supreme Court—"

"That's ridiculous."

"—and that you, whether directly or indirectly, played a role in the murder of Justice Paul Santana. The coroner's had another look at that autopsy report and now he's willin' to testify that a certain gun-barrel-sized bleed under Santana's left temple did not result from the fall, but was more likely inflicted by a certain Colombian hit man often employed by the CIA. He also found it interestin' that Santana had not been drinkin', as was previously reported."

As her heart pumped fear and outrage through her veins, Daryn felt her resolve begin to wane. She hadn't wanted to think about the details of that awful night, about how Paul must have suffered as a stranger invaded his home, threatened his life, forced him to write a suicide note. The assassin must have also threatened Maria or Cristina, otherwise Paul would have had nothing to lose by refusing to cooperate . . .

She lifted her chin as her capacity for fear reached its limits and her emotions veered crazily from terror to fury. "Senator Beatty," she forced the words through lips that felt cold. "I still believe you can't prove anything because there's nothing to prove. But—speaking hypothetically, of course—if I wanted to spare Paul's family the strain of your ridiculous argument, what would you suggest I do?"

"Well, ma'am—" he paused to remove his glasses and rub the bridge of his nose—"I would start by suggestin' that you resign immediately. Let your vice president pick up and carry on until the next election. Frey's an amiable fellow; I don't think we'll have any problem cooperatin' with him."

Translation: Frey was a spineless wimp, and they could easily push him around until the next election. She drew a breath. "And what would you do while Frey is running the White House?"

"Why, just take care of business as usual, Madam President. I don't think we'd feel it at all necessary to pursue this Santana matter if you just stepped aside. After all, the taxpayers wouldn't mind savin' the cost of a special prosecutor, and you and I both know it'd take millions to see this thing through." His eyes narrowed. "Either way, win or lose, your administration would be forever mired in this mess. And somehow I don't think you want the first female president's memory forever reekin' of a pink stink."

Rising, she pressed her hands to the edge of her desk. "You've given me a lot to think about, Senator. Thank you for coming."

"If I may ask, Madam President—" Beatty looked up at her. "When may I expect an answer?"

She rapped on the desk with her knuckles. "Soon, Senator Beatty. I'm not the type to waste time."

Beatty stood, folding his hands as he rose to his full height. "For the good of the country, Madam President, don't force me to make this public. Once we put the story out there, you know every reporter in America's going to jump on it like a dog on raw steak. Think of your infirm parents—think of your public. And my heart breaks to think of all those starry-eyed young girls discoverin' that you're no different from your power-hungry predecessors."

"Thank you for your concern, Senator." She gave him the frostiest smile she could manage. "Your compassion overwhelms me."

●

Bending over the toilet, Daryn surrendered her lunch, then staggered toward the sink. Not wanting her staff to see her upset, she'd fled upstairs to the residence as soon as Beatty left.

After rinsing out her mouth, she dropped the lid on the toilet, then sat on it and propped her arm on the vanity. Somehow she had stumbled into the midst of a surging chaos, or perhaps it had overtaken her while she wasn't looking. But this time, she knew, there was no easy way out. Beatty had presented her with an option, and, considering the risks, she couldn't dismiss it out of hand.

She had wanted to be the first and best female president, but apparently fate never intended her to own both titles. She could be satisfied with the former, but if she continued to strive for the latter she might find history recording her name in the scarlet letters of shame. If she resisted and forced the public to endure an endless round of hearings, investigations, and testimony, she'd run the risk of earning not only their disrespect but also their ire. Investigations of the Clinton administration had cost the nation over 110 million dollars, and she didn't think the public would appreciate learning of a new special prosecutor in the same month she unveiled her "lean and mean" budget.

So . . . she could quietly resign and leave the work to someone else. She could cite her parents' failing health as a reason for leaving office, and while the traditional womanly role as caregiver might arm critics with yet another reason to discredit women in leadership, it would earn her points for sympathy. In the years to come she could still operate as a representative for women, and her value as a public speaker would not be diminished . . .

Her parents would be mortified to think she'd used them as an excuse, but the ignominy of a special prosecutor's investigation would kill them.

She lowered her head to her arm as a fresh wave of nausea assailed her, then crinkled her nose. She reeked of sweat and the musky-sharp smell of fear. She'd have to shower before she went back to the Oval.

Willing her stomach to settle, she exhaled softly. She could almost wish for a genuine illness, something treatable, yet serious enough that her physical weakness wouldn't be viewed as a weakness of women in general. If she were sick, she could leave the office on a wave of sympathy *and* concern.

She could almost wish Paul's contention that abortion led to breast cancer were true. But while breast cancer was serious enough to possibly warrant her resignation, it would prove the medical aspects of *Free Choice Women's Clinic v. Maddox,* and that would never do.

Paul's God, who now seemed firmly intent upon teaching her a lesson, did not seem inclined to fully play the villain and give her a useful disease. Raking her fingers through her hair, she glared up at the ceiling. "Why can't you be more like Zeus?" she muttered. "Now, there was a god. Thunderbolts, lightning, and just punishment for mortal failings." She dropped her head to her arm. "You just keep popping up to make my life difficult."

Every avenue out of this quandary seemed to demand some kind of destruction. The public would have to believe either her family or her body was diseased—or her reputation would be slaughtered. Fate—or God—had left her no easy alternatives.

She closed her eyes and briefly considered the idea of having Beatty murdered, then dismissed it. Too many other people knew too much. And Beatty had friends, while she had . . . temporary staff.

From the bedroom, the phone buzzed. Daryn lifted her head, propped her cheek on her palm, and wearily confronted her pale reflection in the mirror. "Okay, Paul's God," she whispered, closing her eyes. "I'll play your game, and we'll make it winner take all. But I'm going to play my hand first. And I'm going to make it a good one."

THIRTY-EIGHT

FROM HIS NARROW ROOM IN THE HOTEL ADAMS, Clive Wilton tuned his police scanner to the band used by the White House Communications Agency. From the computer in the hotel lobby he'd been able to access a Web page listing all the Secret Service frequencies, even those of the cars that would carry the president (code name Goldenrod) and vice president (code name Casper) to the Capitol Building that evening. The frequencies would be scrambled as the Real Thing went down tonight, but until then Clive was getting an earful.

His month in Washington had been an exercise in frustration. He'd tried just about every avenue of approach he could think of, even attempting to visit Arlington National Cemetery the day they buried the Latino justice. But the feds had sewn that place up tight, and Clive had been forced to return to his hotel without even catching a glimpse of the president. He had also tried to enter the White House, once as a visitor and once as a deliveryman, but both times he'd turned back at the sight of uniformed security guards paying close attention to young men about Clive's age.

A quick call back to the garage in Jackson confirmed his suspicions—the feds had visited his home, talked to the folks at the Sassy Moose Inn and the garage, even tried to intimidate Jimmy Griffin. But no one there knew where he'd gone, so for all their trouble the feds got squat.

"You be careful now, boy," Art had warned him. "Do what you gotta do and then get yourself home. We need warriors back here, too."

We need warriors . . .

The words echoed in Clive's brain, urging him to action. Immediately he shaved off his collar-length hair and his goatee. Now, bald and fresh-faced, he looked quite different from the young man who'd left Jackson. The agents who scanned the crowds at the next presidential appearance would not recognize him on sight.

And the definitive answer had come to him a week ago. Art's words kept repeating in his head, over and over like his brain cells had Tourette's syndrome, and Clive had finally understood what he had to do.

The White Race needed *warriors*—not men like Art who attended True People meetings and then hid the group's literature in a footlocker, but men who were willing to spend their lives for the cause. The White Race had diminished because it had gone underground and allowed the Africans and Latins and Jews and Chinese to take over. The Whites had defaulted because they were unwilling to pay the price.

But he, Clive Wilton, would go to war. He couldn't kill President Daryn Austin—he'd realized that much already—but he could steal her spotlight. All week the Washington papers and TV stations had been buzzing about her budget speech to Congress, and for the last two days the police had been erecting barricades around the grounds in front of the Capitol Building. The papers predicted that thousands of demonstrators would show up to protest budget cuts and vie for a little media attention.

Tonight, while Daryn Austin mounted that polished platform to give her speech to Congress, Clive would be standing outside, as close to the steps of the Capitol as he could get. And while she lifted her red-tipped hand to twiddle her fingers at the crowd, he would lift his arm and spray his clothes with gasoline. And when the witch opened her mouth to speak, Clive would turn to the nearest TV camera and shout out the truth—Behold, the Whore of Babylon!—and then he would flick his lighter.

The coverage would immediately shift to him, and people would forget all about the woman on the podium. Clive would dive under the mesh barrier and proceed up the marble steps as far as he could go before the fire stopped him. The awe-struck protesters would know they were watching a man with more courage than they ever dreamed of having. And later, whenever people thought of May 11, they wouldn't remember the woman. They'd remember the White Race warrior who took his stand in flames meant for the great whore of Babylon.

He'd show his fellow White Men what had to be done. His spilled blood would be like seed, fertilizing the imaginations of other brothers until the sleeping giant of the White Race rose from its lethargy and resumed its proper place.

Summarizing his thoughts, Clive wrote his final letter, inscribed *To whom it may concern* on the envelope, then propped it against the pillow of his perfectly made bed. His equipment stood upon the desk—a pressure-activated sprayer, waiting to be filled with gasoline, his trench coat, and his lighter.

He would not need a gun. A warrior needed but a single weapon, and tonight he would fight fire with fire.

●

At precisely 7:23 P.M., Daryn stepped into the great hall and walked down the red carpeting that led to the portico where the motorcade had assembled. Anson Quinn and a host of other agents were waiting for her, as were Vice President Frey and his wife, Patty.

Daryn greeted the Freys with calm embraces, then sent them to their vehicle in the twenty-four-car motorcade. Turning, she smiled at Quinn. "Which number did the war wagon draw tonight, Agent?"

Quinn didn't return the smile. "Twelve," he said, taking her elbow. He pointed to the black limo that seemed identical to the others, but came with an air filtration system, bulletproof windows, and bomb-proof shielding. All of which seemed vastly redundant tonight, because the Secret Service route involved speeding down a closed-off road, entering the underground parking garage of the Rayburn House Office

Building, and escorting the president through the secure underground tunnel from the Rayburn building to the Capitol. If all went according to the plan, which they'd successfully employed many times before, the presidential limo would be exposed to the public for only a few fleeting seconds.

Daryn paused before going down the steps. "There's been a change of plans, Agent," she said, keeping her voice light. "I understand the police have cordoned off the park in front of the Capitol Building. Since the road will already be blocked, I'd like the motorcade to drive down First Street before we go to the Rayburn building."

Quinn's feathery brows rose nearly to his hairline. "Madam President, you can't do that."

"I can, Agent. And I'm giving you plenty of warning, so tell your people."

"May I ask why?"

Several other staffers had overheard the exchange, and all of them turned toward her now, varying degrees of disbelief registering on their faces.

She spoke with all the quiet authority she could muster. "First Street runs between the Capitol and the Supreme Court. I'd like to pass by the Court in honor of the late Justice Santana." She glanced at Natalie Morgan, White House Press Secretary, who stood among the well-wishers. "Natalie, will you put the word out?" She turned to face Quinn. "After that little detour, Agent, you may take us wherever you like."

Muttering into his sleeve, Quinn stalked away. Daryn moved slowly down the carpeted steps, taking time to say hello to several of the White House residence staff who had come out to see her off. Knowing Quinn would need a few moments to arrange for her detour, she took her time, addressing each of the staff members with a smile, a handshake and a personal greeting.

Her mind vibrated with a million thoughts, few of them having to do with the speech she had planned to give. One sentiment kept pushing its way to the fore: *this may be the last time I do this.*

Five minutes later, Quinn strode toward her, perspiration on his brow and a stream of indecipherable words under his breath.

"This is crazy, you know," he said, directing her toward the twelfth car. "Every zany in America is mugging for the TV cameras in front of the Capitol tonight."

"Including Jehu?"

"Don't even joke about that."

Daryn paused as he leaned forward to open the door. "But you haven't found him."

"No, but don't worry. The mob won't be able to tell which car is yours. Though I still think it's a foolish idea, we'll drive down First Street before heading over to Rayburn, but we're going through there at a decent clip."

"No, we're not." Daryn slid into the back seat. "We'll go at a stately pace. You don't honor someone's memory by zooming by their workplace at fifty miles an hour."

He shot her a look of sheer incredulity.

"I'm not worried." She pulled the hem of her skirt into the car, then smoothed the wrinkles away. "In a bulletproof, bombproof war wagon, who would be?"

"There are other ways to stop a car, Madam President."

"Yes, but we haven't given the terrorists time to bring in their surface to air missiles." She jerked her chin at him. "Get in, Agent, and let's go. I've an appointment to keep tonight."

●

On the greening lawn of the Capitol, Clive moved amid a sea of protesters and fought back the urge to gag in disgust. Dozens of representatives from every alien race crowded the open acreage, many of them singing and dancing while they waved posters and shouted stupid rhymes that made no sense at all. Most congregated under the light posts, the better to be seen by the roving television cameras, but Clive avoided the crowds, preferring to stand alone so he could scope out an appropriate location for his final statement.

The Capitol, long, white, and glowing in the light of a full moon, rose as a fitting backdrop behind him. The tall spire featuring Lady Liberty—a white woman, Clive assumed—crowned the dome at the center of the sprawling structure.

One of the tour guide operators had assured him that the law prohibited any building in the district to stand taller than Lady Liberty, therefore Washington had no skyscrapers. Clive thought the prohibition reasonable enough, but the idea of an uplifted *woman* troubled him. The city's builders should have immortalized a warrior.

Across the street, bathed in brilliant light, stood the mammoth Supreme Court Building. Protesters mingled on the piazza there, too, but not as many, for everyone knew the night's action would center on the Capitol. The police had closed off First Street and Maryland Avenue, but TV vans lined East Capitol, their retractable antennas unfolded and pointed toward receivers miles away.

Clive walked slowly, his left hand gripping the sprayer handle, his trench coat buttoned at the waist. A cool breeze blew through the tall oaks bordering the park, and he felt grateful for the chill. The long coat, which would be downright uncomfortable on a warm May day, did not seem out of place at night.

Near the wide sidewalk running from First Street to the Capitol Building, an olive-skinned man with a transistor radio in his hand boogied to some inaudible music. Clive squinted, certain the man was high on drugs (another failing of the inferior races), then saw that the man wore headphones.

A woman near him walked with her toddler, a little girl dressed in blue jeans, a red shirt, and a star-spangled hat. Bright white lettering splashed across the shirt: *Future President in Training Pants.*

Snorting, Clive turned. The stretch of wire fencing along the sidewalk stood nearly empty, for the crowds had gathered at the street. This would be the best place for him to stand, all alone with the Capitol as his background . . .

"Hey!" The guy with the transistor radio suddenly ripped off his headphones. "The president's coming! She's driving by here!"

Like bees released from a hive, the crowd buzzed in confusion for a moment, then swarmed toward the street. Mounted policemen cantered forward to contain the restless crowd, and Clive felt the corner of his mouth droop in derision. The fools. A moment ago most of them had been protesting Austin's policies, now they were panting like star-struck groupies.

But no matter. In a few moments, they would have forgotten all about the president.

They'd be thinking only of him.

●

Daryn stared gloomily out the window as the limo roared down Maryland Avenue. The time had come. Play or pay, as the man said, time to do or die. Despite her calm exterior, she felt like a one-woman percussion section: heart pounding, pulse thrumming, a sharp pain in her head occasionally crashing like cymbals.

She heard the crowds long before the car turned onto First Street. The police cordon, reinforced every few yards by a mounted officer, successfully restrained the bystanders, most of whom yelled indiscriminately at every passing car. Many people clapped, their eyes vainly searching the opaque windows, while a few chanted her name: *Aus-tin, Aus-tin!*

She closed her eyes. After tonight, would she ever hear that sound again?

As the car rounded the corner, she leaned forward and tapped the driver's shoulder. "Slow down please, as we pass the Supreme Court."

Though Quinn made a violent sound of exasperation, she ignored him and stared out the window.

Rising at her left, the Court seemed majestic and silent in the purple evening sky. The bronze doors gleamed like gold in the spotlights, and the two marble statues, the Contemplation of Justice and the Authority of Law, sat like vigilant guardians on opposite sides of the regal stairs. She bit her lip as a wave of nostalgia passed through her. Now more than ever, she knew Paul had deserved a seat on the Court. Of all the people she could have nominated to fill that vacancy, he alone had possessed the integrity to serve in that marble palace.

Without a word, she opened the door and slid toward the opening. Quinn cried out, the car squealed to a sudden stop, and Daryn used the moment to slip free of the vehicle. Turning, she faced the crowd and lifted her hand.

"There she is!"

"The president, look!"

"Ohmigoodness, it's *her!"*

Skirting the limo's trunk, Daryn walked toward the long stretch of open sidewalk that led to the Capitol. In the hollow of her back, a single drop of sweat traced the course of her spine.

Almost instantly, Quinn appeared at her side. "Madam President, get back in the vehicle."

She waved at a young mother, then blinked as the woman flashed a camera in her eyes. "No, Quinn." She set her teeth in a fixed smile. "I'm walking the length of this sidewalk, then I'm climbing the Capitol steps."

"No, ma'am, you're not."

"Try and stop me."

For a moment she thought he might. His hand came up, blocking her, but he didn't resist as she pushed past him and stepped onto the walkway. Taking a deep breath to quell the pounding pulse beneath her ribs, she lengthened her stride and moved down the sidewalk. Before she had taken three steps, an entire squad of agents flanked her on all sides.

"Gentlemen," she called, continuing her steadfast pace, "give me some room. The crowd is contained, and we've only fifty yards to go."

Reluctantly, the agents parted, but not much, and as she turned to wave to the crowd at her left, Daryn caught one of Quinn's most malevolent looks. If Jehu didn't kill her in the next hour, she realized, Quinn probably would.

●

Clive heard the commotion before he understood what had happened. Homing in on the idiot with the transistor radio, he heard the man yell: "The president's out of the car! She's walking to the Capitol!"

Cold sweat prickled on Clive's jaws. Like Napoleon and Caesar before him, he was about to benefit from a shift in the winds of war.

●

Unable to control the spasmodic trembling within her, Daryn walked forward, aware of the burgeoning crowd and Quinn's glower. She did not move to shake hands—that might cause a riot—but walked down the center of the empty sidewalk, knowing that each step brought her closer to the demise of her dreams. Jehu had apparently given up and gone home, even though she'd done her best to end both their ordeals in a truly memorable fashion.

She flinched as another camera flashed, then managed a wavering smile, too late, for the man who'd wielded the Polaroid. She had spent the afternoon thinking of Lady Macbeth—*screw your courage to the sticking place*—and one final alternative had occurred to her in the silence of the presidential bedroom. She didn't have to quit, nor did she have to outwit a special prosecutor.

A few weeks ago John Hudson had committed suicide by cop outside the White House gates.

She could commit suicide by Jehu outside the Capitol. Any president felled by an assassin's bullet secured the glow of martyrdom. Everyone today knew of John Kennedy's womanizing, Lincoln had presided over the worst war in American history, yet both men were spoken of deferentially and with great affection . . .

Jehu, where are you?

Through fleeting nausea she smiled at a child, waved at his mother, winked at an older man who gave her a saucy thumbs-up. Ahead of her, a sudden break in the barrier sent police and agents rushing forward, forcing Daryn and her protective entourage to stop.

"President Austin!" A young man called, grinning at her with one arm wrapped around his girlfriend. "You got any sisters at home who look like you?"

"Watch yourself." As her heart thumped almost painfully in her chest, Daryn pointed to the girlfriend and gave him a teasing smile. "Or you're going to find yourself all alone tonight."

On the sidewalk ahead, order had been restored. As the crowd cheered its approval, Daryn wiped her damp palms on her skirt and moved on.

●

Clive held his breath as the knot of dark suits approached. There! She walked in the center, her blonde hair shining like a beacon. Smiling and waving and smirking, she bewitched everyone she passed. She was diabolically clever, but this would be her last opportunity to fool the nation. She would not give that speech tonight, for she was about to meet a warrior willing to give his all for the glory of the White Race.

With his right hand he pumped the handle of the sprayer, felt the resistance as the pressure built. With his left hand he pulled the wand free, then smelled the faint aroma of the gasoline. He would have to aim high to spray the stream over the heads of the Secret Service agents, but the witch was an Amazon. She would not be able to hide.

He counted her steps, drew in a deep breath, then silently pressed the trigger on the wand. A wet, squishy sound filled his ears as the acrid scent of gasoline assaulted his nose. The agent nearest her turned, his eyes wide as the gasoline spattered him, but Clive didn't care about collateral damage. As the witch blinked and shook her head in the steady stream of gasoline, Clive pulled out his lighter, flicked on the flame, and looked into the eyes of his enemy . . .

And froze as the world fell away.

The wide blue eyes that met his gaze did not belong to a conqueror. They were the eyes of a wounded animal. Her brows rose and fell, her mouth closed, the long lashes blinked in resignation. And suddenly Clive realized that to lower the flame into the stream would be an act of mercy, and a warrior never showed mercy, a warrior would never—

He crumbled as a battering ram smashed his solar plexus.

●

Staring at the bald man in a paralysis of horror, Daryn felt as though life had suddenly begun to spin in slow motion. Something wet had hit the side of her head, a caressing stream that went on and on, sending her back to her father's lawn in the hot Atlanta summer, and then she'd seen a flame and somehow known this was Jehu, this was her moment, but as she looked at him

Yes, do it!

Quinn lowered his shoulder and rammed the man like a human torpedo. The flame disappeared, and suddenly she was being lifted, carried away from the crowd like a mannequin, and while the agents transported her, she craned her neck, looking back at the pandemonium—

She shall be burnt with fire

—and the kaleidoscope turned, and the pieces fell into place.

Professor Gifford's voice came back to her in a surge of memory: *Janus, the god with two faces.*

She had hoped to die on that sidewalk, to end her public life before Beatty exposed the private one.

Of beginnings, of the past and the future

She had hoped for a different ending, one more final than this, but she had played her hand and now she would capitulate.

Finally, the god of peace.

Winner takes all. The winner here wasn't Janus, but Paul's greedy God, who was probably smiling a smug little smile right now.

The agents, not one of them daring to mutter an I-told-you-so, lowered her to the steps of the Capitol, then whisked her behind one of the sheltering pillars. One of them handed her a handkerchief, while another kept asking, "Are you all right?"

"I'm fine." She dabbed the wetness from her hair, wiped the liquid from her face. She sniffed the cloth in her hand. Gasoline.

A moment later Quinn sprinted up the steps. "We're calling for a car. You're going back to the White House."

"Wrong again, Quinn." She pressed the reeking handkerchief into his hand. "I have a speech to give tonight and I intend to give it."

"But—"

"Agent Quinn." Lightly she rested her hand upon the front of his wet shirt. "Haven't you learned by now that it's futile to argue? But don't worry—our arguments are nearly done."

When she gave him a lopsided smile, Quinn caught her arm. "You sure you're okay?"

"Yeah—I was just thinking of Lincoln."

His expression sobered. "Ford's Theater?"

"No . . . once, after Lincoln lost an election, he said he felt like a boy who had stubbed his toe in the dark. He was too old to cry, but it hurt too much to laugh."

Lifting her head, she gestured toward the tall bronze doors that would lead her into the Capitol where her audience waited. "Lead the way, Agent Quinn. Let's finish this thing."

EPILOGUE

April 19, 2007

Slipping into an empty seat in the back row of folding chairs, Daryn settled herself, then took a moment to adjust the wide brim of her hat. She had nearly decided not to come, but just as Odysseus could not ignore the lovely sirens' song, she could not resist Paul Santana. Even in death, his allure was irresistible.

Peering out through her sunglasses, she spied Maria Santana on the bunting-draped platform. Maria looked as small and wrenlike as ever, but her face seemed to shine with serenity—an emotion Daryn hadn't felt in years. Maria patted the arm of the young woman sitting next to her—Cristina—then turned her attention to the tall man who stepped up and walked confidently to the blue goose.

"We are gathered here," President Lawrence Frey said, his baritone voice rolling over the assembled crowd, "to honor a man who, two years ago today, dared to apply the principles of honesty and courage to an issue few were willing to address. Justice Paul Santana, joined by several of his colleagues on the Supreme Court, recognized that women have the right to know that abortion increases a woman's risk for breast cancer. Because he was willing to speak out about an issue so many have tried to ignore or deny, this winter Congress passed the ABC Rule, requiring medical institutions to warn women of the Abortion/Breast Cancer link. Every three minutes, a woman is diagnosed with breast cancer. It's time we did all we can to help women lessen their risk of this disease."

The president turned slightly, acknowledging Maria. "We are honored to have Mr. Justice Santana's widow, Maria, as well as his daughter, Cristina Santana Wickwire, with us today. Now it is my very great honor and pleasure to award the presidential Medal of Freedom, America's highest civilian award, to Supreme Court Justice Paul Santana."

As the audience erupted in applause, Maria stood to accept the walnut presentation case containing the silver medal. "Thank you, Mrs. Santana," President Frey said, holding her hand as cameras flashed. "The country owes you a great debt."

Daryn breathed deep and felt a stab of memory, a broken remnant from the years she had lived behind these iron gates. Paul had been gone two years, but if she closed her eyes she could still hear his voice, still see him hurrying over the flagstones of the colonnade. The sweet scent of the roses had perfumed the air the last time they spoke in the White House . . . and the last time she told him good-bye, at Arlington.

Pressing her lips together, she dipped her head and let the brim of her hat shield her from the touching tableau on the platform.

Two years ago she had resigned from the presidency, citing personal reasons and offering no explanation. Keeping his promise, Beatty did not call a special prosecutor. The FBI worked vainly to find the assassin Carlos Montoya, but the man had apparently fled the country.

Patty and Larry Frey moved into the White House within hours of Daryn's departure, and as she perused the newspapers every morning, she realized Frey wasn't as spineless as she'd imagined. He immediately announced his desire to affiliate himself with the Republican party (a move that probably infuriated Beatty, who'd been eyeing the White House with such determination), and nominated an African-American woman, Kaye Ball, to fill Santana's seat on the Supreme Court.

Clive Wilton, aka Jehu, had been committed to a hospital for the criminally insane, where he died six months later. According to the official report the death had been caused by an accident in the showers . . .

Maria Santana had remained in Washington amid a circle of fast friends, and last year the *Post* reported that Cristina had married Jason Wickwire, another Harvard student. Feeling that a nice but anonymous wedding gift was in order, Daryn sent the happy couple a set of Waterford crystal.

After her resignation, she went home to Atlanta, remaining there in relative obscurity until her parents died, one after the other. Weary of dealing with the specters of three dead political careers, she sold the family home and moved to Arlington, Virginia, a few miles outside D.C. There she lived quietly in a townhouse, occasionally writing on women's issues for academic journals. Yet her primary occupation was finding the self she'd buried under ambition and public image.

On many occasions, especially in the temperate months when the sweetest part of the day stretched between dinner and sunset, she carried Paul's leather-bound journal out to her balcony and began to read. On one page he had written:

> *One always hates what one wrongs. That is why, God forgive me, I hated Maria all the months I was with Daryn. I didn't display my hate, but now I understand that by not loving her, I hated her. Just as in not loving God, I hated him.*
>
> *But "he has not punished us for all our sins, nor does he deal with us as we deserve. For his unfailing love toward those who fear him is as great as the height of the heavens above the earth. He has removed our rebellious acts as far away from us as the east is from the west. The Lord is like a father to his children, tender and compassionate to those who fear him."*
>
> *God, turn my hate into love, my fears into confidence, my anger into forgiveness.*

The memory of Paul's words drifted away. She didn't know how long she sat in the Rose Garden, but the crowd had dissipated by the time a quiet voice interrupted her thoughts. "Madam President?"

Daryn turned to see Maria Santana standing at the end of the aisle, the medal case in her hand.

"Would you," Maria asked, an uncertain expression flitting across her face, "like to see this?"

Speechless, Daryn nodded. Maria slipped by the other empty chairs, then sat by Daryn's side and placed the walnut case on her lap.

With trembling fingers, Daryn opened it. On her watch she hadn't had the opportunity to bestow the Medal of Freedom, but if anyone deserved it, Paul did.

Lightly, she trailed her fingertips over the five-pointed silver star upon the bed of white satin. "It's beautiful," she whispered, her eyes moving to the silver disk containing the arms of the president of the United States. "I'm sure you're very proud."

Maria said nothing, but her eyes softened.

Daryn waited—what else did the woman want?—and after a moment Maria turned sideways in her chair, her fingertips falling upon Daryn's shoulder. It had been so long since she felt the touch of another human hand that she flinched.

"I know it's presumptuous of me to ask," Maria said, a faint light twinkling in the depths of her brown eyes, "but the Crispins and I are having Sunday dinner together in about an hour. We'd love it if you could join us."

From force of habit, a polite smile rose to Daryn's lips. "I don't think that's a good idea."

"I do." Reaching out, Maria took Daryn's hand and clasped it between her own. "Because whatever else you were to my husband, you were his friend. And while I don't know much about politics, I know about suffering. I know how it feels to yearn for love. I also know how it feels to need—and give—forgiveness."

Daryn stared at her. Had she heard correctly? By all rights, this woman ought to hate her as much as Daryn hated Paul when he decided to love God more than her . . .

But loving God changed him. And apparently it had changed his wife as well.

"Maria," Daryn said, a wry smile tugging at the corner of her mouth, "I don't understand you at all."

A twinkle of sunlight sparkled in the woman's brown eyes as she laughed. "You don't have to, President Austin. Just come as a child to the table and be fed."

After signaling her Secret Service agents with an uplifted hand and an incredulous glance, Daryn stood and followed Paul Santana's wife through the rose arbor.

RESOURCES

No novelist writes without input from others, particularly on the topics covered in this book. I must thank Dr. Joel Brind and attorney John Kindley, who updated me on the status of efforts to inform the public about the abortion/breast cancer link as well as pending litigation revolving around this issue. Thank you, Jim Bell, for your legal-eagle eyes!

Special thanks go to Susan Richardson for proofing rough drafts.

I owe a great debt to Jean Anouilh, author of *Becket* (New York: Riverhead Books, 1960), for ably demonstrating that the story concept would work.

"The Nantucket Girl's Song" was recorded in a journal by Eliza Brock and cited by Nathaniel Philbrick in his book *In the Heart of the Sea: The Tragedy of the Whaleship Essex* (New York: Viking, 2000).

I discovered the information about CIA assassination in an article: "What Did the C.I.A. Do to His Father?" *The New York Times Magazine,* April 1, 2001, p. 60.

I am also extremely grateful for information provided by the following authors and their books:

Henry J. Abraham, *Justices, Presidents, and Senators* (New York: Rowman & Littlefield Publishers, Inc., 1999).

Carl Sferrazza Anthony, *America's First Families* (New York: Simon & Schuster, 2000).

David N. Atkinson, *Leaving the Bench* (Wichita, Kans.: University Press of Kansas, 1999).

Stephen Donadio, Joan Smith, Susan Mesner, and Rebecca Davison, editors, *The New York Public Library Book of Twentieth-Century American Quotations* (New York: Warner Books, 1992).

Ellen Greenberg, *The Supreme Court Explained* (New York: W.W. Norton & Company, 1997).

Meg Greenfield, *Washington* (New York: Public Affairs, 2001).

Peter Irons, *A People's History of the Supreme Court* (New York: Penguin Books, 1999).

Peter Irons, *The Courage of Their Convictions* (New York: Penguin Books, 1988).

C. Brian Kelly, *Best Little Stories from the White House* (Nashville, Tenn.: Cumberland House, 1999).

Suzy Maroon, *The Supreme Court of the United States* (New York: Thomasson-Grant & Lickle, 1996).

Bradley H. Patterson Jr., *The White House Staff* (Washington, D.C.: Brookings Institution Press, 2000).

Barbara A. Perry, *The Priestly Tribe* (Westport, Conn.: Praeger, 1999).

Kenneth J. Vandevelde, *Thinking Like a Lawyer; An Introduction to Legal Reasoning* (Boulder, Col.: Westview Press, 1998).

David Alistair Yalof, *Pursuit of Justices* (Chicago: University of Chicago Press, 1999).

"The Supreme Court of the United States," video produced by York Television, Inc.

Additional Selections by Angela Hunt

The Immortal

A man claiming to be 2000 years old says he is on a holy mission to prevent a global cataclysm. To uncover the truth, heroine Claudia must re-examine her beliefs as she delves into ancient legends of the Wandering Jew, biblical warnings about the Antichrist, and eyewitness accounts of the Crucifixion, the Inquisition, and the Holocaust.

The Note

When PanWorld flight 848 crashes into Tampa Bay killing all 261 people on board, journalist Peyton MacGruder is assigned to the story. Her discovery of a remnant of the tragedy—a simple note: "T - I love you. All is forgiven. Dad."—changes her world forever. A powerful story of love and forgiveness.

Angela Hun

W PUBLISHING GROUP™

Also Available in the Heavenly Daze Series

The Island of Heavenly Daze

To a casual visitor, the island of Heavenly Daze is just like a dozen others off the coast of Maine. It is decorated with graceful Victorian mansions, carpeted with gray cobblestones and bright wild flowers, and populated by sturdy, hard-working folks—most of whom are unaware that the island of Heavenly Daze is not just like the other islands of coastal Maine. The small town that crowns its peak consists of seven buildings, each inhabited, according to divine decree, by an angel who has been commanded to guard and help anyone who crosses the threshold.

Grace in Autumn

It's November, and as the island residents prepare for the coming months of cold and snow, they are surprised by God's unexpected lessons of humility, trust, and hope. Authors Lori Copeland and Angela Hunt revisit the Island of Heavenly Daze in the second book of the highly acclaimed series about a small town where angelic intervention is commonplace and the Thanksgiving feast a community affair.

A Warmth in Winter

Readers have already fallen in love with the quirky personalities that inhabit Heavenly Daze. In *A Warmth in Winter*, the unforgettable characters and humorous circumstances offer poignant lessons of God's love and faithfulness. The story centers around Vernie Bidderman, owner of Mooseleuk Mercantile and Salt Gribbon, the lighthouse operator, who despite the vast differences in their struggles are being taught about the ultimate failure and frustration of self-reliance.